Pr...

"Margaret Dumas's *Speak Now* is as rich and bubbly as a glass of champagne. This series gives you the view from the top in San Francisco."
—Agatha Award–winning author Elaine Viets

"Although set in modern San Francisco, this book really has the feel of a 1930s noir in which everyone is rich, cultured, and beautiful. The protagonist is not only likable but funny, too. I found myself chortling along as the plot unfolded. The author brings just the right touch of sophistication and earthiness to her characters. A very enjoyable read—think of it as a rich, artsy girl comparison to Janet Evanovich's mysteries. We rated it five hearts." —Heartland Reviews

"This is Margaret Dumas's first book, but it is so well written I found that fact hard to remember. The story moves nicely, with well-portrayed characters and an engaging heroine . . . an interesting and unusual outcome." —I Love a Mystery

"Dumas's sparkling debut should appeal to both cozy and chick-lit fans. . . . [H]er engaging voice will keep readers turning the pages." —*Publishers Weekly*

"Comic cozy meets crazed spy thriller in this debut novel. . . . The San Francisco setting is appealing, and the amusing cast of characters will have readers looking forward to subsequent adventures." —*Booklist*

"A fabulous screwball mystery that is reminiscent of the zany 1930s Bob Hope movies. The story line is action-packed, but with a tongue-in-cheek manner."
—AllReaders.com

"With its San Francisco setting; theatrical background; hint of espionage; witty, sophisticated hero and heroine who thoroughly enjoy one another's company; and brisk pace, this humorous . . . tale will entertain readers who like a light mystery with an urban attitude."
—*School Library Journal*

...praise for Spent Now

SPEAK NOW

MARRIED TO MYSTERY

Margaret Dumas

A SIGNET BOOK

SIGNET
Published by New American Library, a division of
Penguin Group (USA) Inc., 375 Hudson Street,
New York, New York 10014, USA
Penguin Group (Canada), 90 Eglinton Avenue East, Suite 700, Toronto,
Ontario M4P 2Y3, Canada (a division of Pearson Penguin Canada Inc.)
Penguin Books Ltd., 80 Strand, London WC2R 0RL, England
Penguin Ireland, 25 St. Stephen's Green, Dublin 2,
Ireland (a division of Penguin Books Ltd.)
Penguin Group (Australia), 250 Camberwell Road, Camberwell, Victoria 3124,
Australia (a division of Pearson Australia Group Pty. Ltd.)
Penguin Books India Pvt. Ltd., 11 Community Centre, Panchsheel Park,
New Delhi - 110 017, India
Penguin Group (NZ), cnr Airborne and Rosedale Roads, Albany,
Auckland 1310, New Zealand (a division of Pearson New Zealand Ltd.)
Penguin Books (South Africa) (Pty.) Ltd., 24 Sturdee Avenue,
Rosebank, Johannesburg 2196, South Africa

Penguin Books Ltd., Registered Offices:
80 Strand, London WC2R 0RL, England

Published by Signet, an imprint of New American Library, a division of Pen-
guin Group (USA) Inc. First US edition published in 2004 by Poisoned Pen
Press. For information, address Poisoned Pen Press, 6962 East First Avenue,
Suite 103, Scottsdale, Arizona 85251, or www.poisonedpenpress.com.

First Signet Printing, November 2005
10 9 8 7 6 5 4 3 2 1

For Mickey

Acknowledgments

This book couldn't have been written without the love and support of my family and friends—especially my parents, Dolores and Keith Dumas. Thank you for everything.

Thanks to the fabulous people at the Book Passage Mystery Writers Conference, who introduced me to a whole new world, and Penny Warner—the most generous person alive—who introduced me to just about everyone in it. Thanks to the lovely people of the CWA, especially Kay Mitchell.

Thanks to Mame Hunt for her invaluable information about the world of nonprofit theatre and to Dave Oberhoffer of the SFPD for answering all my police questions. Commander John Dumas, USN, and Commander Richard Dumas, USN (Ret.), gave me no help whatsoever. Anything I got wrong about the theatre, police procedure, the Navy, or meteorology is entirely my own fault.

Many, many thanks to everyone who suffered through the early and not-so-early drafts: Denise Lee, Robert Hall, Erick Vera, Christine Dorffi, Lilah Koski, Colleen Casey, Carole Dumas, and Rosanne Annoni.

I'm hugely grateful to Barbara Peters, Robert Rosenwald, and the whole gang at Poisoned Pen Press, and to Ann Parker and Claire Johnson for leading me to them.

Finally, inexpressible thanks to Denise Lee and Rosanne Annoni, who held my hands as I jumped off the cliff, and kept reminding me I could choose to fall up.

Chapter 1

Okay, here's the stereotype: A woman will date a serial killer because he has cute eyes and she's the only one in the world who truly understands him. A man will dump a supermodel who holds a Ph.D. in physics because she gets a hangnail.

Right. Well it's safe to say I've never been the kind of girl who fits that profile. In fact, there are more than a few men who might say I start looking for the exit signs on about the third date. And it's true I once broke up with a senior partner at Goldman Sachs because he used the word "surreptitiously" when he meant "vicariously"—and this man had won a George Clooney look-alike contest.

It's not that I haven't wanted a relationship, really. It's just that I seem to have looked for any excuse not to be in one. I mean, why bother? The whole concept of needing someone to take care of me has always rubbed me the wrong way. I have friends for all my emotional needs, and enough money to meet the financial needs of a small country. As for sex—well, just being in a relationship isn't any guarantee, is it?

So I've been called commitment-phobic. Okay, I've been called worse. My friends have concluded that I'm the most romantically challenged woman in the Western Hemisphere. Which was going to make it a little awkward to explain how I came to be sitting in the first-class compartment of the British Airways flight from London to San Francisco beside my new husband.

My very new husband. I checked my watch and realized we'd passed the forty-eight-hour point. I think they say the first two days are the hardest. I looked over at Jack's sleeping profile. He didn't seem to be suffering. Neither was I.

I'd known him six weeks if you count the humiliating incident at the Victoria and Albert museum. He'd been living in London and working as a liaison to the Royal Navy while waiting for his discharge papers from the U.S. Navy. He was thirty-eight and a Commander, which I gathered was a fairly impressive rank. I think James Bond was a Commander.

I'd been in London for the theater. I'd spent the past year working as an intern for one of the oldest true repertory companies working in the English language. Admittedly, at thirty-four I was a little over the hill to be an intern, and as I ran my own nonprofit rep company in San Francisco, it hadn't exactly been an upward career move. But what I'd learned had been priceless. And, of course, if I hadn't done it I'd never have met the man sleeping in Seat 4A.

Jack was a meteorologist. He looked at weather maps and computer screens and told the fleet when they'd run into fog and things. I'd yawned when he'd first explained this to me. Mistake. He'd shown up the next day with that movie where the fishing boat gets lost in the huge storm.

"It's about weather," he'd said, his eyes flashing.

I'd watched it and thought it was more about the noble futility of man's struggle against nature. But then I tend to be dramatic. And anyway, I hadn't been interested in the movie. I had been interested in the man with the flashing eyes. Jack Fairfax.

Now, stretched out in the comfortable airline seat, I studied Jack, willing him to wake up. Tall and lean, with a jawline sharp enough to cut diamonds, he was chiseled without being all muscles. To me he looked like Gregory Peck in his prime. *Roman Holiday* Gregory Peck. It would be nice if I could say I looked like Audrey Hepburn, but I'm not delusional.

Actually, I'm more the Isabella Rossellini type. Curvy. Earthy. Dark-eyed and full-lipped. Unless you catch me on a bad day, in which case I'm fifteen pounds overweight and in need of a brow wax. It's all in the attitude.

One dark curl had flopped onto Jack's forehead, making him appear unexpectedly vulnerable, a look I couldn't imagine on him when awake. There was something powerful and self-contained about him. He was, among other things, the most secure person I'd ever met.

He'd need that when we got to San Francisco. I could predict fairly well how my friends and family would react to my marrying a man I'd known for only six weeks. My uncle Harry, who had taken over-protectiveness to an extreme ever since becoming my guardian twenty years ago, would assemble a team of private investigators to turn over every rock they could find in hopes of something filthy crawling out of Jack's background. That would be if he liked Jack.

My friends, on the other hand, would be surprised but supportive. Then they'd start placing bets on how long it would last.

The flight attendant noticed I was awake and sprang into action. "Good afternoon, Mrs. Fairfax." Mrs. Fairfax. After a lifetime of being Charley Van Leeuwen I hadn't actually decided to change my name yet. "Would you care for a drink? Tea? A biscuit?" She was English, and had that desperately concerned way of looking at you with wide eyes until you let her do something for you.

"Tea would be great," I said, trying and failing to return my seat to an upright position. I would miss English tea. San Francisco is a coffee town.

I turned on my side to face Jack. I knew the questions everyone would ask. Why him? Why now? Why so fast? Why marry at all? And I knew the only way I'd be able to answer them would be to point to Ex-

hibit A, the man in question. I considered rehearsing
some sort of secretive smile that would keep people
guessing.

Jack interrupted my train of thought. "Charley, you
know I can't sleep with you gazing at me adoringly."
He smiled, his eyes still closed. "Stop it right now or
I'll have to do something about it."

"Oh good, you're awake!" I leaned over and
wrapped my arm around his.

"Apparently," he said, finally opening his eyes.

"Did you miss me?"

"While I was sleeping?" He cleared his throat. "No,
Pumpkin, I've trained myself to dream of you so even
when I'm sleeping you're always there." He looked at
me in total seriousness.

I grinned. "I do appreciate a good line of bullshit."
And I kissed him.

"Why else would you have married me? Where are
we?" He glanced at the TV monitor that showed a
little cartoon airplane following a dotted line all the
way to San Francisco, just like in the Indiana Jones
movies. Jack yawned and pulled me closer. "How long
until we land?"

"A while yet." I yawned too. "Don't worry, tea's
on the way."

But by the time the flight attendant came back we
must have fallen asleep, because the next thing I knew
she was shaking me gently and asking us to prepare
for landing. We were home.

I had sold my North Beach flat when I'd moved to
London, so Jack and I were planning on staying at a
hotel until we found someplace together. I wasn't even
sure what hotel. I had left everything up to my friend
Eileen. She'd even arranged for the car that picked
us up.

"Where are we going?" I asked the driver.

"The Mark Hopkins, ma'am."

Jack looked at me. "Good choice for a honeymoon?"

It hadn't occurred to me that this was our honeymoon. I had just thought of it as going home. "It's great," I said. "Although Eileen wouldn't have known to book the honeymoon suite."

"You really didn't tell her?" Jack asked, pulling me across the seat towards him.

"Not her. Not anyone." I made the universal locking-my-lips-and-throwing-away-the-key gesture.

"Won't your friends be mad?"

"Probably. Probably furious." I thought about it. "Eileen will be upset because of the spontaneity. Here was a fabulous opportunity for her to plan something gigantic and I didn't let her."

Eileen lived to organize things. She was a hugely successful financial manager, and had once confessed—after several tequilas—that her secret hobby was alphabetizing.

"What about your other friends?" Jack hadn't asked much about my San Francisco friends before. He'd been kept pretty busy trying to sort out who was who in the London set.

"Brenda will be . . . worried, I think, more than upset. She made me promise once that I'd never get serious about a man until she'd done a Tarot card reading on him." Jack raised his eyebrows. "She's not a flake," I rushed to protest. "She's just . . . she went to Berkeley, and then she taught at U.C. Santa Cruz, and . . . she's very open to alternative ways of thinking."

"She sounds fascinating," he said dryly.

I punched his arm. "Don't mock her. She's one of my best friends."

Jack held up his hands. "I'm prepared to be nuts about her."

"You'd better be." I stroked his jacket sleeve where I'd punched him. "Did I hurt you?"

He grinned. "I'm tougher than you think."

I resumed counting off my friends. "Then there's the gang from the theater, Simon and Chip and Paris and Martha . . . I can't wait for you to meet everyone." I meant it. I wanted to show him off and I wanted him to love all my friends. The gang from the Rep—the repertory theater that I'd established and run before I'd gone to London—could be a little rowdy, and more than a little catty, but I was sure Jack could hold his own.

We turned up Nob Hill toward the hotel. "What about your family?"

He'd asked about my family before, and I'd always successfully dodged the questions. I wasn't about to break that streak now. "Look, there's the hotel!" I pointed. "We're here!" I kissed him quickly to stop him from replying. "God, I can't wait to get into a hot bath!"

There are newer hotels in San Francisco, and swankier hotels. But the Mark Hopkins has the distinction of being the place where Brenda, Eileen, and I had wound up after ditching our dates during a particularly hideous high school dance. We'd produced fake IDs and gotten first silly and then deadly serious over several bottles of mediocre champagne. Sixteen years had passed since then, but we still had a tradition of returning to the Mark for celebrations.

The suite was reserved in my name. After we registered it took a swarm of bellmen led by an intrepid concierge to escort us to our room.

As soon as we stepped through the door Jack summed up the place. "It looks like a duke's drawing room."

At the far end was an elaborate green marble fireplace with an overstuffed couch and two comfy chairs in front of it. Bookshelves lined either side of the mantle. There was a huge armoire which I assumed would discreetly contain a huge television. A round table big enough to seat six was off to the side, buried under a pile of gift baskets, champagne bottles, and flowers. Apparently word of my return had gotten out.

The most spectacular thing about the room was the view. I pulled Jack over to the window and swept my arm out theatrically. A classic, fog-free, pink and orange evening on the bay. Alcatraz Island formed a black silhouette on the purple water. The buildings spilling down the hills to the bay were blushing with embarrassment at being so well-lit. "There it is. Isn't it gorgeous?"

He looked from the window to me and back out the window again. His mouth twitched with a suppressed smile. "I suppose it'll do."

A polite cough interrupted us. We turned to find the bellmen gone and the concierge waiting to give us the grand tour. There were two bedrooms, one on either side of the main room. I'd told Eileen I was bringing a friend from London, and apparently she had assumed it was a separate-bedroom sort of friend, or at least she'd wanted to give me the option.

"Never mind," I told the concierge. "I'm sure we can find everything. Right now all I want is a long hot bath."

Jack tipped the man and closed the door behind him. Then he caught my arm and pulled me towards him. "Are you sure all you want is a bath?"

Tempting. I wrestled with my options as Jack flicked his tongue down my neck. But didn't someone once say marriage was about compromise? "I know," I said, backing away slowly and hooking my finger in his belt. "How about we both take a bath?"

Jack grinned and started unbuttoning. "I knew it wasn't a mistake to marry a smart woman."

I turned and went through the bedroom. It had a massive bed, a walk-in closet, and assorted chaises, benches, and chairs. None of which interested me at the moment.

"How do you feel about bubbles?" I asked, flipping the bathroom switch.

The light was bright on the white tile floor and shining fixtures. At first I blinked, not really understanding what I was looking at.

And then I screamed.

*　　*　　*

Jack pulled me away from the door, but I couldn't take my eyes off it. Off her.

She was about my age, with dark curls half-hiding her face. She was in the bathtub, her left arm hanging over the side. She was naked. She wasn't moving.

"Jack, is she—"

"Don't look. And don't go in there." He put his arm around me as I took a step towards her.

"Jack, her eyes are open. She might—" I struggled to break his hold on me. There had to be something I could do.

He pulled back. "Charley—" he spun me around to face him. "She's dead."

I realized I was holding my hands over my mouth. Part of my mind registered this as a hopelessly theatrical gesture, while the other part knew it was necessary to keep from screaming again. Jack moved me away from the door.

"Just breathe," he said, walking me slowly back to the living room.

He called the police and the hotel manager. The manager, a man with the look of a former high-school jock and an attitude that implied we must have been mistaken about a naked dead woman in our room, was there in roughly seventeen seconds. He made I'm-sure-this-is-just-a-misunderstanding noises until he was joined by the head of hotel security. Then he said "In there?" and gestured in the direction of the bathroom. Jack nodded grimly.

When they came back, the manager had lost his reassuring look. The security man was the first to speak. "You've called 911?"

"Yes," Jack said.

The man nodded, then asked the question that would be repeated at least a hundred times in the next several hours. "Who is she?"

The police came. There seemed to be dozens of them, but only a few actually went into the bathroom. "They must be the crime scene people," I said to Jack, having watched enough television to figure that much out.

We'd been waiting and watching and answering the same questions for long enough that the immediate horror of what we'd seen was fading. I was trying to focus on the activities of the police, hoping if I concentrated hard enough I'd stop seeing the image of that pale white skin in clear still water.

The hotel manager was speaking to a policeman. At least I assumed the man was with the police, because he was making the manager nervous. He was Asian and looked about fifteen years old. He wasn't in uniform. In fact, dressed as he was in a stylishly tailored dark gray suit with a narrow cream pinstripe, he looked like he'd been paged from some ultra-hip club. I nudged Jack. "Who do you think he is?"

The two men turned to look at us. "I think we're about to find out."

They approached, the manager speaking first. "Mr. Fairfax, Miss Van Leeuwen, this is Inspector Yahata. He's in charge of the investigation."

So he probably wasn't fifteen. "Hi," I said.

"I understand you've already given statements to the uniformed officer," Yahata said briskly. He gave us each a slight smile. "I hope you don't mind going over it all again for me."

I didn't imagine it would make much difference if we did mind. The detective seemed to be operating on his own electrical current. He buzzed with energy, from the quick movement with which he produced and opened a small sleek notebook to the overtly curious way his quick gaze shifted from Jack's face to mine. He raised his eyebrows expectantly and I wouldn't have been surprised to see a spark fly up from his tousled, spiky hair.

Jack spoke. "We checked in, we told the concierge it wouldn't be necessary for him to give us the tour, we decided to freshen up, and we found her."

The detective blinked. "You didn't enter the bathroom?"

"Not more than a step or two," I said. "Then Jack stopped me. It was obvious. . . ." I hesitated.

"Quite," the detective said crisply. He was taking notes, writing with a thin silver pen while maintaining eye contact with us. I couldn't help but wonder if that level of multitasking was entirely human. "And you say you don't know the woman?" he asked.

"We don't," Jack said firmly.

"No," I agreed. "Do you know who she is?"

I think the question startled him. "Not yet. And you didn't take anything from the room? From any of the rooms?"

"No," Jack said. "The bellmen took our luggage to another room, but we hadn't opened anything yet."

The detective nodded and noted.

"What would we have taken?" I asked. "Is something missing? Do you think she might have been robbed?"

Again Yahata registered surprise. Maybe I wasn't supposed to ask him questions. Nobody had ever told me the etiquette of being interrogated. After appearing to think about it for a second, he answered. "Everything is missing."

"Her clothes," the hotel manager supplied. "There aren't any. She must have walked down the hotel hallway naked before she . . ." he trailed off, looking over his shoulder towards the bedroom door.

"So you think it was a suicide," Jack said.

"Oh, well—" the manager began.

"We don't think anything, yet," Yahata said.

"Are there security cameras in the hallway?" I asked.

A look of annoyance flashed across the hotel manager's face. "Yes, but—"

"That will be all for now," Yahata interrupted him. "Will we be able to reach you at the hotel if we have further questions?"

"Please," the manager rushed before we could reply. "Accept my deepest apologies for this . . . inconvenience. The management would like to express its gratitude for your understanding, and discretion, by insisting that your stay with us be entirely complimentary."

Call me cynical, but I think the key word in all of

that was "discretion." The if-you-don't-go-running-to-the-papers-with-this-thing-we'll-pick-up-your-hotel-tab kind of discretion. It was probably the man's job to handle damage control, but I was a little miffed that he assumed we'd need a bribe to keep from dashing off to the nearest media outlet.

"Thanks," I said. "We're just moving to the area, and it might be a couple of months before we find a house." I gave him a charming smile. "Let alone go through all the paperwork of buying one. You're very generous."

The poor guy looked like he was reliving some fateful moment of his youth when he'd dropped the ball in front of the whole town during the big game. At around three thousand dollars a night, he'd just offered to comp us to the tune of at least $180,000. And that was before the damage we could do with room service. His left eye began to twitch.

Oh, hell. I can only torture someone for so long. "Never mind." I patted his arm. "It wasn't your fault. Let's just forget the whole thing." I looked toward the bedroom door. "Or try to."

Yahata shut his notebook with a snap. The manager and I both jumped. Jack extended his hand. "Inspector, if there's anything we can do."

"Thank you," the detective replied. He turned to me. "I hope you find a suitable home, Mrs. Fairfax." He stressed my married name slightly. It may just have been a random bolt of electricity, but I think his eyes sparked.

Jack installed me on the sofa in our new suite and poured me a large Glenfiddich on the rocks. I drank it gratefully and watched him pour another for himself. "Jack, have you ever seen a dead person before?"

His face remained neutral as he sat next to me. "Yes."

I'd thought so. He'd been too calm back there for this to have been his first. "How? I mean, under what circumstances?"

"Sad," he said evenly. "Sad circumstances."

I leaned my head back on his arm and didn't say anything for a while. "I'm glad this room is a little different from the other one. It won't seem so . . ." I couldn't think of a word that didn't seem melodramatic, so I gave up.

Jack wrapped his arms around me. "Still a nice view, though."

The room was pretty much the same in layout. A central living room with two bed/bath combinations, one on either side. But the color scheme was different, various shades of blue, and the furniture was more chic townhouse than gentlemen's club.

"This wasn't exactly the welcome home I'd imagined."

"Aren't bad starts supposed to be good luck?" Jack asked. "I'm sure I've heard that somewhere."

"You're such a good liar." I craned my head around to look at the pile of presents that had been transferred to our new room after a thorough examination by the police. "Are you hungry? It looks like there's something to eat." I got up to investigate.

There was the inevitable fruit basket from the hotel management, and a bottle of Tattinger on now-melted ice from Eileen. A bunch of roses was from the gang at the theater. A gorgeous orchid had a note from my friend Brenda. A cheerful bouquet of brightly decorated cookies on stems filled a flower pot. I opened the card that was stuck in among them.

> *Charley,*
> *I expect you and your husband for brunch on*
> *Sunday. A car will pick you up at 11:00.*

Suddenly the whisky hit and I felt the floor go out from under me. The note was from my Uncle Harry. It wasn't signed, but it didn't have to be. Harry was the only person I knew who could make a brunch date sound as casual as a mandatory court appearance. It wasn't an invitation—it was a command.

Damn.

I felt Jack approach me from behind and I took a deep breath. "Want a cookie?" I asked, tucking the note away and hoping my voice wasn't too tight.

He slipped his hands around my waist. "No."

"How about some warm champagne?"

He pulled me closer. "Not now."

I leaned back against him and closed my eyes. "To hell with him," I murmured.

"To hell with who?" Jack asked, exploring my earlobe with his tongue.

"Never mind." To hell with Harry, I thought. And his investigators. And while I was at it, to hell with dead bodies, electric-shock detectives, insecure hotel managers, and everything else except Jack's slow swaying motion.

We stayed like that for a while, then Jack lifted me up, carried me to one of the bedrooms, and did his damnedest to make me forget the past few hours.

It nearly worked. At one point I actually heard bells. How bridal, I thought absently. They were persistent, though, and after a while began to be irritating.

"Jack," I whispered. "Jack!"

"Hmrft?"

"Do you hear bells?"

He paused, breathing heavily. "It's the doorbell. Someone won't go away."

The ringing started again, this time accompanied by voices. Voices I recognized. "Hey!" I tried to disentangle myself from my husband and the bedclothes.

"Pumpkin . . . wait . . . no . . ." Jack protested.

"Jack, I know them. They won't go away until the cops come." The ringing and calling was now accompanied by heavy banging on the door. I grabbed a hotel robe off a hook in the closet. "And I've had enough cops today. Besides"—I threw another robe at him—"don't you want to meet my friends?"

Chapter 2

I opened the door, shouting "Shut up, shut up, for the love of God!" as they came tumbling through in a tangle of arms, legs, coats, and champagne bottles. It was chaos worthy of the Marx brothers.

"Darling! You are here! I was convinced they got it wrong! I couldn't think you'd have gotten back and not called us all instantly!" This was shouted by Simon, the artistic director of the Rep and the most dramatic man I'd ever known—which is saying something. He grabbed me by both shoulders, bent me backwards in an elaborate dip, and kissed me with great flourish. He tasted distinctly of Veuve Clicquot.

It was astonishing that Simon could plant a kiss on me without interrupting his own stream of words. "Charley, you can't possibly have intended to skulk back into town without a suitable greeting, can you? And what in the hell are you doing in a bathrobe at this hour? Not that you don't pull it off admirably, darling, but it's the absolute shank of the evening and your entourage—"

"Charley!" Brenda pushed Simon aside and threw her arms around me. "I can't believe you're back! Why didn't you say something? You haven't called in weeks! I've missed you so much!" She squeezed me, whispering in my ear. "Is everything all right? Are you okay?" She pulled back to give me a searching look.

"I'm fine," I reassured her, squeezing her hands. "In fact—"

"Well, you could have called," Eileen asserted,

standing off to one side. "Oh be quiet, Simon!" This in an attempt to still the running commentary on how I looked, how he looked, and what a lovely pile of presents was over on the table. Surprisingly, it worked. Simon grinned amiably and stopped talking.

"Of course," Eileen continued, "I saw your flight had gotten in all right from the airline's web site, but a phone call wouldn't have killed you." She looked at me severely.

"I'm sorry, sweetie," I said. "But we just barely got settled in the room, which is fabulous and thank you so much—" she waved the gratitude away "—and with one thing and another I haven't had a moment, and I'm so sorry—"

Eileen waved again, impatiently. "You know I'm not angry," she said. "I was just worried that everything might not have gone smoothly."

Somehow, I didn't have it in me to tell her how spectacularly unsmoothly it had gone. I decided the story of the woman in the bathtub could wait. I really didn't want to talk about it any more that night. In fact, I never wanted to think about it again.

"Who's 'we'?" Brenda asked. "You said 'we' just got to the hotel, and with one thing and another . . ."

"And who's this?" Simon asked, catching sight of Jack as he came out of the bedroom tying his robe. "And is he one thing or another?" He crossed his arms and gave Jack an appraising look.

Eileen slapped him lightly on the arm and hissed "Behave! I told you she was bringing a friend."

"Some friend," he murmured.

Jack crossed the room to stand behind me, his arms around my shoulders, and there was a moment when all my friends were speechless. Unprecedented. Jack broke the silence.

"Hi."

Then, of course, they all talked at once.

"And who might you be?" Simon.

"Hello," with hand extended, "you must be . . ." Eileen.

"Hi! I'm Brenda!"

"I don't believe Charley mentioned you." Simon.

"Are you and Charley . . . ?" Brenda.

I tried to shut them up and failed, so I simply shouted over them. I pointed to each, calling off their names in turn. "Eileen, you remember I told you about her? She arranged the car and hotel? She's my financial manager?" And she looked great. Tall and slim with wavy dark hair and dark eyes. Usually her style was businesslike verging on frumpy, but tonight she looked positively stylish in a crisp white shirt with a turned-up collar and black silk pants above high-heeled sandals.

"And this is Simon?" I continued. "From the theater? Simon, shut up and say hello!" Simon paused long enough to toss his head, sending a ripple through his blond, well-cut hair. He had the long, lean, aristocratic look of an Englishman to the manor born, but I'd met his parents in London and I could only conclude that his high cheekbones were a fluke. Simon enjoyed describing himself as "omnisexual," and he lingered as he shook Jack's hand, asking "Wherever did Charley find you?"

Jack looked at me. "Well—"

"Later!" I interrupted, and pushed Brenda in front of Simon. "This is Brenda." I could have continued by saying "the nicest woman in the world," and I didn't only because she would just have gotten self-conscious. But she was.

Brenda and her mother had been the closest thing I'd had to a real family after my parents had died, and there's still nobody who can touch Mrs. Gee for the pure comfort of sticky rice wrapped in bamboo leaves.

Brenda hadn't changed, I saw with relief. She was still slightly plump, her glasses still slid down her nose, she still wore her long straight hair in a clip at the back of her neck, and she still dressed in loose, flowing clothes. She looked wonderful.

"It's great to meet you," Jack said. "Charley's told

me so much about you." If I hadn't known better I'd have believed him.

Then they were off again, firing questions on top of each other, only certain words—"Boyfriend?" "American?" "Staying?"—emerging from the babble.

"Hey, hey, hey!" I yelled, finally audible after the last shout. "Everybody, just calm down!" I straightened my robe, pulling the belt tighter for added dignity. "Sheesh, you'd think I'd never had a man in my room before!"

"Well, darling—" Simon began, but stopped when I gave him a look.

"Everybody," I announced serenely, "this is Jack." Before they could start up again, I added the phrase I'd been rehearsing for two days. "Jack is my husband."

A moment's stunned silence and then—pandemonium.

"Are you serious?"

"Darling, what can you mean?"

"Husband? You got married?"

"You're not serious."

"You got married!"

"You are serious!"

"Darling!"

Jack was great, answering three streams of questions while being pulled and pushed into one set of arms after another. Finally he landed in mine and I held on.

"Okay, everybody! Everybody!" I tried to bring order to the chaos. "Thank you! Thank you!" One last kiss from a tearful Brenda and they finally calmed down. "And now," I paused, "go away!"

I must have sagged a bit because Eileen snapped into action. "Of course you're exhausted, and of course we should go," she said, brushing her lips past my cheek. "We'll have plenty of time to hear all about everything when you've had a chance to get some rest."

"Um," Simon looked awkward, and not just because a weeping Brenda was wiping her glasses on his shirttail. "What about . . ." He looked heavenward.

"What about . . . shit!" Eileen's hand flew to her mouth. "The party!"

"What party?" I asked.

Brenda gulped hugely and stopped crying. "The party!"

"Hello?" I said, getting a little nervous. "Don't tell me more people are about to start banging on the door."

"Certainly not," Simon said smoothly. "They're all upstairs." He registered my look of incomprehension. "In the bar . . ." Patiently . . . "The Top of the Mark?" He pointed up.

Oh, good God. "Who? How many?"

Simon shrugged. "Everybody."

Eileen assumed command. "Well, never mind. It was a stupid idea. We just thought a little welcome home thing. Of course we didn't know . . ." she trailed off and looked at Jack, who was observing the exchange with obvious amusement. "But it doesn't matter. It was thoughtless of us, and you're tired, so we'll just . . ." A crease appeared between her brows.

"We'll just pop upstairs and explain, and . . ." Simon waved his hands magically. "Everything will be fine."

Brenda said "I'm sure everyone will understand."

I looked at Jack. He shrugged. "As long as we're up . . ."

I kissed him loudly on the cheek. "You're wonderful." Then, to Eileen, "Give us five minutes to throw on some clothes."

Simon hadn't been exaggerating. Everybody was there. From the Rep, there was Martha the costume designer, Chip the stage manager, and Paris the set designer. There were also older friends, writers and editors from the literary magazine Brenda and I had started after college, artists I'd come in contact with when Eileen and I had briefly had a gallery in the Mission district, and one or two lawyers and accountants from Eileen's firm that I'd gotten to know over the years.

The Top of the Mark, as its name implies, is on the top floor of the hotel. It has windows on all sides and each view is better than the last, but the spectacle of the city at night was lost on me as I popped from one table to another, exchanging polite air kisses with some and warm hugs with others, completely forgetting how tired I'd been and totally losing track of time.

"Charley, has Simon filled you in on the new play?" Chip got right to the point as soon as we'd said hello. He was in his late twenties and it appeared he hadn't managed to get much of a life since I'd seen him last, although I had heard he'd gotten an assistant, which might help. He was intense and focused and cared deeply about the Rep. Other people were chatting and enjoying the music of Hi Neighbor, the three-piece jazz combo, but Chip wanted to get down to work.

"I just saw him for two minutes, so we didn't get a chance to talk about it."

Chip nodded seriously. "I'll messenger over a copy tomorrow. You'll love it. The playwright is local, from somewhere in the East Bay. Simon's met her but I haven't yet." I listened and smiled vaguely as he went on. "The play is so good. It's funny but touching—"

Simon swooped by and pulled me away before Chip could say anything more. "Charley, I don't know if I shall ever forgive you for not telling me all about this chap." He looked over at Jack.

"I'll make a deal," I bargained. "If you put me in a quiet corner with a martini in my hand I'll tell you everything you want to know."

"Done!" He spun me around and I was facing Eileen and Brenda. "Girls, drag her off somewhere so she can give us the dish. I'll be back in an instant."

A comfortable chair away from the crowd. Bliss. With my friends around, the shock of the evening's discovery seemed miles away. Maybe it was incipient jet lag, or maybe it was the free-flowing champagne, but the dead woman in the hotel room was beginning to feel like something I'd dreamed. It was definitely something I didn't want to think about. Especially not now.

"So," Simon said as he handed me a drink, "tell us everything." He looked meaningfully at Jack, who seemed to be deep in conversation with Chip a couple of tables away. He'd know more about the new play than I would before the night was over.

I cleared my throat and began. "We met at a fundraiser for the Royal Academy of Dramatic Arts."

"Well, la de da," Simon said dryly.

"Not really, it was pretty much your standard gathering of artsy dowagers and theater types at the Victoria & Albert." I turned to Eileen. "It's the most amazing museum. It has the most wonderful costume and textile collections—"

"So anyway," Brenda called my attention back to the point of the story. "Jack was there."

"He was." I couldn't help smiling that mysterious smile that the unromantic find so annoying. "He was the absolute definition of tall, dark, and handsome." I looked over at him now, nodding encouragingly as Chip spoke. "Of course I assumed he was gay. I mean, a room full of actors, all of them fantastically attractive, and he stands out as . . ." I sighed.

"Yes, darling, we've met him. We get the picture," Simon said.

"So did you flirt with him? Did your eyes meet across a crowded room? Did lightning strike?" Brenda's eyes sparkled.

"Did the angels weep for joy?" Eileen contributed, heavy on the mockery.

I gave her a dirty look. "No. It wasn't like that at all." I glanced around the table, making sure I had their complete attention. "I'd caught him looking at me once or twice, but I had no idea who he was— nobody seemed to know. Anyway, the place was packed, and people kept cornering me and hitting me up for donations, so eventually I escaped to the ladies room."

"He followed you in!" Simon accused.

"He didn't!" Brenda protested.

"He did not. I was in there a while, though, because my makeup was starting that transformation from fabulous to frightening and I needed to do some major repair work." There were general nods of sympathy and quick under-eye wipes. "When I came back to the party the crowd was thinning out so I figured the bar had closed. I couldn't find anybody I'd come with."

"Typical," said Eileen. "Ditched by Brits." She looked at Simon, who shrugged as if he wasn't interested in the task of defending his countrymen.

I continued. "I wandered around for a while and wound up in the kitchen, where I got yelled at by some French guy. So I was pretty flustered—"

"Meaning drunk," Simon whispered loudly.

"—and pretty much standing in the middle of the room feeling . . . ditched by Brits." I nodded to Eileen. "When I realized he was right next to me."

"Jack?"

"Jack. Although I didn't know his name. He looked me straight in the eye, smiled just a tiny bit, and leaned toward me. I thought he was going to kiss me—"

"Fresh!" Simon said approvingly.

"—but instead he whispered in my ear."

I paused. I hadn't taken all those acting classes without learning something about timing.

"What! What! What did he say?" They were staring, waiting for the words that had swept me off my feet.

"He said," I breathed, " 'Your ass.' "

"Ugghh. He didn't!" Brenda looked over at him now with deep disappointment.

"He did. And right then my friend Tina came and threw her arms around me and dragged me away. All 'darling, where have you been, you must meet Lady blah blah blah' and she pulled me away from him."

"What did you do?" Eileen looked like she was trying not to laugh.

"Well, you know, I just chalked it up to the fact that even a gorgeous guy can be a complete perv."

"Especially them," Simon said knowingly.

I shrugged. "But I was still a little shaken up by the whole thing when I realized what Tina was saying to me."

"She told you he was married—No! That he was on parole—No!" Brenda was getting out of control.

"No." I cut her off. "She told me I had white powder all over my butt."

They were silent for a moment, registering the facts. Then my closest friends in the entire world burst into laughter.

"Fine, I'm glad you're all so amused."

"So what did you do?" Simon finally asked, after choking on an olive.

"I went back to the ladies, dusted myself off—it was flour, incidentally, from the kitchen—got my coat, and went outside to get a cab."

"That was it? That was your first meeting?" Brenda looked absolutely betrayed.

"I really don't see how you got from there to a shotgun wedding in—how long ago was this?" Eileen asked.

"It was six weeks and almost three days ago, and it was not a shotgun wedding," I said pointedly. "And that wasn't all."

"What, what, what?"

Ah ha! I know how to work an audience. "Well, there I was waiting for a cab, and the next thing I knew he was next to me again. I don't know how he did it. He just sort of appeared."

"And?" Simon demanded.

"And he said, 'I was going to tell you your ass was covered in flour.'"

There was a collective groan of sympathy, which I found very comforting. "I was absolutely mortified. And it didn't help that he looked like he was going to start laughing any second. Then he leaned in again, to whisper in my ear, and he said"—wait for it—" 'But it's a magnificent ass.' "

"Yes!" Eileen and Simon exchanged high fives while Brenda applauded.

"What did you say?" Brenda asked.

"Nothing! It all seemed to happen so fast." I shook my head, clearing the memory. "Then a cab pulled up and the driver said . . . something . . . and when I turned back he was gone."

"Gone?" Eileen exclaimed.

"Poof, vanished, absorbed into the dark and the fog and the crowd."

The three of them turned to look appraisingly at my husband.

By the time we left the party I had hit the wall of exhaustion again. We went downstairs to our suite and slept all night, all the next day, and all the following night.

Well, mostly we slept.

Chapter 3

I was staring at Jack's sleeping profile when his left eye opened.

"Charley—" he cleared his throat—"that's getting to be a very weird habit." The eye closed. "Suppose I get used to it? I won't be able to sleep without you looking at me."

I kissed the corner of his mouth then settled back again, my chin in my hands, regarding him.

"You're still doing it, aren't you?"

"I can't help myself." I sighed elaborately.

At that he let out a laugh, gave up on further sleep, and turned toward me, propping his head in his hand. "Good morning."

"You were wonderful last night."

"You really don't need to tell me that every morning."

"I don't mean that. I mean with the gang. You were wonderful. They loved you."

"Technically," he pointed out, "that wasn't last night."

"Whatever. They still loved you."

"Well," he said, "they were a tough crowd."

"Oh, they're a bunch of pussycats."

"Pussycats?" I sensed a certain skepticism.

"Creampuffs."

"Mmmm. I could go for a creampuff right about now." His smile was just the slightest bit wicked.

"Room service?" I suggested. "Creampuffs and coffee for two?"

"Why is it I think we're talking about different things?" He drew me toward himself just as the phone rang. "Shit," he said, his face centimeters from mine.

"Shit," I agreed. "It's our wakeup call."

"We're awake. Make them go away."

"They won't." I rolled away from him, causing him to let out a very flattering grumble. "We're paying them to do this."

"Then we're idiots."

I laughed and picked up the phone. "Would you believe?" I asked Jack, "it isn't even a person. It's a recording."

"Then I have no qualms about ignoring it. Get over here."

I hung up. "So much for personal attention and service."

"Hey lady," he said, putting on what he must have thought was a Brooklyn accent, "I got your personal service right here."

"Oh, that's sexy," I said flatly. "That's the way to my heart."

"I ain't interested in your heart, doll face," he persisted, and I reconciled myself to being late for brunch with Uncle Harry.

It wasn't until later, when I was dressing, that I started to feel queasy. Why had I wanted to come home so soon? A sane woman would be in Venice or the South of France at a time like this, not worried about bringing the new hubby over to meet the family's lunatic elder statesman.

Ever since he had become my guardian, Harry had taken it upon himself to investigate anyone I was involved with. The fact that he had stopped controlling my finances when I'd turned twenty-five hadn't stopped him from trying to keep control of every other aspect of my life. Possibly because some shady characters had recurring roles in his own personal life, he was deeply suspicious about anyone who came into mine.

Some people thought being over-protective was endearing. These people haven't been on the receiving end of it. I was sure my uncle would be just itching to dig up anything he could find on Jack. He'd probably already started. Not that he'd find anything.

As usual, I took my anxiety out on the inanimate objects around me. I'd already shredded two pairs of pantyhose and caused a pull in the loosely knitted sweater set I'd planned to wear. I had to opt for a celadon-colored Armani sheath dress instead. I was too pale for the color to look good on me, but at least the dress was linen and unlikely to spontaneously unravel.

"Charley," Jack called from the bathroom. "What's your uncle like?" He stood in the doorway, toweling his hair dry and wearing another towel around his hips. Why hadn't we gone to Bora Bora or Fiji or someplace like normal honeymooners so he could dress like that all the time? "You two must be pretty close."

I gave up on my search for the little Kate Spade sandals that I was beginning to believe I hadn't packed. "Close?"

"Well, he invited us over on our second day in town." He shrugged. "Sounds like he missed you." I thought about how to reply while Jack went to the walk-in closet to dress. "He raised you after your parents died, didn't he?"

Sort of, along with the proprietors of boarding schools, camps, and various "retreats" I'd been sent to. "I suppose you could say that."

"So what's he like?" Jack came out looking perfect. Perfectly tailored black trousers and a perfectly fitted charcoal cashmere sweater, a perfect black jacket over his arm. Not only a perfect look for him, but exactly the uniform of choice for gorgeous men attending Sunday brunch in San Francisco. How the hell did he do that? He probably knew exactly where his perfect shoes were at all times. "I'm imagining a sort of Lionel Barrymore character," he said. "The old family patriarch who raises orchids or keeps spaniels or collects first editions."

I laughed. "Hardly."

"What then?"

I thought about Harry. "Picture a Beach Boy gone to seed."

"That's picturing a Beach Boy."

I shrugged. "There you have it."

"Seriously?"

"Seriously." How to describe Harry? I tried. "When he was young he was pretty much a classic bad boy, but on a spectacular scale. His major ambitions involved surfing in the summer, skiing in the winter, and getting laid as often as possible. He smoked a lot of dope and drank a lot of booze and got kicked out of all the best schools."

"As long as they were the best," Jack said reasonably.

"Naturally. He didn't really grow up until he had to. Until my dad died and Harry had to take over . . . things."

Jack pecked me on the cheek in passing. "Such as your lovely self."

"Exactly," I said graciously. "And a couple hundred million dollars."

"Only a couple?"

I ignored him. "But Harry never really matured, if you know what I mean. He was still the same wild man, always pulling outrageous stunts, always just barely on this side of what's legal. And on top of that he got—" I hesitated, not sure how to put it. "Weird. Paranoid and suspicious and mistrustful." I accused myself of being redundant while I held a scarf up to see if it would help the dress.

"Smoking a lot of dope will do that to a person," Jack said. I looked at him enquiringly. "Or so I've heard," he added. "How old is this guy?"

"Mentally? About eighteen. On his driver's license—if they still let him drive—it's more like late fifties. He and my father were almost ten years apart." I gave up on the scarf and went back to the shoe search.

"Your dad was older?"

"Harry says my dad was born old enough for the both of them." I settled for a less-than-perfect pair of high-heel slides. "I suspect when he says 'old' he means 'mature.' Just wait," I warned him. "At some point in the day he'll tell you, 'I may be middle-aged, but someday you will be too, and you won't have lived through the sixties.' "

Jack laughed. "I think I'm going to like this guy."

"Everyone does," I admitted.

"I notice there's no aunt associated with him."

"Oh, there have been." I moved to sit next to Jack on the bed; then I saw the way he was looking at me and thought better of it. "Come out to the living room." He grinned and followed me. "There were . . ." I did a quick calculation, "five official aunts and, oh, probably a dozen whose terms of office were too short to make the record."

"Any kids?"

"My cousin Cece. She's going on thirty now, and apparently she's just like Harry."

"Another black sheep or another surfer?"

"Another pain in the ass. At least she was when she was a little girl," I said, remembering a particularly nasty incident involving maple syrup and my Trixie Belden book collection. "She got kicked out of her share of schools as well. There were always drugs, of course, and the inevitable 'bad crowd' that had corrupted her."

"You sound like a fan."

"Well, you know me." I gathered up my purse, which would have matched the missing sandals beautifully, and checked to make sure it contained the right shade of lipstick. "I hate a cliché. She's the typical spoiled rich girl whose daddy buys her out of trouble."

"I can't wait to meet her. Will she be there today?"

"God, I hope not. It'll be bad enough without that." Too late, I realized what I had said. I looked at Jack, draped elegantly on the couch. He raised an eyebrow. "I mean . . ." I couldn't think of a good way to finish the sentence.

"Family, huh?"

"Yeah."

Harry's driver had arrived on time and waited for us. From the direction he took, heading toward Highway 280, I figured we weren't going to Harry's apartment in the city but to his house in Hillsborough.

Jack interrupted my train of thought with a question. "Is there an aunt in the picture these days?"

"No," I told him. "The last time we spoke he told me he'd just hired some guy to cook for him and sort of run the house. He said at his age that's all he wants from a wife. This way he can have as many mistresses as he likes without ending up in divorce court again." I rolled my eyes.

Jack grinned. "I swear I'm going to like this guy."

"Before you fall in love with him," I warned, "can we agree not to mention anything about finding that woman at the hotel?" I shivered with the sudden sharp memory of her lifeless face.

We hadn't heard anything from Inspector Yahata since we'd left him Friday night. I was curious about whether the woman had been identified yet, but supposed these things took time. Maybe more time than usual during a weekend, although I doubted being a police inspector was a nine-to-five kind of job.

The papers and local TV news hadn't had anything on the story. I could only assume the hotel's public relations agency was earning its keep.

"Why don't you want Harry to know?"

"Because he'd make something of it. He'd assume it had some meaning, like it was a threat or a warning or something. And before you know it he'd have armed guards camped outside our door."

"He's that bad?"

"Trust me," I said. "I'm sure he's already got his entire staff trying to find evidence that you're some sort of gigolo creep bastard—"

"—who's after your fortune," Jack supplied.

"—who's after my fortune," I agreed. "The last thing we need is to give him a reason to think you're a gigolo creep bastard who's putting me in danger."

Jack looked at me thoughtfully. "This should be an interesting brunch."

I'd forgotten how massive the house was. It seemed to sprawl across the landscape, a conglomeration of arches, tile roofs, stucco, and iron work that comprised the architectural style Old California.

Houses of similar size, if not design, were visible through the trees. To the left was an enormous attempt at a château, and to the right a mock-Tudor monstrosity with predictable red geraniums in boxes at every window.

The rear of the property, I knew, faced the Hillsborough Country Club golf course. I had been a member of the club when I'd lived in the house as a teenager. In the stretches of time when I wasn't at school or some camp, I'd escaped the house and its inhabitants by swimming, playing tennis, and golfing. Outdoor activities had had the advantage of being of no interest whatsoever to my cousin Cece, who at that time had been going for the world record in obnoxious behavior.

The car came to a stop at the foot of a sprawling staircase that led up to massive wooden doors, complete with heavy iron fittings. Jack gave a low whistle as he got out of the car. "Cozy."

The doors were suddenly flung open, and Harry stood in the doorway. He threw his arms wide and yelled "Charley!" loud enough to send a flock of doves shooting out of a tree. There he was, wide grin in place, wearing a loose-fitting silk Hawaiian-print shirt, knee-length cargo shorts, and Birkenstocks.

"Baby Doll! Get your butt over here and give an old man a hug!"

I approached him warily, not letting go of Jack's hand until Harry threw his arms around me.

"Damn, girl, you got skinny!" Harry held me tightly. Over his shoulder I saw Jack mouthing, "Baby Doll?" with raised eyebrows. Then Harry pushed me away, positioning me at arm's length to get a better look. "Don't tell me you're turning into one of those damn stick women!"

"Hardly." The only comment Harry ever made to a woman about her appearance was that she looked like she'd lost weight. He figured it was always safe territory. "Harry, I want you to meet Jack."

Harry's eyes held mine for just a fraction of a second before he turned to Jack, but it was enough time to see the flash of anger. "Jack!" he said heartily, simultaneously shaking his hand and clapping him on the shoulder. "The famous Jack Fairfax! Of whom I've heard so much." This last was directed at me.

"It's a pleasure to meet you, sir," Jack said in a voice I'd only heard once before, when he'd been addressing an admiral at a diplomatic party we'd attended in London. It was a long way from the casual, teasing tone I was used to.

I suppose I stared at him in surprise, because there was a moment's awkward silence. Then Harry boomed again. "Well, let's not stand here all day! We've got some celebrating to do! What are you drinking, Jack?" We moved into the house.

There was no foyer or entry hall. Once inside the door, we were in the "great room" that ran the width of the house and nearly the length, at least on the ground level. It was decorated as it had always been, in sturdy oversized mission-style furniture. Dark cherry pieces with straight, clean lines and comfortable cushions were scattered around on area rugs, forming clusters here and there on the enormous expanse of wide-planked floor. The rear wall consisted of four arched windows looking out on a terrace with a pool and garden below and the golf course beyond. Harry kept talking as he led us to the bar, a huge carved altar rescued from a Watsonville church that had been damaged in the earthquake of '89. One of the aunts had discovered it and had it converted to suit Harry's alcoholic purpose.

"Champagne, I think! That only fits an occasion as festive as this! How about a glass of champagne, Charley? Or a mimosa! That's the thing! Mimosas for our wedding celebration brunch! Let me just call Gordon." He pressed a button concealed in the ornate carving of the bar and barked into a hidden intercom. "Gordon! Get up here with some O.J.! We need mimosas up here!" Then he turned once again to Jack, a broad smile not reaching his eyes as he said "Mimosa okay with you, Jack? Not too 'girlie' for a Navy man?"

He didn't wait for a reply. His voice was a rough, gravelly baritone, years of whiskey and cigars having given it its character. "Wait 'til you meet Gordon, Charley, he's only been here about a month but I can't figure out how I ever got by without him. He cooks, he keeps the weirdos away from me"—a weirdo was anyone who asked for money—"and he keeps everything running according to the plan."

Right. The plan. It was pretty clear what Harry's plan was this morning. He was trying to charm us to death. The only problem was that I knew him well enough to see what a strain his I'm-just-so-happy-you're-happy act was to keep up. And the comment about Jack being a Navy man had been thrown in to let me know Harry had begun digging already. I figured it would take about one sideways glance from Jack or one smart-ass comment from me to trigger a meltdown. Right. If that's how he wanted to play it, fine. I can do charm too.

"Harry," I cooed, taking his arm and squeezing it. "The place is amazing. It looks just the same."

"Timeless, much like myself," he responded, winking at Jack.

"I don't know," I teased, reaching up to ruffle his hair. "There might be just a fraction less up here."

"And a fraction more down here," Harry finished, patting his belly. "But I don't care. That's the price of enjoying life. Right, Jack?" Again with the wink.

"Yes, sir."

"And anyway, I may be middle-aged, but someday you will be too and you won't have lived through the sixties!" Jack and I caught each other's eye as Harry laughed at his own wit and called, "Gordon!"

A slight, fortyish man had appeared at the top of the short stairway that led down to the kitchen and dining-room level. "Where's that O.J., dude? Charley, I want you to meet Gordon, my new 'man' as your friends the Brits would say." He took the pitcher of juice that Gordon offered him.

"Pleased to meet you, Gordon. I'd like you to meet my new 'husband' as you Yanks would say." So much for my charm. Harry's smile grew tighter.

There was a moment's hesitation as Gordon picked up on the tension in the room. Jack was the first to speak, holding his hand out to shake Gordon's. "Jack Fairfax, Gordon. Pleased to meet you."

And then a shot went off. Or so I thought, jumping when I heard the loud pop. It was Harry, opening a bottle of champagne and grinning maniacally. "How about we mix these up and then go have some of that great brunch that Gordon's fixed for us, huh Charley? Right, Jack?"

"Sounds like a plan, sir," Jack said, still in his reporting-to-a-superior-officer voice.

"Baby Doll?" Harry handed me a mimosa.

I winced. "Whatever, Harry."

Chapter 4

And so it went, with Harry doing a California spin on the Lord of the Manor, Jack being crisp and polite, and me bouncing back and forth between the desire to keep a lid on the situation and a let's-get-it-over-with urge to provoke Harry. Adolescent, I know, but my uncle brings that out in me.

On the plus side, the brunch was spectacular. Gordon served cured slivers of salmon on buckwheat blinis with crème fraîche and a dollop of golden caviar. Bliss. This was followed by roasted asparagus wrapped in prosciutto, covered in an egg Gordon described as "brullee'd," which presumably meant he'd achieved its caramelized surface with a kitchen blowtorch. He was nothing if not handy. There was a perfect mixed-berry shortcake for dessert.

Throughout the meal Gordon came and went silently and swiftly. He was probably the quietest man I'd ever met. He was thin and pale, with close-cropped light brown hair that was thin on top, but brushed forward to make the most of it. His movements were contained and economical. If I were casting a play I'd pick him for the mild-mannered murderer every time.

It occurred to me at some point that I should ask after my cousin. "It's a shame Cece couldn't be here," I lied. "Is she . . ." The mind boggled at where she could be and what she could be doing.

Harry relaxed into what looked like his first genuine smile of the day. "She's good," he said. "She got out of rehab last week and she's doing just fine." I must have had a look on my face because he continued somewhat defensively. "She's met a nice guy." He looked meaningfully at Jack. "A good man. They're living in Marin."

I choked back the comment I wanted to make and nodded. "That's great. That's really wonderful."

"He's a doctor," Harry continued. "Works with addicts. He's got a good future." He glanced at Jack again. "And a good past." He dug into his food.

Uh-huh. I got it. The doctor had passed the Harry test. Lucky, lucky Cece.

After we'd finally eaten everything we could, Harry pushed himself back from the table and sighed. "Time for a cigar, don't you think, Jack?"

"Well, sir, I can't say I've ever acquired the habit," Jack replied, "but I'll tell you what I would like, and that's to see more of your house."

Who was this man? Whoever he was, I could tell his perfect manners were getting on Harry's nerves. Jack wasn't being polite enough to be interpreted as kissing up, which Harry would have despised. And he wasn't in the least bit ironic; there was nothing that could cause Harry offense. He stayed exactly in the zone of irreproachable behavior, and it was pissing Harry off. Suddenly I had a whole new appreciation of my husband.

We wandered around the house for a while, passing through the rooms while Harry kept up a running commentary worthy of the Style channel. Eventually we wound up in the game room, so called not only because it contained a pool table, pinball machine, and assorted other toys, but because the walls were lined with the mounted heads of assorted "big game," courtesy of a minor, debt-ridden museum that one of Harry's exes had bought out. She'd found the dead animals kitschy.

The house was built on a slight slope, and this room was on the ground level of the south wing. Glass doors looked through impeccable landscaping towards the flagstone terrace and beyond that, the pool. There were board games available on small tables throughout the room, a half-completed puzzle on a poker table, and newspapers and magazines conveniently placed near comfortable leather chairs. It looked like a gentlemen's club for Norman Bates and friends.

And then there were the weapons. Various axes, bows, arrows, and antique guns were mounted on walls, displayed in cases, or simply scattered around on tables. This didn't exactly help my nerves. Harry's attitude had shifted as soon as we entered the room. He was getting down to business.

"I think it's time for a real drink," he said, stepping behind a well-stocked bar and dropping the jovial act. "What's yours, Jack?"

"It's still a little early for me, sir. Thanks anyway."

Harry's eyes narrowed. "Too early? I thought you were a Navy man."

"Since when does that mean a lush?" I asked, stepping up to the bar.

Harry ignored me and poured himself a large bourbon. "What exactly is it you did in the Navy, Jack?" He took a gulp and moved to the pool table. Apparently there was to be no "What would you like, Charley?" for me today.

"Oh, your average things. I joined after college, so I had some officer training, got my commission." He shrugged and grinned engagingly. "I'm afraid I didn't have a particularly distinguished career."

"Jack was a commander," I contributed.

"Really?" Harry flashed a look at Jack, then picked the nine ball off the table. "I thought you guys all had specialties."

"Oh, eventually I got a graduate degree, so I suppose you could call that a specialty."

"Really?" Harry said again, seemingly riveted by this discussion. What did he know that I didn't know? "And just what is your degree in?"

Jack joined Harry at the pool table. He picked up a cue and examined it as he answered. "Meteorology."

He sounded slightly apologetic, as if the degree wasn't interesting enough to warrant Harry's curiosity.

"Meteorology," Harry said, sending the ball across the table.

"Well, if I'm being totally honest"—Jack put the cue down—"the degree is Meteorology and Physical Oceanography." He flashed me a smile. "I only did the oceanography to impress women."

"It's marine biology that gets the chicks," I told him.

"I must have been misinformed." He gave me a grin that made me want to grab him and get the hell out of there.

Harry cleared his throat loudly. "So you're a meteorologist?"

"Yes, sir."

"A weatherman?"

"That's what most people say."

"And the Navy taught you that?"

"Your tax dollars paid for a fine education, sir."

"Hell, man, don't thank me," Harry said. "I'm way too rich to pay taxes." Then the grin receded. "And I suppose you were predicting the weather in 1998 when you were stationed in Jakarta?"

Damn. I didn't know the significance of the question, but I recognized the tone. "Harry," I began, but Jack cut me off.

"No, sir, I wasn't predicting the weather in Jakarta."

"No?"

"No." Jack seemed oblivious to the undercurrent that was making my stomach churn. "I was doing research."

"Research, huh? I'll just bet you were. And—"

"On humidity." Jack spun a ball down the length of the pool table.

"Humidity." Harry said the word the way Sister Mary Bernadette, Mother Superior of the Immaculate Heart School for (Troubled) Girls, used to say the word "lascivious."

"Just humidity?" Harry pursued. "Even though

there were all those riots that year? I think I read
where five or six hundred people were killed before
Suharto was forced out of office. But I guess you just
ignored all that and did your research on humidity."

"Sir, you have no idea what a problem humidity is
for the Navy." Jack moved around the table and stood
in front of a display case of antique arrowheads. There
was silence for a moment, and I let my breath out
slowly. Then Jack turned to face Harry and said one
word.

"Rust."

Harry sipped his bourbon. "Rust?" He seemed to
be considering several things. "Rust a big problem on
a ship?"

"Huge." Jack nodded. "Enormous. And then
there's mildew." He looked over at me. "It was fascinating research."

"Uh huh." I didn't like what I saw in Harry's eyes.
"Harry, why don't you show—"

"And I suppose you were doing research in Bahrain
in '96? When that conspiracy to overthrow the govern-
ment was put down? How many terrorists were
arrested?"

Clearly, someone had been giving Harry some serious
foreign policy lectures lately. I would have laid odds that
my uncle wouldn't know how to spell Bahrain, much
less be conversant in its political history. Not to mention
his newfound knowledge about Jakarta.

"Sir," Jack said, "someday you're going to have to
tell me how you found out so much about me." He
picked up a small flintlock pistol and sighted it out
the window. "And so quickly."

Harry ignored the question. "A lot of humidity in
the Persian Gulf, is there? Rust a big problem?"

"Oddly enough it is quite humid near the shore, but
that's not why I was there."

"I didn't think so."

"No, just the opposite." Jack put the gun down.
"Dust."

"Dust."

Jack grinned. "Dust. Or rather—"

"Speaking of which," I cut him off. "The place looks great, Harry." I ran my finger along the nearest piece of furniture and held it up to show them how clean it was. "New cleaning service?"

Jack gave me a look that seemed equal parts amusement and affection. "Dust storms," he continued, addressing Harry while regarding me. Damned if he wasn't enjoying himself. "Wind," he elaborated. "It's been a problem for every engagement we've had in the desert. Dust storms come out of nowhere. There's no way to predict them."

"Let me guess," Harry drawled. "You found a way."

"Me? No. Made no headway whatsoever." Jack shrugged. "Hell if I know where the next dust-up is coming from." He met Harry's eyes with an expressionless gaze.

Harry was motionless for a moment, returning Jack's bland stare. When he finally spoke, it was softly. "Well, I guess we'll have plenty of time to talk about your career later." He gestured out the doors to the patio and the golf course beyond. "But right now it's too nice a day to stay inside talking about the weather."

I couldn't believe it. Harry was withdrawing from the field. I'd never seen him back down before. I wanted to run over to Jack and throw my arms around him. Something stopped me, though. Probably the knowledge that this was only the first skirmish.

"Jack, I don't suppose you play golf." Harry shifted back into host mode and flung open the patio doors.

"Only when I'm asked, sir."

"Please, I'm Harry. And I'm asking. You come by any time and we'll play." He turned to me. "Pity you gave up the game, Charley."

Jack, for once, seemed genuinely surprised. "You golf?"

I shot Harry a death glance which he, of course, ignored. "I used to."

"You never played after college, did you?" Harry asked. "And that was a shame," he went on, addressing Jack, "because that was right about the time I started playing."

I looked at Jack significantly and he laughed once, then turned it into a cough.

"I never did understand that." Harry was still talking. "You were so good. Why did you give up the game?"

"It was either that or beat you to death with a nine iron," I said, smiling sweetly and taking his bourbon from him. I knocked it back in one long swallow.

Harry looked over at Jack. "What do you make of that?"

"Very wrong, sir." He cleared his throat. "I'd recommend a pitching wedge for bludgeoning, myself."

Which illustrates one of the many reasons why I married the man.

Outside, Jack made appropriate comments about the garden and the view, and we settled into comfortable chairs under an enormous umbrella. Gordon materialized with pitchers of iced tea and lemonade, then just as silently he was gone.

It would have been downright pleasant under other circumstances. We made small talk for a while, on every safe topic I could think of—which no longer included the weather. I was just thinking about making a getaway when Harry leaned forward, elbows on his knees, and cleared his throat. I swear I heard a bell, signaling round two was about to begin.

"Charley," Harry said, "I can see what it is you like about this guy." He did not look at Jack. "He's good-looking, I'll give him that, and he holds up his end of a conversation. Probably pretty smart too if you get past all that polite bullshit."

Jack cleared his throat but made no comment.

"But here's the thing," Harry went on. "You know as well as I do that getting married so fast was just goddamn stupid." He put up his hands to cut off my protests. "Maybe you did it to piss me off, and maybe you did it because he talked you into it, but the point is, we can clear this whole mess up here and now. I've had a lawyer draw up some papers and we can just put this whole thing behind us. Jack won't be able to lay claim to one goddamn cent."

I stared at him, and then at Jack, who seemed fascinated by the scene.

"Are you out of your . . . Who the hell . . . How dare you!" I finally hit the phrase that worked, and hit it at full volume.

"How dare I what?" Harry yelled back. "How dare I look out for you? How dare I get you out of this mess?"

The man was unbelievable. "What makes you think for one minute—" I stood. "We're leaving." I made for the house, heading for the steps that led to the great room.

"Charley," Harry called after me. "This isn't just your decision!" I stopped and turned. Jack and Harry were still where I'd left them. "Don't you think you should consult your husband?"

Jack looked from Harry to me.

"Jack?" Why wasn't he coming with me?

Jack set his tea on a glass-topped table. "Let's hear him out, Charley."

Harry grinned in satisfaction, said "Come with me," and took the path back to the game room. Jack looked at me, then followed.

What in the hell?

When I caught up with them they were in Harry's office, across the hall from the game room. Harry was pulling a folder from his desk drawer. "I think you'll find this is all in order." He tossed it to Jack.

Harry sat behind the massive desk and gestured to Jack to have a seat. He saw me in the doorway. "Glad you could join us." I stepped into the room, feeling more than a little disoriented. "If we can just agree on certain terms, I'm sure we can take care of this today."

"Terms?" Jack enquired.

"Money," Harry said flatly. "How much it will take to make you go away."

"Ah." Jack returned to his perusal of the paper-work.

This couldn't be happening.

"How about five hundred thousand dollars?" Harry said smoothly.

Jack glanced up, then returned to the document, flipping a page.

"Seven fifty?"

Jack looked at him. "May I borrow a pen?"

Harry handed him a silver fountain pen, then watched as Jack underlined something and circled something else. "All right," he said when the pen came down again. "I'll go to a million, but not a penny more."

Jack wrote something on the last page. His signature? Was this really happening? He handed the folder back to Harry.

"I was sure you'd see things my way." Harry looked at me and suddenly seemed much, much older. "Sorry it turned out this way, Charley."

I was about to start screaming and never stop when Jack stood. "Thanks, but no thanks, sir." He looked at me. "Are you ready?" He nodded his head toward the door.

"Goddamn it!" Harry yelled. He held up the last page of the document, where Jack had neatly written "bull-shit" across the signature line. "Listen, you little—"

"Harry!" I was finally able to speak. "You know that part of the wedding ceremony that goes 'speak now, or forever hold your peace'? That's the reason you weren't at my wedding. I won't have you—"

"I don't care what you'll have," he shouted. "That man is not what he says he is, and—"

"Harry, for the love of God," I interrupted. "Jack's a meteorologist. Who in his right mind would pretend to be a meteorologist if he wasn't?" I shot Jack an apologetic look. "No offense, sweetie."

"A meteorologist? You believe that?" Harry brought

his fist down on the desk with a sharp crack. "Any idiot can say anything about the weather!"

"What's your point, Harry?" I asked.

"My point is," he bellowed, "he's a liar. And I'm going to keep digging until even you can see that and have the sense to get out of this mess and get a goddamn annulment!" By the time he finished, his voice was loud enough to shake the substantial rafters.

"It's not a mess!" I yelled back. "It's my life and I can take care of myself!"

"Take care of yourself! You didn't even get a prenup!"

"That's it! I'm out of here! Jack, let's go!" I was storming across the room when Jack spoke.

"Just a minute, Charley."

Not again. I whirled around and saw Jack take a white letter-sized envelope from his inside jacket pocket. "Harry." He shook his head in what looked like admiration. "Please, keep digging. I'm sure whatever you find will be entertaining, if nothing else." He placed the white envelope next to the folder on the desk. "This is for you. It's just a copy, the original is with a lawyer in London." He turned to me. "Now we can go."

What the hell was that?

"What the hell is that?" Harry boomed.

Jack gave me a grin and answered without looking back. "It's a legally binding disclaimer. But you can think of it as a prenup, Horatio."

Chapter 5

I have no idea how Jack found out Harry's real name. No matter how much I begged, he just smiled and said Harry wasn't the only one who could uncover a thing or two. So I had to content myself with the memory of the blank astonishment on my uncle's face as we'd left.

I was a little rattled by Harry's accusations, although I'd have died before admitting it. I hated the fact that he'd found out anything about Jack, be it good or bad. And I really hated that I couldn't ignore what he'd said. Finally, I just had to ask.

"Jack, these places you went for the Navy . . ."

"Um hmm?"

"Harry seemed to think . . ." I cleared my throat. "It does seem kind of funny to send a meteorologist to all those places when all that stuff was happening."

"Does it?" He looked at me with a sort of vague surprise, which wasn't helpful in the least.

I tried to smile. "I know you'll think I'm crazy—"

"You? Crazy? Never." Just a little sarcasm there, which I chose to overlook.

"Jack, were you some sort of spy?" I waited for him to laugh.

He thought about it a minute before answering. "If I had been, I don't think I'd be able to talk about it."

"Not even to your wife?"

"On the other hand," he said, "I can talk about weather as much as you'd like."

Great.

We spent the next few days pretty quietly. No unexpected naked women turned up—living or dead. No belligerent relatives dropped by. I made a few more attempts to trap my husband into an admission of a heroic past, but they were unsuccessful. Pretty tame stuff, all things considered.

On Thursday night we had reservations at Farallon and I was looking forward to an indecent quantity of oysters on the half shell. As we walked into the long, undersea atmosphere of the bar I grabbed Jack's elbow. "It's the detective," I whispered. "Inspector Yahata."

He was standing at the bar, wearing another sharp suit, this time accessorized by an ultra-thin blonde. He spotted us and came over, trailing the date, while we waited for our table.

"Mr. and Mrs. Fairfax. I'm glad to see you've recovered from your unpleasant shock." His speech was as clipped and quick as it had been at the crime scene. I looked at the blonde and wondered if he ever whispered sweet nothings in her ear. And if so, did it sting much?

"Inspector." Jack held out his hand. "We've been wondering about—" his eyes flicked to Yahata's date, then back to the detective, "the young lady."

The detective had one of those smiles where the corners of the mouth go down. "I'm afraid as yet there's been no identification of the young lady." His stress of the last two words was accompanied by the slightest of nods.

Wasn't it nice that we could all be so polite and civilized while discussing a corpse in a swank restaurant? Until I spoiled the mood.

"Was she murdered?"

The blonde looked away, as if I'd said something

unforgivably crude. But since we hadn't been properly introduced, I decided it didn't really matter. Yahata was gazing at me with undisguised curiosity. Again, I had the feeling that the air between us was crackling with energy.

"Yes," he replied. "Are you still sure you didn't know her?"

My mouth had gone dry. Apparently I'd used up my quota of smart-ass comments for the evening. I shook my head.

"We'll know more when we identify the body. But just to be thorough, I'd appreciate it if you could look at the lobby security tapes at some point."

"Do you think there's a connection to us?" Jack asked. "I mean, a deliberate one?"

The down-turned smile reappeared. "It's too early to discount any possibility." His eyes flicked to a point behind us. "I see your table is ready. I won't trouble you any further."

Which was a lie. I'd spent a lot of mental energy trying to convince myself that a total stranger had committed suicide in an anonymous hotel bathroom and it was random chance we'd found her. But a murder implied planning. Had part of the plan been to involve, or even implicate, Jack or me?

"Do you suppose that was a coincidence?" Jack asked after we were seated.

"You mean you think we were meant to find the body?"

Jack frowned. "I meant whether Yahata just happened to be here tonight." He looked over toward the bar, where the detective and his striking date were no longer visible. "But they're both interesting questions."

A few days later Simon called and insisted I meet him, Eileen, and Brenda for lunch and gossip. I decided to make the day complete by doing a little shopping first.

I began with Saks for the basics, moved on to Neiman Marcus, glanced in at Wilkes Bashford, popped into Chanel, and wound up at Prada. A morning well spent, in both senses of the word.

I headed for the restaurant where I was supposed to meet the gang. As I paused to admire a glittering display of glassware in Gump's window, I realized I hadn't done anything yet about finding a place to live with Jack—let alone accessorizing it with the perfect champagne flutes. I felt a little flurry of panic at the thought, so I dashed into Diesel for jeans and some funky tee-shirts. I'd probably wear them more often than anything else I'd bought.

Of course I was late for lunch. I turned into Belden Place, my arms full of packages, and saw the gang sitting at a sidewalk table. Eileen was checking her watch, and as I came up on them from behind I heard Simon say "probably still shagging her brains out—" right before Brenda saw me, kicked Simon under the table, and yelled "Charley!"

We'd agreed to meet at Plouf, one of several small bistros in this alleyway in the financial district. It was one of the few places in the city where you could sit outside and take advantage of the beautiful summer weather, at least on those rare San Francisco occasions when the summer weather was beautiful. It was also close to Eileen's office, and they served the most amazing mussels in town.

"Well, as long as you're late for a good reason," Eileen said, appraising the shopping bags I piled on the pavement before sitting next to her.

"Sorry, sorry, I totally lost track of time—" I began.

"Oh, Charley," Brenda offered, "nobody expects you on time anyway."

"We ordered already," Eileen informed me. "All your favorites."

All my favorites made for a fairly decadent lunch. Mussels in a white wine and garlic broth as well as mussels in a light cream sauce, calamari and fennel tempura, a warm leek and Roquefort tart, and a to-mato and arugula salad with white anchovies. We shared everything, forks clashing as we reached over each other to spear our favorite bites, using chunks of crusty bread to mop up the extra sauces.

After we'd completely stuffed ourselves and the waiter had removed all evidence of the crime, Simon poured me another glass of wine and said "All right, darling, now tell all."

"About your brunch with Harry," Brenda added helpfully.

I should never have told them about the invitation.

"Take it blow by blow," Eileen grinned wickedly. "I want to know how much blood was shed."

"Harry's not that bad!" Brenda exclaimed, then looked around in surprise, as if someone else had said it. Quietly, she added, "I'm sure he was very understanding, once he . . . understood."

I snorted eloquently.

"Was he?" Eileen asked knowingly.

I told all.

When I got to the part about Jack's dramatic presentation of the legal disclaimer, Eileen's eyes narrowed. "A legal disclaimer? So it isn't a prenup?"

"Not officially," I explained. "Because it's not a mutual agreement. I didn't even know anything about it until Sunday. Jack had a lawyer draw it up in London because he figured some people would think he married me for my money."

"Oh, Charley." Brenda seemed wounded by the mere thought of such a cynical perspective, while Simon gazed heavenward and wisely said nothing.

Eileen cleared her throat. "Do you have a copy?"

"With me? Of course not. I didn't even want to look at it."

"Well I do," she said decisively.

I looked at her blankly.

"Charley, I'm your financial manager. I manage your finances."

Still blank.

"I should see any legal document that might possibly impact your financial outlook." She waved away the waiter's proffered dessert menu and ordered cappuccinos for all of us. Turning back to me, she continued. "Even if you don't take an interest in these things, you pay me to."

"I suppose . . ." I hadn't thought of it like that.

"So fax it to me this afternoon," she continued briskly. "After all, I'm not saying that Jack isn't wonderful, but men can be pretty deceitful at times, and—"

"Oh, for heaven's sake!" Brenda exclaimed. "Just because you've married a couple of jerks . . ."

"Is four a couple?" Simon enquired innocently.

It was true that Eileen had been married four times, and each had been a jerk, in his own way. The only positive outcome of her marital experiences was her son Anthony. It was natural for her to be suspicious of Jack's motives, and not just because of her position as my financial manager. She glared at Simon. "The fact," she said icily, "that I have been divorced does not color my judgment in any way."

"Right."

"So anyway—" Brenda gave Simon a warning look—"what else is new?"

Was this the time to tell them about the murdered woman we'd found in the tub? I looked at Eileen and couldn't bring myself to add fuel to her suspicions about Jack. She'd probably point out that I'd never found any dead bodies before I'd gotten married. So I shrugged. "Not much."

Eileen pushed her chair back. "I have to go." She stood. "I have a very new and very rich client. Don't forget to fax me that disclaimer." She bent to air-kiss my cheek. "I am happy for you, sweetie," she whispered.

"You can't go yet," Simon protested. "We haven't talked about work at all. We need to bring Charley up to speed on the Rep and what we're doing."

Eileen consulted a sleek little electronic organizer. "I can move some things and do lunch on Friday."

"Works for me. Charley?"

"Fine." I perked up. "Can we do dim sum?"

"Good God." Eileen gave me a look filled with despair and waved as she left.

"Have you looked at the play yet, darling?" Simon looked at me expectantly.

"I haven't had a chance to read it. But I will by Friday," I promised, seeing his face fall. "Chip said it was great."

"It's good," Simon agreed. "It will be great if we can pull it all together. I've been trying to get in touch with the writer to set up a meeting. You'll love her, darling, she's—"

He might have rambled on forever if Brenda hadn't cut him off. "If you two are going to get all theatrical on me I think I'd better go. Maybe I can still beat the traffic on the bridge." Brenda lived in Berkeley, drove an ancient red Volkswagen, and spent a fair amount of her mental energy figuring out how to get from Point A to Point B without getting stuck in the epic traffic backups that were part of the geography of the Bay Area.

Catching a nasty look from one of the waiters, Simon and I decided to call it a day as well, and he gallantly helped me flag down a cab and cram my morning's purchases into it.

"Don't worry about the Rep," he said earnestly, just before closing the cab door. "Everything will be fine."

Great. Before he'd said that I hadn't been worried.

Chapter 6

"Jack!" I called out as I came through the door. "Are you here?"

Jack stuck his head out of the second bedroom and took in the pile of shopping bags.

"I've had a spree. What do you think?" I reached into a bag at random and pulled out a black Donna Karan dress with a plunging neckline.

He shut the door behind me, then turned to look at the dress. He frowned, wrinkling his brow. "It's just such a waste."

"I beg your pardon?" I wasn't used to having anyone comment on how I spent my money. "What do you—"

"Shhh." He put his fingers to his lips, then came closer and slipped his hands around my waist. "Buying these clothes," he said, "when you look so good naked?"

Oh. All right then. Crisis over. "Why don't I try everything on," I suggested, "and then you can take everything off?"

"How about we start with those?" He pointed to a pair of red stiletto Dolce & Gabbanas that had tumbled out of their box. "Just those."

"Wait right here." I bit his lower lip. "And—"

There was the sound of a throat being cleared awkwardly. "Uh . . . Jack?"

"Mike!" Jack sprang away from me.

It's possible I screamed. Just a little.

"Charley," Jack recovered quickly, "this is my friend Mike Papas."

A tall man with a bad haircut was standing in the doorway to the room Jack had come from. "Hi," he waved weakly.

I raised my hand in a similar fainthearted gesture. Mike who? Who did Jack know in San Francisco? I looked at Mike more closely. He looked enough like Jack to be his brother—his woefully unkempt brother. He was wearing faded jeans, a stretched-out polo shirt, and socks but no shoes.

"Mike's an old friend of mine from grad school, in Monterey," Jack explained, running a hand over his face. "Sorry, Mike, I forgot you were here."

"No problem," Mike assured him. "I totally understand." His eyes sparkled as he advanced toward me, his hand outstretched. "Nice to meet you, if a bit awkward."

We shook.

"Mike got out of the Navy a couple of months ago and he's living in Palo Alto now. I gave him a call this morning," Jack added helpfully.

"Oh." This is why my conversational skills are in such demand at parties. "That's nice."

"I have to admit, I'm trying to steal him from you," Mike said.

I suspect my polite smile began to register incomprehension.

"Mike wants me to join his company," Jack offered. "We set up a sort of a makeshift office in the other room."

"Oh." That seemed to be the only comment I could come up with. I glanced into the second bedroom and saw that the desk and two tables had been pushed together. Two laptops and several piles of paper were scattered across them. More papers, assembled into something that looked like a huge diagram, were spread out on the bed. A pair of well-worn sneakers were visible under the desk. "Oh." Perhaps all the wine at lunch had permanently stunted my ability to speak.

"I'll tell you all about it over dinner, Pumpkin," Jack filled the silence. "Mike, you'll join us, won't you?"

"Um, I don't think so," Mike said. "I'd better be going." He eyed me with what I could only interpret as caution. "It was great to meet you."

"Yes," I agreed. "Great."

The minute Mike had gathered his things and gone, Jack collapsed into a chair laughing.

"I suppose you think it's funny that a perfect stranger walked in on us . . . half naked . . . and . . . and . . ." Oh, hell. It was kind of funny. I perched on the arm of the chair and Jack pulled me onto his lap.

"Hardly half naked yet," he pointed out, reaching for my shirt.

"Don't you for one minute think you can distract me with sex," I said. "I want to know what you two are plotting in there. Who is that guy? What does he mean he's going to steal you from me?"

Jack grinned and looked me in the eye as he deftly unhooked my bra. "Trust me, you have nothing to worry about."

Maybe I was wrong. Maybe he could distract me with sex. "But Jack . . ." I began, then lost my train of thought.

"I'll tell you all about it later." He shifted my position on his lap. "First, I think you owe me a fashion show."

Much later, as I surveyed the morning's purchases strewn around the bedroom, I reflected that they didn't look much different from the clothes I already owned, strewn around the bedroom. I wasn't exactly well-known for taking care of my things. Although it really was too much, I thought, to tie an Hermès scarf to the bedpost. I began working the knot as Jack emerged from the shower. "Hey, Pumpkin." He shook his head, sending water droplets everywhere. "What about sushi for dinner?"

Could life get any better?

We walked down the hill to a restaurant on Geary where you sit at a bar and the sushi floats past you in little boats so you can take what you want. It wasn't the best sushi in town—for that I'd have to take Jack to the place on Ninth Street near the park—but we hadn't felt like dealing with a cab.

After I'd had a salmon skin hand roll and the obligatory California roll dusted with tobiko, I felt sufficiently fortified to ask Jack about Mike and the job he had mentioned.

"He's just getting started. He's putting a team together, and he wants me to be a part of it from the beginning."

"Oh." There was that incisive comment again.

"You'll like Mike once you get to know him," Jack assured me, mistaking my reservations entirely.

"Sure."

"But?" His eyes met mine.

"It's just that," selfishly, "I didn't really think of you as . . . having a job, I suppose." Even I heard how weak that sounded.

He looked at me blankly. "Charley, of course I'm going to work."

Of course he was going to work.

"You knew that, didn't you?"

I shrugged in what I hoped was a charming, rather helpless way.

"Charley," he said intently, "you didn't think I'd just live off you, did you?"

"Well . . ." Did I? "I don't think I really thought about it."

"Well think about it. I couldn't just loaf around doing nothing and spending your money. What kind of a guy would do that?"

A lot of guys. But I didn't say so.

"And how long could you stay interested in a guy like that?"

Not long. That was a good point.

"You're right," I said, finally. "Of course you're

right. I think I'm just a little thrown. I mean . . . it seems so soon."

"I haven't agreed to anything yet," he reminded me. "Besides," he wiggled his eyebrows, "we have many things left to accomplish in that hotel suite."

"Oh." Well then. "If you're talking about taking a job *eventually*," I grinned, "I'm totally with you."

"Right. Eventually we're going to find a place to live, and I'm going to find the right work, and . . ."

"And?" I enquired.

"And we're going to live happily ever after." He kissed me lightly, tasting of Japanese beer and wasabi. A good combination. "Besides," he asked, "what about you?"

"What about me?"

"Aren't you going to be working on the new play at the Rep?" He reached for a spicy tuna roll, still looking at me out of the corner of his eye.

"I don't know." I watched the passing fish. "I haven't read the play yet, and I don't know if they need me for anything." Simon probably had things completely under control, damn him.

"That's not what that guy Chip said at your welcome home party." He dipped the spicy tuna in extra wasabi—brave man—and popped it into his mouth.

"What did Chip say?"

Jack swallowed and reached for his Sapporo, his eyes watering a bit. "He has you practically running the place. Said they were falling apart without you. Said you'd come back just in time."

"Really?" Is that why Simon had told me not to worry in that way that had made me worry? "Chip said that?"

Jack nodded. "I got the impression I'd be lucky to see you for more than ten minutes together between now and opening night."

"Don't be silly." I reached for a shrimp tempura roll. "I'm not going to abandon you for some play." Simon had said it was a great play.

"And I'm not going to abandon you for the first job that comes along from an old Navy buddy."

I thought about it, chewing. "But, Jack," I asked, "is it a good job? Is it something you'd like?"

"It may be. I'd have to hear more about it."

"What kind of company is it?"

"Computer security." He saw the look on my face and grinned. "It sounds boring, I know, but Mike's a brilliant guy, and he thinks it's possible he's figured out a pretty innovative encryption methodology that could radically—why are you smiling?"

Because I couldn't help it. Because he looked so intense and I had no idea what he was talking about. "Because you sound excited about it." And he did. He sounded happy and energized and purposeful. "You should go geek out with your friend and see where it leads." After all, I would probably be pretty busy myself. "Maybe you'll love the job."

"You really wouldn't mind?" He looked doubtful.

"Not at all. Not if it's something you want." I sipped my sake demurely. "I'm sure I'll be able to find something to do with my time."

In the hotel elevator I found myself wondering if I could call the conversation we'd had about Jack getting a job our first fight. If so, I could reasonably expect to enjoy our first make-up sex. I put my hands under Jack's leather jacket in the hallway as he slipped the card key into the reader, and turned straight for the bedroom as soon as the door was open. Jack reached for my belt and pulled me backwards, saying "Not so fast." I pushed him against the closed door and slid the jacket off his shoulders. I wasn't paying attention to anything but the texture of his shirt beneath my hands and the feel of his mouth on mine when the lights came on.

"Oh, don't," I whispered.

"I didn't." Jack straightened, looking past me. "Hello, Harry."

This time I definitely screamed.

Jack kept my back to Harry as he pulled my shirt down, then he released me. "What the hell do you think you're doing!" I demanded as soon as I was decent. "And how the hell did you get in here?"

Harry held his hands up innocently. "Can't an uncle drop in to say hello?"

Jack moved to the bar cart. "Can I get you anything, Harry?"

"No thanks, I just stopped by for a little chat."

"How nice." Jack poured whiskey over ice. "Charley? Something for you?"

The pair of them were completely insane. "How about a gun?"

Harry made a "tsk, tsk" sound and came over to kiss me on the forehead. "Is that any way to make an old man welcome?"

"An old man who lurks around in the dark, in my hotel room, waiting for God knows what . . . and you wipe that innocent smile off your face or I'll—"

"I was just admiring the lights of the city." Harry gestured towards the window. "Some view you've got here."

"We like it." Jack joined us and handed me a large whiskey. "What can I do for you, Harry?"

"I just have a couple of questions," Harry replied easily. "I hope you don't mind?"

Jack smiled. "Fire away."

"What the . . . Would you two . . . For the love of . . ." Of course they ignored me.

"In 1994," Harry began, "you were an attaché to the royal house of Oman."

"Was it that long ago?" Jack seemed surprised, whether by Harry's information or the swift passage of time, I couldn't tell. And frankly, at that point, I didn't care.

"I wonder," Harry pressed, "just how you got that position."

"Funny story. One of the sultan's daughters—I forget her name—was a huge fan of American music." Jack eyed the stereo system. "Loved classic rock. Anyway, the admiral wanted to score some points with the sultan, and I had the biggest CD collection on the ship, and one thing led to another."

Harry grunted.

"So, really, attaché is a little bit of an exaggeration. I was more like a music advisor."

"And you expect me to believe that?"

I did. I could see quite clearly the image of a voluptuous Arabian princess in a silk-lined harem wearing something sheer and midriff-baring, reclining on pillows while being fanned by nubile maidens. And at her feet was Jack, naked, proffering *Quadrophenia* on a silver platter.

Bastard!

"You were some sort of an attaché in London, too, weren't you?" Harry asked.

"More of a liaison, actually."

"It seems you were quite the little diplomat." Harry said the word distastefully. "Don't we have a State Department for things like that?"

Jack raised his hands. "What can I say? Once the word gets out that a guy can tango, the offers just start pouring in."

"I didn't know you could dance," I said. "Why haven't we ever gone dancing?"

"You don't like dancing," Jack remarked, accurately.

"Maybe if you'd had a decent wedding," Harry said, "you'd know these things about a man."

"We had a lovely wedding," I told him. "And as far as the dancing part of it goes, we're perfectly open to the idea of having a lavish reception now that we're back."

"We are?" Jack looked a little startled, then agreed with me. "We are."

"Well, that's just fine." Harry bit off the word. "People are already calling, wanting to know if they should send a gift or wait for the annulment."

"And I'm sure I know just what you tell them," I said icily.

"How the hell would I know what to tell anyone,

when you don't tell me a goddamn thing!" he bellowed.

Neither of us responded, and Harry made a visible effort to get himself under control. I felt a twinge of guilt, but I hadn't forgotten this was the man who'd tried to buy off my husband in front of me.

"Are you sure you wouldn't like a drink, Harry?" I rattled some ice in my now empty glass to get his attention. "Or do you need to be going?" The sooner he left the sooner I could find out some pertinent details about this sultan's daughter.

Harry sat on the couch, facing Jack. "Oh, I'll be out of your way soon enough."

"Harry," I demanded, "why are you so fixated on what Jack did when he was in the Navy? Have you noticed he's not in the Navy anymore?"

"I've noticed a lot of things. I've noticed that your *husband*—" the word was layered with speculation— "was in some very interesting places at some very interesting times."

I gave him a look that said "So?"

"But he wasn't doing anything very interesting himself. In fact, as far as I can tell—and believe me, I'm still looking—he's never done anything interesting at all."

This time I said it. "So?"

"So your boy's too sharp to be that dull."

That was the weirdest compliment I'd ever heard, even from Harry. "What—"

"He was up to something, Charley." Harry looked at Jack fiercely as he addressed his words to me. "And I think he's still up to something."

I looked at Jack and saw a slow smile spread across his face. "Harry, I'm flattered."

Harry made a sound that was part growl and grabbed his coat. "You watch your step, boy," he said to Jack. "And you"—he looked at me—"be careful." He slammed the door behind him.

I stared at the door for a moment before I turned to Jack.

"You know," I said, "you sometimes remind me of Cary Grant."

"Only sometimes?" He grinned.

"And right now you remind me of Cary Grant in *Suspicion*."

He set his drink down, crossed the room, and put his hands on my shoulders. "Was that the one where he was devastatingly handsome?" He began to massage my neck. "Or was that the one where he was fantastically charming?"

I broke free and took a step back. "That's the one where his wife knows he's hiding something."

Chapter 7

I woke up the next morning satisfied that I knew everything there was to know about the social lives of Arabian princesses. The most pertinent fact, to me, was that a particular Arabian princess had been only thirteen years old and prone to fits of giggling when she'd known my husband.

I sighed. If only I could be equally satisfied that I knew everything about Jack's increasingly murky-sounding past. I turned over, and was disappointed to find a note instead of Jack's sleeping profile on the pillow next to mine.

> C,
>   The concierge found a racquetball partner for me. I should be back around 1:00.
>   —J

Racquetball. Right. I stretched, wondering what to do with the day. The clock said 8:32, so sleeping a few more hours seemed reasonable. Then, guiltily, I remembered I'd promised to read the play Chip had sent over. I padded out to the living room and found it under a pile of newspapers and magazines.

I called room service for coffee and a bagel, then turned on the television, flipping among the channels of morning programming. There was still no news coverage about the murder of the woman in our suite, and I wondered why. If they were trying to identify her, it seemed reasonable to put her picture on the news. But either the hotel really had some pull with the media or the police didn't work that way.

I kept switching channels after breakfast had been delivered. Various stars were shilling for their various new movies on various talk shows. Various chefs were creating various masterpieces on various cooking shows. I hovered on the Weather Channel for a moment, picturing Jack on screen, telling me all about pressure systems over the Pacific. Then I pictured him shirtless. I turned the TV off and sighed. Maybe it was time to deal with the subject I'd been trying to put out of my mind. I picked up the phone and pushed the button for the hotel operator.

"Could you connect me with the head of security, please?"

"Is there a problem, Mrs. Fairfax?" When would it stop startling me when someone called me that?

"Just put me through, please."

"I'll give you Mr. Shepherd," she answered, after a slight hesitation, and I heard music for a minute or two. I scrunched my forehead, trying to remember if Mr. Shepherd was the name of the security man I'd met the night we'd found the body. I drew a blank.

"Mrs. Fairfax," a robust voice assaulted my ear. "Bill Shepherd here. How may I help you?"

"Mr. Shepherd." The voice clicked with a face, but not the right one. "Aren't you the hotel manager?"

"Yes ma'am. How may I be of service?"

Well, for one thing you could let me talk to the person I wanted to talk to.

"I'm afraid there's been some mistake," I told him. "I asked for the head of security. Mr. . . ."

"Oh."

Now it was my turn to ask if there was a problem.

"I'm afraid the man you're thinking of is no longer with us." The regret in his voice was completely manufactured. The tension wasn't.

"What? Why?"

"Mrs. Fairfax, I'd be happy to help you in any way I can."

"Did you fire him?"

A pause. "I'm sure you'll understand I can't comment on the matter."

Right. But I didn't like it. I'd had the crazy idea of questioning the security chief to see if he had any theories about the body in the bathtub. And maybe to get a little information out of him. Like whether the police suspected me or Jack. But I doubted I'd get anything from the corporate Mr. Shepherd. I thought quickly. "Well, maybe you can help me. I was wondering if now would be a good time to look at the tapes."

"Tapes?"

"Inspector Yahata mentioned there were tapes from the lobby security cameras. . . ."

"Yes, of course. But I'm afraid the police still have them."

So much for that.

"Mrs. Fairfax?" I suppose my silence was unnerving the man.

"Can't you just tell me whether you fired Mr. . . . the security chief, or if he . . . left?" As in left, shrouded in mystery and casting suspicion on himself and what his role in the murder of an unidentified woman might have been?

"I'm sorry, but—"

"Never mind then."

"Is there anything else?" His voice held the hope that there wasn't.

"Nothing. Thank you." I hung up and stared vacantly at the phone. Apparently I was no good at this sort of thing. Instead of learning anything useful, now I just had more questions. Was the missing security chief sitting in a bar somewhere nursing a whiskey and a grudge over having been fired because a murder was committed on his watch? Or was he relaxing on a South American beach, congratulating himself on having pulled off the perfect crime?

Damned if I knew. And damned if I knew how to find out. I said "oh, hell" out loud, downed some coffee, and picked up the play. I was better off sticking to what I knew.

"It's brilliant!" I met Simon in the hotel lobby Friday afternoon practically gushing with enthusiasm.

"This?" He looked down at his shirt. "It's just a Kenneth Cole I've had for ages, but—" He saw the look on my face and realized I hadn't complimented his wardrobe. "Oh, the play," he recovered smoothly. "Of course it is. I chose it."

"When do I get to meet the writer? Have you heard back from her?" I peppered him with questions as he dragged me outside to where Eileen was waiting behind the wheel of her gray Volvo.

"Hello to you, too," she said, interrupting me as I continued to harangue Simon for details.

"Have you read it?" I demanded.

"I don't read them, I just budget them." She turned out of the parking lot. "I'm not allowed to fall in love with the material, remember?"

"That's our clear-eyed Eileen," Simon said from the back seat. "Guiding us to financial security."

Eileen gave Simon a squinty look in the rearview mirror.

"Eileen," I told her, "you just have to read it. It's so good. Really, it's funny, and true, and there are wonderful characters, and you'll just—"

"I'll just wait for opening night," she assured me. "If I don't fall in love with it, I'll have an easier time turning you two down when you come asking for enough money to build a medieval fortress or a replica of the Mayflower or something equally extravagant."

"Not this time, darling," Simon said with satisfaction. "A simple, one-set design. Nothing extravagant about it. I took your admonishment to heart, you know."

"What admonishment?" I asked. "What have I

missed in the last year? And when have we ever had to worry about budget?"

"Later, darling," Simon answered. "First I want you to tell me more about what a fabulous play I picked. Don't you just love the title? *All About Me.*" He sighed with contentment.

"If Neil Simon had grown up a girl in suburbia in the late fifties instead of a guy in Brighton Beach in the forties, this is the play he would have written," I announced. "And I intend to make sure at least one reviewer says exactly that."

Simon beamed. "You do like it."

Eileen took us to the Richmond district. There are hundreds of good restaurants serving every conceivable variation of Asian cuisine along Geary and Clement streets in the Richmond, and we usually relied on parking karma to determine which one we'd choose. I must have done something good in a previous life, because Eileen found a space across the street from Ton Kiang.

It wasn't until she stepped out of the car that I realized Eileen was wearing a killer outfit—a snug black skirt that hit just above the knees topped with a form-fitting black jacket that left a dramatic V opening at the neck. "Look at you!" I said. "Where's the fashion shoot?"

"Oh, this?" Eileen looked down at herself. "It's just a simple suit." She put quarters in the meter while I exchanged a look with Simon.

"Elegantly simple, tastefully simple, stunningly simple," I said.

"Sexily simple." Simon nodded his approval.

"Don't be ridiculous. I've always worn suits to work." Eileen looked rather desperately for a break in the traffic so we could cross the street.

"Sweetie," I told her, "I've known you since you were sixteen years old and I've never seen you in a suit like that, especially not with knee-high boots." I took a closer look. "Those are Prada!"

Eileen looked down at herself again, and this time when she looked up she was grinning. "The whole thing's Prada," she confessed. "Do you like it?"

"Woof," Simon said.

"Really, Eileen, you look fabulous," I told her. "It's such a change!" Then, realizing how that might sound, I tried to come up with something else to say. "I mean—"

Simon cut to the chase. "Who is he?"

"Let's cross at the corner." She abruptly walked away.

Simon gave me raised eyebrows as we followed.

At the restaurant Eileen refused to tell us anything more about her new look or the new man responsible for it. "This is a working lunch," she said. "I'm billing you for it, Charley, so we'd better cover everything we need to before degenerating into a fashion discussion."

"Uh huh," I agreed absently, my attention diverted by the passing trolleys, piled high with buns, dumplings, and other steaming treats. "Do you see any shrimp balls?"

After the waiters had deposited barbeque pork buns, crab claws stuffed with shrimp, foil-wrapped chicken, scallop shu mai, stuffed mushrooms, steamed Chinese broccoli, and the coveted deep-fried shrimp balls, we got down to the serious business of eating and planning the future of the Rep.

"I won't sugarcoat it, Charley," Eileen began. "We had some serious cost overruns last season."

Simon suddenly looked miserable. "It's my fault," he confessed. "Remember how well your last season went when we put on *Five Gay Men and Three Straight Women*?"

I nodded. It had been a runaway success. Before that we'd staged mainly classics. We'd built up the Rep on Shakespeare, Ibsen, and the occasional Restoration comedy that we'd sometimes dared to update with modern dress. *Five Gay Men* had been our first contemporary, and we'd loved every minute of its extended run.

"Well, because that was such a hit, last year I decided to do another contemporary—along with a dreary *Hedda Gabler,* a boring old *Faustus,* and a creaking *Twelfth Night.* So I picked this fabulous futuristic science fiction parable—"

"Simon . . ." Eileen interrupted.

"Right." He came back down to earth. "It was called *Up There* and it was . . ." He seemed at a loss for the perfect description.

"It was a disaster," Eileen said flatly. "Nobody came."

I looked at Simon.

"I simply got carried away," he admitted. "That bloody space thing practically ruined—"

"Ticket sales were abysmal," Eileen stated. "The reviews were terrible and we don't have enough of a season ticket-holder base to carry us through something like that." Simon looked truly wretched, but Eileen continued relentlessly. "The repertory company is a business, and at the end of last season we were over budget."

I looked up in alarm.

"It's all right," Eileen reassured me. "We just had to dip into this year's budget to make up the difference. When we set up the funding for the Rep we knew this kind of thing might happen."

"Right." I also knew that when I'd bought the theater building outright I had taken care of a major expense for the company. The rest of the budget went to salaries for the few year-round employees like Simon and Chip, payroll for the actors and staff who were employed just for the season, sets, costumes, electricity bills, publicity, and a thousand other things.

"It's all my fault," Simon repeated. "If it hadn't been for that bloody space disaster we'd have done all right." He stabbed viciously at a pork bun with his chopstick.

"Water under the bridge," Eileen reassured him briefly. "Except . . ."

This was going to be bad. "What?"

Eileen cleared her throat and reached for her tea. Simon smiled weakly. "Darling," he began.

"What?" I was starting to panic.

"I felt like an idiot for having wasted the Rep's money," he told me. "I thought the right thing to do, the proper thing to do, the only decent thing to do—"

"Simon!" Eileen set her cup down with a bang. "Tell her."

"We found someone to give us a little dosh to get us through the rough patch." He held up his hands. "That's all. We thought that way we wouldn't have to bother you in London, and you would never even have to know about it."

Someone else had put money into my Rep? I looked at Eileen. "Who?"

"It's a private, one-time donation that will cover last year's shortfall and enable us to get through this season without cutbacks."

"Who?"

"Well," Simon said smoothly, "does it really matter who? The important thing is that he was there at the right time with the right amount."

"Why didn't you just tell me?" I asked Eileen. "You know I would have made up the difference."

"Charley," she explained, "if I were just the managing director of the Rep I would have asked you in a heartbeat. But as your personal financial manager I couldn't advise you to invest any more than you already have."

"Besides," Simon volunteered. "I wouldn't let her. It wasn't Eileen's fault. And it wasn't yours either. You didn't pick that bloody space—"

"Simon!" Eileen gave him a warning look, then turned back to me. "We're really very lucky this donor came along," she continued. "It isn't as though people are lining up to support a nonprofit enterprise these days."

"I know," I said, still not thrilled at the thought of someone else getting involved in my company.

"Right. Is there any more tea?" Simon asked.

"Who is it?" I looked at each of them in turn. "I don't believe you're not going to tell me." Simon focused on the teapot. I focused on Eileen.

"Charley, there were certain conditions associated with the donation," she said.

That was so not what I wanted to hear. "Such as anonymity?"

She pursed her lips, then gave a brief nod.

"Why?"

"Darling," Simon said gently, "we were looking for a white knight. We really couldn't afford to be choosy."

"And along with anonymity comes silence," Eileen said. "The donor will have nothing whatsoever to do with any decisions about the company. He's just a money man." She stressed this last point, but it didn't make me feel much better. One thing Uncle Harry had taught me is that, in most things in life, money equals control.

"Just tell me one thing," I addressed Eileen. "Look me in the eye and tell me it's not Harry."

Eileen looked at me with perfect clarity and said, "Never. Not in a million years. Not if I had to put up the money myself. I would never do that to you."

"Good Lord, darling," Simon sputtered, "Harry? Surely you wouldn't think? I mean, it's bad enough—" Eileen must have kicked him under the table because he winced and recovered himself. "And of course I blame myself entirely and that bloody space fiasco for putting us in the situation—"

"Oh, shut up," I said, "and tell me how you found the new play."

Simon had gushed on uninterrupted for a solid ten minutes about how brilliant the play was and how brilliantly he had secured it for us before Eileen was finally able to get a word in.

"Hang on," she said. "Before you two start designing the costumes, I need to go over one or two more things with Charley." She looked at her watch.

"You don't have to leave?" I asked.

"I have a three o'clock," she apologized. "I couldn't move it."

"Ah ha!" Simon exclaimed. "I'll just bet this mysterious three o'clock is the reason for the fantastic new suit."

She ignored him. "So before I have to go, I wanted to go over the housing situation."

I looked at her blankly. "What housing situation?"

She sighed. "Yours, Charley. Where do you plan to live? Have you lined up a realtor or would you like me to send you one? Do you know what neighborhood you want? Are you thinking house or condo?"

All perfectly reasonable questions, and I probably should have had an answer to at least a few of them. "I don't know."

Eileen sighed again and looked at Simon. "Excuse yourself," she said.

Simon looked at me with pity, placed his napkin on the table, stood up, and wandered away.

As soon as he was gone Eileen looked at me intently. "Charley, are you serious about this marriage?"

"Of course I am!"

"You didn't fax me that disclaimer," she reminded me.

"I have it right here." I pulled a thin envelope out of my purse and passed it to her. She pushed the teapot towards me and took it, and read while I sipped.

When she'd finished she looked at me over the edge of the paper. "Have you read this?"

I'd thought about reading it when Jack had given it to me, but I couldn't bring myself to do it. "No."

She nodded. "It's good. Simple and straightforward." She folded the paper and replaced it in the envelope. "He gets nothing, ever, under any circumstances, regardless of when or why you two might break up."

I sipped again. "He did tell me it was only a commitment on his part. That's why he didn't mention it earlier."

"That's true. It's not so much a prenup as a unilateral declaration." She paused to consider something. "Of course . . ."

Oh, hell. "What?"

"It could be very clever. I mean, it's so unfair towards Jack that it's possible a judge would simply set it aside."

"Eileen—"

"I'm not saying that's the case." Her eyebrows contracted as she slipped the envelope into her purse. "Charley, if this guy is on the level you're the luckiest woman on the planet."

I nodded. "I think I might be." Now was definitely not the time to bring up my recent musings about Jack's previous career. Or the possibility that we were about to become involved in a murder investigation.

She reached over to squeeze my hand. "I hope so, sweetie." Then she cleared her throat and was all business again. "So if you are going to set up house with Mr. Wonderful, you should start thinking about where you're going to live."

Simon cruised back to the table and looked at Eileen with wide eyes. She waved him into his chair. "Charley," he said. "You should let Eileen take care of finding you a house. We need you too much at the theatre. You simply can't be off playing wife when we've got a new production starting up."

"I'm not playing wife." At least not yet. "I just need to concentrate on my personal life right now." I turned to Eileen. "I think Jack is getting a little tired of the hotel."

"What's he going to do?" she asked, seemingly casually.

"Work," I replied helplessly. "He's already got an offer from an old Navy buddy in Palo Alto."

"Charley!" Simon yelped. "You're not thinking of moving to the provinces! Tell me you're not!"

"I'm not," I assured him. Good God, was Jack?

That decided me. "No, I need to find a house and find it quickly, so we can get on with . . . things."

"Good," Eileen approved. "I'll have a realtor call you tomorrow."

"Excellent," Simon said. "But don't get too wrapped up in floor plans. We start casting next week."

"Haven't you got a director for that sort of thing?" Chip had said something about a new guy, from LA, who had signed on to direct the first two plays this season.

"Brian," Simon grimaced, "is turning out to be a complete prick." In response to my startled look he rushed on. "Furiously talented, I'm assured, but an absolute shit of a human being, as far as I can tell."

"I can't wait to meet him."

"I'm probably exaggerating," Simon admitted. "But I do want you to come to the auditions." He saw me hesitating. "We've already narrowed down the field, so you'll just be seeing the callbacks."

"I'll come," I caved, "but don't count on me to help out much this season. I've got a lot to do." I shot Eileen a glance. She was checking her watch again.

"I've really got to run," she said. "Do you two want to come now? Or do you mind cabbing it?"

"We haven't had dessert yet," Simon pointed out. "We're staying."

I got up to peck Eileen on the cheek as she stood. "Thanks for everything. And I still expect you to tell me all about whatever motivated your new look."

"Whomever, you mean." Simon blew her a kiss.

Eileen waved at him dismissively and left.

Simon flagged down a waiter and asked for sesame balls and custard tarts. He waited until all the plates had been cleared, then leaned towards me conspiratorially. "Darling, I give you two weeks of domesticity before you come screaming into the theater demanding something useful to do."

"Simon!" Of course, he was probably right. Nevertheless . . . "I have every intention of making a good home for myself and my husband. That includes decorating and gardening and cooking—"

His laughter cut me off. "Charley, darling, this is me you're talking to," he choked. "I know you. You can barely manage to keep gin, vermouth, and olives in your house concurrently. Do you really think a ring on your finger is going to turn you into Suzy bloody Homemaker?"

When I got back to the hotel, Jack was on the phone. "Here she is now," he said, "I'll ask her." He put his hand over the mouthpiece. "Charley, it's Harry."

"Tell him no." Whatever his question was.

"He wants to know if you've heard from Cece."

Hear from my cousin? Voluntarily? Never in my life. "No. Why should I have?"

Jack spoke into the phone. "No." He listened, then asked me, "You're sure?"

"Of course I'm sure. What's going on?"

But Jack was speaking into the phone again. "Yes. Of course. The minute we hear. And you too." He hung up.

"What's going on?" I repeated.

Jack kept his hand on the receiver for a moment after hanging up, then he looked at me. "Your cousin is missing."

Chapter 8

There was no word from Harry on Saturday. I kept telling myself it was just Cece being Cece, and that she was probably on some secluded island resort with her new boyfriend, laughing at Harry and spending his money. I still didn't like it.

According to what Harry had told Jack over the phone, Cece had been expected to bring her boyfriend, the doctor, to the Hillsborough house on Thursday night for dinner and one of Harry's friendly family interrogation sessions. She hadn't shown. At midnight Harry had finally given up and called her, and found the number disconnected. Her cell phone had given a "customer out of service area" message. That's when he'd called one of his private detectives and told the guy to find her.

The next morning the detective had reported that the house where she'd been living with the doctor in Marin was empty, and looked like it had been for at least a few days. There was no trace of Cece or the boyfriend. There had been no activity on her credit cards for a week, which was about the length of time since she'd spoken to anyone the detective had been able to find.

"Wasn't Harry having her watched?" I'd asked Jack.

"Why would he have?"

"Habit." But I hadn't really wanted to get into a

discussion of Harry's methods of demonstrating familial affection to a person, so I dropped it.

Harry and the detective had made the usual calls to friends, emergency rooms, airlines, and anybody else they could think of. Nothing. Other times when Cece had disappeared Harry had always been able to drag information out of her more marginal friends, but this time he couldn't find anyone who appeared to be holding anything back.

Cece had cut herself off from everyone except her new man after she'd gotten out of rehab. Initially, Harry had interpreted this as a sign that the treatment was working this time, but now it meant there was nobody she'd confided in. There was nobody to blackmail into giving her up. There was no trace of her.

I spent Saturday trying not to listen for the phone. The only call that came was from Eileen's realtor. I'd practically hung up on her, explaining that I was waiting for an important call and it wasn't a good time. I watched a lot of TV, read two newspapers cover to cover, and refused to worry about Cece. Jack played racquetball again and only once suggested that I should call Harry for news.

We spent the afternoon curled up together on the couch, watching the end of a Greer Garson movie followed by a Giants game. There was something infinitely comforting about having someone to share a worry with—even a worry I wouldn't admit to feeling.

On commercial breaks or in between plays I told Jack about other times Cece had disappeared. When she was fourteen she'd hooked up with a roadie and gotten on Screaming Blue Messiah's bus as it left town after a concert. Then there was the time she ran away from school with some friends to go pick psychedelic mushrooms in Oregon. The worst had been when she'd joined a cult at seventeen. Harry had tracked her down to some smack-in-the-middle-of-nowhere Texas town, then had her kidnapped and deprogrammed. He nearly went to jail for that himself, but a few discreet political donations kept him out of serious trouble.

Cece's twenties had been more gruelingly predictable, the disappearances every year or so usually signaling a bottoming-out with drugs that led to another stint in rehab. Each time there was the almost-certainty she'd be found too late.

Jack didn't say much to any of this, which was a relief. There wasn't much to say. We watched the game.

I couldn't sleep that night, which was probably why I was groggy and grumpy at breakfast the next morning. "I need fresh air," I announced. "I think I'll go for a run."

Jack tried to disguise his surprise with a gulp of orange juice. "A run?"

"I run sometimes," I said, breaking off a piece of croissant and not looking at him. "And I've been eating too much since we got back," I slathered strawberry preserves on the pastry and popped it in my mouth. "It'll do me good," I said through the crumbs.

He cocked an eyebrow. "If you want to work out, why don't you come to the gym with me? The concierge set me up with a temporary membership."

I made a face. "I'm not really a gym person. If I'm going to be gasping for air I want it at least to be fresh air." And I'd rather not have my new husband watching my first workout in ages. It was bound to be ugly.

It took a while to find the appropriate shoes, jog bra, shorts, and tee-shirt among the piles of clothes on my side of the closet, but I managed. All the while I was getting ready I was fighting a strong impulse to stay parked by the phone for another day. But I'd made a good effort during the night to convince myself that Cece was fine, and I was determined to stick to that conviction. I was even more determined not to let Jack see how scared I was.

When you grow up with money, there's always fear. Fear that people will like you for how much you can give them. Fear that who you are is secondary to how much you have. And fear that one day someone will pull a bag over your head and hold you hostage. If you're not going to go crazy one way or another, you have to be careful. And Cece had never been careful.

When I came out of the bedroom Jack whistled. "I didn't know I married a jock." I did look the part, with my blue lycra tee-shirt and my hair pulled back in a ponytail. I had tied a sweatshirt around my waist. No sense in parading my spandex-covered ass around in full daylight.

Jack tossed a cell phone to me. "Thought you might like to take this along."

"Where did you get it?" The phone was silver and about the size of a cigarette lighter. "When did you get it?"

"I thought it might come in handy."

I flipped the top of the phone up and saw Jack had programmed both the hotel's number and Harry's into it.

"I'll call you if I hear anything, okay?" Jack said. "Don't worry."

I nodded and slipped the phone into a snug pocket inside the waistband of my shorts. "Okay." Having the weight of it made me feel more secure somehow. I suddenly and ridiculously felt like I was about to burst into tears, so I grabbed my room key and some cash, called "see ya" over my shoulder, and left.

I took a cab to the Embarcadero. I figured I'd run when I got there, so there was no need to be fanatical and walk all the way. I had the driver let me out under the Bay Bridge, and began stretching. I wasn't as stiff as I'd expected to be. Although I hadn't formally worked out very often while in London, as an unpaid intern for a busy theater company I'd done more physical labor than at any other time in my life. Apparently it had paid off.

It was overcast and windy, typical of summer in the city, so I was glad to have the sweatshirt. I started out slowly, heading toward Fisherman's Wharf. It felt good to breathe the sharp salty air of the bay. I started to find my pace as I kept moving, passing the working piers and then the ferry building.

The wide sidewalk was almost empty. Other runners, couples walking hand-in-hand, a few tourist groups, and clusters of skateboarders practicing their moves for one another were about all the company I had.

And a motorcycle. Because there were no cross streets on my side of the road, I didn't have to wait at corners. But the street traffic did, and I found myself passing the same group at each light as I caught up to them while they waited. There was a red motorcycle with some sort of muffler problem that just about deafened me every time I passed it or it passed me on its way to the next light.

I was already irritable and the engine racket just about put me over the edge. I tried to give the biker a filthy look as I passed, but his matching red helmet enclosed his whole head and I couldn't even tell if he'd seen me. He finally turned down a side street when I neared the always-congested area around Pier 39, and I started to relax and breathe easier at just about the time the sidewalk became too crowded to keep up a regular pace.

To hell with it. I came to a stop near a bench and watched some girls demonstrating racing kites as I stretched and cooled down.

Pier 39 is a tourist mecca. The people there generally look cold and surprised, as if the brochure hadn't told them about the fog. The sweatshirt vendors do a brisk business and the air smells of waffle cones and fried calamari, with the occasional acrid whiff of sea lion.

As a self-respecting native San Franciscan, I was expected to run through the out-of-town crowds with my head held high, getting through the area as quickly as possible on my way to the Marina Green. But today I didn't care. My heart wasn't in the run and I wanted a latte.

I don't know how long I spent sipping coffee and watching the sea lions from the railing of the pier. I was startled out of my stupor by a gull, screeching as it flew past my head. I jumped and automatically turned to see where it had gone, and I was almost sure I saw someone watching me. He turned immediately and walked quickly away across the landing of a second-story balcony. But in the moment I'd seen him I had recognized, or thought I'd recognized, the red-helmeted biker from the noisy motorcycle.

Great. I was getting as paranoid as Harry. Time to take a deep breath and—I yelped as the cell phone in my shorts started chirping and vibrating. "Shit!" I dug it out and flipped the top up. "What?"

"Charley?" Apparently Jack hadn't been expecting to be yelled at.

"Jack!" The latte I'd just drunk began to re-froth in my stomach. "What's happened?"

"I'm not sure. Harry called and told me a car was on its way to pick me up. He's at his apartment in the city."

"Has there been another call? What about Cece?"

"I don't know. He just said that I was supposed to come over and you were supposed to stay here and he'd explain when I got there. The car's probably downstairs by now. I should go."

"Wait!" I yelled, scaring the seagulls, "I'll meet you there! At Harry's!"

"Charley, I don't know what's up, but he said he wanted me to come alone. You should come back here and I'll call you when I know what's going on."

"Like hell!" Now tourists were pulling their children away from me as I ran toward the street, looking for a cab. "I'm not going to sit around waiting while—"

"Charley." Jack's voice stopped my crazed dash. "Listen to me. Do what Harry says. Come back here and I'll call you when—"

"What aren't you telling me?" I demanded. "What's going on?"

"Just do this," he said. "Just do this." He hung up.

"Shit!" It not being possible to slam a cell phone receiver, I threw the phone at the ground. "Shit!"

"Ma'am?" A young woman was looking at me with mixed concern and fear. Maybe they didn't have lunatics in spandex who scream obscenities in public where she came from. "Are you all right?"

I took a deep breath. I picked up the phone. I nodded at the woman. I went back to the hotel.

Jack didn't call until he left Harry's, and then it was only to say he was on his way back.

The instant the door closed behind him I pounced. "What did he say? What did he hear? Why did he want to talk to you and not me? What's going on?"

Jack kissed me quickly on the cheek and said, "Cece is alive." Then he headed for the bedroom. He pulled his gym bag out of the closet and dumped its contents onto the bed.

I followed him to the doorway. "And?"

He was sorting through the drawers where his clothes were neatly stacked. "She's been kidnapped." He looked up at me briefly. "They made contact this afternoon. They've made their demands. Are you all right?" I was hanging onto the doorpost, but I nodded mutely. "They want six hundred thousand in cash. Harry's getting it now. We don't know when they'll call back and tell us the terms of the exchange. You're not all right."

He took me by the arms and led me to a chair. "Put your head between your knees if you need to—you look like you might pass out."

I took a few deep breaths instead. "I'm fine. It's just . . ."

Jack nodded, keeping his eyes fixed on mine.

I straightened my shoulders and pulled myself together. I'll be damned if I'll faint in a crisis. "Well," I said. "What are we going to do to get her back?"

Jack gave me a careful look, which I didn't like one bit. He resumed packing. "Your uncle has asked me to take care of it."

"Uh huh." I pulled another bag from the closet and

started throwing things at random into it. "How are we going to do that?"

"Charley." Jack grabbed my bag and threw it back into the closet. "There's no time. I don't know how long this is going to take or where I'll have to go, but I have to leave for Harry's right now. They expect him to be at the Hillsborough place in—" he looked at his watch—"twenty-three minutes. They could call any time after that. I have to be there."

"Alone?" He couldn't be serious. "You and Harry?" Harry had asked Jack to deal with the kidnappers? And Jack had agreed? "Why?" I said it like an accusation. "Why did Harry ask you for help? Why didn't he call the cops? Or one of his famous detectives?"

"We don't have time for this now," Jack said.

"If you think I'm going to let you go alone you're completely insane."

"You're not the first to suggest that." He zipped his bag, not breaking his pace. His movements were precise and economical. He took a last look around the room. Everything he had taken was black. That meant he thought the meeting would take place at night. Tonight?

"You'll need me," I told him.

"Pumpkin," he held my eyes, and suddenly the room seemed unnaturally calm. "The last thing I need is to be worried about you. Stay here. Be safe."

That stopped me for a minute. It was the way he looked at me. Then I registered what he had said. "First of all—" I followed him into the living room— "don't 'Pumpkin' me at a time like this." He ignored me. "And secondly, what makes you think you need to worry about me? I'll have you know I'm perfectly capable of taking care of myself."

He grabbed his leather jacket from the back of a chair. "Really?"

"Really." I disregarded his sarcastic tone and stood, feet shoulder-width apart, knees slightly bent, hands relaxed at my sides. "You probably don't know I have a black belt in Tae Kwan Do."

"Impressive." He paused. "Why is it that I've never known you to practice?"

"Well," I held my stance, looking (I hoped) defiant and athletic, "getting the black belt was my goal. After that I sort of . . ."

"Stopped?"

"Well, reduced the frequency and intensity—"

"When?"

"What?"

"When did you get your black belt?"

I lifted my chin. "A while ago." He raised his eyebrows. "All right," I admitted, "I was seventeen."

"That is impressive, a black belt at seventeen. Luckily my mother raised me to be a gentleman, so I won't point out how long ago that was."

Bastard. "The point is, I can take care of myself."

He finally lost his cool. "Yes, I'm sure I'd feel much better knowing that when some psycho pulls a gun on you you'll be able to wow him with a rusty roundhouse. Look," he cut off my response, closing the distance between us to grab my shoulders, "these guys are professionals. They took Cece with no trace, and they've made no mistakes so far in dealing with your uncle. They are undoubtedly highly armed and highly alert. You cannot pull a Nancy Drew and save the day. I'm going to go wherever they tell me, do whatever they tell me, and I'm going to give them the money to get your cousin home. That's all."

I looked into his eyes and I didn't believe him. He kissed me quickly and made for the door. If he thought I was going to stand helplessly by and tell him to be careful—like hell I would. "Jack!"

"Charley." He looked back at me as he opened the door. "I'll call as soon as I know anything. Stay here. Stay safe." And he left.

Damn. "Be careful!" I yelled after him.

I looked at the closed door, trying to get my breathing back under control. Then I picked up the phone and dialed. "Brenda? You have to come over right away. With your car."

Chapter 9

I knew it would take Brenda close to an hour to make it over the bridge and across town to pick me up. I put the time to good use, pacing and fuming and pacing and worrying and pacing and cursing. Why the hell didn't I smoke?

Finally I heard a knock on the door. "Thank God! You made great time—" I choked back the rest of my words when I opened the door. It wasn't Brenda.

"Inspector Yahata."

"Mrs. Fairfax." The detective inclined his head slightly, and in the time it took him to look up and say my name I swear he made a comprehensive visual survey of me, the room behind me, and probably the hotel hallway in both directions. "Were you expecting someone?"

I had a momentary brain freeze. "Expecting?" I echoed.

Suddenly he was in the room, although I don't think I actually saw him move. "Are you alone, Mrs. Fairfax?"

Okay, I had to get control of this situation. I had to get rid of him. "Yes," I said giddily. "Yes, I'm sorry but Jack had to go out, so if you need to speak with both of us, I'm afraid we'll have to do it another time. I'd be happy to come down to the station. Do you have a station?" I chirped. "Of course you have a station, so if you just tell me where it is, Jack and I can come see you as soon as he gets back."

The inspector kept his gaze on me as I babbled, and I was starting to feel like a bug being seared under a magnifying glass until he released me with a slight smile. "But it's you I came to talk to."

"Me?" Another brain freeze.

"I have a few questions." The slim notebook appeared in one hand, the glittering pen in the other. "About your husband."

"Inspector, really, another time would be—I beg your pardon?"

"How long have you known your husband, Mrs. Fairfax?"

"Excuse me?"

The man who noticed everything didn't seem to take note of my confusion. He continued crisply. "I know you arrived from London on the day you discovered the victim."

"Have you found out who she is—was?" This was the one topic that could divert my attention from the fact that Jack was probably risking his life right now to save my cousin's sorry ass.

"I also know that you were married only two days before your arrival."

"So?" What was he writing down?

"How well do you know your husband, Mrs. Fairfax?"

Was he saying he suspected Jack? "What does that have to do with anything?"

There must have been something in my tone that caused the detective's eyebrow to raise a nanometer. "In the course of my investigation I have come across certain facts, certain discrepancies, in your husband's background."

Oh, great, that. But I really didn't have time to hear Yahata's take on the information Harry had already come up with.

"Inspector, my husband's background has nothing to do with the woman who was in that bathtub." I stared at him with as much cool confidence as I could muster, but admittedly I wasn't having much of a day for mustering cool confidence.

"I find it difficult to accept that conclusion without knowing who the woman was. Or, for that matter, who exactly your husband is."

That was a fair point, but I was in no mood to acknowledge it to the detective. "Jack had nothing to do with that woman's death."

"Are you quite sure of that?"

I was quite sure I didn't want to have this conversation. "Yes."

"Then I can only ask you to impress upon your husband the importance of sharing any information he might have . . . forgotten in the shock of finding the body. I would be very interested in anything he might now remember."

"Fine." If it would get him out of there, I'd agree to anything.

The detective paused before speaking again, and seemed to choose his words with surgical precision. "Mrs. Fairfax, I urge you to be cautious. Extremely cautious."

He held my gaze for a moment, then nodded infinitesimally and was gone.

I stood staring at the closed door, which seemed to vibrate slightly behind him. "Great," I breathed out. "I'll be cautious. But first I have to go on a ransom drop."

When Brenda finally showed up I was waiting for her on the corner, wearing sensible black clothes and silent black shoes. I hadn't bothered to tell Brenda to wear something black, because she nearly always did. True to form, she showed up in a loose-fitting black sweater and dark gray pants. Good enough.

"What are we doing? What's going on?" She was a little breathless, tossing papers, folders, half-empty water bottles, and snack wrappers into the back seat. I swept everything that remained on the passenger seat onto the floor and threw myself in.

"Head for Hillsborough. Hurry!" I strapped myself into the little VW, hoping she'd floor it.

"Not until you tell me what's going on. Where's Jack?" Brenda used her most serious I'm-the-teacher-and-you'll-tell-me-what-you're-up-to-young-lady voice. I'd gotten her to come over with no explanation, but now it looked like she'd had enough mystery.

"Brenda, just go!" I pleaded. "I'll tell you on the way!" She hesitated for a moment, then sighed and pulled out into the traffic.

I told her an abbreviated version of events. She kept her eyes on the road, nodding and gasping at appropriate intervals. By the time I got to the part about Jack ordering me to stay at the hotel we were approaching the Seventh Street onramp to 101 South. She slammed on the brakes and pulled over to the side of the road.

"Where are we going?" she demanded.

Wasn't it obvious? "To Harry's."

She nodded, and damned if she didn't look angry. "Even though he and Jack told you to stay put."

"Yes." What did that have to do with anything?

"Charley, I don't like this." She gave me a stubborn look. "You have no idea what's going on at Harry's. We could show up at the wrong moment and ruin whatever they're planning."

"Exactly!" I nodded eagerly, dismissing the second part of her argument. "I have no idea what's going on and I'll be damned if I'll let Harry pull Jack into something dangerous—"

"It doesn't sound like Harry pulled him into anything. It sounds like he's a willing participant. And Charley, it sounds like he knows what he's doing."

"But—"

"So if you're worried about it being dangerous," she insisted over my protest, "don't get in the way!"

"I'm not going to get in the way!" I hollered.

"Then what are you going to do?" she yelled.

"I don't know!" I shouted.

We glared at each other.

Brenda was the first to speak. "Oh, hell."

I took a deep breath. "Yeah."

She waited a moment, running her hands along the steering wheel. Then she turned to me. "Okay." She paused. "Okay?"

"Okay."

"What do you want to do?" She was all practicality now.

"I want to go there."

"Okay. And then what?"

Damn her. "We'll watch."

She nodded. "From where?"

"From down the street, where they can't see us." I knew the perfect spot, hidden from Harry's house as well as the neighbors' by a grove of eucalyptus trees.

"And that's all?"

"We won't go in. We'll just watch." Until something happened.

"If I say no, what are you going to do?"

First, never speak to her again. Then, "Take a cab. Or rent a car. Or something. But time is running out and I'm going crazy and I just have to know what's going on."

She thought about it, then nodded again. "Okay." She got on the freeway.

Part of me knew she was right, and that I was being irrational, but when Brenda slipped the car between the eucalyptus trees with Harry's driveway in clear view, I felt like I could breathe again. At least now I'd know what was happening. I couldn't stand the thought of waiting impotently by the hotel phone.

The light was starting to fade when we got there. I had no way of knowing whether Jack was still in the house or had gone out to meet with the kidnappers, but I figured I'd see him either leaving or coming back. Unless something went horribly wrong . . .

"Charley." Brenda interrupted my thoughts before I could get too far down the Path of Mental Terrors. "Why do you think Harry wanted Jack to help?"

I'd asked myself that question at least a dozen times. "I'm not sure," was the truthful answer.

"But what do you think?" she persisted.

"I think . . ." How to put it? "I think Harry thinks Jack is not being entirely truthful about his past." I knew Inspector Yahata would agree with that opinion.

"So? Harry always thinks the men in your life are liars."

She made a good point. "Right . . . but in this case he thinks Jack is something more than he says, not something less."

"Something more? Like a higher rank or something?" She reached into the back seat for a bottle of water.

"Something more like . . ." It seemed ridiculous to say it out loud. "Maybe a spy or something."

She digested this. "Why would he think that?"

Reasonable question. I told her about Harry's digging, and the coincidences he'd found about Jack's proximity to political upheavals and terrorist crackdowns. It sounded pretty thin, but what Harry had said about Jack being too smart to have had such a weak career had rung true to me, and I pointed it out to Brenda.

She didn't say anything for a while. She took a gulp of water and offered the bottle to me. I shook my head. "What do you think?" she asked.

"I don't know." Wouldn't I know if my husband was a spy? Is that the sort of thing a woman just knows? Or is it the sort of thing the wife is the last to know? And what exactly did Yahata know?

We waited and watched.

It got darker, and lights began to show at the windows, but we weren't close enough to see what was going on inside the house. I thought about suggesting I get closer on foot, but figured Brenda wouldn't appreciate the idea. I didn't want to blow the fact that despite her initial misgivings she seemed to be getting into the spirit of the thing. At one point she exclaimed "oh!" and started rummaging around in the back seat. Based on the amount of discarded clothes she had back there, we wouldn't need to worry about getting cold. Eventually she emerged triumphantly with a black beaded evening bag.

"Ta da! I knew it was here!"

I looked at it. "Is this a formal stakeout?"

She opened the bag and pulled out a tiny set of onyx binoculars with inlays of mother-of-pearl. "My opera glasses. I thought they might be useful."

"Fabulous! What else have you got in there?"

She poked around. "My 'star red' Chanel lipstick that I wore to *Carmen* last season . . . ticket stubs . . . some cash . . . oh! I thought I lost these earrings!" She pulled out two big clusters of deep red crystals. "Horribly uncomfortable, but gorgeous, aren't they?"

I had to admit they were. I tried them on.

"Perfect with your basic black," she told me.

They were horribly uncomfortable. I handed them back. "Anything else as useful as these?" I picked up the opera glasses and swung them open, trying to get my bearings on Harry's house.

"Just a tin of tiny fruit sucky candies." She took off the lid and held it out. It was filled with yellow, orange, and pink candies, each the size of a pea. "Want some?" I took a couple and popped them in my mouth. I suddenly realized I hadn't had anything to eat all day except a croissant for breakfast and about thirty cups of coffee. Then I realized I had to pee.

"Why do you keep your evening bag in the car?" I asked, trying to take my mind off my bodily needs.

"I only carry it to the opera, and I always drive to the opera, and so this way I always know where it is."

I couldn't argue with that. The glasses weren't very powerful, but then we weren't very far away, so they worked well enough to help me see shadows behind the closed curtains. Multiple shadows. That meant multiple people. So probably Jack was still there, right? I'd told the hotel switchboard to forward any calls to the cell phone, so I knew he hadn't called to tell me it was all over. If he was still there it meant it hadn't begun yet. So we'd keep waiting.

Brenda killed time by telling me all about the previous opera season. She and Eileen had gotten a box every season since we were in college, regardless of

whether the men that came and went from their lives
cared to participate. I went with them occasionally,
but didn't have nearly the appreciation, or fanaticism,
that they had. Brenda was in mid-diatribe about the
new Ukrainian soprano who'd been a grave disappointment as Dorabella in *Così Fan Tutte* when I
grabbed her arm. "Shhh! Something's happening!"

The garage door was opening.

I trained the opera glasses on the garage. "Start
the car!"

Brenda didn't argue. It was fully dark now, but she
didn't put the headlights on. We saw a black Lexus
SUV pull out of Harry's garage. I focused the glasses
on the windshield, trying to see the driver, and caught
a glimpse of a silhouette before I was blinded by the
SUV's headlights.

"Is it Jack? Is that Harry's car?" Brenda whispered.
"What should we do?"

"I can't tell," I said, squinting but failing to see
anything behind the dark glass on the driver's side of
the SUV as it passed us. It turned and headed uphill.
It had to be Jack. The driver was too tall for Harry,
and if it had been one of Harry's detectives he would
have taken his own car, not Harry's Lexus. Well, presumably it was Harry's Lexus because it had come out
of his garage and it was just the sort of car he'd own.
Which meant, presumably, it was Jack behind the
wheel. "Follow it!"

I looked at Brenda and she nodded. "Okay." She
eased out of the trees and kept her headlights off until
Jack had turned a corner.

There were hardly any cars on the road so it was
easy to keep track of the big SUV as it made its way
along the winding hillsides leading to Highway 280.
At least that's where I assumed it was headed. I knew
I was right when it turned and picked up speed on
the frontage road. He was headed for the city.

It was harder to follow him as we merged into the
traffic heading into town. I cursed myself for not having done something useful like breaking into the ga-

rage and kicking out the taillight while we were waiting, but it was too late now.

Brenda was fantastic. She stayed close enough so we could see the SUV in the distance, but let other cars come between us and didn't always stay in the same lane.

"Have you done this before?" I asked.

She grimaced. "Remember Malcolm?"

A Stanford paleontologist who'd broken her heart into a million pieces a few years ago. "You followed him?"

"I was completely out of control." She gave me an apologetic grin. "I didn't want you or Eileen to know because you'd worry."

"Like hell we'd worry, we'd have helped you."

"You did help me. You brought over a huge box of cannoli and told me I was better than him."

"You were! You are! How long did you follow him?" Long enough to get good at it, clearly.

"A few weeks." She winced. "Long enough to confirm my worst fears."

"Oh, sweetie." We followed Jack in silence as he left 280 and took Highway 1 towards Pacifica. He took a right on Skyline, then a left onto the Great Highway. We had to stay back now, because we were practically the only cars on the two-lane road that ran the length of Ocean Beach.

"Oh, I hope he's not going to get into a boat or something," Brenda said. "We'd never be able to keep up with him."

"I bet he's going to the park." But we drove past the silent windmill that marked the western end of Golden Gate Park. He stayed on the Great Highway as it turned and went uphill at the Cliff House. In a few blocks the street turned into Geary and traffic picked up.

"Where the hell is he going?" I asked. "Why would he have taken this route if he's just going downtown?" But he wasn't. He turned left on 25th and headed towards the Presidio.

Brenda realized it before I did. "The Presidio! It has to be! It's perfect for a ransom drop!"

She was right. The former military installation would be almost completely deserted. It was on a huge piece of land and had spectacular views of the city, the bay, and the Golden Gate Bridge. But it had been caught in epic political battles over what should be done with it once the military moved out. There had been speculation that everyone from Mikhail Gorbachev to George Lucas was going to take it over, but while its fate went undecided it went largely unoccupied.

"You're right!" I felt a surge of excitement and wondered if Jack was feeling the same in the big black Lexus ahead of us.

Eventually Brenda had to turn off her headlights. We stayed as far back as possible and pulled off the road quickly when we saw Jack turn into a small parking lot on the hillside overlooking the last onramp to the Golden Gate Bridge.

The opposite side of the narrow road was lined with small white houses, officers' quarters from days gone by, abandoned in the weak moonlight now. Without speaking, Brenda and I quietly got out of her car. The dome light came on for an instant when I opened my door, but Brenda quickly reached up and flipped it off. We heard nothing from the parking lot ahead. Silently, I crouched and dashed across the street to the side of one of the houses. Brenda followed.

The overcast summer day had turned into a chilly night. We could see our breath in front of us, but we couldn't see what was happening in the parking lot.

I looked at Brenda. This is where things could get dicey. "Are you in?"

She only hesitated for an instant, then nodded. "Okay."

We crept closer to the lot, staying behind the houses, dashing from one backyard to another and pausing in unkempt hydrangea bushes at each stage to see if we could tell what was happening.

About five houses along, we finally had a good view. We could see Harry's Lexus parked alone near the tree-lined edge of the lot. There were no lights and no other cars. We settled in to wait.

After a few minutes Brenda tugged at my sleeve. "I'm cold."

I nodded. "Me too. We should have brought something from the car." But neither of us wanted to go back. "I forgot the opera glasses too."

A few minutes later there was another tug. "Charley?"

"What?"

"I need to go to the bathroom."

Damn. I'd been trying to put my own need out of my mind. "Me too."

"What should we do?" Her voice was urgent.

"Hold it." But for how long?

A few minutes later: "Charley?"

"What?"

"I can't hold it." She looked like she was in pain.

"Then go in the bushes."

"Here?" she squeaked.

"Not right here," I said impatiently. "Go over there." I gestured to what looked like a clump of oleander a few yards away.

"You think?" She seemed doubtful.

"Oh, for the love of God. Stay here." I dashed to the bushes. I could no longer see the parking lot or Brenda, so I quickly pulled down my pants and did what I had to do, trying to keep it as quiet as possible. I vowed never to drink coffee again.

I was distinctly uncomfortable on the dash back. "See?" I glared at Brenda. "No big deal. Go."

She looked reluctantly from the bushes to me. "What did you use to—"

"Brenda! I swear to God I'll—"

"Okay!" She crept off.

She'd just left when I heard a car approaching. It came slowly up the road with no headlights, and I prayed whoever was in it didn't notice the VW off in the bushes. I could see it more clearly when it got closer, a dark van with no side windows. Was Cece inside? Was she all right? In all my worrying about Jack I'd forgotten that the point of the whole thing was to get my cousin back safely, damn her.

The van slipped into the space between the SUV and the trees that lined the parking lot. In the darkness I couldn't make out anything except one shadowy figure getting out of the van and one shadowy figure getting out of the Lexus. I strained to make out what they were saying when I heard a sudden liquid sound coming from behind me. I froze as the figure from the van looked towards me. Brenda seemed to go on forever. I had counted to fifteen by the time she stopped. The figure from the SUV—Jack? Was it Jack?— seemed impatient with the other figure's distraction. He reached into the car and pulled out a bag.

"It wasn't that bad," Brenda whispered, and it was everything I could do not to scream. "It took me a while to get started—"

I put my hand over her mouth and nodded my head in the direction of the street. Her eyes widened when she saw the van.

The bag had been exchanged, but now the two figures were arguing. The one from the van made a move to get back in, but the other one pulled him back. "No way!" I heard him say. Was it Jack's voice?

The kidnapper pushed him away and laughed. I heard the word "choice" and assumed he'd said something like "you have no choice." In any case, he threw the bag into the van and then turned back. He seemed to be telling the other man to leave. There was a brief argument, but eventually Jack, if it was Jack, got back in the SUV. Before he shut the door, I heard him say quite clearly "If you're fucking with me—" before the wind took away the rest of the threat. But it had been enough. It wasn't Jack's voice. Whoever it was gunned the engine and pulled out of the lot.

The kidnapper watched the SUV until it was out of sight, back down the hill where we'd come from. Then he looked up at the sky, and in both directions of the street, and across the street. Again I had the feeling he was looking straight at us. Brenda gasped softly but didn't move.

He got back into the van, and I was just starting to breathe again when I saw a shadow high in the trees separate itself from the rest of the branches. A dark figure dropped silently onto the top of the dark van just as the engine started.

"What the—" Brenda began, but I was pulling her up.

"Come on! We have to follow it!" I ran for the car, Brenda following. The van had pulled out by the time we got to the VW, but we'd both seen where it had gone. The onramp to the bridge. The van was heading for Marin County and I was sure Jack was clinging to the top of it.

"What's happening? Do you see them?" Brenda had floored it getting onto the bridge, but didn't want to draw attention to herself by speeding once we got into traffic. I looked at my watch. One o'clock in the morning and there was traffic on the bridge. And they say New York is the city that never sleeps.

I was scanning the taillights in front of us, looking for higher, wider-set lights that could indicate the large van. "There!" I pointed ahead. "In the fast lane just going into the tunnel!" Brenda sped up and we got close enough in the lighted tunnel to see that it was the dark van. But I didn't see anyone on top. Was it just the angle or had he fallen off? Had we passed him, crushed and bruised on the side of the road, and not even known it? What if . . .

"Charley!" Brenda yelled. "He's taking the Stinson Beach exit! We'll never be able to follow him on that little windy road without being seen!" She was right, we'd never be able to make it over Mount Tamalpais without the kidnappers realizing they were being followed.

"Keep going! They may turn off before then."

They did, taking the road to Mill Valley. Brenda

fell back as far as she dared. There didn't seem to be anyone else headed for the woodsy little town at this hour. I knew we were passing isolated houses, and I wondered if Cece was being held in one like them, too far away from neighbors to yell for help.

"Charley?" Brenda asked. "Do you think they still have Cece? Why wouldn't they have brought her?"

"I don't know." But I could think of a million reasons. All of them bad.

The van slowed and Brenda quickly pulled her car off to the side of the road. We saw the van turn into a long driveway and cut the headlights. We were too far away to tell what happened then, or to hear doors.

Brenda looked at me. "Well?"

Well. Cece was probably in a house up there. And— if he wasn't dead in a ditch—Jack was probably there too, looking for a way to get her out. "Let's get closer."

For the second time that night we left the car quietly. For the second time we forgot jackets and opera glasses. We crossed the street and I blessed the tall trees that obscured the moonlight, brighter on this side of the bay where there was less fog.

We made our way to the van. It was at the corner of an L-shaped driveway, pointed toward the road as if for a quick getaway. It was about twenty yards from a large house, where either the lights were out or there were very effective blackout curtains. I couldn't see or hear any activity. We waited in the shelter of the van for a while, eyes and ears straining.

Finally I couldn't take it any longer. "Stay here," I hissed to Brenda. "I'm going to see if I can peek in a window."

"Charley—" but I put my finger to my lips and moved away from her.

I stayed under the trees for as long as I could. I was eyeing the open space between the last trees and the house when I heard a crunch behind me. Like a footstep. I turned, but not in time. I heard a wooshing sound, then there was a moment of splitting pain, then nothing.

Chapter 10

I woke up in a rush of adrenaline, trying to escape the attack I hadn't seen coming. Unfortunately my hands and feet were tied and my sudden frenzy of motion only succeeded in launching me out of a chair and onto the ugliest carpet I'd seen since 1979.

I looked around, my brain catching up with my body, and tried to make some sense out of the situation.

"Hey Charley, glad you could join us." It was Cece's listless drawl, and coming from behind me. I flopped around on the floor, trying to turn around. "I see you're still as graceful as ever."

I rolled onto my back, and from that position managed to sit up. Cece and Brenda were bound, as I was, with crossed ankles and hands behind their backs. They, however, had managed to stay seated on a pair of violently flowered vinyl dinette chairs. "Cece," I said, "are you all right?" She looked thinner than usual, if that was possible, and her blond hair was held back in a stringy ponytail. There were dark craters under her eyes, but no visible bruises.

She shrugged, as much as she could in her current position. "I've been better."

"Are you okay, Charley?" Brenda spoke.

"Brenda." An enormous wave of guilt sloshed over me as I looked at her. "I'm so sorry. Did they hurt you? Are you okay?"

"I'm fine, Charley," she answered, her eyes filling

with tears. "I was just so worried about you. I didn't know how hard they hit you, and it took you so long to wake up—"

"Oh, for christsakes," Cece interrupted. "She's fine. You're fine. I'm fine. We're all fucking fine except for being trussed up like goddamn turkeys waiting for who knows who to do who knows what to us." She blew out her breath explosively, then inhaled slowly, as if she were counting. "Not that it isn't nice to have a little company."

Brenda and I exchanged worried glances. "Cece, tell us everything you've learned about the people who took you," I said, doing my best to sound firm and in control. Doing my best to sound like Jack. "Jack!" I yelped. "Brenda, what did you see? Did you see where he went? What—"

"I didn't see anything." She shook her head. "I saw you go down before I even saw the guy who hit you, and the next thing I knew there was a bag over my head and somebody holding my arms and pushing me ahead of him until we got here." Her eyes brimmed with tears again.

"Imagine my surprise," Cece said dryly. "Hardly anybody just drops in anymore."

Clearly her experiences hadn't made my cousin any less bitchy. "Cut the crap, Cece," I ordered. "Did you see anyone else? Did they bring Jack here?"

"Who's Jack?"

I couldn't answer. A knot had lodged itself in my throat. If they hadn't brought him here with the rest of us it could mean they hadn't caught him. Or it could mean something I refused to think about.

"Oh, that's right, you don't know," Brenda announced, pulling herself together and putting on a shaky smile. "Charley's married!"

For just a flash Cece looked genuinely stunned. "Married?" She looked at me blankly, then her lips twitched. "Does Harry know?"

I glared at her.

"Really?" She turned to Brenda for confirmation.

"Really." Brenda nodded. "And he's great, he's just won—"

"All right," I cut her off. "The point is he's not here." There was silence while we all let the various possible reasons for that sink in.

"Oh, Charley." Realization dawned on Brenda's face. "He's just going to kill you when he finds out we followed him."

For some reason this cheered me. A Jack who was going to kill me for following him was not a dead Jack.

"Don't worry, honey," Cece said. "I'm sure these freaks will kill you first." She gestured toward the door with her head.

Right. Right. I had to put Jack out of my mind and deal with the situation. Right. I addressed Cece. "Who are these freaks, and what the hell—" I looked around the room—"is this place?"

The long rectangular room looked like it had been decorated by the Brady Bunch on 'shrooms. Two walls had fake wood paneling and two had a wallpaper of ugly, uglier, and ugliest stripes of green. The carpet was a deep shag, in a color I had once heard a set designer describe as "burnt orange." At the far end were two mustardy vinyl beanbag chairs in front of an oak-and-smoked-glass entertainment unit that housed a television set and VCR. A pile of videos was in the corner near it. At the other end of the room, which had two closed doors facing each other in the corner, was a brass-and-smoked-glass dinette set and a fourth of the vinyl floral chairs. A stack of puzzles leaned drunkenly against the wall, and a pile of paperbacks had been dumped on the floor.

The room appeared to be a basement. The only windows were near the ceiling and, unfortunately, painted black. The only light was supplied by a fixture near the table. It consisted of a collection of irregularly shaped green and gold orbs suspended by a thick antiqued-brass chain.

We had been placed in the center of the room, and behind me was a long reddish-brown leatherette couch with pillows and a blanket heaped at one end. Suddenly every muscle I owned was sore, so I butt-crawled over to the couch and scooted myself up until I was sitting on it, facing the two women. It felt a little better.

Cece watched me with undisguised amusement, waiting until I was seated before answering. "This place," she announced, "is Kay Harrison's rumpus room."

The kid had a flair for the dramatic, I had to give her that. "Are you saying," I asked, "that you know where we are?"

She shook her head. "I just know what this is a re-creation of."

"Excuse me," Brenda asked, "but who is Kay Harrison?"

Cece ignored Brenda and eyed me coldly. "You didn't know her, did you, Charley? I was ten when I met her, and you were gone that year. Which boarding school was it?"

I sighed. I hated it when Cece played the let's-walk-down-memory-lane game. But I knew her well enough to know that I'd have to humor her if I was going to get her to tell me anything. "If you were ten I'd have been fifteen. That was the year in Vermont. As I recall I had to freeze my ass off in the middle of the woods so I wouldn't be a 'corrupting influence' on you."

Cece nodded. "You know, I always felt bad about planting my stash in your jewelry box." She paused, considering or remembering, I couldn't tell which. "But not too bad."

Enough of this. "Cece? A little focus please? Can we talk about our current situation?"

Brenda hadn't lost sight of the pertinent question. "Who's Kay Harrison?" she repeated.

Cece acknowledged her this time. Her voice took on the tone of someone beginning a well-worn fairytale. "When I was ten years old Kay Harrison was my best friend. And what's more," she continued, "she was the only friend of whom my father, Harry—" she rolled her eyes—"approved."

She seemed to have finished, lost in a pleasant memory. It crossed my mind that perhaps she wasn't just being her usual pain-in-the-ass self. Maybe the strain of her captivity had taken a toll on her mind. Brenda gave me a worried look. I shrugged with my eyebrows. She turned back to Cece. "And . . ." she said encouragingly.

Cece's head slowly pivoted to her. "And he shouldn't have." A fond smile played across her face. "My God, the things we got up to in her rumpus room." She sighed deeply. "First time I did coke, first time I did speed, first time I did pills of any sort, really." She looked around the room absently as she continued. "First time for hash, not the first time for booze, of course, but the quantity. . . ." She trailed off.

"You were ten?" Brenda squeaked.

"Hmm?" Cece seemed to come around in some way. "Yeah. Anyway, the point is, this room is pretty much an exact recreation of the scene of the crime, or crimes, or whatever."

"Oh, Cece, you poor—" Brenda began.

"Fuck that," Cece said sharply. "And fuck you."

I could tell Brenda's feelings were hurt but we didn't have time for that now. "Okay," I said. "Let's just look at the facts here. Someone . . . who? Who would have . . . ? Who could have . . . ? And why?" My head was throbbing.

Cece cleared her throat. "Well, I've had some time lately to think about that." She looked at me and smiled weakly, her defenses for one moment down. "The why gets complicated, even though it's basically simple, and the who. . . ." She hesitated just for an instant. "Is Tom Nelson."

"Who's Tom Nelson?" Brenda and I said together.

Cece's face became bitter. "My boyfriend." The words left a sting in the air. When neither of us spoke she continued. "I met him in rehab." She grimaced.

"The last one. The program was mostly group therapy. He was in my group."

"Oh," I said as realization dawned, "and you talked about Kay Harrison."

"Bingo."

"And you continued to see him after you got out?" Brenda asked.

"Yep. Of course it was against the rules but what the hell, you know? He was great."

I struggled not to make the obvious comment regarding evidence pointing to the contrary.

Cece continued. "He wanted to know everything about me. It was part of the therapy to talk about specific details. He wanted me to describe my bedroom as a little girl, and my college dorm room. . . ."

"And this room," I finished.

She shrugged and closed her eyes. "Ain't love a kick in the head?"

After a moment Brenda spoke up. "Um, Cece?"

"Yeah."

"What about the why? You said it was simple and kind of complicated?"

"Why don't you ask my cousin? She's the one with the brains in the family."

Brenda looked at me. "What's the simple part?"

"Money."

"Oh. Of course." She waited a moment, then prompted, "And the complicated part?"

I didn't answer. I was watching Cece as she slowly raised her head and opened her eyes. "He. . . ." Her voice came out in a croak and she swallowed forcefully, then began again. "He wants to fuck with my head."

"He wants," I pointed out, "for you to know it's him." A thought struck me. "Has he been here?"

She shook her head. "That's the weird part, or one of the weird parts. All I've seen are these guys in black."

"Have you seen their faces?" I asked.

"Ski masks," she replied. "They all wear exactly the

same clothes, black jeans and black turtleneck sweaters, and they all wear the same black ski masks."

Brenda seemed to perk up. "I think that's a good sign," she said. "Because I saw in a movie once that if the kidnappers can hide their identities from the victim they don't have to—Oh!"

"Uh huh," Cece finished for her. "They don't have to kill you."

I decided not to dwell on that line of conversation. "How many of them are there? The guys in black?"

"I don't know for sure. They come in two at a time, every time, but sometimes I can hear others when the two are here. They only come in twice a day, with breakfast and dinner. They never speak. The couple of times they wanted to tell me something they just handed me a sheet of white paper with a message typed on it."

"What did they say?"

"The first message was on the first day. They'd tied me up like this when they'd brought me in, and the message said I could be released if I behaved myself. After that I had the run of the place. Of course I spent the first few hours trying to find a way out." She shrugged. "But no such luck. After that I just watched movies and played solitaire. The note said all I had to do was sit on the couch with my hands on my knees when they came in the room."

"And you did it?"

"Would you do it if someone offered to untie you right now?"

I would.

"What were the other messages?" Brenda asked.

"Just one, yesterday. It said I should be patient and soon I'd be rescued."

"Rescued? Why would they say that? Why wouldn't they say you'd be released?" Yesterday would have been the day they spoke with Harry. "Harry agreed to the ransom, so I don't get it." I looked at the two of them, Brenda's face just as clueless as mine, and Cece's suddenly curious.

"Speaking of which," she asked, "what's a wayward daughter going for these days?"

"Six hundred thousand." I spoke without thinking, still puzzling over the wording of the second note.

"Six hundred? That's a fucking insult!"

I tuned her out. Why would the note from Tom Nelson have told Cece she'd be rescued? The implication was that he had no intention of setting her free in return for the ransom. Was he going to ask for more? Did he think that asking for more would provoke a rescue attempt? He seemed to think a rescue attempt was a foregone conclusion, which was ridiculous considering the small amount of ransom he'd asked for. Of course Harry would pay. Harry wouldn't even miss an amount like that.

"Harry wouldn't even miss six hundred thousand!" I realized Cece was still speaking, heading into a full-blown rant. "I mean, do the goddamn math!" She was addressing Brenda. "If there are four guys in black, and there have to be at least that, but just say four guys in black, plus Tom makes five, that's only a hundred and twenty thousand each. And that's before expenses. I mean, you don't just find a room like this, you have to put it together. So, say they went to garage sales or something, it still adds up. And where the hell are we? Someplace with enough property that they don't worry about the neighbors, right?" Brenda nodded quickly. "So that's rent, and probably a lease, because what kind of place rents by the month? I mean—" She realized I was listening and turned to me furiously. "Why the hell bother? For that amount of money, what's the fucking point?"

"What if—" I began, but three sharp raps at the door caused us all to jump. The door opened and two black-clad men stepped in. They were exactly as Cece had described—black jeans, black turtlenecks, black ski masks. One was holding a sheet of white typing paper. They advanced into the room together and stood side by side. Their features were hidden and their builds were similarly tall and athletic. I could see why Cece had a hard time telling how many there were. The one on the left, without the sheet of paper, was a little taller, but that was the only noticeable difference. He closed the door behind them.

The man with the paper took the first step forward. He was headed for Cece, and, although my first reaction had been relief that Jack wasn't being brought in as another prisoner, that was quickly replaced with an overwhelming curiosity about what the message would say.

Before I quite realized what was happening, the second man made a swift smooth gesture and the man with the paper sank silently to the floor. Brenda let out a short yelp and the second man, who was crouching over the first, looked up at her quickly with his finger to his lips. Then he looked at me and, I swear, winked.

What the hell— "Jack!" I whispered urgently. "Is that you?"

He was busy cutting through the tape that bound Cece's wrists and ankles. Then he did the same for Brenda. They rubbed their wrists and looked dazed as he stood to face me. "Hi, Pumpkin," he said through the mask. "You ready to go?"

Chapter 11

"What the hell—" I stammered as Jack cut my hands and ankles free. "How the hell—"

He pulled his mask up, kissed me quickly, then pulled it down again. "We'll talk later, okay?" He turned to Brenda. "Nice to see you again."

She nodded blankly. "Hi, Jack."

"And you must be Cece." My cousin had been eyeing the man on the floor with loathing. She looked up when Jack said her name.

"Let's get the fuck out of here."

"Nice to meet you, too. Are we ready?" He looked at the three of us. "Nobody's hurt? You can run if you have to?"

"We're fine," I said.

"Okay. Here's the plan. I'll lead the way and you follow me closely. As far as I can tell there's a force of five tonight." He looked to Cece for confirmation, but she was focused on the fallen man again. He went on. "So with this one down and the one I took out to get this," he gestured to his clothes, "that leaves three more we need to worry about."

What the hell did he mean, the one he "took out"?

"I heard two of them playing a video game in another part of the house, so they should still be occupied. If we're lucky the third will be calling in to report on the mission, so we should be able to get out of here all right." He pulled a gun from the small of his back and made a deft one-handed movement that caused metallic snapping-into-place sounds.

"I'll go first, up the stairs as far as the kitchen door. If I don't see anyone there, you follow me. We go straight through the kitchen and out the back door, then straight to the van in the driveway. The keys are in the ignition. Everybody clear?"

Brenda and I nodded mutely. "Cece!" Jack said sharply. "Do you understand?"

She looked at Jack, looked back at the man on the floor, then at Jack again. Then she viciously kicked the bound man in the head. "I'm ready."

Jack nodded and went to the door. He gestured that we should all line up along the wall behind him. I stood closest to him, then Cece, and Brenda brought up the rear. Jack stood with his back to the wall, holding the gun in both hands at chest level. Then he spun quickly and opened the door, pointing the gun. He looked at us and nodded. All clear. We heard him mount the stairs swiftly. I peeked out when I heard the door to the kitchen open. He turned back and waved us on.

We got up the stairs as quickly and silently as we could. The kitchen was lit up like a football stadium, and open space stretched for about a mile to the back door.

While we waited, Jack stood beside the hall doorway in the same commando stance he'd used downstairs. Again he spun quickly to see what lurked beyond, and again he turned and waved us forward. "Go!" he hissed. We went.

At the other end of the kitchen, I peeked out the door. I didn't see anyone on the driveway. "It's clear," I whispered to Jack, who was still guarding the hall.

"Run!"

I could have sworn my feet never touched the ground, but I heard the crunch of the gravel so I knew that couldn't be true. Cece stumbled and fell halfway down the drive. Brenda and I picked her up and half-dragged her the rest of the way. She mumbled

"Weaker than I thought," and we both hissed "Shut up!" I looked back and saw Jack silhouetted in the kitchen doorway, gun drawn.

We had almost made it to the van when I heard the first shout from the house.

"Get in!" Jack called, sprinting toward us. We piled in the driver's-side door. I went first, then pulled Cece in behind me while Brenda pushed from behind. Jack spun and crouched in the shadow of the van, gun pointed at the kitchen door. He shouted over his shoulder, "Start the car!"

Brenda was in the driver's seat. She looked wildly at me. "Do it!" I yelled, and she fumbled to find the key in the ignition.

Then the shooting started.

I screamed, and Brenda screamed, and I threw myself across her trying to get to Jack. She pushed me off, still screaming, but finally managed to get the van started.

Cece, in the back of the van, seemed to snap into focus with the sound of the first shot. When a bullet hit the van Brenda and I screamed again, but Cece yelled "Shut the fuck up!" and pulled open the heavy sliding cargo door.

I vaulted into the back of the van, calling for Jack, who I could now see was still firing from his position by the rear wheel. He turned around, yelling "Go!" and dove for the door opening.

Brenda hit the gas with Jack's legs still dangling outside, and Cece and I hauled him in just before the van made a sharp turn onto the main road that could have sent us all flying out.

I lay on the floor of the van with Jack on top of me, both of us gasping for air, as Cece dragged the big door shut. The sudden quiet was deafening.

"Is everybody okay?" Brenda called from up front. "Is anybody hurt?"

"We're fine," I yelled. "Cece, find a light or something."

She felt along the ceiling until she found a switch. The rear of the van was suddenly brightly illuminated.

"Pumpkin," Jack said from on top of me, "I think I'm going to need a little help here."

I looked down, saw the blood, and screamed.

My scream set Brenda off again, and this time Cece joined in. Over us all, Jack shouted "Calm down! Just calm down!" but it took us a while.

Brenda pulled off the road. "Why are you stopping?" Jack yelled. "Don't stop! Keep going!"

"You're hurt," she shouted. "And besides—" she looked in the rearview mirror—"I don't think anyone's following us."

"Still, keep going." Jack struggled to sit up.

"Stay where you are," I told him, wiggling out from under him and making him lie flat on the floor. "Where are you hurt? How bad is it?"

He managed a rakish grin. "Just a flesh wound, baby." Then his eyes fluttered closed. "I've always wanted to say that."

"Brenda, get us to a hospital," I ordered. "Where's the nearest one?"

"No!" Jack's eyes flew open. "No hospital. They have to report gunshot wounds."

"Which is what you have, which is why we're going to a hospital."

He leaned on his right elbow and managed to get himself to an upright position. "Charley, no hospital. It just grazed my shoulder. I'll be fine. Brenda," he said with raised voice, "how fast can you get us to Harry's place in Hillsborough?"

She looked from me to Jack, then turned and put the van in gear. "Fast."

"Don't get arrested," Jack warned. "Just get us there, okay?"

"Okay," she said grimly.

Cece and I helped Jack to a fairly comfortable position leaning against the side of the van. Then I tore the black sweater from around his neck, using the bullet hole as a starting point. There was a lot of blood.

"Jack," I said softly. "Please let us take you to a hospital."

"It looks worse than it is," he said. "Just make a compress for now to slow down the bleeding." He closed his eyes.

I looked around for something to make a compress from, then settled for pulling my shirt off and tearing it into pieces. I ripped the sleeves off, then folded the rest into a large bandage, and used the sleeves to tie it around Jack's arm and hold it in place. The wound was on his left shoulder, about three inches from his neck. I tried not to think about what would have happened if it had been a little further down or to the right.

"Hey," Jack said, eyeing my bra as I tightened the bandage. "What are you trying to do? Give me something to live for?"

"I swear to God if you keep joking about it I'll kill you myself," I told him.

"Toll plaza!" Cece called from the passenger seat. "I need to turn off the inside lights if we don't want questions."

I nodded and she flipped off the light. Outside, we could see the beginnings of sunrise on the city.

We made the rest of the trip in silence. I wedged my body between Jack's and the cold steel side of the van, and held on to him until we got to Harry's.

Chapter 12

We made it to Hillsborough as the neighborhood was waking up. Papers were being delivered, landscapers were unloading equipment from battered pickup trucks, nannies were putting executive children into Volvo station wagons. It all seemed so normal. Except for us.

Brenda had begun to cry quietly as she turned onto Harry's street, brushing her tears away angrily. Cece, who had been alternating between silent stupor and manic fidgeting for most of the trip, now kicked the fidgeting up a notch. By the time we turned onto the drive she was simultaneously biting her nails, tapping her feet, twitching, and humming tunelessly.

I held on to my bleeding husband.

"See? We made it. No problem," he winced as the van lurched one last time before stopping. "Thanks, Brenda."

She turned back to look at us, blinking back tears. "I'm sorry," she said, gesturing helplessly to her face. "I can't stop."

"Well, stop," Cece snapped. "We're here, right? And everything's fine, right? So cut it out." She fumbled with the door handle, couldn't open it, so settled for slamming her fist against the window.

"It's okay," Brenda said softly, and reached over to unlock the door. "It's okay."

Harry chose that moment to explode out the front door, running down the stairs and sprinting across the lawn yelling "Where is she? Is she all right?"

Cece squared her shoulders and took a deep breath,

then hopped out of the van. "Hey, Pop," she called with complete nonchalance.

Harry nearly knocked her over, throwing his arms around her and repeating "Thank God, thank God, thank God." He just rocked her for a moment, then seemed to remember there were other people present. He pushed his daughter away, demanding "Are you all right? Did those bastards hurt you? If they did anything to you I'll—"

"I'm fine, Harry," Cece said. "Nothing a triple espresso can't fix." Harry clasped her closely again, and she submitted, but only for a moment. She pulled away, jerking her head in the direction of the van. "I think the new hubby is the one you need to be worried about."

Harry looked up in panic as Brenda pulled the van door open, revealing Jack and his sodden bandage, me, shirtless, trying to help him up, and a whole lot of blood. "Goddamn!" he yelled.

"Not as bad as it looks, I'm sure," said the calm voice of Gordon, who had materialized behind Harry with a blanket in his arms. He hopped lightly into the van and touched Jack gently on his wounded shoulder. "All right?" he asked.

"Never better." Jack allowed his uninjured arm to be draped across Gordon's shoulders. "What's for breakfast?"

Gordon handed the blanket to me, averting his eyes from my bra. "We wouldn't want the neighbors to talk," he said, and helped Jack out of the van.

"What the hell happened?" Harry demanded. Then, registering the fact that Brenda and I were present, "What the hell are you doing here?"

"Perhaps," suggested Gordon, "we might better have that discussion indoors?"

"Absolutely," agreed Jack.

"Well—What—Right!" Harry sputtered. "Yes, first things first, let's get you taken care of." He put his arm around Cece and followed Jack and Gordon up the path to the house. I opened the blanket for Brenda to come in with me, and we followed.

Gordon deposited Jack on one of the sofas in the great room and hurried off for bandages. He returned in seconds pushing a cart containing a variety of surgical-looking stainless steel instruments laid out precisely on clean cloths, along with a collection of medicinal bottles, cotton swabs, bandages, and white tape. Jack looked from the trolley to Gordon's face and back to the trolley again.

"I thought some preparation for this possibility might not be inappropriate," Gordon explained.

"Certainly not," Jack agreed.

"Do you know what you're doing?" I asked the chef, as he picked up a small, sharp pair of scissors.

"I have had some medical training, yes," he replied, snipping at the makeshift compress that used to be my DKNY long-sleeved silk tee.

"Then have at it." Jack leaned his head back on the cushion and closed his eyes.

"Shouldn't we call a doctor?" Harry asked doubtfully.

"No," said a voice from across the room.

Jack opened his eyes and turned toward the stranger. "Hey, Mike."

Mike? Computer guy Mike? He stood silhouetted in the doorway, but I saw it was the same guy who'd surprised me, in a rather similar state of undress, in my hotel room a few days ago.

"Mike," I said, realization dawning. "You were driving the Lexus."

He grinned at me. "Hi, Charley." He closed the big front door and joined us around the couch. To Harry he said "You really should keep your doors closed when you're harboring a possible fugitive, sir." And to Jack, "Is that bad enough to need a doctor?"

Jack looked at Gordon, who narrowed his eyes and shook his head. "No."

"Fugitive? What do you mean fugitive?" I demanded.

Mike gestured toward Jack's shoulder. "I'm guessing that wasn't the only shot fired in Mill Valley last night."

"How did you know it was Mill Valley?" Cece spoke up suspiciously.

"It's all over the news." He looked at her. "You must be the girl in question." He held out his hand. "Glad you're all right." She extended her hand automatically, and they shook. "What do you say we go scare up some coffee?" She nodded mutely and followed him to the kitchen.

Harry watched his daughter walk away. "Well I'll be damned." He turned to Brenda. "Are you all right? Do you need anything?"

She smiled weakly. "A hot shower and a week of sleep."

"The first shouldn't be a problem. Come with me." As Harry led her out of the room Brenda looked over her shoulder to shoot me a "should I?" look. I gave her a "go ahead" wave.

"How would you feel about a painkiller?" Gordon asked Jack.

"Not yet."

"Don't be silly," I said, sitting next to him, out of Gordon's way, and reaching for his hand. "At least have a slug of whiskey and a bullet to bite on."

Jack smiled. "That's my girl." He squeezed my hand, then just about wrenched it off as Gordon started cleaning the wound and assessing the damage.

"Could have been a lot worse," he summarized after a few minutes of swabbing and probing, enough to cause a fresh sheen of sweat to appear on Jack's face. "A couple of stitches wouldn't be out of place."

"Later," Jack said. "When you can give me something for the pain. Just bandage it up for now, okay?" Gordon looked like he was going to argue, then shook his head and reached for a stack of gauze pads. Jack took a deep breath. "Right now I want to hear what

Cece can tell us, before she's had a chance to sleep off any interesting details."

"Not fucking likely," Cece said, carrying a tray of mugs into the room. Mike followed her with an enormous coffee pot. I know I swore off the stuff in the oleander bushes, but to hell with that. I reached for a mug.

Harry returned without Brenda. He threw an oversized gray T-shirt in my direction and I quickly put it on. He spoke to Cece. "Do you think you can talk about it?"

"Hell yes."

"I'll get some breakfast," Gordon murmured, and slipped away.

Cece told us pretty much the same version of things she'd related to Brenda and me back in the basement. Jack and Mike stopped her frequently to ask for details about Tom Nelson. They probed her for an exact description, including voice characteristics and any mannerisms she could remember. There wasn't much. He'd told her he was thirty-eight, and a doctor who'd graduated from Harvard Medical School.

"That part checked out," Harry volunteered. Cece gave him an accusing look, and he protested, "Of course I checked him out! You think I'm going to let you shack up with someone you just met and not verify a few facts?"

"How did you verify them?" Jack asked, before they could open up an old argument.

"Hmm? Oh." Harry broke off a staring contest with his daughter. "I used McIntyre and Zipfel. They did some sort of Internet search." McIntyre and Zipfel was the firm of private investigators that Harry regularly used for background checks. He had a different agency entirely for tailing people and tapping phones, and yet another for providing security.

Jack and Mike exchanged a look. "Simple," Mike said.

"Excuse me?" I asked. "What's simple?" Mike was

beginning to get on my nerves. I kept forgetting he was in the room and then jumping when he spoke.

"Simple enough to hack into the Harvard registrar and add a name and a degree," he explained.

"That's simple?" Harry seemed shocked.

"For the right guy, yeah." Mike nodded.

I could see that McIntyre and Zipfel were in for a Harry-style ass-kicking at some point in the not too distant future.

"What else did you find out about him?" Jack asked.

Harry thought. "No marriage records. No criminal records. They didn't check his job history, so I don't know where he worked before the rehab center—"

Cece cleared her throat. "About that . . ."

We all looked at her.

"He didn't exactly work there." She looked up at the beamed ceiling.

"What in the hell do you mean he didn't work there?" Harry sputtered, but Jack held up his hand to quiet him.

"Cece, he was a patient?" I suggested.

She nodded.

"And you let Harry think he worked there when you told him the guy was a doctor," Jack continued.

She nodded again, then turned to face her open-mouthed father. "Well, what was I going to say? That he was a junkie? It happens to a lot of doctors, you know!"

"Right, except he wasn't a doctor," Mike pointed out.

"And probably wasn't a junkie," Jack agreed.

Cece seemed frozen in mid-protest. "Then why? . . . what? . . ."

"Are you suggesting," I asked, "that this guy checked himself into a rehab just to meet Cece?"

Neither my husband nor his know-it-all friend answered.

"No," Cece said. "It was all a setup?" She raised her voice. "Answer me!"

"It's possible," Jack said.

None of us spoke until Cece uttered a heartfelt, "Bastard!"

When the rest of the group went to the dining room in search of Gordon and breakfast, I went upstairs to see how Brenda was doing. I found her coming out of one of the guest rooms.

"Brenda!" I could hardly believe it was her. "You're gorgeous!"

With her hair uncharacteristically loose and hanging luxuriously down her back, and her face flushed from a hot shower, she looked positively glamorous. She was wearing a form-fitting silk robe that hugged her curvy figure. It was green and blue and violet, patterned in peacock feathers, and the colors were perfect on her.

"Well, I admit it's a little more . . . something . . . than what I normally wear," she said, looking down at herself. "Is it too tight?"

"It's perfect!" Why did she always hide her body under drapey folds of fabric and oversized sweaters?

She grinned. "Harry left it out for me in the guestroom for after my shower. Along with these." She stuck her foot out from beneath the robe to reveal purple feathered mules. She giggled. "I feel like a Chinese princess."

"You look like one," I agreed. "How are you feeling?"

"Famished! Is there anything to eat?"

"Come with me. Gordon—and I'm beginning to suspect he's actually Clark Kent—has been up to something in the kitchen."

In between mouthfuls of huevos rancheros and corn muffins, we told Cece what had happened in her absence.

"You mean you didn't even notice I was gone for six days?" she interrupted the narrative.

"Well, it's not like you stay in touch!" Harry said

defensively. "If I called in the cavalry every time you didn't pick up the phone, we'd be in a constant state of alert around here!"

"Well if you didn't attack me every time I talked to you, maybe I'd want to call more often!"

They glared at each other.

Lovely. I changed the subject by asking Jack the question that had been bothering me since the ransom drop. "How did you know where the exchange was going to be? How did you know to be hiding in the trees?"

He and Mike exchanged glances, and again I felt a wave of irritation. Mike seemed to know more about what was happening to my family than I did.

Jack cleared his throat. "They gave us two hours' notice for the drop. As soon as they told us where it was supposed to be I called Mike and we came up with our plan."

"Why?" Brenda asked. "Why didn't you think they'd bring Cece? Why did you think you'd need to follow them?"

"Good question." Harry looked at her approvingly.

Mike answered. "It wasn't enough money."

"That's for damn sure," Cece agreed. "Six hundred thousand!" She snorted and pushed her plate away from her. She'd hardly eaten anything.

Jack continued. "We suspected it wasn't about the money. It seemed to be more about . . ." he faltered.

"Fucking with my head," Cece finished for him.

Jack nodded briefly. "And Harry's. All of ours."

Mike spoke up. "Kidnapping isn't really about the victim, usually. They're just, um, a tool that's used to get the ransom. A cause that's used to create an effect."

Mr. Sensitivity didn't seem to notice Cece flinch at being called a "tool." He went on. "But in this case the desired effect doesn't seem to have been the money."

Gordon cleared his throat. We all turned to look at him, standing in the doorway to the kitchen. "Speaking of money . . . This was in the van." He held up a bag. It took me about two seconds to realize where I'd seen it before.

"The ransom!"

Harry and Mike trampled each other in their rush to take the bag from Gordon and open it. Stacks of cash spilled out onto the breakfast table. We all stared at it, stunned into silence.

When someone finally spoke it was Brenda, sounding like the professor she was, working out a logic problem. "All right. If it wasn't about the money, what was it about? It seems like everything was orchestrated just to lure us out to Mill Valley to rescue Cece." She looked at Harry as if struck by a sudden thought. "When they called you, did you ask to send someone else to bring the money or was that their idea?"

As Harry realized the implication of the question his face twisted in anger. "Goddamn! That sonofabitch said I should send someone else! Said he didn't want me keeling over from a coronary in the middle of everything!" His fist came down on the table. "Goddamn!"

"So," Brenda cut off what would otherwise have become a full-blown rant. "They got you angry, which distracted you from questioning why they didn't want you involved. It wasn't you they were interested in luring, Harry." Her eyes went to Jack. So did mine. So did everyone's.

"And another thing," Brenda continued. "Why did they give you so much notice about the ransom drop? It seems pretty stupid. It gave you enough time to set up an ambush." She looked around the table. "In the movies they always call the person on a cell phone after he starts driving around."

"You're a very bright girl," Harry said. I did not like the glint in his eye when he looked at her in that robe. "What do you think?" he asked Jack.

"I think they expected to be followed back to Mill Valley."

His words hung over the table. "Oh, my God!" I remembered. "The note! They told Cece she was going to be rescued!"

Jack nodded. "It was all a little too easy. They let us take her."

In response I looked pointedly at his bandaged shoulder. They hadn't let us take her without a fight.

"Although I'm not sure they counted on the full force of the rescue team," Mike said, a little too sarcastically for my taste, "until you showed up at the Presidio."

"You knew?"

"First rule of a stakeout, Charley," Jack said, his eyes twinkling. "Use the bathroom before you get into position."

Mike muffled a laugh. "And try to park somewhere other than the middle of the road."

Brenda's eyes began to glisten. "It was my fault. I drove and I parked, and it was me you all heard—" She clamped a hand over her mouth.

"You just stop teasing this girl!" Harry ordered, putting a protective hand on Brenda's shoulder.

"I think they were teasing me, Harry," I seethed. "Sorry Brenda."

"Sorry, Brenda," Jack repeated.

"Yeah, sorry," Mike said.

"Hello? How about 'sorry, Charley'?" I turned on Jack. "If you had bothered to tell me one little piece of all of this maybe I wouldn't have felt I had to follow you! Did you ever think of that?"

"Sorry, Charley." His mouth twitched. Bastard!

"By the way," Mike offered, "you really were good at tailing me all over town, Brenda. I didn't notice a thing until we got to the Presidio."

"Really?" She looked pleased, then startled. "Oh, I need to go get my car! What time is it?" She put her napkin on the table and started to rise. "I have a class at two."

"Um, Brenda, about your car . . ." Mike said.

"What?" Then she registered his tone of voice and repeated "What?" with dread.

"I was in position down the road from the house, and I saw you guys in the van on your way back here at dawn."

She looked baffled. I suppose I did too.

"Jack and I were in contact until he changed into the goon's clothes and went down to the basement," he confessed. "He'd told me to wait there."

I looked at Jack. "I couldn't risk the other guy seeing the cell phone." Of all the things he could have explained, that wasn't high on my list.

"So you saw us in the van," I prompted Mike.

"Right. And I wanted to give you a few minutes to make sure you weren't being followed." He looked at Brenda. "Which is when I saw your car. With five guys crammed into it."

Brenda's mouth made an O.

"I followed them across the bridge. They went to the Marina Green, where they transferred to another car. I hung back and followed them, but the early morning commute was pretty heavy by then and . . . I lost them." He grimaced. "In the financial district."

"So my car is at the Marina Green?" Brenda asked.

"Uh, no," Mike said. "I went back there, thinking they might have left something in it, and it was gone."

"Gone?" she said faintly.

"Whoops," Cece said.

"What do you mean, gone?" I demanded. "If all five guys were in the second car, who could have . . ."

Mike shrugged.

"My purse was in the car." Panic was beginning to surface in Brenda's voice. "My wallet, my keys—I left them in the ignition—everything!" She looked at me wildly. "My students' papers! I graded them on Saturday and had them in the car to hand back today! What am I going to do?"

"It's okay, it's okay," I assured her, lying. I got up and took her hands in mine, looking into her eyes. "It's okay. I'm sure all of your students did their papers on computers, and have backup copies, right?"

She calmed a little. "Probably."

"And we can start making phone calls about your license and credit cards, and everything else you had in your wallet, right?"

She gave an exhausted moan. "Right."

"And I'm sure we can find a locksmith to make you some new house keys. And I'm sure the school has duplicates for your office, right?"

"Um, about that . . ." Mike began.

I whirled at him. "Mister, you are parked on my last nerve. Stop saying 'um' and spit it out!"

"I don't think it's a good idea for her to go home," he said.

I looked at him, then at Jack. "Jack?"

"They have her wallet, which has her address, and they have her keys." His voice was perfectly calm, but the look he gave me was filled with meaning.

"Goddamn!" Harry exploded. "Gordon! Get me a phone!" he hollered, then asked Brenda, "What's your address? I'll get security over there this minute. Don't you worry about a thing. Gordon!"

Brenda looked dazed. She sank back into her chair.

Gordon appeared with a phone and Harry's address book. "Here you are, sir." Then he turned to me. "And if you've finished your breakfast, Mrs. Fairfax, perhaps you'd let me take a look at that lump on your head. Then"—he eyed Jack—"time for those stitches, I think."

I was pulled away and fussed over, then I stayed with Jack while Gordon stitched his wound. When I returned to the dining room I found Harry holding Brenda's hand and speaking softly.

"Charley," Brenda greeted me, "Harry thinks I should stay here for a while. What do you think?"

I looked at my uncle. Certainly it sounded like it might be dangerous for her to go home, but I wondered if another kind of danger lurked for her here. "Why don't you stay at the hotel with us?" I suggested.

She looked horrified. "You're on your honeymoon!"

Somehow I suspected the honeymoon was over.

"You and Jack should stay here, too," Harry said. "I've called in a security firm to stand a twenty-four-hour watch. That hotel isn't nearly as safe as here."

"Nevertheless," I said icily.

He held up his hands. "I won't try to force you. God knows you're a grown woman now, and make your own decisions."

"Harry, I'm way too tired for this right now. Jack needs to rest, and so do I. How about we sleep for a few hours and talk about it then?"

He grunted. I took it for agreement.

"Brenda," I asked, "what about your class this afternoon?"

"Harry talked me into calling in sick," she said, with a trace of guilt.

"They won't miss her for a few days at that girls' school," Harry said confidently.

"Women's college," Brenda corrected him.

"Sure."

We went back to the great room, where we found Mike and Jack in conference. "I'm outta here," Mike said. "I didn't find anything in the van, so I'll take it somewhere, make sure it's clean, and dump it."

"Make sure it's clean?" I asked.

"The police are looking for it. A neighbor saw it pulling out during all the shooting."

Oh.

"I hardly think they'll be looking for a bullet-riddled van in this neighborhood, but we might as well be on the safe side. And we want to make sure if they do find it, none of your prints are in it."

This time I said it. "Oh."

He grinned and held out his hand. "Take care, Charley. I hope to see you again soon."

I shook, grudgingly.

"Sir." He gave Harry a mock salute. "Brenda." He nodded at her. "Call me if you need me, Jack." And he left.

I looked at Jack, propped up where Gordon had left him. "Sleep?" I suggested.

"Sleep," he agreed.

Chapter 13

We wandered into the first available guest room and were asleep before touching down on the mattress. When I woke up the light was dim. I couldn't tell if it was dusk or dawn.

I rolled over to check on Jack. He seemed to be sleeping peacefully, although I wasn't sure if it was from exhaustion or the shot Gordon had given him. If past history was any guide, though, he'd wake up if I stared at him hard enough. I decided to let him sleep. He'd need his strength. I had a lot of questions for him.

I realized I was still wearing my blood-stained pants and Harry's shirt over my blood-soaked bra. I left the bed as quietly as I could and stumbled into the adjoining bathroom. I took what was arguably the best shower of my life.

Someone had hung two sets of silk pajamas with matching robes on the towel rack, one creamy beige and about my size, and the other a deep bronze that would fit Jack. I dried off and slipped into the soft fabric. By the time I tied the belt I felt ready to face the world, or at least the household, again.

I slipped out the door and headed for the kitchen, figuring if anyone was awake they'd be eating. A glance at the hall clock told me it was evening after all. I'd slept for about nine hours.

I heard voices coming from the kitchen. It sounded

like a private conversation so I hesitated outside the door.

"Do you need anything?"

It was Gordon's voice. I couldn't hear the answer.

"Understand this is not a conversation I'll be sharing with your father." So the other person must be Cece.

"All right then, the truth. Are you clean?"

Cece hesitated, but I heard her answer. "I'm clean." Her voice got stronger, and harsher. "Haven't you heard? I turned my life around for the love of a good man."

Gordon cleared his throat. "I think it's best to focus on the result, rather than the cause. Will you be all right here?"

Cece's voice had the mocking defiance that indicated trouble. "You mean will I go back to my badass ways if I'm back in my old environment?"

"Something like that."

There was a long silence. Then, "I don't know."

Well, at least she wasn't kidding herself. I felt guilty for listening, so slipped quietly down the hall. It occurred to me to wonder why Cece was having such a personal conversation with Harry's cook, but then I figured it was better not to wonder too much about Gordon. The man had hidden depths.

I heard Harry's voice and followed it to his study. He was in position at his desk, feet up, with a half-empty bottle of the Macallan and a plate of sandwiches in front of him. He slammed the phone down as I entered the room. "That useless sonofabitch! Calls himself a security specialist!"

Ah. No doubt it had been the firm of McIntyre and Zipfel on the other end of the line.

"Feel like sharing?" I gestured to the bottle as I slumped into an enormous leather chair opposite him.

He poured an inch or so into a heavy crystal glass and pushed it across the desk. "How are you? How's Jack?"

"Still sleeping." I took a sip of the amber liquid. A mellow warmth slid down my throat. "What have I missed?"

"You didn't answer my question." He poured himself another. "How are you?"

I raised my eyebrows. "Me? Well, gosh, let me see. My husband has been shot, my best friend is afraid to go back to her own house, I've got a lump the size of a golf ball on my head, and the only thing I know about the guy who's behind it all is that he's still out there." I reached for a sandwich. "All in all, I'm pretty good. Mmm." Rare roast beef and gorgonzola on thick crusty bread.

"Not to mention . . ." Harry said, leaning back in his chair and rocking.

I nodded slowly and regarded my uncle. "Not to mention, I don't know who the hell I'm married to or who his friends are."

"Oh, you know who he is, I guess," Harry said reasonably. "You're just not sure what he is. Or was."

"Right." What a lovely distinction.

"So—" he gazed at the ceiling—"not too bad."

We munched and sipped for a while in an oddly companionable silence. I broke it after a while. "Harry, I'm sorry." It must have been the single-malt talking. "I should have invited you to my wedding."

He stopped rocking for a moment, then resumed. "Yes."

I struggled not to get irritated. "I didn't want you to . . . but you did anyway . . . and now I just . . ." Perhaps I'd had enough to drink.

"Charley, for what it's worth, I haven't found out one goddamn thing about that man of yours that doesn't make me like him more."

I let that sink in. "I don't suppose you're going to tell me what you did find out? Why you got Jack involved in all of this? Why you trusted him with Cece?"

"As far as what I found out . . ." He seemed to choose his words carefully. "Let's just say that I am of the firm conviction that Jack Fairfax is less of a pussy than his official records indicate."

"Right." I knew Harry well enough not to press it. Besides, I didn't want to hear Jack's secrets from Harry. But I damn sure wanted to hear them from Jack.

"And as far as why I trusted him with Cece . . ." he continued, clearing his throat. "Well, I trust him with you, don't I?"

I looked him in the eye. He was offering me a truce. "Right," I nodded.

In other families there might have been a hug at that point. This wasn't other families. Harry opened his desk drawer and pulled out a box. "I want you to have this."

A wedding present? I opened the box. "A gun."

He held up his hands to ward off my expected protests. "Now, I know you don't like guns, but this is one goddamn situation we've got here, and—"

I slammed the lid shut. "I'll take it."

He blinked.

"On one condition."

His eyes narrowed.

"Promise me you won't . . ." How to put it? "While Brenda's staying here . . . don't . . ." Ugh.

A slow grin spread over his face. He reached for a cigar and twirled it between his fingers. "I'm flattered." He held the cigar up to his ear and listened to the crackle of the tobacco. "But you know I'm just a harmless old man."

Right.

I went back upstairs and looked at Jack, still sleeping, solid and familiar. Or possibly a complete stranger, some action hero I'd met the night before. In any case, I slid back into bed next to him and slept all the way through to morning.

When I woke again I had the oddest sensation. I opened my eyes and found Jack, inches away from my face, staring at me. "Cut that out!" I jumped away.

"See? It's funny until you're on the receiving end of it."

I thought about hitting him with a pillow but decided I'd check on his shoulder first. "How are you?"

"Damn good, or so I've been told." He wiggled his eyebrows.

He must be feeling better. I noticed he'd showered and shaved and was wearing the bronze silk ensemble. "How's the shoulder?"

He did a Pete Townsend windmill air-guitar move. "Great."

"Very nice. Now how about the one with the bullet in it?"

He moved his left arm gingerly. "It hasn't got a bullet in it. The bullet went through."

"Uh huh. Has Doctor Gordon had a look at it?"

"He changed the dressing after I showered." Jack moved closer and got that look in his eye. "And I shaved. Did you notice?"

"Just get one thing straight, mister," I told him. "I'm not having sex with you in this house no matter how cute and clean-shaven you may be."

He looked at me. "Then let's get out of here."

Jack had rounded up some clothes while I'd been sleeping. A black jogging suit with a red stripe down the sides and a matching red shirt for me, presumably left by one of Harry's more fitness-minded conquests, and jeans with a gray sweater for himself.

I scooped my hair back into a ponytail, wincing as I ran the brush over the bump on my head. When I saw myself in the bathroom mirror I was surprised. No makeup, no styling products in my hair, and borrowed clothes, but I didn't look bad. There was a not-unpleasant flush to my cheeks, and I had to admit, now that the danger was past, I was finding our whole adventure pretty exciting. It was wrong, I knew, because what I'd told Harry the previous night had been true—the person responsible was still out there and we didn't know why he'd done it or if he'd try something again.

But it was also true that I wasn't afraid as long as Jack was around. Even the new Jack, who was apparently accustomed to sprinting through a hail of bullets. The idea of figuring out who the kidnapper was and finding him had a certain appeal. I could picture us, Jack and me, as this incredibly cool crime-solving couple. Something along the lines of the Avengers, but with massive amounts of sex. I was wondering if I could pull off a black leather jumpsuit when Jack stuck his head in the door.

"Are you about ready? I'm starving."

I jumped and dropped the hairbrush. Not a particularly smooth secret-agent sort of move, but, unlike my husband, I was new to this.

Gordon offered to fix something for us, but I was bursting to get out of the house.

"Where's everybody else?" I asked him.

"Your uncle took your cousin and Miss Gee shopping."

"Shopping?" Of course he did.

Gordon smiled briefly. "The security people sent some of Miss Gee's things over, but not everything she needs, and your cousin's things were all lost in the . . . recent events."

Cece and Brenda shopping together was hard enough to get my head around, but Harry tagging along behind them was simply too much. I looked at Jack. "Let's get out of here."

We borrowed Harry's Lexus and headed downhill to the little town of Burlingame. There we sat at a sidewalk table and ate mountainous stacks of the world's best pancakes, while watching what my friend Simon calls "the suburban dog and baby show."

I wanted to ask Jack some serious questions someplace with no distractions and nobody to overhear us, so I suggested we head over to Half Moon Bay and the beach. Jack looked doubtful. "Will it be warm?"

"Of course not," I scoffed. "It'll be foggy and windy, but the fresh air will do us good."

We took Highway 92 to Half Moon Bay, then turned north on Highway 1. It wasn't as foggy as I'd predicted, and we stopped at the first of the state beaches that dotted the way up the coast.

We took off our shoes and walked along the beach near the water, where the sand was wet, cold, and hard. We held hands, which was corny but nice. I had to remind myself we weren't here just to relax and enjoy the moment. I had an agenda. What I didn't have was a clear idea about how to approach the subject of my husband's apparent wealth of experience in covert operations. Finally I just took a breath and plunged in.

"Jack?"

"Hmm?"

I pointed to the sky over an outcropping of rocks to the north. "What kind of clouds are those?"

He stopped, shielding his eyes from the hazy light of the sun. "Well, that one looks a little like a pony." He gestured. "And over there I think I see a bunny."

I looked at him. "Hilarious."

He spread his hands. "I hope I wasn't too technical."

We walked a little further.

"Jack?"

"Still here."

"You really do have a degree in meteorology?"

"And physical oceanography. Yes."

"And when you were in the Navy, on a ship or something," I pursued, "you predicted the weather?"

"I did." He nodded. "Here's an interesting bit of trivia. On a ship, the meteorology officer gets a porthole. It's very handy to be able to look outside when you're writing the weather report."

"This is my own fault," I said. "I did tell you I liked your line of bullshit."

We strolled in tandem for a while, with Jack's arm

draped around my shoulders, stopping occasionally to let the water lap towards our toes or to exchange a brief nibble on the neck. We looked just like any of the other windblown couples out braving the elements on a summer day. Then I tried again.

"Jack?"

"Charley?"

"Was predicting the weather the only thing you did for the Navy?"

He stopped and squinted out to sea.

"Because," I tried, "for a meteorologist, you do a damned good impression of a spy."

The sand suddenly became fascinating to him. "Don't spies, uh, spy on people?"

"All right, then, a secret agent, an undercover operative, an espionage . . . person. Whatever you want to call it." I turned to face him. "Seriously, Jack. Are you one?"

He pulled me toward him and wrapped his arms around me. "I'm retired."

"Yes, but a retired what?" I persisted. "And who the hell is Mike, really? And what has Tom Nelson got to do with any of us?"

"If I say Mike's an old Navy buddy and I have no idea who Tom Nelson is, will you let it go?"

"Probably not."

He looked at me long and hard. "Charley, I will do everything I know how to protect you."

That was comforting. The list of things he knew how to do was turning out to be rather extensive. "Jack." I pulled away. "Do you know who kidnapped Cece?"

He held my eyes with his. "I think so."

I nodded. "Is he another spy? Because the whole thing seems pretty elaborate for just a run-of-the-mill kidnapper. Is he someone you used to . . . work against?"

Jack's jaw tightened. "Someone I used to work with."

"What?" I reached for the only explanation that made sense. "Does he want money?"

Jack picked up a stray piece of driftwood. "If it's the guy I'm thinking of, there's more to it than money." He squinted into the distance. "If it's the guy I'm thinking of, it's more personal than that."

"Why? Who is he?"

Jack threw the stick into the sea. "I can't, Charley."

"You mean you won't."

His mouth twisted in frustration. "Look, aside from any other reasons I have for not spilling my guts, I may be wrong. This all feels like something this guy would do, but it can't be him. It's impossible."

"Why?"

"Because he's in solitary confinement in a maximum-security military prison." He paused. "I put him there."

Oh.

On the way back to the city I tried to adjust to my new reality. Imprisoned psycho killer toying with us in order to punish husband. Check. Husband undoubtedly some sort of ex-spy, apparently accustomed to shootouts. Check. Husband's friend Mike presumably the same. Check. Uncle setting up militia-like encampment with best friend. Check.

I should have felt a lot worse.

But the same little bubble of excitement I'd felt that morning was percolating again. And as I turned the facts over, one thing became increasingly clear.

"Jack," I said. "This isn't over."

He kept his eyes on the road. "No."

"Tom Nelson, or whoever he is, is going to strike again."

"Strike?" Jack echoed.

"So we have to do the sensible thing."

"Good . . ."

"And the only sensible thing is to find him before he finds us."

"Charley!" Jack slammed on the brakes and pulled over to the side of the road. "Don't even think about it! Have you forgotten that lump on your head and this hole in my shoulder? This isn't a game!"

I'd never seen him angry before. God, he was sexy. "Of course, Jack," I agreed. "Whatever you say."

He pulled back onto the road after muttering a few things I didn't quite catch, which was probably just as well. I looked out at the ocean and tried to come up with a question he might actually answer. Which wouldn't be easy. An hour of demands to know more about the former colleague he'd put in prison had gotten me exactly nowhere.

I chewed my lip for a while and went over the events of the last thirty-six hours. "Jack." I decided to tug on a loose thread. "Why did you let Gordon practically perform surgery on you? I mean, he's Harry's cook but we all just meekly accepted that he knew what he was doing."

Jack waited a few beats before answering, "Didn't I mention I knew Gordon before?"

"Let's not get into the whole list of things you didn't mention," I suggested. "How do you know him?" He didn't reply. "Jack!"

"All right, all right, calm down." He glanced over at me. "Gordon and Mike left the Navy at the same time I did, around four months ago. Mike went to Palo Alto to get his company started, and Gordon had plans to go to San Francisco and open a restaurant, but he did some traveling first. I ran into him in London about two weeks after I met you." He shot me a quick glance. "You'd told me where you were from, and you'd mentioned Harry, but you always avoided any questions about your family."

"Can you blame me?" I asked. Then it hit me. "You sent Gordon to spy on my family?"

Jack had the decency to look embarrassed. "Well, Pumpkin, you did seem too good to be true—I mean, can't you see why I was a little suspicious?"

"Oh my God!" I stared at him. "You did! You sent Gordon to spy on my family!"

"Just to verify what you'd told me—nothing more. But then when Gordon met Harry, and it turned out Harry was looking for a cook . . ." Jack looked over again to see how I was taking it.

Not well. "Don't tell me—he decided to stay and spy some more?"

"No," Jack said. "He decided to earn some money and maybe meet some other rich foodaholics through Harry. He still wants to open a restaurant." Jack tried on a smile. "Really, that's all."

Okay, this was another big chunk of information I somehow had to process. My husband had checked me out when we were dating. The way Harry had always checked out men on my behalf. The way I had refused to have Jack checked out. In all my obsession about not letting Harry investigate Jack, it had never dawned on me that Jack might want to investigate Harry. That he might have planted someone in Harry's house.

Normally I would have been outraged. But somewhere along this line of thought I started to giggle. Inappropriate, I know, but I couldn't help myself.

"Do you mind letting me in on the joke?"

"One aspect of all of this is just priceless," I told him. "I mean, all these years Harry's been spying on me, and now we have a mole in his house!"

"Gordon's not a mole," Jack said quickly, looking faintly alarmed. "He's just a cook. And we should be glad he's there to keep an eye on them—I mean look out for them."

"Sure," I agreed, putting on a completely sober face. "Of course."

"Charley," he said warily. "You're scaring me."

My husband, the commando.

When we got back to the hotel I was feeling wired. Possibly because I'd slept too much the day before. Or possibly because I'd married James Bond.

"Jack," I said as he was opening the door. "Do you

mind if we go out again? Maybe call Simon or Eileen? I feel like talking to people."

"Excellent," said a crisp, polite voice from inside the room.

Jack and I both froze. The door swung open of its own will.

"Because I'd very much like to speak with you." Inspector Yahata stood motionless in the center of the room. He was once again dressed immaculately, his suit a dark gray with a microscopic violet pinstripe. And once again he was looking at us with hyper-alert interest.

"Inspector," Jack said, recovering almost instantly. "I'd ask you to come in, but . . ."

The detective displayed a fleeting down-turned smile. "I took the liberty of waiting for you here. I hope you don't mind."

"Do you have a warrant?" I surprised myself with the question.

Jack looked at me as we came in and closed the door. "I can't imagine why the Inspector would need a warrant, Charley."

Maybe that was because I hadn't gotten around to telling him about Yahata's little chat with me on Sunday afternoon.

"My intent is not to search the premises, Mrs. Fairfax," the policeman said. "Simply to ask you a few questions."

"Have you identified the murdered woman yet?" Jack asked.

Yahata produced his ubiquitous notebook. "My questions pertain to more recent events," he said. "Events in Mill Valley in the early hours yesterday morning?" The look of mild enquiry did not extend to his eyes. There was nothing mild about them.

I sat down, since my legs threatened to go out from under me. How the hell did he know we were involved?

Jack sat next to me and gestured for the detective

to make himself comfortable. "Yes, I was just about to call you."

"I have no doubt," Yahata said quietly.

"Why—" My voice cracked, so I had to try again. "Why would we know anything about something happening in Mill Valley?"

A flicker of impatience crossed the detective's face. "Mrs. Fairfax, please don't make this difficult. You were clearly in a state of some distress when we spoke on Sunday afternoon, and your cousin's fingerprints were found in great quantity in one of the rooms where shots were fired less than eighteen hours later. During which eighteen hours your whereabouts were unaccounted for." He ended the statement with an air of expectation.

Jack had flashed me a look of surprise at the mention of Yahata's previous visit, but he answered the implied question smoothly. "We were there," he said. "My wife's cousin was kidnapped, and her uncle chose not to involve the police. I followed the criminal's instructions to deliver the ransom."

Yahata's expression registered nothing. His eyes flicked over to me.

"I followed Jack." I left it at that.

"I see." Inspector Yahata stood. As he had on Sunday, he seemed to consider his words with infinite care before speaking. "Mrs. Fairfax, we seem to be experiencing something of a crime wave since your return."

"You can't think Charley is involved in any of this." Jack rose and faced the detective.

"No, Mr. Fairfax, I don't." Yahata locked eyes with Jack. "You, on the other hand . . ."

"Don't be ridiculous!" Now it was my turn to stand. "Jack rescued Cece, and Brenda and me! He nearly got himself killed—" I caught the expression on Jack's face and stopped myself from saying more. There was a charged silence.

Finally Yahata spoke, softly and with precision. "Mr. Fairfax, you intrigue me. When I try to find out more about you, I find the standard avenues of inquiry are inaccessible. Yet there are certain facts which suggest you are," he paused, "a person of interest." Again he met Jack's eyes.

I didn't want to hear any more of this. I'd had enough of half-truths and innuendo for the day, and I was sure Jack had as well. I spoke up. "What other fingerprints did you find?"

The detective gave me a frankly startled look. Which was very satisfying. "An excellent question," he surprised me by answering. "The federal authorities have identified two sets, both belonging to known mercenaries."

"Mercenaries?" I echoed. "What does that mean?"

The detective looked back to Jack as he answered. "It means a number of things. It means they're probably all long gone by now. And it means they were hired by someone. The interesting question, then, is who hired them?"

"Good luck with that," Jack said evenly.

That night I woke up at about three and saw Jack standing at the window, looking at the city. I propped my head on my elbow and watched him.

After a while he spoke. "You know I can see you."

I smiled. "But do you know what I'm thinking?"

His lips twitched. "You're afraid you pulled my stitches out."

"I hate you."

After a while I sat up. "Jack?"

"Hmm?"

"Do you think the woman in the bathtub was related to all of this?"

He cleared his throat. "Remember when you asked me not to mention it to Harry? You said he'd assume it was some sort of a message or warning."

"You think it was? She was?" The thought of some innocent person being murdered just to send us a message made my stomach flip a few times.

Jack frowned. "We'll know more once Yahata identifies her." The detective had remained singularly un-

informative on that point. Which was only fair—Jack
had remained equally uninformative about his past
professional associations with the person he believed
to be behind Cece's abduction.

"We should tell Harry about the murder." He might
go ballistic, but if there was a chance the same man
who had kidnapped Cece had also killed someone,
Harry should know.

"I thought so too. I already told him. While you
were sleeping back at the house."

I didn't want to know what his reaction had been.
I could add that to the increasingly long list of things
I didn't want to know.

"Jack, what are we going to do?"

He looked at me. "Well, for starters, I'm going to
make sure that guy I told you about is still in prison."

"Do you think he was Cece's Tom?"

"No," Jack said. "But Tom could have been working for him."

"Jack, for the sake of convenience, what should we
call this guy?"

He shrugged. "Dave?"

I wrinkled my nose. "That's not much of a name
for a villain."

"What did you have in mind? Moriarty?"

"It would help if I knew something more about
him . . ." I trailed off suggestively. "Like maybe what
crime he's in prison for?"

Jack looked at me briefly. "Treason." He wiped a
hand across his face. "Selling things—secrets,
information—to the highest bidder. He made millions
before we caught him. Who knows how many have
died because of it." He turned back to the window.

"Oh." I'd actually gotten an answer from him. Not
that I quite knew what to do with it. But a name for
a traitor did suggest itself. "How about calling him
Macbeth?"

"Great. Now that we've gotten that cleared up,
there's something I want you to have." Jack reached

into the nightstand drawer and pulled out a small object wrapped in a Burberry scarf.

When I unwrapped it, the metal was dull in the dim light. I looked at Jack. "A gun."

"I'll teach you how to use it," he said. "I'm sorry if it makes you uncomfortable, but it's for the best, Charley."

Wordlessly, I got out of bed and went to the bag I'd brought from Harry's. I reached in and pulled out the box he'd given me. I put it on the bed in front of Jack.

"Should I be worried that all the men in my life want to arm me?"

Chapter 14

Kate Spade doesn't make a holster. I asked. For some reason the salesgirl seemed to regard it as an odd question, but I'm thinking it might just be an untapped market opportunity. I settled for a black zippered makeup bag with a hot pink lining. The gun fit beautifully.

It hadn't been hard to choose between the two guns. Harry had given me a Smith & Wesson .38, a revolver that held five rounds and was, he'd assured me, a favorite of policemen as a backup gun. Since I didn't have a license for it, I didn't think I should ask Inspector Yahata for an opinion.

The present from Jack was a Walther 9mm automatic that held a ten-round magazine. It was sleek and silver and deadly looking, and it won me over just on style points. It was also lighter and, according to a comparison of the two owner's manuals, it should have less recoil than the .38. Besides, James Bond carried a Walther, a fact I pointed out to Jack.

"Great. Except he's fictional," he replied.

I managed to surprise Jack, which pleased me no end, when I told him I knew how to shoot. Harry had sent me to an elite self-defense camp between my junior and senior years of high school. I didn't like guns then and I still don't, but I'd gotten revenge on Harry by making donations in his name to every anti-gun cause I'd come across since, and now I had to admit I was glad of what I'd learned at Camp Readiness.

Jack took me to a firing range in South San Francisco. Even though it had been a while, I didn't disgrace myself. Jack didn't shoot. From what I'd observed, he didn't really need much practice.

With just the shooting and the holster-shopping, the occasional dinner at Harry's, and trying to make sure Jack didn't pull his stitches out, we spent the rest of the week pretty uneventfully. Jack took calls from Mike out of my hearing, and I came up with an unimaginative series of excuses for not meeting with Eileen's realtor, who called daily. I figured it was more believable to tell her that I had the stomach flu than to mention that hired thugs had kidnapped my cousin and shot my husband.

I didn't have time for real estate if I was going to look for Macbeth.

It took me a while to figure out where to start. But I reasoned that Macbeth wouldn't have had any cause to target me, my family, or my friends before I'd gotten involved with Jack. So I figured I should investigate anyone who'd shown up in our lives recently to see if they, like Cece's Tom Nelson, could be an operative of the criminal. It's possible Jack might have disagreed with this approach, so I chose not to discuss it with him.

The two people I thought warranted immediate attention were Eileen's new client/love interest and the new director Simon had hired at the Rep. I figured I'd meet Brian, the director, later in the week during the auditions for *All About Me*, so I put him on the back burner and called Eileen.

Her assistant put me through immediately, and I wasn't able to get out the word "Hello" before Eileen tore into me.

"Oh, now you call! Now that you don't need any help getting kidnapped and rescued, now that you don't need someone to get shot at with. Now you pick up the phone." She paused for breath.

"Hi Leenie, how've you been?"

"Charley, I could just kill you."

"Never mind, it's been tried."

Not funny. "Don't you dare joke about this! You could have been killed! Brenda could have been killed! Jack nearly was killed!"

"I take it you've been talking to Brenda?" I asked.

"It's a damn good thing someone calls me, since you don't!"

"Eileen, sweetie," I tried, "please don't take it personally—"

"Why didn't you call me?" she demanded.

"Well, I've been a little distracted lately . . ."

"I don't mean now, I mean when you followed Jack! Why did you call Brenda instead of me? I was closer, I have a better car—"

"You would have said no," I interrupted. "No way would you have gone along with it."

"Exactly!" she said triumphantly. "Any sane person would have said no. How you managed to talk Brenda into it I'll never know."

"Did you know Brenda is really good at tailing people? Hey, remember that Stanford paleontologist she used to go out with?"

"Don't think you can change the subject. I'm mad at you!"

"I'm getting that," I said. "Leenie, I'm sorry. I did think about calling you that day, but I knew you'd talk me out of it, and I didn't want to be talked out of it."

"Brenda said she tried to talk you out of it."

"Yeah, but she couldn't. You might have."

I heard her take a deep breath on the other end of the phone. "Don't ever do that again," she said.

"Never," I agreed. After all, the same situation would probably never come up again. I put on a breezy voice. "So, what's new with you?"

"You're unbelievable," Eileen said flatly.

"I know. You want to tell me about the new man in your life? Or do I have to call Brenda for the good stuff?"

Eileen sighed. "Whatever. It's over."

"Over? You never even admitted it had begun."

"It was short and not at all sweet," she said tersely. "Look, I'm late for a presentation. Can you meet me tonight? Get me drunk and I'll tell you all the sordid details."

"Absolutely. Where and when?"

"The Bubble Lounge at eight, okay?"

"I'm there." I felt a pang of disloyalty to Jack, but it had been quite a while since I'd had an honest-to-goodness girl's night out.

"See you then. And, Charley, are you going to call Brenda?"

"I was just about to."

"Make her come along. Oh, and Charley?"

"Still here."

"Why don't you ask her about her new car?" She hung up.

Damn.

Brenda couldn't afford a new car. As an untenured professor living in one of the most expensive areas in the country, she could barely afford to put gas in her old one. That was one of the reasons I intended to call her. I was going to try to talk her into letting me buy her a new car, since it was my fault she'd lost her beloved VW.

Brenda had never accepted a loan or an extravagant gift from me in all the time I'd known her, despite my doing everything short of forcing her on several occasions. But in this case, since I was to blame for the loss, I was sure she'd allow me to make it right. Apparently someone else had made her the offer first.

Harry, of course.

Damn.

Brenda was staying at the Hillsborough house, which now resembled an armed compound. Gordon answered the phone on the second ring. After asking me several questions about the state of Jack's bullet wound, he went off to find Brenda.

"Hello?" she said, breathlessly, a few minutes later. "Charley! I was going to call you right after my swim!"

"What's new?" I asked innocently.

"I'm just having the best time here," she told me. "It's like being at a luxury resort."

"Harry does appreciate the creature comforts."

"And he's such a nice host. I feel a little guilty because of why I'm here and everything, but Cece seems to be doing really well, and, you know, sometimes I forget that there's a sociopath out there with my house keys and just . . . you know? And Gordon is an amazing cook."

"So I guess you found someone else to handle your classes?"

"Well, I'm only doing the one seminar until August, when fall semester starts. So yesterday I went in to meet with the class—we only meet once a week, on Mondays—and Harry insisted I bring this man named Flank with me, for protection. Charley, what kind of a name is Flank?"

"I'm guessing it's the kind of name that goes with a big neck."

"You'd be right about that. He stood at the back of the room and looked dangerous the whole time we were having a discussion on contrasting feminist explorations of current social ethics."

"I'm sure he got a lot out of it."

"I don't really think so. He didn't say a word all the way back to Harry's place."

"Maybe he was concentrating on his driving," I fished.

"No, I was driving. Oh! Charley, guess what?"

I didn't have to guess. "Harry bought you a new car."

"Yes! How did you know? Did he ask you what kind I wanted? I never would have picked out something so expensive, but Charley, it's so beautiful. Did you pick it out?"

"I didn't hear a thing about it until I talked to Eileen this morning."

"Really?"

It made me nervous to hear how pleased she sounded about Harry's sole responsibility for the gift. "What is it?"

"A Saab. A red convertible Saab with leather everything and the most amazing stereo. You should see how it just scoots right on to the freeway without having to think about it."

Oh, what the hell. I'd wanted her to have a new car and now she had one. That didn't mean Harry was trying to woo her, did it? "It sounds like you love it."

"I love it. Do you know what Harry said when he gave me the keys?"

"Could be almost anything."

"He said Volkswagen cabriolets want to be Saab convertibles when they grow up. Isn't that cute?"

Right. I had to get her out of that house.

"Brenda, come have drinks with Eileen and me tonight," I commanded.

"Yay!" she said. "Where are we going?"

"The Bubble Lounge. We're meeting Leenie at eight."

"Yay!" she repeated. "I'll pick you up at the hotel so you can see the new car, okay?"

"Yay," I said.

Jack didn't grumble when I told him my plans for the evening. Perversely, I found that disappointing. Intellectually, I know I want to be in the kind of relationship where we have our own lives and are comfortable spending time apart. Sort of like Katharine Hepburn and Spencer Tracy—or at least like the characters they played. But emotionally, I guess I wanted Jack to at least pretend he'd miss me, even if it was only going to be for a couple of hours. There was only one solution. I had to dress to kill.

At 7:40 precisely I emerged from the bedroom

wearing a sleeveless black dress by MaxMara with a V-neckline that dipped to the exact optimum cleavage point and a flirty little ruffle that skimmed just above the knee. It showed off the good stuff, camouflaged the bad stuff, and hinted at the stuff in between. Insanely high-heeled strappy sandals completed the look. I had blown my hair dry with my head upside down for volume, then given the ends a hint of a flip, and used every makeup brush in my arsenal to achieve that smoky eye thing the magazines are always going on about.

When Jack saw me he dropped his book. That made all the effort worthwhile.

"You're wearing that?" His eyes swept from head to hot-pink toe.

I was nonchalance personified. "Don't you like it?"

"To meet the girls for drinks?" he asked.

I gave him a "didn't we already discuss this?" look.

"At a bar?" he completed the question.

"The Bubble Lounge. It's a champagne bar, a little too yuppified for me, but it's close to Eileen's office." I'm so informative.

"Uh huh," he said. "I have a better idea."

Success. "Oh?" I said innocently.

"Room service. With me."

The look he gave me melted all my resolve. My instinct was to say "okey dokey" and stand up my two best friends. Luckily, I had planned the timing perfectly, and Brenda knocked the instant before I caved.

I gave Jack a bright smile. "Too late, that's Brenda."

Okay, so it was an old-fashioned, sexist ploy, but I left knowing Jack would miss me after all. So there.

The car was beautiful and Brenda was glowing. She gushed about it all the way downtown, pointing out its perfect little accessories and clever little designs. She left it with the valet, and watched longingly until it was out of sight.

She gave a small sigh. "Charley, you know I've never really been into material possessions."

"I know, sweetie."

"And I'm probably being a traitor to my little VW." She bit her lip. "But I just love that car." She looked at me.

"Don't worry, sweetie. You're still a good person." I put my arm around her shoulders and dragged her inside.

The bar was lit with a soft amber glow and decorated with velvet drapes and clusters of comfortable upholstered seating around low cocktail tables. Eileen was waiting for us at a table in the back corner, perched on a crescent-shaped banquette. She waved us over.

"I didn't feel like champagne, so I've got three dirty martinis on the way. If you don't want yours, I'll drink it for you," she announced.

"The hell you will," I said.

"Oh, Eileen, what's the matter?" Brenda asked.

Eileen sighed and drummed her fingers on the table. She looked around the room. "Men," she said heavily.

There were a lot of them in the bar. All clean-cut and aggressive, vying for the attention of equally sharp-looking women. Suit jackets had been flung off, and ties loosened at the collars of Thomas Pink shirts that revealed gym-honed torsos. It's not that there weren't any drab, dumpy guys in the financial district, it's just that they didn't venture into the same bars as the esthetically elite. Frankly, I thought the joint could have used a few balding heads and beer guts just to break up the monotony.

"We shouldn't have come here," Eileen said. "They all look like Ben."

"Ben?" Brenda asked.

"Drinks!" I saw the waiter heading our way. "Who's Ben?" The waiter, yet another perfect specimen, set down three martinis, heavy on the olives, and walked away with the attitude of someone used to

being watched. Too bad, we were focused on Eileen.
"Is Ben the guy?" I asked.

"What guy?" Brenda demanded. "Are you seeing
someone? Why didn't you tell me?"

Eileen delicately removed the olives from her drink,
then tossed back half of it in one gulp. "Why," she
asked, "just once, can I not get interested in a normal guy?"

We sipped and considered.

"Maybe you don't meet any," Brenda offered.

I was less concerned with Eileen's love life at that
point than I was with figuring out if her Ben was actually Cece's Tom Nelson—in which case he was certainly in league with Macbeth. "Tell us everything," I
demanded. "Leave nothing out. Start with when you
met him and take it from there."

"Blow by blow," Brenda said.

Eileen nodded, polished off her drink, and signaled
to the waiter for another. I turned around to make
sure he'd seen her and caught a flash of something
out of the corner of my eye. I wasn't sure exactly
what it was. A sudden motion, someone turning away,
maybe, but it bothered me. I scanned the crowd but
didn't see anything beyond the usual activity. I turned
back to Eileen with a prickly feeling on the back of
my neck.

Brenda pushed her drink, barely touched, toward
Eileen. "Here," she said, "I'm driving." Eileen took
the martini, giving me a highly significant look.

I refused to be diverted from my investigation by a
discussion of Brenda's new car. "When did you meet
him?"

She grimaced. "About a month ago."

Ah ha. That would have been a week before Jack
and I had gotten back—which was exactly the time-
frame I was worried about. "How did you meet?"

"He came in as a new client. He's worth over a
hundred million, so they sent him to me." She
shrugged. "We had a perfectly normal first consultation. I didn't really see why he needed to change firms,

because his portfolio was doing fine as it was, but I wasn't going to turn down his business just because of that."

But if he was Macbeth—or working for Macbeth—he'd have sought Eileen out for reasons other than her skills as a financial manager. And he would have had millions, according to Jack. "How did he behave toward you?" I asked. "Was it obvious he was interested from the beginning?"

"Not really," she said. "Like I said, it was all perfectly normal, right until the end of the meeting."

"What happened then?" Brenda asked before I could.

"He asked me out."

"Just like that?" I asked.

Eileen nodded. "We were standing at the door, and had made an appointment for the following week for me to show him some suggestions I'd come up with, and he said 'I really don't want to wait that long to see you again. How about dinner tomorrow?' "

"Smooth," I accused.

"Nice," Brenda said.

"Where's that waiter?" Eileen finished Brenda's martini and looked around for replacements. I turned to look towards the bar, and that's when I saw it. At the far end of the bar, on the floor, was a red motorcycle helmet. It was only visible between the legs around it in intermittent flashes, but it was definitely a helmet. I turned around quickly. Would I sound paranoid if I asked Brenda whether she'd noticed a red motorcycle in her rearview mirror?

Eileen continued relating the story of Ben, but I was only able to give her half my attention. I'd remembered the day I'd gone for a run, the day we'd gotten the call from Cece's kidnappers, and the red motorcycle that had kept pace with me. That day, too, I'd caught a flash of something out of the corner of my eye and thought it had been the biker, carrying his red helmet, watching me.

"He was nice enough, and very attractive, but I

should have known there was something weird about him from that first dinner." That caught my attention.

"What?" I demanded. "What was weird about him?"

Eileen looked startled at the intensity of my interest. "He was a neat freak," she said. "He kept straightening things on the table, lining up the silverware perfectly, adjusting the angle of the little lampshade on the candle, repositioning the bread basket every time the waiter or I moved it."

"Maybe he's obsessive-compulsive," Brenda suggested.

I'd have to find out from Cece if it was a characteristic of Tom Nelson.

"You don't know the half of it," Eileen said. "His apartment was unbelievable."

"When did you go to his apartment?" I asked sharply.

"Good. More drinks," Eileen said. When the waiter came back to the table I took the opportunity to glance over to the end of the bar again. The helmet was gone. Was that a good sign or not? Did he know I'd spotted it? Was he still there? Or was I just freaking out for no reason?

"What about his apartment?" Brenda's question brought me back to the conversation at hand.

"It was perfect," Eileen said.

"Wait," I interrupted. "When did you go there? On the first date?"

"Why, are you worried I'll get a reputation?" Eileen bit into a fresh olive.

"I just want to be clear on the timeline." They both looked at me like I was crazy, but Eileen shrugged and answered.

"No, it wasn't on the first date. We went out a couple times. Dinner, drinks, and that play at the Curran. You'd hate it," she told me, then came back to her story. "So it was the fourth date by the time he invited me over. He cooked."

"Nice," Brenda said again.

"You'd think," Eileen agreed.

"So what was it about his apartment that was weird?" Men in black ski masks hanging out in the dining room, maybe?

"It was just so perfect," she said. "Hardwood floors you could see yourself in with white rugs and white furniture. Glass and chrome tables with surfaces like mirrors. And you should have seen the kitchen," she went on. "It looked like you could perform surgery in there. Not a speck on anything."

"What did you think?" Brenda asked.

She gave us a guilt-wracked look. "I thought, if it got serious, he'd have a hard time adjusting to Anthony."

"Ouch." I adored Eileen's nine-year-old son, but I had to admit he was a neat-freak's nightmare.

"Yeah," Eileen said. "So I just spent the evening trying not to spill anything or let my glass make a mark on his furniture." She finished her third martini. "I swear to God, when I used the bathroom I flushed four times." She giggled, then looked surprised.

"So did you spend the night?" I asked.

She shook her head. "He didn't ask. That was another weird thing. In all this time he'd only given me pecks on the cheek or forehead. Nothing else. No moves whatsoever." She looked a little mournful. "Even though I got a new haircut and all those new clothes."

"You look fantastic," Brenda assured her. "He's probably gay."

"Absolutely," I agreed loyally. "It's obvious he was either gay or a lunatic. Otherwise he'd have been all over you." But I wondered. Cece had never explicitly said she'd had sex with Tom Nelson. I'd just assumed that, since they'd moved in together, they'd been intimate. Something else I'd have to check on. I was beginning to regret not bringing a little notebook.

"Thanks, guys." Eileen straightened up. "You're right. He was a nut case."

"What finally convinced you?" Brenda asked. "Did he want to spit-shine your boots or something?"

"No," Eileen shook her head. "Can I have that?" She pointed at Brenda's second barely-touched martini.

Brenda slid the drink towards her. "What happened?"

Eileen took an olive and sucked on it. "I made a move."

"That night?" I asked. "At his place?"

"At his place, but it wasn't until the next time." She dunked the olive back in the drink. "Even though Anthony's with his dad this month, I didn't want to invite Ben over to my place. I mean, of course I'd told him about Anthony, but it's one thing to hear 'I have a son' in the abstract, and another to see the PlayStation-hooked-to-the-TV, model-airplane-parts-everywhere, train-set-in-the-dining-room reality." She looked to us for understanding. We understood. A man has to be eased into these situations.

"So you went back to his place . . ." I prodded.

"Saturday night," she said. "After dinner."

"And you made a move?" Brenda probed.

"I did," she admitted. "We were talking on the couch, and I . . . pounced."

"What happened?" Brenda asked.

"Well, we're kissing, and then we're taking each other's clothes off, and I figured he'd move into the bedroom, but no."

"No?"

"No. Instead he pulls me down onto the floor."

"That can be nice," Brenda said, then looked embarrassed.

"Most things can be nice," I said. "What did he do then?"

"It's not what he did." Eileen cringed. "It's what he said."

"What?" Brenda asked.

Eileen swigged the last of the martini. "He said, 'Try not to get the rug messy.' "

"Eeeyyuu." Brenda made a face.

"You're kidding," I said.

Eileen raised her right hand. "I swear."

"What did you do?" I asked.

"What could I do? I gathered up my clothes, and what was left of my dignity, and I left. Are you going to finish that?" She pointed to my martini.

I took the last swallow. "Yep. You've had enough anyway. It's a school night."

She sighed heavily. "Is it me?"

"No!" we protested. And we took her home and tucked her in, telling her all the while how fabulous she was and how much better off she was without a pathologically clean boyfriend.

Privately, I thought there were worse things than bad boyfriends. There were too-good-to-be-true boyfriends who turned out to be kidnappers. Maybe Eileen had been luckier than she would ever know.

Chapter 15

When I woke up the next day Jack had already left for the gym. He'd promised not to play racquetball until his shoulder was fully healed, but apparently there were other ways he could find to torture himself.

I hadn't told him about Eileen's suspicious boyfriend. My going-for-a-drink-with-the-girls outfit had been a little more effective than I'd bargained for, and I hadn't had a chance to say much of anything at all. Now that I thought about it, I wasn't sure how to introduce the topic without revealing that I was interrogating my friends. If he knew what I was up to, Jack would probably tell me to let him handle the situation, and that was a conversation I'd rather not have.

I sifted through everything Eileen had told us about Ben. Point one, he was rich. That fit. Point two, although he'd asked her out, he'd waited for her to make the first move. I had to remember to ask Cece whether that matched her experience with her perfect boyfriend. Although the thought of probing into Cece's sex life was not an appealing one.

And then there was the obsessive cleanliness thing—unless it had been an act. But why? If Ben was working for Macbeth, and trying to get as close to Eileen as Tom Nelson had to Cece, the behavior had worked against him. Why would Macbeth hire someone with habits that would drive his intended victim away? How could Macbeth hire anyone from solitary confinement anyway?

The whole mental exercise began to seem pointless. After all, both Tom and Ben were out of the picture now. I should be spending my time worrying about those people who were still around. I decided to head for the theater and check out the new director.

I came in through the stage door, hoping to slip in unnoticed so I could observe my suspect during the auditions. No such luck. I wasn't three steps into the building when I heard Simon cry, "Darling!" He strode towards me, gracefully flinging a sweater from around his shoulders. "Charley, my angel, my pet, how we've all missed you!" There was a reason Simon had chosen the life of the theater.

"Simon," I greeted him, as he kissed both my cheeks, grabbed me by the hands, and dragged me to the stage, talking all the time.

"Darling, it's all so thrilling! Don't you just adore auditions? They spell the dawn of a new day for our little troupe. Will we find genius today? Will we all write about this in our memoirs, as the day we discovered a breathtaking new talent?" As we reached the stage he pulled me close and whispered in my ear. "Sorry for camping it up so, darling, but the money man is here and one has one's image."

I smiled, relieved that Simon hadn't gone completely over the top. Then I took in what he'd said. The money man. The anonymous donor, who apparently wasn't that anonymous any more. I felt a stab of jealousy that he would be in my theater. Then I realized he was yet another stranger in our lives. "Where is he?" I muttered.

"Fifth row center," Simon said softly, then, with boisterous energy, "Look, kittens! Look who's come back to the fold! The prodigal producer has returned!" I saw a lot of familiar faces, but more who looked confused and annoyed at the interruption.

Everyone had stopped what they were doing with Simon's announcement, and the pause was getting awkward. I looked toward the orchestra seats, but the lights prevented me from seeing who was seated fifth row center.

"Charley!" I heard, and turned to find Martha, the costume designer, waving from a group of people at the back of the stage. "Charley!" That was Paris, the set designer, calling down from the balcony. Then, "Charley!" from offstage, as Chip emerged from the gloom. A small crowd began to form, and Simon clapped his hands imperiously for attention.

"All right, all right, everybody! We'll all have a chance to socialize with Charley later on. For now, we must be all business!" He grabbed my hands again and pulled me offstage in the opposite direction from where we'd come. "A few brief words in private I think, darling, and then we'll get down to work. Chip!" he interrupted himself. "We'll see the Annas first."

Offstage, Simon propelled me up two flights of stairs and down a narrow, brick-walled hallway to the theater offices. He shoved me in the room marked *Artistic Director* and flung himself at the door to close it behind us.

"Chaos!" he proclaimed. "Disaster and ruin! Thank God you got here when you did!" He sank into a red velvet sofa which had seen better days, and looked up at me like a man on his way to the scaffold.

"Problems with the new production?" I guessed, sitting on the battered antique desk and crossing my legs.

He snorted. "How I've missed your gift for understatement."

Now that I could look at him more closely, I saw how tired Simon was. There were dark circles under his fjord-blue eyes, and his hair, usually a perfect blond wave sweeping back from his brow, flopped down across his forehead. Worst of all, his clothes were rumpled. "Good Lord, Simon, you look like hell," I said, causing him to wince. "What's the matter?"

"Brian bailed," he said flatly.

"Brian?" Brian the new director? The Brian I was

here to investigate? The Brian who was now my leading contender for the role of Macbeth's henchman? "What do you mean he bailed?"

"As if enough hadn't gone wrong with this bloody production already," Simon said bitterly, "I got here bright and early this morning to find a note." He shot me a glance of pure hatred. "A note! That sodding—"

"All right," I interrupted. "I get the picture. What did the note say?"

Simon collapsed back into the cushions again and gestured toward the desk. "It's right there. I wanted to keep it so if I ever see him again I can ram it down his ungrateful throat."

I looked around the desk and realized I was sitting on the edge of a piece of paper. I adjusted my position and retrieved the note.

> *Simon,*
>   *I'm really sorry, but I just got an offer that I really can't refuse. I know it really sucks for me to leave you like this, but it's Broadway and I've really got to go.*
> *Brian*

I cleared my throat. "That's it?"

Simon glared at me. "That's it. That's *really*"—he spoke the word with an exaggerated American accent—"it." He shook his head. "Eileen will sue him, of course, for breaking his contract, but that doesn't help us now."

"And you're supposed to be auditioning today?" I asked.

"Yes, we're auditioning, and to make matters worse, the Begley excrescence is here. Anonymous investor my ass!" He gave me pleading eyes. "Charley, you've just got to help out. You've just got to go once more into the breach for dear old Simon and the good of the company. You've just got—"

"Simon," I cut him off. "What do you want me to do?"

"Isn't it obvious? Darling, I want you to direct!"

"What?" I responded, and then something he had said earlier caught up with me. "What do you mean by 'the Begley excrescence'? What's going on?"

We heard a clatter of footsteps in the hallway. One good thing about having concrete floors and brick walls in the theater office area was that a producer could never be surprised by a mob of angry actors. In this case, though, I had the horrible feeling we were about to face a mob of something worse.

"Where are they?" demanded a voice I knew and loathed.

"Simon! Charley!" sang another voice, Chip's, trying hard not to sound desperate. "Rix would like a word with you, if it's convenient!"

Simon had only time enough to entreat, "Follow my lead," before the door burst open.

Chip darted in ahead of the crowd, but the man that followed swept him aside as he entered. He stood at the doorway. Tall, lean, handsome in an impossible, matinee-idol sort of way. He took in the shabby room and its inhabitants with distaste. Several other people stood behind him, trying to peek in the doorway at whatever scandalous exchange might take place.

Rix Begley. Damn.

"Rix." I preempted any attempt he might make to speak. "It's been a long time." I crossed the room, smiling in what I hoped was a relaxed, charming manner. "Simon was just telling me how delightful it's been working with you on this production." You miserable bastard.

Simon snapped forward. "Yes, Rix old sock, we've just been doing a little catching up before we carry on with the auditions. Isn't it marvelous of Charley to step in for us? What a trouper! Honestly," he moved closer to the scowling man and spoke in a low, confiding tone, "I think this is the best thing that could possibly have happened. I mean," he rushed on, when it looked like Rix might respond, "she's simply head and shoulders above Brian. So talented! I would have died before hiring him if I'd known Charley was coming back. It's simply wonderful." He paused for breath. "Don't you agree?"

Rix regarded me darkly. The look on his face, angry embarrassment mixed with frustration, matched exactly how I felt, but for Simon's sake I wasn't about to show it. Of all the people who could have put money into the Rep, why the hell had they gotten involved with this back-stabbing, filthy, lying, scum-sucking bastard? I was going to kill Eileen the next time I saw her, and then I was going to kill Simon.

Need I say I had dated Rix? He had pursued me energetically, romanced me relentlessly, seduced me tirelessly. I was just beginning to get bored with his unflagging perfection when he'd asked Harry for two hundred and fifty thousand dollars to get out of my life. Apparently he'd had a pile of gambling debts. He'd told Harry that if he didn't get the money he'd propose. Harry, the idiot, had thought I might accept. So he'd done me what he'd thought was a favor and had bought the creep off.

Rix interrupted my short trip down memory lane. "Charley," he said. "What the fuck are you doing back?"

Charming. My smile grew brighter. "How could I stay away?" I practically purred. "When everyone I love is here." I moved closer to Simon and put my arm around his shoulder. "This is my home." Then, with more force than I should have given it, "This is my theater."

The pause that followed lasted too long. I turned to Simon, as much energy and enthusiasm as I could muster in my voice and on my face. "Shall we get to it, sweetie? The actors have suffered long enough, don't you think?"

"Absolutely, darling!" I was probably the only one to see the relief in his eyes. He turned to Rix. "As much as we'd all like to catch up . . ." He maneuvered himself past the group at the door, dragging me behind him, and practically sprinted toward the stairs when he hit the open hallway. "Work, work, work!" he called as we fled. "That's the way to ensure a successful production!"

But by the time we reached the stage we knew we hadn't made a clean escape. "Bannister!" Rix's voice commanded. "I want a word with you."

All conversation, both onstage and backstage, ceased. Experienced actors, recognizing the tone of a pissed-off backer, exchanged worried looks.

Rix's group had come to a halt at the bottom of the stairs. Simon raised his eyebrows as if he couldn't for the life of him imagine what the man might want, and walked nonchalantly back across the stage to him, discreetly pulling me along. "Yes?"

Rix took him by the arm and dragged him away, out of earshot. What they said I could only imagine, but Rix was a picture of ill-contained fury and Simon did his best to maintain his British sangfroid. The members of Rix's entourage, two men who looked like bodyguards and an efficient-looking girl with thick glasses and thin lips, followed the action.

The argument went on for a few moments, but Simon must have scored some winning point, because eventually Rix shut up, glared at him for a moment, then looked over at me. He approached me with a set face, coming close enough to speak without being overheard.

"Charley, I'd hate to think you'd fuck this show up just to screw me."

I decided not to reply.

"But your boy Bannister has made the very good point that you can't screw me without screwing yourself, so I'm willing to go ahead with you as the director."

Big of him. When I still didn't reply he grunted to his entourage, then walked swiftly to the stage door, his faithful followers faithfully following.

After he left there was a tangible release in the theater, as if everyone had been holding their breath.

Simon was suddenly standing next to me. "Well," I murmured, "I hope my upper lip is as stiff as yours."

He kissed me lightly on the forehead. "Only way to play it, darling," he said softly. Then he came to attention, clapped his hands sharply, and called "Chip! We'll see the Annas now!"

Everyone on stage snapped into action as Simon and I took the makeshift stairs from the stage to the orchestra seats. A desk with a few small lamps had been set up among the seats, and I saw a stack of head shots. Seated in the relative darkness of the orchestra seats, I realized I was still wired after seeing Rix, and still feeling blindsided by Simon's request that I direct. I looked at my watch. I'd been in the theater for half an hour and I felt like I'd just run a marathon.

"All right, darling?" Simon was looking at me closely.

I reached for the first pile of head shots, all twenty-something women who were auditioning for the female lead, Anna. "When we're finished here," I replied, "we're going out for the biggest margarita this town has to offer."

"Done," beamed Simon.

"And then," I continued, "you're going to tell me what the hell has been going on around here." I gave him my most serious, don't-even-think-of-bullshitting-me look.

His smile faltered. He swallowed and nodded. "Done."

I took a deep breath. "Can we start now? Is the playwright here?"

"She still hasn't returned any of my messages. She has casting approval, but we can't just wait forever."

"Maybe we should call Eileen and ask her if we're going to get into legal trouble if we cast without her," I suggested.

"Maybe the author ran off with Brian and we need to sue them both," Simon responded darkly.

"Okay!" Chip called from the stage, "We have Heather Magruder here. Heather is going to give us a monologue from *A Doll's House*. Quiet everybody!" The first actress took center stage, smiled out confidently to where she couldn't see us, and began.

The first several actresses were competent, but unremarkable. Chip's assistant efficiently ushered them on and off the stage, but I have to admit that I only gave them half my attention. I couldn't even begin to think of the ramifications of Brian's disappearance to my Macbeth investigation, or of how I was going to deal with the Rix situation. I also wondered how, exactly, I was going to explain to Jack that I'd been pulled into this project. Especially after I'd made a fuss about him even thinking of taking a job.

Of course, I knew I could back out. My response to Simon's panicked entreaties could hardly be considered binding. But did I want to back out? I loved the play. So what if I had been manipulated into the seat I was now occupying? That didn't mean I couldn't do the job. In a bizarre way, I felt good. I felt comfortable. I was in my theater and I was home. And I would probably be much better at this than at chasing down criminals.

"Thank you," I said to the actress who had just finished a selection from *The Crucible*. "Very nice." She bounced on her toes a little, beamed, and said "Thank you!" with a little wave before surrendering the stage.

"Next," Chip announced, "we have Regan Welsh. Regan will be giving us a selection from *Cyrano*." In the picture of Regan Welsh I had in front of me, she was stunning. Perfect features, radiant skin, startlingly clear eyes staring frankly at the camera.

"Ah." Simon shifted in his seat beside me. "The lady in question."

"Who is she?" I asked. She hadn't stepped into the light yet. "Do you know her?"

"Only by reputation. She's a friend of our friend," he said, his voice loaded with innuendo.

"Who's our friend?" Then I caught his tone. "Rix? She's Rix's . . . what?"

"Friend."

She stepped forward. The photograph hadn't done her justice. She was extraordinary. Her hair shone under the lights, and her face, dominated by those amazing eyes, was classically beautiful. But what struck me the most was her presence. She was the first of the actresses to look like she actually belonged on the stage. In fact, she looked as if she couldn't exist anywhere else.

She gazed out into the orchestra seats, and I could have sworn she was looking straight at me. Then she lowered her eyes and began the scene.

I wanted so much for her to be terrible. I wanted her voice to be thin and her acting to be wooden. That's the only way it would make sense for her to have anything to do with Rix. I wanted her to be the worst actress we'd seen that day, the worst actress I'd seen in my life.

She was brilliant.

When she finished, the theater was completely silent. I had to shake my head a little to break the spell she had cast. I looked over at Simon, who was staring with an open mouth. He blinked.

"Bugger me," he said. "It can act."

Chapter 16

After the auditions, my promised drink with Simon turned into something more like a staff meeting. No doubt wanting to delay our conversation about Rix, Simon had invited Martha, Paris, and Chip to join us.

The auditions had gone on for several hours after the revelation of Regan's performance. As much as I had hoped to find someone else, we'd cast her as Anna, the lead. Connections to miserable bastards aside, she was the best actress by far for the part.

We'd cast another unknown, Paul Collins, as the love interest. He was about as bland as his name implied, but there hadn't been a wealth of male talent to choose from.

The remainder of the cast was filled out by actors we had cast repeatedly from season to season. They were all known quantities—not without their quirks, but at least these were quirks we knew how to handle—and it was a relief to know we'd be able to count on them with two newcomers in the lead roles.

So, satisfied we'd put the production back on track, we headed down O'Farrell Street to Foley's, the best Irish bar in town, or at least the best within walking distance of the theater.

Simon, unsurprisingly, chattered incessantly, while Paris and Chip settled into a technical discussion of the rigging necessary to achieve a particular effect the script called for in the second act. Martha walked silently beside me, looking distinctly upset.

I put my arm around her. "What's the matter, sweetie? Too many costume changes in this one?"

She smiled quickly. "No, it isn't that." She looked at me sideways, then back down at her feet. "I'm just expecting to hear from a friend."

Simon pounced on her. "A friend? Martha darling, have you got a beau? Please don't tell me you've fallen for an actor. You deserve so much better than that. Oh, but I know," he rushed on, "it must be the dishy Paul, our new leading man. I knew he had to know someone because he came in without an agent. It's him, isn't it darling?"

"Simon, it's possible Martha would rather keep her private life private," I said, although Martha's red face should have spoken for itself.

"Private? I'm not familiar with the word."

We stepped into the bar. Martha mumbled something and made for the ladies' room. I glared at Simon.

"What?" he asked innocently. "Mary, my love," he called to the woman behind the bar, "five pints of your best, if you please. We'll be in the back room."

"Anything for you, Simon, my dear," she called back cheerily.

Simon was something of a regular.

"Do you really think Paul's dishy?" I asked him as we snaked through the tables to the back room, a comfortable, wood-paneled space with portraits of Irish poets and politicians on the walls. There were six tables, only one of which was occupied by a couple of men deep in conversation.

Simon pulled two tables together in the corner. "Dishy, dreamy, de-lovely, whatever you want to call it, that boy is it."

Paris snorted. "When are you going to grow up? There's more to life than a pretty face." He spoke from experience. In his mid-fifties, Paris had been in a solid, happy relationship for eighteen years with one of the ugliest, nicest men in the world. It was a classic San Francisco story. Paris had come from Dallas in the seventies—where it was hard to be out and impossible to be black and out—only to end up falling in love with someone who'd come from Fort Worth for the same reason.

"But when you've got a pretty face, who needs more? Ah! Spirits!" Simon gave the waitress his most endearing smile.

"Speaking of a pretty face . . ." Chip said.

"Regan," the three of us replied in unison.

"She's something," Paris said. "And the girl can act, too."

"I thought she was amazing," Chip agreed.

Martha joined us again, looking a little red around the eyes. "Are we talking about Miss Glamour Face?" she asked, picking up her pint.

"Put your claws back in, darling," Simon said.

"Didn't you like her?" I asked. This was important. If there was something off-putting about Regan it might come across to the audience.

Martha made a face and shrugged. "She's just so perfect. It isn't interesting. I stopped making costumes for Barbie when I was eleven." Martha herself would never be called perfect in the age of supermodels, but she was definitely interesting. She had an exotic look that she played up with lots of black eyeliner and a wardrobe she designed and constructed herself, consisting mainly of column-like knit garments overlaid with drapey, drippy scarf-like swaths. It gave her an Indian/Asian/something else look that would have worked better, admittedly, on someone taller than her five-foot-two self, but she made the best of every inch she had.

"Well, I have no problem with her perfect, uninteresting, gorgeous face," Simon said. "No problem whatsoever. In fact—"

"Simon," I interrupted. "Promise."

He widened his eyes in innocence. "Promise what, darling?"

"Promise you won't get involved with her," I said

firmly. "Not during production. The last thing we need is broken hearts on opening night."

Simon pointed to himself in a gesture that said "Moi?"

"And . . ." I continued threateningly.

He sighed, and lazily raised his right hand. "I promise, in front of all these witnesses, not to get involved with our leading lady."

I gave him a stern look.

"Or our leading man," he finished.

"It doesn't matter anyway," Chip commented. "About Regan, at least. She's otherwise engaged."

"Yes," I said. "She is. A friend of our new patron." I put an extra helping of venom on the word.

"Ah." Simon made a strangling sound. "Darling, have I thanked you properly yet for agreeing to direct? You simply can't know how fabulous you are, and—"

"I can't believe that bastard Brian," Chip interrupted. "We should find out who hired him in New York and let them know what he did to us. We're suing, right?"

"Completely unprofessional," Paris agreed. "I thought so all along. The man didn't know the first thing about stage lighting. And it wouldn't surprise me," he lowered his voice, "if he'd never worked in a union shop before."

I suddenly remembered that the point of my attending the auditions had been to learn more about the mysterious Brian. I could wait until later to berate Simon for his involvement with Rix.

"What made you think that, Paris?" I asked. "Did he seem inexperienced?" I turned to Simon. "What had he done before he signed on with us?"

Simon shrugged. "He seemed solid. He'd been doing a lot of decent-sounding work in Seattle and LA."

Chip made a sound that was halfway between a "ha" and a "hrumph."

"What?" I asked him.

He shook his head. "I don't believe half of what was on his resumé."

Simon looked surprised. We all must have, except for Martha, who still looked miserable.

"Why not?" Simon demanded.

Chip leaned forward intently and began counting on his fingers. "One, he claimed to have directed *Midsummer Night's Dream* but when I said something about a certain person making a perfect Bottom, he had no idea what I was talking about. Two, he was supposed to have worked at the Pasadena Playhouse two years ago, but he didn't know the name of this guy I went to Cal with—who happened to be the set designer that season. Three, when I asked him where he'd lived down South, all he said was 'near the beach.' Nobody who lives in LA would be that vague. They'd say 'Venice' or 'Malibu' or something. Not just 'near the beach.' " He gave a disgusted shake of his head.

"So you think he was a complete fake?" I asked. "Everything?" That would fit if he was working for Macbeth, but then why would he have left? Was keeping up the pretense too much for him as the actual production got closer?

"I can't believe that," Simon protested.

"Neither can I," Martha spoke up. "I don't know why you all hated him. He knew you did. That's probably why he left. He couldn't stand your petty—" she choked back her words and stood. "I have a headache. I'm going home." She practically ran from the room.

"Well," Simon said dryly. "I think we can guess who's broken young Martha's heart."

"I should go after her," I said, reaching for my purse.

"Let her go," Paris said. "She's a big girl. She'll be fine."

Chip looked stunned. "I'm sorry," he said. "I had no idea. I never would have said all those things about him. . . ."

"Never mind," Paris said. "Let's have another round. This one's on me." He headed for the bar.

I looked at my watch. "I need to call Jack if I'm going to be much later."

"Darling, if you have to go . . ." Simon said hopefully.

"You're not getting off that easily," I assured him. "Give me your cell phone." Reluctantly, he handed it over.

Jack wasn't there, but I left a message on the hotel voicemail. I was a little relieved he wasn't in, because that meant I didn't have to explain why I was out drinking with friends instead of being with him for the second night in a row. Then I started wondering where he was. Probably with Mike, I assured myself, still hunting through the records of a certain maximum security military prison. And if I hadn't left the cell phone he'd given me in Brenda's VW on the night of Cece's rescue, he'd have been able to call and tell me so.

"What's the matter?" Paris asked, returning with four fresh pints and giving me a shrewd glance.

"Not a thing," I told him. Probably not a thing. "So, about Brian—"

"Enough about Brian," Paris interrupted. "The boy is gone and good riddance to him." He raised his glass, and Chip and Simon did likewise.

"Oh, all right," I agreed, joining them in the toast. I could always do some digging into his past on my own.

"Now, Charley," Chip said, leaning forward expectantly. "I'm worried about the second act. Do you think the whole comedic thing with the mother subverts the dramatic tension?"

Oh, hell. I was directing a play.

We talked shop for a while, and I was surprised to see how far Chip had come professionally while I'd been away. He was still dauntingly intense, in a squirrelly sort of way, but his instincts were good and his ideas, particularly for specific pieces of business, were impressive. I wondered how long he'd be satisfied with his current role of stage manager at the Rep. It occurred to me that Chip might be training his assistant to take over when he moved on. Clearly, he was ready for bigger and better things. Equally clearly, I had to spend a lot more time with the script.

"Shall we have another?" Chip asked, and I realized we'd all drained our glasses while talking. "It's my turn, I think."

"Ah." Simon was looking at the doorway to the main bar with a mixture of nervousness and relief. "Reinforcements have arrived."

I turned to see Eileen approaching us. Reinforcements indeed. Simon had probably called her when he realized I wasn't going to go home without hearing how Rix Begley had come to be a patron of my theater company.

"Eileen, darling!" Simon enthused. "So glad you could make it. You know everybody, of course? Have a seat. Chip was just off to get another round."

"Please." Eileen sat heavily in the chair next to me. For a size four, that's not as easy as it sounds. "No alcohol." She grabbed my hand with both of hers. "Promise you'll never let me drink again."

"Maybe not four martinis on an empty stomach," I agreed, wondering how she'd made it through her work day in her hungover state.

"I think it's time for me to go," Paris said, rising. "It's my turn to cook tonight, so I'd better stop for a pizza somewhere. You want to come over?" He gave Chip a look that translated roughly into "let's run for our lives."

"Oh." Chip looked from Paris to the rest of us. "Oh. All right. See you tomorrow."

As soon as we were alone, Simon began to babble. "Eileen, darling, what's all this about four martinis? What were you up to last night? Something to do with the new man in your life, I suspect. Darling, you know what I always say—"

"Simon," I interrupted. "Shut up and tell me how you got involved with Rix Begley."

Eileen jumped, her eyes seeming to focus for the first time. "Is that what this is about?" She turned to Simon. "You told her?" she demanded.

"He didn't have to," I stopped her. "He was there."

"There?" Eileen looked at me blankly. "Who? Rix? Where? At the theater?" She turned on Simon again. "How did you let that happen?"

Poor Simon. He had expected Eileen to be on his side, and now he was faced with two angry women and he was all alone. He smiled weakly. "He wasn't supposed to be there."

"Damn right he wasn't." Eileen reached into her purse for her phone. "I'm calling his lawyer. He was supposed to be one hundred percent hands-off. That was the only way I'd ever have agreed to it," she explained to me. "You would never have to know where the money came from, because he'd be invisible, and it was only for one season, and—" She must have seen the betrayal on my face, because she put the phone down and grabbed my hands with hers. "Oh, Charley, I'm so sorry. We didn't even know if you'd be back in town for this season, and his offer, and the timing, and his promise to stay away, were just too good to be true."

"Clearly."

"We really are sorry, darling," Simon said. "If we'd known from the beginning who he was, we'd never have entertained the idea—"

"He used a lawyer," Eileen interrupted. "Until Rix showed up to sign the final paperwork, we didn't know who we were dealing with, and by then . . ."

They both looked miserable. "Oh, hell," I said. "It doesn't matter. It's not like I'm some fragile flower who has to be protected from every guy who's ever turned out to be a jerk."

"Darling," Simon said, "you're too forgiving. I simply must kiss you." Which he did, twice on both cheeks.

"Okay," I said, "but now I want the details. I've been thinking it over, and I can't figure it out. The basic question for Rix is always 'what's in it for me?' Why would he, of all people, want to help the Rep?"

Neither of them answered.

"Eileen, you say his lawyer came to you? You didn't go out looking for backers?"

"No." She shook her head. "That was what made it all so easy. Right about the time Simon finally convinced me to go for outside funding, in marches Rix' lawyer with an offer to bankroll one third of our seasonal expenses."

"When was this?" If she said it was in the time between my meeting Jack and coming home, I thought I'd scream.

Eileen looked even more miserable. "That's the awful thing. Charley, if we'd known you were going to be back for the season . . ."

"Eileen, when did he give you the money?"

"We finalized the deal about a week before you came home. Charley, if I'd known you were coming—that you'd have to deal with him—"

Surprising myself, I didn't scream. But I admit I tuned out their apologies for a few moments as a hundred other questions presented themselves. I started with an obvious one. "How did Rix know you were looking for funding?"

"Aren't theaters always looking for money?" Simon asked. "I assumed it was a given."

"No," Eileen said, speaking slowly. "That's true for most theaters, in fact for most of the arts, but anyone who knows anything about the Rep knows that Charley always financed it one hundred percent." She looked at me. "What are you getting at, Charley?"

"I'm not sure." I knew I was looking for signs of Macbeth everywhere, but I honestly didn't see how he could fit in to the reappearance of Rix Begley in my life, despite the suspicious timing. How could the vicious killer and the smarmy playboy be connected? And why?

Those were not questions I was comfortable asking Eileen and Simon. Particularly since I had no intention of telling them about Macbeth.

"Okay, here's what I want to know," I said. "One, how did Rix know that we'd need money and know the exact time to offer it? And two, why would he have wanted to offer it? Since when does he want anything to do with the Rep? Or me?" I remembered the look on his face when he'd first seen me that morning and realized that he had been as unpleasantly surprised as I had. I held up a third finger. "But most important is three. Where the hell did he get the money?"

They didn't have any answers, and no matter how long we stayed and speculated, we weren't going to be able to figure it out. I wanted to talk it over with Jack. Maybe he'd see a pattern or a signal that we'd missed. But I wondered if it was really appropriate to discuss the professional complications caused by an ex-lover's finances with my new husband. Perhaps Miss Manners has a chapter for just such questions.

"Well, you can count on one thing," Eileen said. "Rix won't come back to the theater. Not for rehearsals, not even for opening night. I'll get a court order if I have to." She was making furious notes in her little electronic organizer.

"He was only there today for Regan," Simon said.

We both stared at him.

"It's the only part of this I've been able to figure out. Why he came to the theater." He looked at me. "Rix obviously didn't know you were back in town. He wanted to bring Regan in personally and see that her audition went well."

"Simon, you didn't make him any promises, did you?"

He looked genuinely shocked. "Charley, of course

not. I may be a complete balls-up as an artistic director, but I still have some integrity."

"I'm sorry, sweetie," I said. "I'm just a little—"

"Excuse me," Eileen interrupted. "But who's Regan?"

Simon answered. "Oh. She's . . . that is to say . . . she . . ."

"She's Rix's girlfriend. She's an actress," I finished for him.

"Uh huh," Eileen said. "And Mr. Investor brought her to the auditions today to get her a part in the show." She grimaced. "At least some things never change."

"Casting the money man's girl is a time-honored theatrical tradition," Simon agreed.

"Well, at least you won't have to worry about her." Eileen snapped her organizer shut. Then she saw our faces. "You didn't."

Simon shrugged nonchalantly. "She was very good."

Eileen turned to me. "Tell me you didn't cast her."

I followed Simon's example and shrugged. "She was brilliant."

Eileen slumped back in her chair. "Shit."

I decided I'd let Simon do the explaining. Suddenly I was very thirsty. "Another round?" I asked, and without waiting for an answer I grabbed my purse and headed for the bar. The back room had filled up since we'd arrived, and I had to squeeze past two pudgy stockbroker types who were arguing loudly over whether Bono's portrait should be added to the pantheon of Irish heroes decorating the bar.

When I popped out on the other side of the twosome, I was propelled into a tall man who suddenly turned his back on me. I nearly knocked him over.

"Sorry," I said, recovering myself and gesturing vaguely behind me. "It's a madhouse in here—" and that's when I saw it. The red motorcycle helmet in the man's hand.

He was already several steps away from me. I didn't stop to think. I ran after him and grabbed his arm. "Hey—"

He shook me off and kept moving. If the bar hadn't been so crowded, he'd have gotten away. But just as he got within reaching distance of them, the double doors burst open with the force of an entire sweaty, filthy, victorious rugby team.

A cheer went up from the crowded bar as the team poured in, calling to friends, swearing at one another, slapping and hugging and punching and generally basking in their sporting glory. The motorcyclist didn't stand a chance. He was thrown back into the room and spun around until he stood directly in front of me.

"Mike!"

Chapter 17

Once he realized he'd been caught, Mike tried a pathetic bluff. "Charley!" He assumed a look of surprised delight. "What are you doing here?"

The wave of rugby players crested around us, then left us in a sudden calm by the door.

"Don't bullshit me, Mike."

He looked around at the mayhem of the bar, but a clever answer failed to appear. When he looked at me again it was with an apologetic grimace. "I was only trying to make sure nothing happened to you."

After my initial shock, it all made sense. "Jack?"

He nodded miserably. "Charley, don't—"

"Don't you—" I snapped, intending to finish with *dare tell me what to do!* But I suddenly hadn't seen the point in arguing with him. "Go home, Mike."

I ducked past him out of the bar and hopped into the first cab I could find. It wasn't that far to the hotel from the bar, but with one-way streets and Union Square gridlock, I had plenty of time to work myself into a first-class fury.

In the cab, I called him names that would have made a drill sergeant blush. After I'd finally escaped from a lifetime of Harry's private detectives, Jack had done the one thing that was guaranteed to make me crazy. I didn't care that he'd done it out of concern for me. I didn't care that he'd used his best friend and not some impersonal agency. He'd sent someone to spy on me.

Of course, what did I expect? He'd admitted that he'd sent Gordon to check me out when we'd first gotten serious. Why wouldn't he think it was perfectly reasonable to have Mike shadow me all over town? Well it *was* different! Doing a background check on a new lover is one thing, but spying on your wife is not acceptable—not to this wife.

And to think I'd been afraid I was getting paranoid! I hadn't told Jack about the feeling that someone was following me because I didn't want him to worry! The bastard!

I went on in that vein, muttering profanities and occasionally punching the front seat or slapping the door, causing looks of concern from the driver. "You okay, miss?" he asked.

"Fine," I barked, and he kept his eyes on the road for the rest of the trip.

I would kill him. I would scream bloody murder at him. I would tear his head off. I would rip him to shreds. I would turn him into a quivering pile of apologies. I would kill him.

When I stepped out of the cab into the night air, I felt like I'd been doused with ice water. Suddenly I wasn't angry anymore. Suddenly I was terrified. Because I knew what I'd do.

I heard Jack as soon as I opened the door.

"Here she is," he said into the phone, relief clear in his voice. "Charley, where have you been? Eileen is on the phone and she's worried sick. She's—"

I took the phone from him and spoke into the receiver. "I'm fine. I'll talk to you tomorrow." I hung up. I looked at my husband.

"What the hell were you doing?" he demanded. "You had us frantic, disappearing like that. What were you thinking?"

I didn't answer.

"What the hell is going on? What happened?" The balance was swiftly shifting from concern to anger.

The phone rang.

"Aren't you going to answer that?" I asked.

"To hell with it. What's going on?"

I picked up the receiver and held it out to him. "It's for you."

He grabbed the phone "What?"

It was Mike. I was only surprised that Eileen had gotten through first. I watched Jack's face as comprehension dawned. He hung up without saying another word. He met my eyes. "Charley—"

"Jack," I cut him off. "I will say this once." I stood directly in front of him and, when I was sure I had his complete attention, I spoke quietly. "If you ever have me followed again, for whatever reason, by whatever person—" I swallowed hard, but knew what I had to say. "We're finished."

I don't know what I expected—explanations, apologies, justifications. He didn't say anything. He just kept his eyes locked on mine. I could see the exact moment when he understood I was serious. Slowly, he nodded. "I will never have you followed again."

I took a deep breath. "All right, then." I sat down, dizzy suddenly.

"But," he said.

My chin snapped up.

"You have to agree to a bodyguard. At least until I can figure out whether . . . Macbeth . . . is still a threat." He stumbled on the name I'd given his former colleague, but he was deadly serious.

"I'm already carrying a gun," I pointed out.

"That isn't enough." He sat beside me. "I promise you, I swear to you, that I will never ask your bodyguard where you've been, who you've been with, what you've been doing, anything." He took my hand, forcing me to look at him. "I'm not Harry. I will never spy on you." His face hardened. "But I won't have you unprotected."

"You realize how patronizing that is," I said. "The implication being that I'm incapable of taking care of myself?"

"Charley, I believe you're capable of damn near

anything," he said. "But I also know what Macbeth is capable of." He swallowed. "I won't have you unprotected," he repeated.

I leaned back into the cushions and thought about it. Of course I didn't need a bodyguard, but it wouldn't be the first time in my life I'd had to put up with one. And it wasn't really the fact that Jack didn't think I could take care of myself that had made me crazy, it was the fact that he'd had me watched. Having me protected, with my full knowledge, was a different matter entirely. And I felt I'd made my point.

Finally, I spoke. "I hear Brenda knows a nice man named Flank."

"Charley, how could you say something like that?" Brenda's face bunched into a mask of concern. "You didn't mean it, did you? You wouldn't leave him?"

We were at Harry's house, drinking iced tea on the terrace overlooking the pool. I was telling Brenda all about the events of the night before. Well, not all about them. Not about the extremely satisfactory way in which we'd sealed our new agreement. But pretty much everything else.

The poolside setting would have been downright idyllic if it hadn't been for the occasional glimpses of armed men through the trees. God only knew what the golfers thought, catching sight of the large unsmiling men who observed their drives from the fifteenth hole with studied disinterest. At least Harry had kept their presence to the "perimeter." So far there were no mercenaries in the breakfast room.

I sighed and answered Brenda. "I did mean it. I think I would leave him." I closed my eyes briefly. "That was the scariest thing."

She gave me a silent, reproachful look.

"Brenda, I will not be spied on," I said firmly. "I don't think it's too much to ask my husband to respect that."

"Oh, Charley," she said sadly. "He was only trying to take care of you."

"Never mind, it's all worked out. Jack is probably asking Harry for the use of one of his bodyguards right now." I gestured toward the game room with my glass. "Maybe you and I can work out a time-share with Mr. Flank."

"Just Flank, no Mister," she said absently. "Charley, if I understand you correctly, you're not upset because Jack thought you needed protection, you're upset because he was secretive about it. Yes?"

"Yes," I agreed. "He's my husband. I expect him to be honest with me. If he thinks I'm in danger he should tell me, not have me watched like I'm some sort of child."

She nodded thoughtfully. "Full disclosure."

"Why not?"

"Uh-huh." She sipped her tea.

"What?" I demanded.

"Well." She cleared her throat. "I was just wondering if you might be just the slightest bit hypocritical on that point." She gave me an apologetic look. "About full disclosure."

"What?" I said again, this time as a protest of innocence.

"Well." She bit her lip. "I could be wrong, but I'm guessing you haven't told Jack about Rix Begley." She waited for my reaction.

Damn.

"Have you been talking to Eileen?"

"Of course I have," Brenda said. "She called me this morning. She was furious with you for disappearing like that. She wanted to know if I knew what was going on."

"Oh." I'd called Eileen that morning to explain, but apparently I hadn't been early enough.

"And then she told me about Rix showing up at the theater." Brenda's face returned to the look of concern she'd been wearing most of the day. "Charley, how awful for you."

"I'll admit it was a something of a shock."

She nodded. "Don't you think you should tell Jack?" she asked.

I shrugged. "Why make a big deal about it?" Thinking things over in the night, I had pretty much resolved not to have the Rix discussion with Jack until I could figure out if there really was a connection between my bastard ex-boyfriend and Jack's bastard ex-partner.

"Isn't it a big deal?" Brenda asked. "Eileen said the three of you were going crazy trying to figure out why he'd shown up offering funding right when the Rep needed it. Don't you think that's suspicious?"

"Well, yes," I shrugged. "But—"

"And don't you think it's a good idea to tell Jack about anything suspicious?" she pressed. "And anyway, don't you think you owe it to Jack to tell him about Rix anyway? In the interest of keeping your relationship honest?"

"It's not the same thing," I said.

She raised her eyebrows just the slightest bit.

"It's *so* not the same thing," I stated firmly.

She pursed her lips.

"Is it the same thing?"

She raised her glass. "To full disclosure."

I sighed. "Fine. I'll tell Jack about Rix." Ugh. But maybe he'd be able to see the connection that I couldn't.

She beamed. "Oh, Charley, you'll be so glad."

Maybe. "Anyway, how are you?" I changed the subject before she could make any further suggestions. "You look fabulous."

Brenda was wearing a linen sundress in a shade somewhere on the border between raspberry and orange sorbet. It made her skin glow and the slit up the side showed a lot more leg than usual for her.

"Do you like this?" She looked down at herself. "Harry seems to think shopping and going for spa treatments are the only acceptable pastimes for Cece and me." She smoothed out a wrinkle on the dress.

"Can you believe this is a Calvin Klein? I'm sitting poolside on a weekday afternoon wearing Calvin Klein." She shook her head.

"And unless I miss my guess," I commented, "those are no Birkenstocks on your pedicured feet."

She looked down at the two thin straps of buff leather holding a high heel on her foot, wiggled her bright orange toes, and sighed. "They're pretty, aren't they?"

"Mmm," I agreed.

"They'd probably get me blackballed from the faculty lounge."

"A small price to pay."

"Maybe." She contemplated her footwear.

"Charley," she said after a while.

"Um hmm?"

"When do you think I can go home?"

"What's the matter?" If Harry had done something to upset her, I'd kill him.

"It's just that . . ." she gestured, taking in the pool, the grounds, the house. "I'm getting used to all this." She turned to me. "I think wealth can be dangerously addictive."

Oh. As long as it was the lifestyle she was getting used to, and not the company of a certain bad-boy uncle of mine.

"I don't know, sweetie," I said. "Jack and I have some leads, but I don't know when . . . things . . . will be safe again."

"You and Jack?" Brenda replied skeptically. "You and Jack have some leads?" She leaned back in her chair, letting the sun hit her face. "If you don't mind my saying so, it's no wonder Jack wants to borrow Flank."

I decided not to be insulted. Brenda had been through a lot, most of it—okay, all of it—my fault.

"Do you only take him to school?" I asked.

"Who? Oh, Flank," she said. "I only have one more class. We were supposed to have two, but I decided to make the final a take-home assignment that they can email me when they're done. So the last class is on Monday, but I'm not bringing Flank."

"Won't Harry freak out?"

"I'm bringing Harry."

Oh?

"He's such an idiot," Brenda went on. "He's convinced we're all going to bring cupcakes or something for the last day."

I stared at her. Did she just call Harry an idiot?

She saw my look and made a face. "I know he's your uncle, Charlie, but really. He insists on believing that Women's Studies is another term for Home Economics. He thinks I'm teaching girls how to cook and sew."

She did call Harry an idiot! "Brenda," I said, grinning so hard I thought my cheeks would split. "I'm so happy! What's the last lecture on?"

She smiled slyly. "Well, it was scheduled to be a survey of feminist ethical issues as portrayed in the mainstream media." She paused and rattled her ice cubes. "But I've decided to substitute a session on media representations of subversions of the patriarchy." She looked at the pool and stretched contentedly. "What do you think?"

I beamed. "I think it's just what your students deserve."

"I thought so too. Oh, look, here come Jack and Harry."

They were squinting in the sunlight after the darkness of the game room. Harry, in his trademark cargo shorts and Hawaiian shirt, moved as though he'd just gotten off a surfboard, taking wide strides and holding both arms up to wave hugely at us. Jack, beside him, looked like a sleek thoroughbred in his dark gray tee-shirt and black jeans.

"Pour me some of that tea, Baby Doll," Harry said, pulling up a chair to join us. "Um, I mean—" He shot a look over to Jack. "I'll have a glass of tea," he cleared his throat. "Charley."

I stopped in mid-reach and stared at Harry. He

glanced again towards Jack, who kissed me lightly on the cheek before folding himself into the chair next to me, the slightest of smiles on his face.

"I'm about as parched as an old man can get," Harry announced, pouring his own tea.

I looked at my watch. "Really? I'd have thought the sun was over the yardarm somewhere in the world." Harry had never really been a stickler for which time zone he was in when he declared it the cocktail hour.

"Ah, but Baby—um, Charley," he said, grinning broadly, "it's the new Harry!" He swallowed the drink in one gulp. "Clean and sober!" He patted his not inconsiderable midsection. "Never felt better in my life!"

I looked at Brenda for confirmation.

"Harry got rid of all the alcohol in the house," she explained. "Because of Cece. He said if she could stay straight, he could stay sober." She smiled warmly at Harry. "And he has."

"I tell you, Charley, I'm like a goddamn teenager again!" Harry held up his arms, bodybuilder style.

"Wow." It was all I could come up with. "Really, wow. Good for you, Harry." I suppose wonders would never cease. I'd been so busy worrying about Brenda falling under my uncle's influence, I'd never stopped to think what might happen if Harry fell under hers.

I realized I should say something else. "How is Cece?"

Brenda had told me that my cousin was out with Gordon that morning, shopping at the local farmer's market. In fact, she'd told me that Cece and Gordon were practically inseparable these days.

Harry beamed. "She's a different person, Charley." He shook his head. "I'd never have believed it. I think this thing got through to her more than any of the rehabs and clinics and treatments ever have."

"She's learning to cook," Brenda said.

"You're kidding." Cece around food? The woman

hadn't eaten a full meal since the day Nancy Reagan had implored her to just say no. Personally.

Harry nodded. "Gordon's teaching her. She's put on weight, hasn't she, Brenda?"

"She has," Brenda confirmed. "It's so nice not to see her bones sticking out."

"Wow." It seemed to be my word *du jour.* "Amazing. Wonderful. Good for her." I resolved to keep my fingers crossed that this time she'd stay clean for good.

Jack changed the subject. "Harry's going to loan us one of the men who works for him."

I looked at Harry. "Flank?"

"Flank," Harry said.

"Oh, goodie." My sarcasm fell on deaf ears.

"He'll stay in a room down the hall from us at the hotel," Jack explained. "He'll be in the suite with you whenever I'm not—in another room, out of your way," he shot down the protest I'd been about to make. "And he'll go with you and stay with you whenever you go out without me." He met my eyes. "Deal?"

"When he's at the theater he stays up in the balcony, not in everybody's way," I negotiated.

"As long as he can see you from there," Jack conceded.

I thought about it. "He doesn't come into bathrooms or dressing rooms with me."

"But he checks them out before you go in."

I took a deep breath. "Deal."

Harry slapped the table. "Well, all right then. Let's go find the guy and tell him he's got a new job."

Flank looked something like a cross between a Samoan hit man and a mastodon. The size was not completely unexpected for someone in his line of work. But the hair . . . It sprouted from the backs of his hands and his knuckles. It crept up from his shirt collar. It merged from his temples into his eyebrows. Eyebrow, to be fully accurate. The only place he didn't have hair was on the top of his head. But he'd let what remained on the sides grow long enough to be held in a ponytail that trailed down his back. I prayed I'd never have occasion to see him in a tank top.

When Harry explained his new assignment to him, Flank looked at me and grunted a word which may have been "cool."

We took him home.

I decided to stage a relaxed, romantic dinner that night. I had to tell Jack I'd agreed to direct the play, as well as provide full disclosure on the whole Rix thing. This called for heels and a slinky dress. This called for soft music and softer lighting. This called for discretion in the wait staff and an almost psychic level of anticipation from the wine steward. This called for an eight o'clock reservation at Postrio.

The setting was perfect. The colors and lighting were subdued. Decorative flourishes of hammered copper glinted in the candlelight. Icy martinis appeared with the menus and a basket of delectable artisan breads was placed reverently between us.

We started with Miyagi oysters on the half shell and a blini with smoked salmon and caviar, both of which we shared. Then Jack ordered the squab with polenta and a surprisingly chocolaty Madeira sauce, and I went for the Chinese duck served with fried rice and bok choy. Jack ordered a perfect crisp white wine that worked with it all, and I silently congratulated myself on having picked the perfect venue.

It wasn't until the entrées were served that Jack said, quite casually, "So what is it you don't want to tell me?"

I held up my finger and took one bite of the amazing duck. "There," I said, having finished chewing like a proper grown-up. "I'm ready now."

I started with an update of the goings-on at the theater, beginning with the news that Brian, the director, had decamped for the East Coast. That led naturally to my nomination by Simon to take up the job, and from there I segued into the auditions and what a talented actress we'd found for the female lead.

Jack nodded and commented appropriately, pausing only to ingest the occasional tidbit of squab or to spear a forkful of duck off my plate. He was more curious about Brian than I had expected him to be, and we went over everything I'd learned about him from the gang at the theater.

When I'd finished, Jack looked at the table thoughtfully. "So this whole elaborate evening out was for you to break it to me that you've taken a job?" His right eyebrow raised fractionally.

I reached for the last of my wine. I gulped. "That," I said, "and a little something more."

The waiter chose that moment to whisk our plates away, brush any offending crumbs from the table, and place dessert menus discreetly before us. Jack pushed his away.

"You haven't accidentally shot anyone, have you?" he asked.

I made a face, took a breath, and told him everything about Rix.

Chapter 18

Although Jack rose above any prurient interest in my past with Rix, he wanted every detail surrounding Rix's reappearance and his new involvement in the theater. Jack may have had some illusion that investing in a Rep company could be lucrative, but once I explained the concept of nonprofit status to him, he had to admit he couldn't come up with any logical reason for Rix to have supplied funding.

"Is it possible he just wants to mess with your head?" he asked.

"I don't think so. I'd swear he was just as uncomfortable seeing me yesterday as I was seeing him." I toyed absently with the dessert menu, sliding it from one hand to the other on the tablecloth. "And Eileen said he'd agreed to total anonymity, so I don't see how I would have even known about it if I hadn't accidentally run into him."

I overshot the menu and came close to knocking the candle over. Jack smoothly intervened. "What's really bothering you?"

I made a face. "I know you'll think I'm being paranoid, but I can't help thinking there must be a connection. With Cece's kidnapping. With the woman in the bathtub, maybe. With Macbeth." I picked up a spoon and began flipping it over and over.

Jack didn't even blink. "It's possible."

"What?" I dropped the spoon. "Hell, Jack, I thought you were going to tell me I'm crazy."

"That's possible too."

"Thanks."

He frowned. "The thing that bothers me about Rix is where he got the money to put into the Rep. He was broke when he dated you, and Harry's money can't have lasted long if he really used it to pay off gambling debts, so someone must be bankrolling him."

"Macbeth?" I swallowed hard.

"But even if that's true, I can't figure out why. What do either of them have to gain by it?" He shook his head. "Maybe we're just looking for patterns that aren't there. It's probably something much simpler."

"Like an unbridled love of drama? A sort of sudden-onset thespiophilia? Why don't I believe that?"

"Maybe he's still in love with you," Jack suggested. Then he shot me a look. "Did you make that word up?"

"He was never in love with me. He was in love with my bank balance."

"He's an idiot."

"Of course he is, but why is he back?"

"My best guess is that he expects you to buy him out." Jack leaned forward. "Think about it—despite all the conditions of anonymity in his agreement with Eileen, he expected you to find out about him. When he showed up at the theater he might not have known you'd be there, but he knew you'd hear about it. And he probably figured that when you found out he'd put money into the Rep, you'd give him a nice return on his investment just to be rid of him."

"Well if that's the case he's seriously deluded. Harry paid him once to go away and I don't intend to make a habit of it."

We left it at that and took our dessert to go. Banana milk chocolate pie is a dessert best eaten in bed.

The next morning I woke up completely happy. Brenda had been right. It felt good to have told Jack about Rix.

I stretched contentedly. It was Saturday, and the only thing I had to do all day was meet Martha at a vintage clothing store in Palo Alto so we could look for authentic fifties costume ideas. At least, that's what she'd be doing. I would be ever-so-subtly digging for information about Brian, my directorial predecessor and her missing boyfriend. What I had heard from the Rep staff had convinced me that there was something fishy about him, and I figured anything fishy should be examined for connections to Macbeth.

But that wasn't until the afternoon. I had the whole morning ahead of me. And the sound of the shower told me Jack hadn't gone off to the gym.

I had a clear conscience and a clean husband. Life was good. It was even better after I joined Jack in the shower.

"How long until you're ready?" Jack asked later, toweling me off in a way I found pretty. fabulous.

"Again?" I asked. "What kind of superman are you?"

He chucked the towel at me. "Ready to go to lunch, you maniac." He walked away, and I was a little preoccupied by the way the few remaining drops of water sparkled on his butt, so it took me a minute to realize what he'd said.

"Lunch where? Do we have lunch plans?"

"We're meeting Mike."

"Who?"

He stuck his head back in the room. "Didn't I mention it?" He vanished again.

"You know damn well you didn't mention it!" I wrapped the towel around myself and marched into the bedroom. "Mike?"

"He's my best friend, Pumpkin." Jack sat on the bed in a pair of jeans, one shoe in his hand. "I really want you to get to know him better."

I sat next to him. "Do I have to get to know him today?"

"You're going to Palo Alto anyway, right?" He nudged me. "And it's just one little lunch."

I nudged him back. "I suppose it is just one little lunch."

"Good."

"But I don't have to like him."

"Understood."

We made a striking group as we crossed the lobby and waited for the valet to bring Harry's SUV (now apparently on permanent loan) from the garage. Jack, looking perfect as usual, me, looking a little sulky but cool, and Flank, looking like a balding silverback gorilla who'd been captured in the Virunga mountains and forced into a Brooks Brothers suit.

Palo Alto had spent most of its existence happy just to be called the home of Stanford University. Quiet, tree-lined streets named after poets crossed the central thoroughfare, University Avenue, which was occupied by bookstores, movie theaters, and student-oriented restaurants.

But sometime in the eighties the unassuming town had become ground zero for the digital revolution. Now, even after the dot.com bubble had burst, it's impossible to parallel park without grazing the khaki-clad ass of a venture capitalist or denting the fender of a twenty-five-year-old entrepreneurial genius. At least that's how it seems.

We met Mike at Zibibbo, a relatively upscale restaurant off University. After passing through an open-air space with a fountain and olive trees that served as both the entrance and bar seating, the place turned into one of those lots-of-blond-wood, funky-lighting-fixtures, whimsical-cocktail-glasses kinds of scenes where the digerati like to hang out. If I hadn't still been full from the previous night's dining excess, I might have gotten more enthusiastic about the menu. If we hadn't been meeting Mike I would have loved the place.

Flank took a position at the "one for lunch" counter that faced the exhibition kitchen and watched us as we were led to a table against the back wall.

"Who's your friend?" Mike asked, nodding his head in Flank's direction.

"Your replacement," I said.

"Oh." He slid into his seat. "Um, look, Charley, about that—"

"Never mind." I waved dismissively.

"No, really," he insisted. "I want you to know I really wasn't spying on you. I was just watching your back. Really."

"Right," I said agreeably. "But now my back and I are happy to report that we are no longer in need of your services."

Mike looked uncertainly at Jack, who must have made a "just drop it" face, because he did.

"So, what's good here?" Jack asked enthusiastically.

I sighed and decided to act like an adult. We ordered a bunch of small plates to share: olives, a cheese assortment with hazelnut crackers and honey, roasted eggplant with pine nuts, marinated mushrooms, an heirloom tomato salad, and lots of crusty rustic bread to accompany it all.

What amazed me was how Jack and Mike were able to act so perfectly normal—as if they weren't spending all their waking hours trying to track down any possibility that an imprisoned former colleague might be waging some sort of war of retribution against us. But no, the conversation was all about Mike's computer-security company. I had wondered if that had been some sort of cover story, but they both seemed serious about it. Apparently, Mike was "retired" too. And, after all, I supposed a crowded restaurant was no place to compare notes on the activities of a certain traitorous ex-spy currently code-named Macbeth.

Mike, despite the whole spying-on-me thing—which really did call into question his undercover skills—wasn't so bad. When he spoke about technology and computer code, all of the "um's" and "uh's" that peppered his ordinary speech vanished. I decided the guy was just poorly socialized. And there was a cure for that.

He also seemed to have a good business head. At least it sounded that way to me—he said things like "intellectual property" and "market capitalization." I wondered if I should put him together in a room with Eileen and see what happened.

"So, Mike," I said, inserting myself into a lull in the conversation. "Do you have a girlfriend?"

He choked on a mushroom and, I swear, blushed. "Um, a girlfriend?"

I nodded encouragingly. "You know, like someone to go to movies with. That sort of thing."

"He knows what a girlfriend is, Charley," Jack said dryly. "At least in theory."

Mike had recovered enough to protest. "I've had girlfriends!"

"But at the moment . . ." I pursued.

He tried to sound casual. "At the moment, I'm, uh, between relationships." He actually looked proud of the way he'd put it.

"Really?" I sounded fascinated. "Because I have this friend—"

"Pumpkin, I really don't think—"

"And I think you might like her," I finished.

Mike got that trapped male look so common among unmarried nerds of a certain age.

"Charley, why don't you tell Mike about your new job?" Jack said.

I looked at him like he was insane. "My new job?"

"You know, at the theater . . ." he gave a very leading emphasis to the last word.

"The theater?" I repeated. "I'm directing a play," I told Mike, shooting Jack a "where are we going with this?" look. "We just finished casting."

Jack grinned. "Tell him about the actress."

"The actress? Oh, right, she's . . ." And then I saw it. "Regan?"

"Her name's Regan," Jack told Mike. "And Charley says she's drop-dead gorgeous."

"I don't think those were my exact words," I said. "And in any case, I was thinking of Eileen."

Jack shook his head. "Eileen's great, but Regan . . ." He endowed her name with untold sexual possibilities.

"Regan?" Mike asked. "An actress?" He looked at me. "You, um, think she'd like me?"

I looked at Jack, then at Mike. Right. If that's the way they wanted it.

"You know," I said, "I think we should have a dinner party. Don't you think so, Jack?"

"I think so."

"And that way"—I brushed some crumbs away—"everybody can get to know everybody." I smiled at Mike.

He grinned nervously. "Sounds good."

And I could seat him next to Eileen.

After a while I glanced at my watch and realized it was time to go meet Martha. Ugh. Now that I'd mellowed over lunch I really wasn't looking forward to providing a sympathetic ear to her tale of a broken heart. But, if that was how I could find out more about Brian . . .

"Right." I turned to Jack. "You guys are going to the office?"

He nodded. "And you're going costume shopping?" I nodded.

"And what aren't you going to do?" he asked.

I looked over at the counter, where a large pile of dishes cluttered space in front of my bodyguard. "I'm not going to ditch Flank."

I was reaching for my purse as a shadow fell across the table. I looked up expecting to see the waiter, and got a nasty shock.

"Inspector Yahata."

The detective stood before us, a pristine figure in a fawn linen suit. He looked brightly from me to Jack. "Mrs. Fairfax, Mr. Fairfax. How fortunate. I was planning to see you later today." He gave Mike one of those politely quizzical looks that usually sear through my flesh. "I don't believe we've met."

"This is Mike Papas, Inspector," Jack said. "He's an old friend of mine."

"Ah." The detective produced a microscopic smile.

"Um, hi," Mike offered.

"Why were you planning on seeing us today?" I asked. I didn't add "as if we believe you're here by coincidence."

"I have a few questions."

I waited for the notebook and pen to materialize, but they didn't. Did that mean this was off the record?

"Inspector, please join us," Jack offered.

Another slight smile. "Thank you, no." Of course not. Sitting might put a crease in his suit. "But as long as I have you here . . ." He targeted me with his gaze. "Mrs. Fairfax, we have learned that the man your cousin knew as Tom Nelson was an actor."

He waited for my reaction, which I suppose was something between shocked and stunned. Then he went on. "He was hired for what he was told would be a new reality television series—*How to Marry an Heiress*."

My jaw dropped.

Yahata continued. "He believed he was playing a part, and that his seduction of your cousin was being filmed by hidden cameras."

"That's insane."

The detective granted me a barely perceptible shrug. "Nevertheless."

"Inspector," Jack said. "Do you know who hired him?"

Yahata flicked his glance toward Jack. "As with the mercenaries, that remains the critical and unanswered question." He turned back to me. "And the one on which I hoped Mrs. Fairfax might be able to shed some light."

"Me?" I squeaked.

"As someone who has, herself, hired actors."

Jack spoke. "If you're implying—"

"I imply nothing." The detective showed a flash of impatience. "I merely enquire of someone with greater experience in the matter than I."

I put a hand on Jack's arm. "Inspector, what would you like to know?"

"Thank you." He focused on me. "In your opinion, is it credible that an actor would quit his job, leave his apartment, and check himself into a drug rehabilitation center with the goal of achieving a romantic conquest over a woman he has never met, based solely on one phone call?"

"What was his job?"

"Waiting tables."

"Did he live alone?"

"He had four roommates."

"What was his last acting job?"

"A local pet store commercial eight months ago."

I have to admit, firing questions off at the inspector felt good. And the answer was obvious. "He'd have done it in a heartbeat."

The inspector's shoulders descended a millimeter, which I assumed was his version of slumping in disappointment.

"Based on one phone call?" Jack was skeptical.

"He was told a contract and a check were in the mail," the inspector informed us.

I grinned. "Oh, well, if the check was in the *mail* . . ."

But I could tell they still didn't believe me. I sighed. "Look, actors live on dreams. When it comes to telling them they're about to be rich and famous, they're the most gullible people in the world." I shrugged. "If they were sensible, they'd be doing something sensible with their lives." Like producing. "Now, if that's all, I need to go shopping."

The inspector inclined his head, which I interpreted as "Yes, thanks, you've been so helpful. Have a good time." I gave Jack a peck on the cheek, picked up Flank at the bar, and left Yahata in the company of my husband and his Navy buddy.

*   *   *

We walked to a shop called Trappings in Time, only a few blocks from the restaurant. Flank followed three steps behind me and I tried to ignore him.

The store was small, and filled to bursting with clothes from the twenties through the seventies. Above the racks of dresses, suits, evening gowns, and lounging pajamas were shelves displaying hats, purses, scarves, gloves, and any manner of vintage accessories. There was fringe everywhere.

Martha was in the back, near a rack of highly painful-looking underthings. She was wearing her standard knitwear layers. Today's ensemble was in shades of gray—a long straight skirt and a gray funnel-necked sweater accented by a long gray-striped scarf. She had pulled her hair into a knot on the top of her head, then jelled the ends into spikes that stuck out at odd angles, rather like the Statue of Liberty's crown. Her eyes were rimmed with black liner and her lips had vanished under a nude lipstick that perfectly matched her skin tone.

Anyone else would have looked like a lizard poking out of a steam pipe. Martha looked like the queen of another planet. And she was already hard at work.

"Okay," she briefed me. "We're mostly looking for the graduation dress for Regan in the first act, and whatever else we can find along the lines of housedresses for the mother or fabulous bowling shirts for Paul and the father." She waited for some sign of comprehension from me, then turned her back and began critically assessing a rack of what looked like ancient bridesmaid dresses.

Looking around, it seemed to me that we'd have had better luck if we were trying to costume a drag show set in 1973, but I followed Martha's example and started digging for gold. We were mainly looking for ideas and vintage pieces to deconstruct for patterns. Martha would use these as a jumping-off point and build the show's costumes based on them, but in a color palette integrated with the show's overall artistic design.

Although "fabulous" and "bowling shirts" didn't normally occur in the same sentence for me, I did manage to find a couple of men's shirts with what seemed to me to be a fifties sensibility. One was brown with a large raspberry-colored flamingo appliquéd on either side of the chest, and a logo for a drive-in in Ft. Lauderdale on the back. The other was white, with black sleeves and black silhouettes of bowling pins stitched randomly across the body. As if they'd just been hit by a ball. Clever.

While I was shopping, I was thinking about the conversation I'd just had with Inspector Yahata. Cece had told us that Tom Nelson had only appeared at her rehab clinic two weeks before she'd been released, but that he'd left the program at the same time she had. Once out of the clinic, they'd set up house together. So, including the time in rehab, they'd been together for almost a month before the kidnapping. Could an actor really stay in character that long? Especially without getting any direction? And without a script? It didn't seem likely. No, the more I thought about it, the more I was convinced that, even if the actor had uprooted himself and gone after Cece based on one phone call, someone had to have been directing the show from the wings. And that someone had to be Macbeth.

So, the way I saw it, we had to find out how Macbeth had communicated with the actor. If we could trace the communication back to Macbeth, we'd be able to prove that Jack's ex-colleague was behind Cece's kidnapping.

I had to talk to Jack. I turned to make some excuse to Martha, and gaped at the gorgeous gown she was holding triumphantly. "Look!" she demanded.

"It's amazing," I admitted. "Beautiful." It dawned on me that even if I did abandon Martha, I didn't know where Jack was. They'd have left the restaurant by now, and I had no idea where Mike's company was.

"It's a private label," Martha said. "But obviously modeled on a Dior."

"Obviously." Damn. I'd have to wait to talk to Jack.

So I might as well focus on why I was talking to Martha anyway—to get information about Brian. Even though I still wasn't sure where his disappearance fit into things.

Martha was caught up in examining the dress. It was strapless with a tight bodice and full skirt, made of a pale pink satin with an overlay of black lace. It looked like something Elizabeth Taylor would have worn in *A Place in the Sun*. It looked like something Anna, the lead character in our play, would have killed for.

"Wrap it up."

Martha came close to smiling. "And this, too, I think." She hung the gown and pulled out a "housedress." I hadn't really known what to expect, but immediately recognized something that looked like what Lucy and Ethel used to wear. It was a short-sleeve shirtwaist style dress in a soft shade of aqua, with cream polka dots and a cream detail at the neck and on the sleeves.

"Classic design," Martha pronounced. "What have you found for the boys?"

She nodded approvingly over both of my discoveries, and we made our way over to a wild-haired woman who was repairing a piece of lace behind the counter.

When the woman was ringing up our purchases, Martha slumped over the glass case and said, "Charley, come look at this."

I assumed she'd found an interesting piece of jewelry, but when I bent close to see what she was pointing at, she muttered "Don't look now, but I think we're being watched."

I had a momentary adrenalin surge, then glanced at the front door. Flank stood motionless on the sidewalk outside the store. He probably would have looked right at home outside a SOMA nightclub at one o'clock in the morning, but his station next to a rack of swimsuits that might have been worn by Dorothy Lamour didn't really work for him.

"Don't worry, he's with me."

Martha's eyes widened.

I patted her hand reassuringly. "Don't worry," I repeated. "He can carry the packages."

We loaded Flank down with shopping bags. "Do you mind?" Martha asked hesitantly, then backed away from him.

Flank grunted something that may have been "sure" and relapsed into stoic expressionlessness.

I cleared my throat. "Where to now?"

Martha jumped, then tore her eyes away from Flank. "Oh, the bridal gown place. It's just up and over a couple of blocks."

I was trying to figure out how to get the conversation onto Brian as we walked, when Martha gave me the perfect opening.

"Simon has some pretty firm ideas about how we should dress Paul, you know," she told me.

"I'll just bet he does," I said, remembering Simon's appreciation of our leading man's talents. "Let me guess, tight tee-shirts?"

"What else?"

"We'll see about that." Then it hit me. "Martha, what did Brian think about the costumes? Did you guys come to any decisions I should know about?"

Her step faltered and her face fell. It was a good thing she'd decided on a theatrical career that didn't involve acting.

"Martha? Sweetie? Are you all right?"

She looked down at her feet.

"Martha," I said, in as big-sister a way as I knew how, "were you and Brian involved?"

She looked startled. "How did you know?"

"I'm very perceptive," I assured her. "I'm sure nobody else has a clue." Nobody who was blind and deaf, anyway.

She covered her mouth with her hands. "Oh, Charley, I just don't understand. I can't believe it was all lies. I can't believe he'd just run out like that, with no word, no note, nothing."

"He hasn't contacted you since he left?" I asked.

"Nothing!" she wailed. "Not one word. After all we . . . after everything he . . ."

I put my arm around her. "Shhh, sweetie, it'll be all right."

But it wouldn't. Because either Brian had been a jerk who'd forgotten her the minute she was out of sight, or—if he had worked for Macbeth—he'd never been who he said he was in the first place. I wondered which of those possibilities I'd prefer if I were in Martha's boots.

"Martha, he didn't leave you a note?" I asked.

"No!" she cried. "Nothing!" She wiped her face, leaving streaks of eyeliner.

A thought occurred to me. "Had he ever given you a note?"

She looked at me, curiosity behind her damp eyes. "Why?"

"I wondered if you'd recognize his handwriting. Did you see the note he left for Simon?"

She shook her head.

We turned right, heading back toward University, and I was insensitive enough to notice a lingerie store with some gorgeous lacy things in the window.

"Charley," Martha said hesitantly. "I would recognize his writing."

"Oh." I tried to think how best to say it. "Then maybe you should take a look at the note he left Simon."

She grabbed my arm. "Do you think something happened to him? Do you think he didn't just leave like that? Do you think someone else wrote the note?"

I couldn't tell if she was frightened or relieved at the prospect. "All I think right now is that it's pretty strange he hasn't contacted you. So it wouldn't hurt for you to take a look at the note he left."

Of course, she might be so eager to believe Brian's farewell had been forged that she'd say just that when she saw it.

"Martha, do you still have anything Brian wrote to you?"

She sniffed. "I did until the other night." She made an effort to collect herself. "It isn't true, you know, what Chip and Paris were saying. Brian wasn't unprofessional, he was just so insecure. This job meant everything to him. He said it was a huge break. He was terrified of messing up somehow."

Interesting. For someone with the experience Brian had claimed to have, it didn't seem like directing at our Rep company would be that big of a break. Maybe he had lied about his past only to land a job that was beyond his qualifications. But if that were the case, it seemed unlikely that he'd have been whisked away by a fabulous offer from Broadway.

I sighed. "What do you mean, you had the notes until the other night?"

Martha hesitated again. "Well, do you know the Psychic Eye?"

I knew it was a New Age sort of bookstore that had on-site Tarot card readers and did something of a business in occult supplies. San Francisco is that kind of town.

"The bookstore, right?"

"Right. Well, I went to get my cards read after I left you guys at the bar the other night."

"Uh-huh . . ." I encouraged.

"And while I was there I bought a candle."

"Okay . . ."

"It was a special candle." She looked at me nervously. "You know? A ritual candle. A Wicca candle."

"I can imagine." Was Martha telling me she was a witch? A Wicca practitioner? A witch?

She was. "I'm not very experienced with performing rituals. I haven't been practicing Wicca very long, and this was . . . difficult for me emotionally. But I had to do something when Brian just left like that."

"Of course you did." My costume designer was a witch. Several questions presented themselves, but I tried to stay focused on the important ones. "So, when you used this candle . . ."

Martha nodded eagerly, apparently relieved that I hadn't started calling for the villagers to burn her at the stake. "I threw all of Brian's notes into the flames."

"Was that some sort of a spell?" I tried to keep my voice nonjudgmental. I don't think I quite got it.

She winced. "A ritual. To bring him back."

Wow.

"Has it worked?"

She looked at me sharply. "It was only the day before yesterday."

"Of course." Right. Presumably there was a scarcity of fast-acting rituals to bring back errant boyfriends.

"Is this the store?" I asked. We were in front of a shop called Ages Ahead that had a window filled with vintage wedding gowns.

Martha took one look at the window display and burst into tears. "Oh, Charley!" She put her head on my shoulder and I put my arms around her, giving her back little pats.

"There, there, sweetie. It'll be all right. You'll hear from him."

But, magic rituals notwithstanding, I didn't think she would.

Chapter 19

"You think she's a witch?" Jack asked.

"Oh, I know she is," I nodded. "She told me all about it."

"A witch?" He seemed the slightest bit doubtful.

"A practitioner of Wicca. A Wiccan. Yep. She cast a spell to bring Brian back."

Once we'd established that Martha wasn't up to looking at vintage wedding clothes, I'd whisked her off to the nearest bar and she'd told me everything. Not only about the whole Wicca business, but excruciating detail about every tender thing Brian had ever said or done. Then she'd cried some more and Flank had taken us home, Martha to her loft in Hayes Valley and me to the hotel, where I couldn't wait to tell Jack everything.

"Wow."

"That's just what I thought," I told him.

"I have no other response."

Jack was helping me to get over my skittishness about the bathtub, a natural-enough response to finding a dead body in one, by sitting on the edge of the tub and occasionally splashing me while I soaked in a cloud of steamy bubbles.

"What do you think about Brian?" I asked him.

His forehead creased. "It's weird. It's one more weird thing."

"Paris and Chip think Brian didn't have a clue about what he was supposed to be doing and was just faking his way through the job. But Martha, who's admittedly biased, thinks he was brilliant and just needed the chance to prove it." I loofahed my legs reflectively. "But it really doesn't matter which of them is right."

"Why not?" Jack watched the movement of the sponge with interest.

"Because Broadway doesn't just call some guy in San Francisco who lied on his resumé and tell him to pack his bags and catch the next plane."

"Mmm." I couldn't tell if that indicated Jack's agreement with me or his increasing level of concentration on splashing away some of the more strategically placed bubbles remaining in the bath.

"Anyway"—I thought I'd try to use Jack's distraction to my advantage—"did you and Mike have fun with Inspector Yahata after I left?"

"He stayed for a while."

"Jack, I think I should call him."

"You haven't shot anyone, have you?"

"I wish you'd stop saying that." I gave him an expert splash, which he took like a man. "No, I was just thinking about that actor who romanced Cece, and I really don't think he could have gone for a month without some sort of direction."

"Oh, well, you left too early. We heard all about that." Jack reached for a towel. "Tom Nelson—that's his real name—was sent a digital video camera and instructed to keep a secret video journal and upload all the files to a Web site whenever he could."

"That sounds like something they'd do on a TV reality show," I admitted. "But could he do that from rehab?"

"He got to leave the clinic twice a week, and he used an Internet café to send in the files. The next time he checked the Web site, there would be instructions for him, based on what he'd said on the video. That's how he found out he was supposed to pretend to have a house in Marin and ask Cece to move in with him."

"So he did have someone coaching him from the outside." I shivered despite the heat of the water. "Arranging everything."

"And once they were out of the clinic, and Nelson had access to a computer from home, the communication was daily."

"Until the kidnapping."

"Right. Nelson's story is that he was instructed to propose to Cece on a certain day. If she accepted, the show would be over, and he would win a million dollars. Then the producers would appear and tell her it had all been a game. If she still wanted to marry him after she found out about the TV show, he'd win her and her whole fortune."

"I bet they didn't tell him her fortune includes Harry."

Jack grinned. "Anyway, that's how they got rid of him. He proposed, and Cece accepted—"

"She what?" I sat up, sending bubbles flying everywhere. "What kind of a—"

"So anyway"—Jack wiped a fleck of scented foam from his face—"Nelson had been told to leave her alone in the house after the proposal. He thought the TV crew would show up after he left."

"And instead the kidnappers did."

Jack nodded.

"And let me guess—when Tom Nelson checked the Web site, he was told Cece said she never wanted to see him again."

"Right. So he believed he'd lost the game and he went back home and he's just been waiting for the show to be on TV and make him a star."

"And the Web site he used?"

"Gone."

I'd said it a lot that day. "Wow."

Since Jack was in such a talkative mood, I decided to press him for information. "I don't suppose you told Inspector Yahata about your buddy Macbeth?" I reached for a towel.

Jack grimaced. "He knows we're not telling him everything, and I think it's driving him a little nuts."

"Probably." I stood and wrapped myself in the towel, not without enjoying an appreciative glance from my husband. "But I don't suppose it matters. I mean, it's not like you have anything concrete to tell him about Macbeth." I attempted an elaborately casual tone. "Do you?"

Jack shot me a focused look. "I thought you'd never ask."

"What?" I splashed my way out of the tub. "What have you found out about Macbeth? Is he doing all of this from prison? Could he have hired Tom Nelson? Or Brian?"

"No."

Something in his tone chilled me, despite the steamy room. "I'm getting a very bad feeling here."

"It's been next to impossible to find anything out," Jack explained. "Even for Mike, and he can usually get in anywhere—" He stopped himself before he said anything more. "But this morning he found out why all the information on Macbeth had been sealed up."

Somehow I knew. I forced myself to say the words. "He's dead."

Jack nodded briefly. "He killed himself. Six weeks ago."

Our eyes met. We were back to square one.

We stayed up for hours trying to figure out what to do next. Jack told me that Mike was hard at work attempting to learn the details of Macbeth's death, but it was only the suicide ruling they doubted, not the actual death.

"I just can't accept that he'd kill himself," Jack explained. "Particularly if he was behind setting Cece up and that woman in the tub. He wouldn't just leave it all unfinished."

"But it wasn't unfinished," I pointed out. "Someone finished it."

Jack gave me a meaningful look. "If Macbeth is—or was—behind all of this, it isn't finished yet."

"Jack, why are you so convinced it's related to him? I mean, it was my cousin who was kidnapped, and it's a director from my theater· who's gone missing, and that woman's body was left in a hotel room booked under my. name. Suppose this isn't about you? Suppose it's about me?"

He stopped pacing for a moment to look at me with a frown. "I have thought about that. Everything has been directed against you, but the way it's all been carried out sends a message explicitly for me."

"From a dead man?"

Jack blew out a deep breath and sat down. For once in my life I shut up and let him think. I was rewarded for my uncharacteristic patience when he spoke. "When I found out Macbeth had been selling us out," he began, "we were in the middle of a . . . project."

I bit my tongue and waited for more.

"The tactics used by Cece's kidnappers—the identical clothes and masks, the instructions on typed paper, everything—was what we'd been doing. How we'd been operating when we—" He stopped.

When he what? When he'd been working undercover? Had he kidnapped someone? I probably wasn't going to find out. I wasn't sure I wanted to find out.

"And the way Tom Nelson met Cece," he continued. "The way he manipulated her—it's classic Macbeth."

"It's classic schmuck," I countered. "If every guy who lied about being a doctor—"

"Charley," Jack spoke quietly. "There's something else."

Not good news, I was willing to bet.

"It was because of a woman that I found out what Macbeth was doing. She told me about it. She betrayed him."

I knew by now that any questions I had about what Macbeth was doing would go unanswered. So I asked the other obvious question. "What woman? Where is she now?"

"She's dead." Jack's tone was flat. "I found her the day Macbeth was arrested."

"Don't say it." But I knew. And I had to say it. "She was in a bathtub."

He met my eyes. "She was his wife."

I took a minute to wait for the room to stop spinning. "Right," I said, my voice cracking. "So I guess this is about you."

I spent Sunday in bed with the covers over my head, but Monday morning I had a plan. Not a plan to figure out who had assumed Macbeth's tactics in order to terrorize the people around me and torture my husband, but a plan nevertheless.

First, I had figured out how I would explain Flank's presence at the theater. I would tell people he was my personal trainer and a sort of food watchdog. The trainer bit was entirely believable, given the man's physique. The watchdog thing would account for him going everywhere with me. I'd tell people it was Flank's job to knock doughnuts out of my hands and force broccoli down my throat. Presumably that's what trainers did. It was a stretch, but it sounded better than telling a roomful of actors that I might be in danger, and that by association they might be in danger, and the only thing between them and a homicidal maniac might be the oversized gentleman in the balcony.

Part two of the plan was to make Chip my assistant director. He was obviously ready for the job. If I was totally honest with myself I would have to admit that he was more qualified to direct the play than I was. I looked guiltily at the script that I'd managed to ignore since Thursday, even though I'd vowed to study it before the first read-through, scheduled to begin at eleven o'clock.

But I also had a much more selfish reason. With

Chip as my AD, I'd be able to delegate a lot of work, which would leave more time for figuring out what had really happened to Brian, why Rix was meddling in my theater, and whether either was connected to the dead woman in the tub or Cece's kidnapping.

Of course, I wouldn't tell my husband any of this. He'd made it very clear that he and Mike were still handling any investigations. They'd already started checking out all of Macbeth's former associates, but I figured if I approached the puzzle from the other end, they'd never have to know about it until I found some crucial piece of information. And then it would be too late for them to be angry.

So I smiled innocently at Jack when he emerged from the bedroom. "Just to let you know—I'm brilliant."

"I already knew that. I have something for you." He was holding a shopping bag, which he placed on the table in front of me.

"Not another gun?" I eyed the bag suspiciously.

"Open it."

A cell phone. "Oh. Thank you."

"Try not to lose this one," he suggested. "There's something else."

It was one of those tiny electronic organizers that everybody seems to have these days. I regarded it suspiciously. "Do I have to learn some weird way of writing?"

"You'll manage. You're brilliant, remember?"

I flipped the cover open and turned it on. "There's stuff already in it." I looked up at Jack.

"I filled in the address book with everyone I could think of," he said.

"When did you have time to do that?"

He grinned. "You sleep a lot. I also put a few things on your to-do list."

I pushed the button that looked like a list. The first item to appear said "Screw your husband senseless." I gave him a sideways look.

"That one's set up to appear daily."

" 'Cuz otherwise I might forget," I nodded.

The next item said "Call Realtor." I turned the thing off and shut the cover. "It's great, Jack. Thanks." I slipped the two gadgets into my purse, which was getting unfashionably bulky, and grabbed the script. "I'd better get going if I don't want to be late for the read-through." I opened the door and crashed directly into Flank. God only knew how long he'd been standing in the hallway.

"Have a nice day, dear," Jack called after me. There was more than a touch of mockery in his voice.

I walked to the theater at a brisk pace. I figured if I was going to pass Flank off as my trainer I should make an effort to look like I exercised occasionally. I knew how demanding the rehearsal schedule would be, and that it would leave no time for indulgences like long runs along the waterfront. We only had six weeks to pull the show together. That would include all the time for rehearsals, technical run-throughs, building the sets, creating the costumes, and a thousand other things.

I got to the theater early, counting on the assumption that Chip would be there before anyone else. I was right. He was heartbreakingly naïve about the new position. He worried that he wouldn't be up to the job. He promised earnestly that he would justify my faith in him. And even though he was leaving the union protection of his current position, he didn't ask about a pay raise.

He did ask whether he could promote Lisa, his assistant, to replace himself as stage manager. Although I'd seen her around, I hadn't actually met the woman yet.

"She's up to it?" I asked him.

"She's amazing," he assured me.

"Go for it." If only everything could be that easy.

The cast started filing in around ten thirty. Because the Rep owned the building outright, we didn't use the kinds of rental rehearsal spaces other companies had to deal with. We'd be able to hold all rehearsals right in the theater. Chip had stopped for muffins on his way and made coffee before anybody else arrived. As expected, people began congregating around the food as they came in.

A large table had been set up center-stage. The first read-through of a play was often grueling. The actors all sit around the table with their scripts in front of them and simply read the play. It sounds easy enough, but it was the first real work the cast would do together, and egos would be at their most fragile.

We would need the whole cast to be present. A few minutes before we were scheduled to start I came down from the office, sent Flank up to the balcony, and assessed the situation.

Regan was there, looking ready to get to work in comfortable jeans and a long-sleeved T-shirt. Her hair was in a simple ponytail and she wore no discernable make up, but she was still, in Jack's vernacular, dropdead gorgeous. She also seemed a little nervous, a fact which I noted with some satisfaction. Thankfully, today she had no escort.

Two of our regulars, actors we'd cast in several productions in the past, played the parts of the parents. Olivia Hamilton was the mother. Hearing her voice come belting across the stage, I figured she would need to have her standard direction reiterated. Tone it down, Olivia. Not quite so far over the top, Olivia. But she learned her lines quickly, and was generous with the other actors.

Victor Swartz would play the father. Victor, I knew, was capable of brilliant moments on the stage, but he wasn't the most dependable of performers. He had a hard time getting his lines, and tended to blame those actors around him for his inadequacies. Once he got it, he'd be letter-perfect. But getting him to that point, I knew, would take patience and hard work.

The tomboy little sister was played by Sally Carter. At twelve, she already had more experience than some actors get in a lifetime. She'd danced in a Gap ad, played with a golden retriever for an allergy medicine, and eaten french fries for a major fast-food chain. Knowing her mother, I felt confident Sally would cause no serious problems during the production and, honestly, that's about all you can hope for in a twelve-year-old.

I noticed with a flicker of annoyance that Paul Collins, the "dishy" Paul, hadn't shown up yet. Although he didn't have any lines until the second act, everyone was expected to participate in the full read-through. I didn't care how fabulous Simon thought the guy looked in tight clothes, he wouldn't be exempted from the rules. There was a stand-in waiting in the proverbial wings, and I wouldn't hesitate to use him if I had to.

I looked around. Paris and his master carpenter were going over some drawings at the far rear of the stage. In the shadows of the wings stage left, Martha was murmuring quietly to her head stitcher and tailor, the three of them looking with professional, critical eyes at the bodies they'd be dressing over the next few weeks. I tried to refrain from thinking they looked like a trio of witches, muttering incantations.

Chip was with his serious-looking assistant in the first row of the orchestra seats. They were talking intently, presumably about her new duties as stage manager. If she was half as capable as Chip, things would be fine.

Looking at her closely, I realized she was older than Chip—at least in her late thirties. Her sleeveless shirt revealed the kind of defined arms I would have killed for. This woman was no stranger to the gym. She looked up suddenly, directly at me. I jumped as if I were guilty of something other than over-burdening her boss. Then she gave me a confident smile.

Chip followed her gaze and waved me over. "Charley, come meet Lisa."

I went to the edge of the stage and crouched down to shake hands with the woman. "I hope Chip's letting you know the full range of insanity you'll be dealing with as stage manager."

She grinned. "I live for insanity."

"Then I'm sure you'll be great."

"Thanks, Charley. I won't let you down."

The only other person I had expected to show up was the play's author, Nancy Tyler. I was surprised she hadn't arrived yet. I imagined it would be pretty exciting for an author to see her work come to life for the first time. I also wanted to meet her for my own sake. I'd worked on so many plays whose authors had been dead for several hundred years, I was looking forward to collaborating with a live one on this production.

I was catching up with Olivia and keeping an eye on the stage door when I saw Simon come in. He looked like he hadn't slept since I'd seen him five days before. He glanced around the stage wildly, saw me, and headed straight over.

"Olivia, darling, how nice to see you again," he said automatically. Then, "Charley, a word if I may." He grabbed my arm and pulled me toward the stairs that led up to the office.

"Simon," I gasped as he dashed up the stairway, still holding my arm, "didn't we play this scene before? If you're going to tell me that another of my ex-lovers is about to walk through the door, I really don't think I can take it."

He remained tight-lipped until we got to the office, where he closed the door, released me onto the battered couch, and stood, hands on hips, towering over me.

"Charley, what's going on?"

I was completely baffled. "Well, for one thing, we're about to be late starting the read-through."

He let his breath out impatiently, running a hand through his already-disheveled hair. "Don't kid me, Charley. When you left the pub the other night Eileen was manic with worry. I thought she'd gone mad until she told me about your cousin being kidnapped and you and Brenda chasing after her and getting caught, and Jack getting shot and . . . bloody hell, Charley!"

"Oh, look, Simon, I would have told you about all that, but—"

At that moment the door burst off its hinges and Flank filled the doorway, then filled the room as he grabbed Simon and threw him against the brick wall, holding his arms behind him.

Simon, understandably, screamed. I screamed. Flank hollered something unintelligible and held Simon's arms tighter.

"Let him go!" I shouted, banging on Flank's arm with my fist. "Let go of him! He wasn't hurting me!"

Flank released Simon with evident reluctance. I think he said "Sure?"

"I'm sure," I said. "Look, I should have given you some signal that it was all right for him to pull me away like that."

Flank grunted in agreement.

"In the future I'll wave at you if I need your assistance, okay?"

Another grunt, possibly in assent.

"Now please put the door back on its hinges and wait outside, all right?"

He gave Simon one last look, then picked up the door and, from the hallway, propped it back into position.

Simon was rubbing his elbows eloquently. "What," he asked, sitting cautiously on the couch, "the bloody hell"—he winced as I sat next to him—"is going on?"

"Oh, sweetie." I reached out to touch his arm, but thought better of it when I saw the look in his eye. "I'm sorry. It's just that Jack, after the whole thing with Cece, got worried about me."

Simon looked pointedly at the door, then back at me.

I nodded. "So he hired that guy to watch after me until we find the person who kidnapped Cece."

It was an abbreviated version of the truth, at best, but I though Simon deserved more than the "oh, he's my personal trainer" line I'd prepared.

Simon closed his eyes and leaned back into the

cushions. "You're so buying me a massage after rehearsal tonight."

"I promise," I said. "At your favorite spa."

I waited a moment in silence.

"Do you think we should go downstairs now? I think everyone is here except for Paul—"

Simon's eyes flew open and he jumped back to his feet. "Seriously? Is she here? Nancy? Did she show up?"

Nancy? Had we cast a Nancy? "Oh!" I got it. "The author!"

His head bobbed impatiently. "She's here?"

"No."

He sagged down into the chair.

"Simon, what's the matter? Did you talk to her this weekend? Did she have a conflict—"

"She wasn't home," he said dismally. "I left her a message."

That didn't seem to warrant his current level of depression. "Well, maybe she got the dates confused, or something came up, or—"

"That's not what the police think."

"Police? What police?"

"The ones who showed up on my doorstep this morning." He ran his hand through his hair again, not without some signs of stiffness from his experience with Flank. "They're investigating her disappearance. They heard my message and thought I might be able to shed some light."

The word "disappearance" seemed to echo in the room. Or maybe it was in my head.

"Disappearance?"

He nodded. "Her sister called the police after she hadn't heard from Nancy in a week. Gave them a story about Nancy having met the man of her dreams and apparently run off with him."

I gulped.

"So after what Eileen had said about Cece running off with some guy and winding up held hostage . . ."

Simon looked at me mournfully. "Charley, what's going on?"

"Charley?" We heard Chip's voice through the door. "What's going on?"

It seemed to be the question of the day.

"This guy won't let me in," Chip said, sounding more than a little irritated.

"Flank, let him in!" I shouted.

Beefy hands appeared on each side of the door, which was lifted away long enough to let Chip slide in.

"What are you two doing up here? Everyone's on-stage and ready. It's quarter past." He looked at us in exasperation.

"Has the author shown up?" I asked, with a faint flicker of hope.

"Not yet. We don't have to wait for her, do we?"

I looked at Simon. "We'd better not."

Chapter 20

I went down to the stage with Chip, after telling Flank to stay the hell up in the balcony unless I waved at him. Chip gave Flank a "who are you?" stare, but didn't ask.

Paul had shown up at the last possible moment, earning a frozen smile from his stand-in, and Simon joined us at the table onstage after a few minutes. He'd changed his shirt, brushed his hair, and splashed cold water in his face. "Hello, darlings!" he called in a general greeting and, for all the world knew, he was as exuberant as ever.

After air-kisses all around and a bout of introductions, we opened our manuscripts and the actors began to read.

I have to say my attention was divided. Now and then someone would make a statement or raise a point that would involve the whole group, and I'd find myself listening with interest, arguing for or against something, or telling them to move on. But more often I was turning the news about our playwright's disappearance over in my mind, exchanging furtive worried looks with Simon, and counting the minutes until I could tell Jack what I'd learned. On the bright side, Chip was off and running as my assistant director. At least someone was giving the script and cast his full, feverish attention.

I staggered out of the theater at nine that night. The read-through had dragged on until six, and then Chip had insisted on a point-by-point review with me. I was too tired to even regret that I hadn't found the time all day to pull Martha aside and get her opinion on the handwriting of Brian's purported farewell note.

I'd sent Simon off to the Kabuki Hot Springs in Japantown for a soak and a massage around eight. I felt it was the least I could do to make up for Flank's enthusiasm.

I was just about to ask that gentleman to hail us a cab when I saw Jack double-parked in front of the theater.

"Hey!" I waved and squeezed between two parked cars to knock on his passenger-side door.

The window slid down. "Excuse me, ma'am, but I'm looking for someplace nice and quiet to take my girl tonight."

I grinned. "Lucky girl."

He peered at me. "Forget her. What are you doing? You want to lose your buddy and run away with me?"

I looked over my shoulder, then back to my husband. "I could do that." I directed a shooing gesture toward Flank, climbed into the car, wrapped my arms around Jack's neck, and started to snore.

"Long day?" he guessed. He's very clever.

"How did you know when I'd be leaving? How long have you been here?"

He pulled out into the traffic with a frown on his face. "I called you."

"I know I'm tired, but I don't think I blacked out an entire conversation."

"I talked to Chip half an hour ago. He said your purse was ringing, so he picked it up."

"Oh." I sat back and buckled up.

"Oh?" Jack said frostily.

"What?"

He cleared his throat. "Charley, why didn't you hear the phone?"

I was baffled. "I guess I left my purse somewhere."

He nodded. "And where did you leave your gun?"

Oh.

"Charley, unless you want Flank to stand next to you every minute of the day—which I'd like, by the way—you have to promise to keep your gun within reach." He took his eyes off the road long enough to give me an I'm-totally-serious look.

"Okay," I said.

"Okay?"

"Okay. Where are you taking me for a nice, quiet dinner?"

He sighed in a god-give-me-strength sort of way. "Noodles?"

"Yum."

He headed for Mifune in Japantown, and it wasn't until I was steaming my face over a bowl of soba with big pieces of shrimp tempura floating on top that I remembered Simon was probably somewhere nearby.

Simon. "Oh!" I yelped. "I can't believe I haven't told you what Simon told me this morning. Jack—"

"Hang on a minute," Jack said, having slurped a mouthful of noodles in that effortless, completely dignified way that only the truly dedicated noodle-eaters of the world can master. "I need to tell you something, too."

I hated it when he sounded that serious. So far that tone of voice had only meant danger and disaster. "What?"

"Inspector Yahata called today."

I stopped swirling my noodles. "They've identified the woman? From the tub?"

He nodded.

"Who is it?" I asked. "Is there a connection?"

"Her name didn't sound familiar to me. I told Yahata I'd ask you. Does the name Nancy Tyler mean anything to you?"

I must have dropped my chopsticks because I heard what sounded like a very loud crash. I looked at Jack with a weird sort of tunnel-vision. Then I didn't see him at all. I only saw the pale face and lifeless eyes of a woman who'd written a beautiful play.

* * *

I honestly don't remember anything else until we were back at the hotel and Jack was pressing a glass of brandy into my hands. I sipped, then registered Jack's worried face. I gulped.

"Inspector Yahata is on his way," Jack told me.

I nodded and held out my empty glass. "We should probably call Simon, too."

They arrived within minutes of each other. Jack hadn't told Simon why he'd called, just that it was an emergency. Although he looked more like himself than when he'd left the theater, and smelled refreshingly of eucalyptus aromatherapy oils, the color drained completely from Simon's face when Inspector Yahata introduced himself.

"Bloody hell." He sank into the nearest chair. "What now?"

The detective lasered a look at me, which I took as an invitation to explain things. I told Simon about finding the dead woman on our first day back in town. "And now she's finally been identified," I said. "Simon, it was Nancy Tyler."

Simon let out a sort of strangled cry. He reached blindly for the drink Jack offered. "How?" he asked. "Why?"

The corners of Inspector Yahata's mouth went down infinitesimally. "How was with a combination of sedatives, first introduced in powder form with red wine—probably to disguise the taste. Following that, the fatal dose was administered by a hypodermic needle into the back of the right thigh." He held his notebook at the ready, but he didn't consult it. "Although the body was discovered nude"—he paused long enough for his eyes to flicker toward Simon—"there was no evidence of a sexual aspect to the crime."

"Good Lord," Simon whispered. "The poor woman. She was . . ." He turned to me. "I can't . . ."

I shook my head. I didn't trust myself to speak.

"Why, for God's sake?" Simon finally demanded. "Why would anyone kill her? And why leave her in a hotel bathtub?" His eyes widened. "Your hotel bathtub." He looked wildly from me to Jack. "You hadn't even met her yet. What possible reason . . ."

"Yes," the detective said, when it became clear Simon was incapable of finishing his sentence. "I was wondering about that myself." The air around him buzzed with the question.

Jack and I both knew exactly why Nancy had been left in our hotel room. But—given the fact that Jack was under some obligation not to go blabbing to the authorities about whatever clandestine operations he'd once been a part of—helping Inspector Yahata in his investigation was going to be a little tricky. Which is why I let Jack do the talking.

He was taking his time. When he finally spoke, I realized he was leading the detective in the direction I would have taken if I hadn't known about Jack's past.

"It appears as though someone is trying to terrify my wife," he stated. "This woman's death and Cece's kidnapping must be related in some way."

The detective raised his chin. "I'm not generally a believer in coincidences."

"The way Charley was set up to find the playwright's body," Jack continued. "It indicates the killer knew exactly when we were coming home, where we were staying—"

Yahata's personal electrical field began to crackle. "Who knew your travel plans?"

"Everybody." Simon sounded surprised that he'd answered. We all looked at him. "The party, remember, darling?" He bit his thumbnail. "Everyone from the Rep knew. Brenda, some people from Eileen's office . . ." His eyes wandered, then focused on the detective. "Lots of people."

Yahata turned briskly to me. "I'll need a full list."

I nodded with a sinking feeling. Taking the Inspector's focus off of Jack was going to be a full-time job.

The detective stayed a while longer, and he and Jack kept talking, but I had trouble focusing on the conversation. When Yahata had gone, and Simon had staggered down into a taxi, I finally let out my breath and gave the tears permission to come. But they didn't. Maybe I was still in shock.

Jack held me. "It's all my fault," I said eventually. "She's dead because of me."

"Shhhh," he whispered. "It's not your fault." Then, grimly, "It's mine."

The next day, early, I called Eileen. I knew, as the person who'd made our travel arrangements, she'd be on the top of Yahata's interrogation list. I told her all about Nancy Tyler.

It took her a surprisingly short time to start asking questions. "Did you know her?"

"No. I think Simon was the only one who actually met her in person."

"Really?" she said. "How did the police treat him? Do you think they suspect him?"

"Simon? Why would anyone suspect him?"

"Maybe I've just been married to too many lawyers, but I have the impression that it's not a bad idea to assume you're a suspect whenever you talk to the police."

"Don't be silly," I said. "In that case Jack and I are suspects—and you will be too, and so will everyone else who was at the homecoming party you threw for me."

"Maybe," Eileen said cautiously. "But Simon knew her, and none of the rest of us did."

"Oh, come on," I insisted. "Can you really imagine Simon murdering anyone?"

She thought about it. "Only if they got between him and a marked-down Armani at the Saks men's sale," she admitted. "So did they tell you why it took so long for them to identify the body?"

"Nobody realized she was missing," I said. "The only family she had was a sister. She thought Nancy had gone off with her new boyfriend, and she only got worried enough to call the police a couple of days ago when she went to Nancy's place and found her cat nearly starved to death."

"New boyfriend?"

"Yeah."

"Cece went off with her new boyfriend, too, and ended up held hostage."

"I know."

I heard a quick intake of breath. "Charley," Eileen said slowly, "when you had all those questions about that guy I was seeing, did you think he was the same one who kidnapped Cece?"

That was the problem with having a smart friend. "Um . . ."

"You did," she stated. There was a pause. "He might have been."

I've seen Eileen go through childbirth and four divorces. She doesn't get hysterical. The worse things get, the more she freezes into a big, calm, block of ice. About this time in the conversation she could have given the Titanic a nasty bump.

"Leenie? Are you all right?"

"Certainly," she said. "I'm simply taking a moment to absorb the fact that there appears to be a serial criminal, who has killed at least once, roaming freely around the city and targeting women connected to you. That's all."

Oh. That's all.

Chapter 21

The police were a constant presence at the theater for the first few days following the identification of our playwright's body. They questioned everybody. Judging by the number of interviews, they were especially interested in what Simon had to say. Although it could have just seemed that way to me because Eileen had suggested him as their favorite suspect. She quietly lined up a lawyer for him just in case.

As far as I could tell, the authorities had made no progress towards finding Nancy Tyler's killer. They speculated that the murderer might have sneaked into the suite behind a maid or a bellman who had delivered the assorted homecoming presents during the day, and done something to the lock in order to bring the body in unobserved some time later. Either that or he'd stolen a passkey. And she might have been only unconscious when he brought her to the room. She might have still been clothed. The fatal dose might have been injected somewhere else or right there in the tub. There were no clues.

Inspector Yahata finally made arrangements for us to view the tapes from the lobby security cameras, but they didn't show anyone suspicious. Jack and I spent an afternoon watching the grainy black-and-white images. People came and went in jerky motions, but Jack recognized no one, and I thought everyone looked equally sinister.

There was no security tape of our hallway. The camera that was supposed to film it had developed mechanical problems about an hour before we checked in. Like Yahata, I'm not a big believer in coincidences.

Flank was joined at the theater by three more bodyguards. My clever story about him being my personal trainer had never seen the light of day. After learning about the playwright's murder, the cast and crew were more than happy to accept the existence of a security force at the theater.

The next time I saw him, I told Inspector Yahata about Brian's disappearance. He listened with intense politeness but didn't seem terribly interested in pursuing the matter. I didn't blame him. I wasn't so sure there was anything suspicious about Brian's disappearance anymore. Eventually I'd gotten around to showing his resignation note to Martha, who'd admitted the possibility that the handwriting was her ex-boyfriend's hurried scrawl. Then she'd burst into tears and I'd had to send her home for some therapeutic time at her knitting machine. Or her cauldron. Whatever.

Nancy Tyler's sister flew the body back to Boston to be buried in the family plot. When I got in touch with her, to see if there was anything I could do, she asked if she and her husband could come see Nancy's play on opening night. Life went on.

After two weeks of rehearsals, I wanted to slap the entire cast. Olivia, playing the mother at top volume as a semihysterical neurotic attention-seeking bitch, wasn't acting. And Victor, although he played the father nicely, was clinging to his script like a life preserver.

When I'd coaxed him into going paperless for one tiny bit where he only had one line, he'd completely frozen, then, turning red under everyone's critical gaze, had hissed, "Line!" at Lisa. Her tone dripping with condescension, she'd given him the line, "Hello, Anna." Victor had stormed off to his dressing room, trailing a surprisingly versatile string of obscenities behind him. Lisa had looked from his retreating back to me and shrugged.

"I've heard worse," she said. I instantly labeled her a treasure.

I suspected Victor was drinking. And I suspected Paul, playing the love interest, was on drugs.

"Perhaps he's just excitable," Simon protested when I shared my thoughts with him. We were seated in the dark orchestra seats, comparing notes on the first run-through of Act One.

"Excitable? He sweated and twitched his way through three scenes this morning, then came back after a break absolutely fine." I scribbled furiously in the margin of my script. "A complete personality change in the space of a ten-minute break has got to scream drug use, don't you think?" That's the way it had always been with Cece, anyway.

"Assuming you're right, what should we do?" Simon asked.

"I don't know," I admitted. "I don't actually have proof he's on anything."

"Although that would explain the sleeves," Simon said reflectively.

"What sleeves?"

"I, ah, suggested to Martha that we might want to show a little bicep on the boy. Costume-wise, you know."

"Uh-huh." I knew.

"But she said he had tattoos. Not period, of course, so it was either sleeves or makeup, and sleeves are easier."

"And hide things like track marks," I said.

"Well, darling, what are we going to do?"

I thought about it, then sighed. "I think, for the first time in my life, I'm going to ask my cousin Cece for advice."

"Good Lord," he said. "I think I just saw a pig fly up to the balcony. Perhaps it was fleeing hell, which has just frozen over. Or—"

"Shut up and tell me about the advance ticket sales."

The news had been full of the story of the murdered playwright for a few days, and, in a sad commentary on our society, that had sold a lot of tickets. Although it had never been mentioned that I had discovered Nancy's body in my hotel room—I suspected Harry's influence had something to do with that omission—it had been repeatedly reported that a play written by the murdered woman was in production by the Rep. Curiosity being what it is, we were now close to sold out for the first few weeks of the run.

Which was scheduled to begin in exactly one month. Which accounted for the squeezed-accordion feeling I had in my chest most of the time.

"How are things with the rest of the cast?" Simon asked. "It's clear you loathe Olivia and Victor, and you think Paul's a junkie, but aside from that?"

I squinted at the stage, now blissfully free of actors. "Sally's fine when she's on, but she's a kid." I shrugged. "She gets bored waiting around so she goes looking for trouble."

"And," Simon's voice took on a reverent tone, "how is The Girl?"

"Regan?"

"The very one."

"She's . . ." I hated, absolutely hated, to say it. "She's great."

Simon patted my hand. "Don't worry, darling. I'm sure she's bad at something."

I'd gotten into the habit of walking to the theater in the mornings with Flank, and usually Jack picked me up at night. But he called around eight and said he and Mike were going to work late, so Flank would drive me home. The staff of bodyguards may have increased, but Flank was still pretty much stuck to me. At least it cut down on the conversational burden.

I was too tired to think straight when I got back to

the hotel. I curled up on the sofa, considered ordering room service, and worried about Jack.

He'd been spending most of his time with Mike, and if anyone asked I told them he was working on the business plan for the computer start-up. Of course that was a lie. He and Mike were hunting for the killer.

Jack remained the irritatingly strong and silent type when it came to the investigation. At first I expected him to come home any day announcing he'd captured the killer and made the world safe again—or at least as safe as it had ever been. But no announcements were forthcoming. It was maddening how little he told me about it all. I'd come to expect only a few frustrated words now and then, followed by a quick change of subject.

As time went on, I became more and more convinced the truth was they'd found nothing. Which meant, once again, that the killer would have to find us.

I must have fallen asleep because Jack woke me up when he unlocked the hotel door.

"Sorry, Pumpkin, I thought you'd be in bed by now."

It was only eleven, but I'd been coming home so tired lately that I'd drop off regardless of the time. The catch was, I'd wake up at about three every morning and obsess for a few hours about the pace at which the actors were coming up to speed, the safety of everyone I knew, the three pounds I'd gained, who might be carrying on Macbeth's work, whether my husband had ever killed anyone, and anything else that popped into my head.

I referred to that as my thinking time.

"What's happened?" I moved my legs to make room for Jack on the sofa.

"Hang on." He stuck his head into the second bedroom, where Flank was at his post, and told him he could leave for the night. I heard a response that may have been "okey dokey," but probably wasn't.

When we were alone Jack sank down next to me and pulled my feet onto his lap. "How'd it go at the theater today?"

"The usual. Tears, obscenities, possible drug abuse . . . all in Act One." I stretched. "What about you?"

He rubbed my feet absentmindedly. "Nothing. We thought we had a lead in Johannesburg, but . . . nothing."

"Johannesburg? As in South Africa?"

"Have you eaten?" And that was the end of the discussion. Maddening.

"I thought about room service before I drifted off."

He made a face. "I don't know if I can face that menu again."

"It's a little late anyway," I said, knowing full well that late dining had played a significant part in the three pounds I had sprouted. "Maybe just some toast?"

"I'll call." But he made no move toward the phone.

"It's not too late to order a pizza or some Chinese," I suggested. "We could get that good crispy duck thing again, if you're really sick of room service." If I remembered where it had come from.

"Charley, don't you miss real food?" he asked, in a tone I'd never heard him use before. He was exhausted, yes, but also . . . plaintive or mournful or something. Verging on pathetic. It was unnerving.

I sat up. "Real food? You mean like . . ." What did he mean?

"Food that you cook yourself. You know, so when you come home late and you go to the refrigerator you find leftover spaghetti and meatballs or something."

"Spaghetti? Meatballs?" He looked positively tragic, and I didn't think it was just because he was craving pasta. "Sweetie." I rubbed his shoulder sympathetically. "If you want to find an Italian place that's still open I'm sure we can."

He let his head slump back into the cushions. "I don't want Italian. I just want a home-cooked meal."

Something icy slithered down my spine and landed in my belly. "Home cooked?" I repeated.

He looked at me. "I like going out just as much as the next guy, but, to be honest, this hotel life is starting to get on my nerves." His head slumped again. "Especially the food situation."

Situation?

"Um, Jack . . . I don't quite know how to say this." Could I just come out and say it? Did it really need to be said? I took a deep breath and embraced my personal truth. "I can't cook."

He gave me a startled look.

"Really," I insisted, "I can make coffee in a French press, and I can usually manage to do toast, but not necessarily to butter it without tearing holes in the bread. Jam's easier. People keep telling me pasta is so simple, but they're wrong. And, you know, you can do popcorn in a microwave, but you have to be really careful not to burn the bag, and—why are you laughing at me?"

He was. Bastard!

"Look, mister, just because I don't possess some archaic feminine skill is no reason for you to—" and then his mouth was on mine and I couldn't argue any more.

Eventually he came up for air and mockery.

"I wish I had a camera. The look on your face is priceless."

"What the hell is so funny?" I demanded.

He gained control of his features. "I cook."

Oh.

"*Oh*," I said, "so the home-cooked meals would be . . ."

"Supplied by me."

I considered the scenario. "I think I like that idea."

"Something told me you would," he said dryly. "Although . . ."

"Although what?" I snuggled closer to him, visions of gourmet meals dancing in my head.

"Although if a person's going to cook it helps to have a kitchen."

Damn.

I sat back up. "Jack, I know I said I'd deal with the realtor, but with everything that's happened, and with as crazy as things are at the theater—"

He shut me up by kissing me again. Not the worst way to be silenced, I reflected.

"Jack," I said when he released me, "the play will open before you know it, and then I'll devote myself full-time to finding a house."

He pulled me towards him. "Perfect."

"I just hope," I said before he covered my mouth again, "that we won't need a guest room for Flank."

Chapter 22

The question of real estate settled, or at least postponed to a more convenient time, Jack and I had found something more creative than dinner to occupy the rest of the evening.

I was just the slightest bit stiff in the morning, having drifted off in a somewhat unorthodox position. And for once I hadn't woken with my usual three o'clock case of insomnia. But the stiffness was nothing a brisk walk to the theater couldn't work out. All things considered, I was in a damn fine mood.

Which was destroyed the instant I set foot on the stage.

"Charley, dear, I must speak with you immediately!" Olivia's strident voice didn't simply project to the upper balcony, it slapped the far wall and stampeded back. "Chip made some ridiculous comment about shortening my pot roast speech, and I think you'll agree—"

"Charley, we have to talk," Paris called out from his position high on a ladder. "First thing!" He shot Olivia an evil look.

"Charley, there you are!" Victor strode forcefully towards me. "We need to discuss the attitude of certain people." He glared at Lisa, who had fed him his famous line the day before. "And the complete lack of respect—"

"Charley! You're simply not going to believe the printer costs for adding one bloody page in tribute to our dead playwright!" Simon waved a mock-up of the program at me, his sense of fiscal outrage having rendered him tactless on the subject of our dead playwright.

I wondered if this was how preschool teachers felt, always having children climbing on them as they tried to make their way across the classroom. This reflection was cut short by the sight of Sally walking along the balcony railing as if it were a balance beam.

I pushed away the program that Simon had thrust under my nose. "Simon, sweetie, go make sure our child star doesn't kill herself." I gestured toward the balcony.

"Christ on a bike," he muttered. "You! Infant! Come down from there immediately! Where's your mother?"

"Don't worry." Lisa appeared out of nowhere, the way all good stage managers should. She set off purposefully. "I'll take care of it."

I couldn't watch. I turned and came face to face with an indignant Olivia. "Really, Charley, this simply can't wait. If you intend to have Chip do your dirty work for you, I completely understand," this said in a way that was not at all understanding, "but I'd like to hear it from you if you intend to butcher the most soul-defining speech my character makes in this entire—"

"Olivia, sweetie, let me talk to Chip," I said. "We all know the first act is running long, right?"

Her eyes flared. "That's no reason—"

"So doing a little trimming here and there—" I ignored her sharp intake of breath, "isn't out of the question. But I'll talk to Chip," I rushed on, "all right? Martha! Isn't it time for Olivia's fitting?" I thrust the old girl into Martha's surprised arms before she could respond.

"Charley!" Paris called. "When do we deal with the refrigerator problem?"

Refrigerator problem?

"Can it wait until lunchtime, sweetie? It looks like we're already going to get a late start on Act Two."

That was mainly due to the fact that, although Regan was sitting quietly at a table looking over her lines, there was no sign of Paul.

"If you say so," Paris said. "But don't come crying to me when you've got no kitchen on opening night."

Where was Paul? "Chip!" I called, looking around the stage. Where was Chip?

"He's upstairs," Victor pronounced in a tone of grim satisfaction. "Probably getting blown by that bitch stage manager."

This was a new side to Victor.

"Charley, I insist you get rid of her," he pressed, following me as I headed for the stairs. "The way she treated me yesterday was inexcusable. I won't have some fucking nobody making a fool of me in front of the entire cast and crew. Who the hell does she think she is? She's worked at this theater for all of five minutes, and she thinks she can—"

"Victor." I turned on him at the foot of the stairway. "That's enough. I'll talk to her about her attitude but nobody has time to find yet another new stage manager, all right?"

His eyes narrowed. "If she ever—"

"Thanks, Victor." I walked away.

I found Chip behind the desk in the office. "Oh, Charley, there you are." He looked pointedly at his watch.

If my gun hadn't been buried at the bottom of my bag I might have shot him. "Chip, what the hell—"

"We're running late," he interrupted, and threw in an accusatory look for good measure. "And I've got this whole list of issues to go over with you before we get started. Do you need coffee?"

I sat on the couch and rubbed my temples. "Lots."

By the time we made it through Chip's issues list, the cast had been waiting for over an hour. Except for Paul, who'd only just rushed in, late and full of excuses again.

The day's goal was to get through all of Act Two.

The first scene, which included only Regan and Paul, was relatively painless. But then came the scene where Regan had a heart-to-heart that was supposed to turn into a heated confrontation with her father, Victor.

It was excruciating. Despite the fact that her character had the bulk of the dialog, Regan was already off book. Although nobody expected the same from Victor, he seemed to take it as a personal insult that the girl could do what he couldn't. He played the scene like a sulky child—a sulky actor—instead of as a well-meaning father.

When we broke for lunch, I pulled Regan aside.

She began with an apology. "I'm sorry, Charley, but I don't know what I've done to get Victor so upset." Her huge green eyes were twin pools of sincerity. I wished I could get over the impulse to slap her.

"I think you're just a little intimidating for him," I told her.

She looked stunned. "Intimidating?" She shook her head, sending her smooth golden ponytail rippling. "But he's so old."

I assumed by "old" she meant "experienced."

"Well, yes, that's part of the problem," I said reasonably.

She gave me a blank look.

"You're very young, and you're coming up on your lines faster than he is."

"Oh." She looked at me with an expression that clearly said she had no idea what to do.

"Regan, sweetie," I began.

"Yes?"

Sometimes a woman can appear to be very beautiful just by the way she looks at you. I've seen it happen with actresses who know just how to turn their heads, just how to gaze with the right mixture of . . . something. It's as if they can blind you with their personality so you don't see their little laugh lines or the bumps on their noses. They can dazzle you.

Regan had this gift. On top of being extraordinarily beautiful. And enormously talented.

So what the hell was she doing in my beloved but admittedly second-rate Rep company? And why on earth had she thought she needed Rix's influence to get her there?

And then it hit me. And I knew. And I had to talk to Jack.

"Um, Charley?" Regan said hesitantly.

"Just hold your script when you're working with Victor, okay, Regan? I know you don't need to, but it'll make him feel better."

The tiniest of vertical lines appeared between her perfectly shaped brows, but she shrugged and said "Okay."

"Charley!" Paris yelled from somewhere up in the rigging. "If you go running off before we talk about the refrigerator situation I swear I'll never speak to you again!"

Right. The refrigerator situation. I told Regan to go get some lunch and turned my face toward the dark catwalks above the stage. "Chip's got some sandwiches," I called into the darkness, not entirely sure where Paris was. "Come up to the balcony."

I had started carrying a messenger bag (Kate Spade, of course) instead of a purse. I usually wore it hands-free, with the strap across my chest, because I knew Flank would rat me out to Jack if I ever wandered away from it—and what was in it—again. Now I fumbled in its depths to find my cell phone. I had to tell Jack what I'd just figured out. I pulled out the phone and started punching buttons.

"Oh, I don't think so," Paris said from behind my left shoulder. He plucked the phone out of my hand, hung up, and handed it over. Then he stood back, making a gesture that would have smoothed every hair into place, except he'd been shaving his head bald for the past several years. "We need to talk."

I sighed and dropped the phone back into the bag. "Let's find Chip."

He was in the balcony. He said "What's up?" through a mouthful of tuna salad and handed me a tomato, basil, and fresh mozzarella on foccacia. Paris grabbed a ham and Gouda. "Charley, I know we used a refrigerator in that ridiculous outer space play we did last season." He turned to Chip. "Didn't we?"

Chip nodded and swallowed. "It's what the frozen replacement body parts were kept in."

I'm so sorry I never got to see that play.

"Well, where is it?" Paris demanded. "I need to outfit a whole kitchen, and I can re-use that." He turned to me. "After remodeling it, you know, painting it that fifties green and sticking on some chrome." Back to Chip. "So where is it?"

Chip took a swig of grape soda. "That's right. You went on vacation before we closed last season."

Paris looked at me. "Girl, that last play was just about all my nerves could handle."

I nodded sympathetically and drained my mango iced tea.

"We took out a lease on Mangia's back room," Chip informed us. "They made us an offer we couldn't refuse." He grinned.

"The restaurant next door? We leased their back room?" I hadn't heard about that.

"Their storage room. They weren't using it, and it's where that door in the back of the prop room leads to. Their building used to be part of the theater before it was cut down."

I thought back to all the documents I'd read when I'd bought the theater. The building had been built in the 1930s, and originally had included office space occupied by song writers, music publishers, talent agents, and assorted other theatrical types. The office building had been separated from the theater and sold off sometime in the sixties. It now had a decent Italian restaurant on the ground floor and an Asian import/export business on the other three.

"Weren't all the connecting doors sealed up?" I asked.

"Sure, but just with one layer of brick. Mangia's

said we could break through, then they'd seal up their door to the room and we could have sole use of it."

"Is that legal?" I asked.

"Simon approved it," Chip said. "We took sledge-hammers to the brick wall after the party on closing night."

I wondered if Simon had consulted Eileen. Or a structural engineer.

"And you're saying that's where the refrigerator is?" Paris brought us back to the point.

Chip nodded. "All the big stuff that was crowding the prop room. Remember the pool table? And the purple couch?"

"Well, what are we doing here?" Paris exclaimed. "Let's go have a look."

I checked my watch. We were due to resume re-hearsing Act Two in ten minutes. Looking over the balcony, I could see Olivia and Regan sitting on oppo-site sides of the stage, and Lisa bustling around efficiently.

"Let's make it quick," I said. I really didn't need to go with them on a refrigerator hunt, but I was curious about the new storage room.

"Simon's got the key, I think," Chip said. "I'll go get him and meet you there." He dashed off, calling back over his shoulder, "Charley, we'll have to plan on stay-ing extra late tonight, since we're wasting lunch."

Perfect.

Paris and I headed for the prop room, which was quite a bit tidier than I'd ever seen it before.

"Someone's been busy," I said.

"I'll bet it was Lisa," Paris said. "That girl is amazing."

"She is, isn't she?" Neatly typed labels marked the proper places for everything on the wall-to-wall shelves.

Paris turned a footstool upside down to look at the workmanship. "I think I'll ask Chip for help the next time I hire someone. He's got the magic touch."

I looked more closely at the labels. Were they alphabetized? I wondered when Lisa ever found the time to sleep.

Simon barged in with Chip. "Charley, didn't I mention the new storage room? It was just what we needed." He gestured at the shelves filled with candelabras, paintings, swords, and other bits and pieces from productions gone by. "This place was bursting at the seams."

"It looks a lot better than the last time I was in here," I said.

He flourished a key and headed for the new door at the back of the room. "I don't suppose we need to lock it, really," he said. "Oi, that's weird." He turned the handle. "It wasn't locked."

"Really?" Chip asked. "I thought we agreed, since the more valuable pieces were in there . . ."

"Someone must have forgotten." Simon opened the door and fumbled for the light switch.

The room was musty, with an undertone of the olive oil and Parmesan that Mangia's must have stored there before abandoning the room. The light showed furniture under dust covers and various out-of-place-looking portions of sets. Against the back wall was the refrigerator.

Chip frowned. "Aren't there regulations about how abandoned fridges are supposed to be kept?" he asked. "Aren't you supposed to remove the door?"

"I don't really think any unsuspecting child is about to come in here and play in it," Paris scoffed.

"But we do have a child in this production," I pointed out. "And the door was unlocked." I reached for the refrigerator handle. "Although I don't think any harm's done."

I opened the door. There was something in it.

"What's that?" Chip asked, right about the time I screamed.

Slowly, stiffly, as if against its will, the body fell from the refrigerator to the floor.

"Good Lord," Simon whispered. "It's Brian."

Our missing director. With a small round hole between his eyes.

Chapter 23

Simon moved toward the body, reaching slowly for the dead director's shoulder.

"Don't!" a voice commanded from the back of the room.

We all jumped. I may have screamed again.

"Don't touch him!" It was Flank, standing in the doorway with his gun drawn. Finally, he'd said something I was able to understand. And agree with.

"He's right," I said. I looked at my three colleagues, staring wildly at the body, at Flank, at me, at each other. Flank advanced into the room, holding his gun upwards and moving more swiftly than I'd have given him credit for. He looked down at the body, then at us, and holstered his gun.

"Out," he said to me, then he tapped the earpiece he was wearing and began muttering into his sleeve.

"We need to get out of here without disturbing anything," I said softly. "We need to call the police."

We took a collective step backwards. Chip bumped into a birdcage and knocked it off its stand. Simon yelped.

"Calm down!" I yelled. "There's nothing we can do for him now except try not to mess up the crime scene." Paris started to protest, but Simon cut him off.

"Listen to her, guys, this isn't her first dead body."

I stared at him. "Can we leave now?"

We left. We didn't stop in the prop room. We didn't stop until we were onstage and realized everyone was looking at us. I didn't suppose we were a sight to inspire confidence in cast or crew. The four of us stood in a cluster, turning various shades of green, trying not to let our legs go out from under us. Flank hung back in the shadows. He was soon joined by the rest of his squad.

"Do something with them," I whispered to Chip, nodding at the cast. "Take them somewhere."

"Where's Lisa?" he said automatically, having learned the finer points of delegation from me. When he didn't see her handy, he made a visible effort to pull himself together. "All right, everyone!" he called, clapping his hands. "Can I have everyone's attention here!" I thought for one horrible minute that he was just going to blurt out our discovery. But once everybody was looking at him expectantly, he seemed to run out of steam. "Um . . ."

"Nobody panic." Simon took over, his clear, aristocratic voice lending him authority. "I'm going to have to ask that everybody stop what they're doing and leave the building immediately."

There was a general murmur of surprise and protest. "Please, darlings, as quickly as you can," Simon went on. "Everybody just take the rest of the day off and be back here bright and early tomorrow morning."

"What the hell is going on?" Victor demanded, stepping forward importantly.

Simon looked from the aging actor to me with a feverish light in his eye. Then he took a deep breath. "Bomb scare," he said loudly. "Probably nothing, but better to be safe than sorry. Now, if you'll all just . . ."

But he didn't have to continue. People began grabbing for their things and rushing toward the doors.

"Calmly! Calmly!" Simon yelled. "Paris, go make sure everyone is out of the basement workshops."

Paris opened his mouth as if to reply, then just nodded and dashed off.

"Chip, go upstairs and make sure there's nobody in the office." Chip set his face grimly and headed for the stairs.

Suddenly we were alone, and I stared at Simon in amazement. "We didn't actually have to clear the building."

He was trembling visibly. He sat down and ran his hands through his hair. "Thanks, but I didn't see you coming up with any clever ideas."

"Yes, but the police will probably want to talk to everyone."

"Oh, please. The man had obviously been in that refrigerator for weeks." He turned a deeper shade of green and swallowed forcefully. "I hardly think whoever put him there is still hanging about."

That was a point.

"Can I get you a cup of tea?" He really did look awful.

"You can get me the hell out of here," he snapped. Then he sighed and reached for my hand. "Failing that, you can get me that charming detective chap."

I sat down, pulled out my cell phone, and thought how optimistic Jack had been not to have put Inspector Yahata on speed dial. He had, however, included the policeman in the address book of my organizer.

I dialed the number with a certain fatalistic dread. "Inspector? Charley Fairfax. I've found another body."

Once again, I was amazed by the meticulously detailed approach the police took to violent death. Inspector Yahata had arrived within minutes of my call. The crime scene team had shown up only a little behind him. When the detective asked me to show him the body, Simon held me back in my seat. "I'll do it," he said, swallowing. I was profoundly grateful.

After we'd told Yahata everything we knew, he accompanied us up to the office to go over every piece of paper regarding Brian we had. Chip pulled the file that held the employment information he'd provided, including his local address. I dug up the note he'd left when he'd gone. I'd tossed it in the desk drawer after showing it to Martha.

"Martha!" I yelped.

The detective gave me a curious glance.

"She's our costume designer," Simon explained. "What about her?" he asked me.

"She . . ." I paused. Oh, hell. This was no time to keep a girlish confidence. "She was in love with Brian."

Chip looked thunderstruck. They all did, except Yahata. "Were her feelings returned?" he asked.

"She seemed to think so. She couldn't understand why he'd just gone off like that without . . ." My voice trailed off. It seemed pretty clear now why he'd just gone off like that.

After more questioning the detective left us alone in the office. For a while we just sat around in still-stunned silence.

There were a thousand questions running through my mind. Eventually Chip gave voice to one I hadn't thought of yet.

"What are we going to do about the play?"

"We'll just do whatever we can," Paris said defiantly.

Simon cradled his head in his hands. "What can we do?"

I checked my watch. It was a little after five. I should have called Jack hours ago. It didn't cross my mind for an instant that Brian's murder might be unrelated to Nancy's. Or to Cece's abduction. I reached for my phone.

"Good," Simon said when he saw me dialing. "Call Eileen. She'll know what our options are."

I stared at him. At the three of them. And I knew I was responsible for everything that had happened. And that I couldn't abandon them now to go chasing after a criminal shadow figure that I hadn't even told them about. Who was probably long gone. I sighed, hung up, and dialed Eileen.

"Of course you have to go on." Eileen knocked back the glass of whiskey Simon handed her and held it out for a refill. After we'd called her, Simon and I had sent Paris and Chip home. It was the theatrical equivalent of not arguing in front of the children.

"How can we just go on?" I asked. "Our playwright and our director have been murdered. Don't you think that's going to have an effect on morale?"

"Morale be damned." She tossed back the second whiskey.

"Eileen, if it's about the money . . ."

"Money be damned."

Money be damned? Who was this woman? "Leenie—" I started.

"Charley," she interrupted. "This company is not strong enough to survive a cancelled season."

"Maybe not the whole season," Simon said, "but surely one play."

"On top of one disastrous play and three mediocre ones last season?" She raised her eyebrows. "If you cancel now, you may as well just shut down the Rep and sell the theater."

Simon began to sputter. "Naturally I admit that the bloody space thing was a disaster, but I really don't think—"

"Look," Eileen cut him off. "I'm sorry to be so harsh about this." She turned to me. "Really. But the fact of the matter is that the company is already on the brink of collapse. People already regard it as the vanity project of a wealthy woman with too much time on her hands, and we can't keep carrying on in an unbusinesslike—"

Too late, she saw the effect her words had had on me. "Oh, God." She closed her eyes. "Charley, I didn't mean that."

"Do they?" My voice came out in a croak. "Do they think that?"

"Of course not!" Simon said.

Eileen shook her head mutely, looking like she'd give anything to take it back.

I was stunned. I don't know how long we sat in silence before I spoke. "We haven't exactly done anything earth-shattering here, have we?" It was painful to admit, but I knew it was true. "We're just . . . And now with . . ." I was depressing myself to the extent that I couldn't go on.

Simon looked from Eileen to me and back again. "Balls!"

Eileen and I jumped.

"Absolute bloody bollocks."

We blinked at him.

"Complete crap!"

"Simon," Eileen said.

"Shut up, Eileen. Both of you. You two need to stop wallowing in whatever it is you're wallowing in and figure out how we're going to get on with things." He glared at us.

"We are wallowing a bit," I admitted.

"Bloody right you are. Darlings," he said earnestly, "since when have we cared what people say about us? And so what if we haven't achieved brilliance yet? We do this because we love it, and sometimes—just sometimes—it isn't complete crap. Isn't that enough?"

"Simon," I protested, "a few minutes ago you were moaning and wailing and wondering how we could ever go on."

"Right," he said. "I'm over it. We're bloody well going on."

Eileen looked at me expectantly.

I thought about it. It was true that a lot of theatrical companies fail. And yes, the Rep might one day go under. But if we did, it would be because of our own mistakes, not because some homicidal maniac was terrorizing us. And it damn well wouldn't be without a fight.

"Charley?"

I met their stares. "We're bloody well going on."

I finally called Jack. He arrived at the theater nine minutes later and went directly into a consultation with Flank and his team. Then he had a few words with Inspector Yahata.

Jack and the detective seemed to have reached some sort of unspoken agreement in the weeks since we'd discovered Nancy Tyler's identity. I knew they'd spoken almost daily, and had shared what little information there was. Jack still hadn't told the policeman about his own covert past—at least not that I knew of—but Yahata seemed to have taken Jack off his personal list of the five most suspicious men in San Francisco. I didn't exactly know why.

When Jack and I finally left the theater, I was surprised to find it dark outside. We climbed into the Lexus and Jack headed for the freeway.

"We're going to Harry's," he said. "Mike will meet us there in half an hour—"

"We have to make a stop," I interrupted him.

He slammed on the brakes. "What's the matter? Are you all right?"

"I'm fine," I told him. "But we have to go see Martha. I don't want her finding out from the police."

Jack looked like he was about to argue, then relented. "Fine. Where's her coven?"

"She lives in Hayes Valley, off of Gough." I gave him a warning look. "And no witch jokes."

Martha's home was a perfectly normal live/work loft space. With the exception of the enormous knitting machine in the middle of the living room, it could have been anyone's. I could sense Jack was a little disappointed not to find black cats and cauldrons. Although we did find the lady of the house clad in a filmy black knit sort of Stevie Nicks number.

She looked terrified when she opened the door. "Did the building explode? I've been watching the news but there hasn't been anything on."

"There was no bomb," I told her. "But there is bad news."

She took it better than I expected. She sniffled and said that when Brian hadn't responded to her summoning ritual she'd known that something was preventing him from returning to her. To his credit, Jack refrained from rolling his eyes.

It was to Jack that she turned when she finally began to cry. Or maybe *weep* is a more accurate description. The tears fell gently down her pristine cheeks and she folded herself gracefully against my husband's chest.

He looked at me over her head, trying to keep his face away from the dangerous-looking spikes of hair protruding from her French twist.

"I know the woman just found out her lover is dead," I said when we were back outside, "but if she puts some sort of spell on you I'll kill her."

Finally on the road to Harry's house, we were able to talk about Brian's murder.

"Do you think he was just another warning?" I asked. "Like Nancy?"

Jack shook his head. "No. Nancy was left deliberately where we would find her. Brian was hidden. And he was shot, not poisoned. I don't think his murder was planned. At least not in the same way."

"But you do think they're connected?"

"It's either that or your theater is cursed. And even your witchy friend isn't going to convince me of that."

"That's what the cast will think, though," I told him. "Theater people are completely superstitious."

"They might be, but Inspector Yahata isn't."

"What does he think?"

"You won't like it," Jack warned. I braced myself. "He's looking at Simon."

I was shocked. But then I wasn't. "That's what Eileen said would happen."

"Why?" Jack asked sharply.

"He was the only one who'd actually met Nancy."

"He was also the one with the key to the storage room where Brian was found."

"Jack, you can't think—"

"Of course I don't think. But Yahata's leaning in that direction."

"Jack, you and Yahata are pretty chummy these

days. What did you do to make him stop suspecting you?"

"Maybe he hasn't."

"Oh."

We drove for a while in silence. Then I remembered what I'd wanted to tell Jack earlier in the day. Had it just been that morning? My conversation with Regan seemed weeks ago.

"Jack, what do you think of Regan?"

"She's not my type."

"I don't mean that. What do you think of her as a suspect?"

"Regan?"

"Well, we've talked about how weird it was that Rix showed up at the right time with the right funding for the theater, right?"

"Right."

"The thing is, if he meant to infiltrate the Rep, he didn't really put himself in much of a position to do that."

"Right."

"But," I said emphatically, "he did supply Regan. And she's in a position to do just that."

"Regan?"

"Why do men never suspect beautiful women?" I asked. "That's what made me think about it this morning. She's so beautiful, and she's so charming, and so talented."

"And?"

"And so much better than Rix."

"You think?" Heavy sarcasm from my husband.

"I think. I also think she's better than some second-rate theatrical company run as a vanity project by a wealthy woman with too much time on her hands." Eileen's words still stung.

"Where did that come from?"

"Never mind. The point is, the whole reason for Rix to have come up with the money we needed might have been to plant Regan, on Macbeth's behalf, within the Rep."

"Maybe." Jack sounded doubtful. "But if she's as good as you say she is, why would she need Rix?"

I hadn't thought of that. "Damn." I was quiet for a while. "Before Regan, I had been thinking of Paul."

"Based on what?"

"I was thinking he might have a drug problem. And that might make him easy for someone to manipulate."

"Are you sure he's on drugs?"

"I don't have proof. I thought I'd ask Cece for advice."

He took that in without comment.

"Charley, there's something you should know." Jack shot me a look. "The man we've been calling Macbeth . . ." He hesitated. "He hadn't been selling secrets just for the money. He'd been involved with someone in one of the organizations we were . . . investigating."

"I thought you told me he was married?"

Jack gave me an eloquent look.

"Okay, okay, so he was cheating on his wife," I said. "And—Jack, is that why his wife turned him in to you?"

"I'd like to think her patriotic duty had something to do with it as well," he said.

"But you're saying Macbeth was in league with a woman. A criminal woman."

"I don't think I would have phrased it quite like that, but yes. That's the gist of it."

We turned off the freeway into suburbia. "So this woman could be the person who's been carrying on with his plans. Who, even before his death, was making things happen for him outside of prison."

Jack frowned. "That doesn't really fit. Mike and I believe her group was behind his death."

"It really wasn't a suicide?"

He shook his head.

I digested that. "I guess it wouldn't make sense for her to kill him and then carry out his scheme."

Jack didn't respond.

As we turned into Harry's driveway, I brought the conversation back to its beginning. "Jack, could Regan fit anywhere in this? What do you think?"

He frowned. "I think I'd better ask Mike to keep an eye on her."

Chapter 24

We were up all night, debating what our next move should be. Harry still assumed the reason behind the mayhem was financial rather than personal, and that the criminal would eventually demand money to leave us alone. Jack didn't correct him.

Brenda's first priority when we'd arrived had been to insist that Jack and I eat steaming bowls of home-made chicken noodle soup, but once we'd complied with that, she joined us in our analysis of the evidence and speculation about what move we should make next. Not that it did any good. Hours later we were still where we'd started.

Cece had already gone to bed when we got there and nobody thought it would be a good idea to wake her. I did the next best thing and asked Gordon about my Paul-as-addict-informant scenario, but he wasn't sold on it.

"The behavior you describe might just as easily be symptomatic of nerves," he pointed out. "Or even an extreme case of low blood sugar. It does indicate the possibility of drug abuse, but that's not the only possibility."

He suggested I take a look around the dressing room Paul shared with Victor, and gave me ideas for typical places where addicts hide their paraphernalia.

"How do you know so much about all this, Gordon?" I asked.

He looked at me in a way I couldn't read. "I think I'll make more coffee."

The next day Jack took me straight from Harry's to the theater.

"Are you sure you want to do this?" he asked for the third time.

I thought about what Eileen had said the day before. If we cancelled this show we might as well close the Rep for good. "I'm sure I have to."

Flank stuck his head out of the theater door, looked both ways down the near-deserted street, and came out to the car. It didn't look like he'd slept. Or changed his clothes.

"What are you going to say?" Jack asked.

With a little luck, something that would keep the cast and crew from panicking. "I wish I knew."

Simon strolled into the office just moments after I got in. "What are you wearing, darling? Aren't you cold?" He took his leather coat off and hung it on my shoulders.

"Thanks." I slipped my arms into the sleeves gratefully. I'd been freezing in the UC Santa Cruz T-shirt I'd borrowed from Brenda.

"We've called everyone in," Simon told me. "Paris' crew from the workshop," the huge building in South San Francisco where the sets were built before being loaded into the theater, "and all Martha's staff, as well as the lighting and sound crews. Everyone we need for an old-time revival meeting." He looked at me. "Coffee?"

After the past night at Harry's, another cup of coffee would probably make me gag. "Simon," I said, "before Chip gets here, there's something I need to tell you."

I closed the office door and brought him up to speed on the investigation, such as it was. I thought it was only fair, given that Simon seemed to be the police's favorite suspect at the moment.

For once, he let me get through an entire story without interrupting. He didn't say a word until I let slip the name Jack and I had been using to identify the man we believed to have set everything in motion.

"Charley!" he exclaimed, and clapped his hand over his mouth.

"What?"

"What you said! The Scottish play! We're in a theater, for God's sakes!" Simon grabbed me by the shoulders and pushed me towards the door. "No! Wait! Is it turn around three times and then leave the room, or leave the room and turn around three times?" He stared at me.

Of course. The Scottish play. How could I have been so stupid? It's a common superstition in the theater that bad things happen when a company stages a production of *Macbeth*. Sets collapse, actors are hurt in combat scenes or fall off the stage in rehearsals. People sicken and die mysteriously. When we'd staged the play in our second year, Simon himself had been accidentally stabbed with a dagger. But since he'd sustained the wound in the prop room, while engaged in a game of "lift the sporran" with the actor playing Macduff, I hadn't thought it could really be blamed on the play's curse.

In any case, the superstition is so bad that it's considered an invitation to disaster simply to say the M word in a theater. That's why it's referred to as "the Scottish play."

I shook Simon's hands off me, knowing the cure for my indiscretion. I turned around three times, left the room, spit on the floor, knocked on the door, and asked permission to re-enter the office.

Simon opened the door. "Darling, if you had to give an evil criminal mastermind a nickname, why did it have to be something that would bring us even more bloody bad luck?"

"Jack did suggest we call him Dave," I said.

Simon opened his arms. "Come here." He hugged me for a minute, then said, "At least all this means there's a possibility our friend Yahata won't be arresting me for the murders."

I broke away. "Has he threatened you?"

Simon shook his head. "Not in so many words, but when you lead as debauched a life as I do, darling, you get to know when someone's starting to think you're a bit fishy. Ah, Chip."

Chip stood at the door with a thermos of coffee and a stack of paper cups. "Do we know what we're going to do yet?"

I responded on Simon's behalf. "We're bloody well going to go on."

Chip had asked Lisa to assemble everyone on the stage. Before going down, I tried to put my messenger bag on the way I'd been wearing it, with the strap diagonally across my chest. But with Simon's bulky leather coat on it didn't fit right. I knew I'd leave the bag behind somewhere if I just slung it over my shoulder, and Jack would kill me if I wandered off without the gun again.

The guys had left me alone in the office, so I took out the makeup pouch that served as a holster. I slipped the gun out, made sure the safety was on, and tucked it into my waistband at the small of my back. The oversized Diesel Jeans label held it in place nicely. It seemed secure enough, and I'd seen people wear guns that way in the movies. I jumped up and down a few times and it didn't jiggle free, so I figured I was good to go.

Downstairs, I looked around and saw everyone but Martha. No surprise there. I also saw Inspector Yahata, waiting in the wings. No surprise there either.

"Everybody, could I have your attention?" I called. Which was a bit unnecessary, since the entire cast and crew were looking at me expectantly.

"Did they get the bomb, Charley?" Lisa asked.

"There was no bomb," I announced. A ripple of relieved sighs went through the crowd.

"You see," Lisa said, "I told you all it was nothing."

"There was something." My words brought all conversation to a halt.

"Are we expected to stand around all day, Charley?" Olivia demanded. She was front and center in the group and clearly assumed she spoke for them all. "I demand to know why I was rushed out of here yesterday. It completely destroyed the moment I had created for my pot roast speech."

"Your pot roast speech?" Victor yelled. "Nobody gives a shit about your pot roast speech, you stupid bitch. Chip's already cut it twice! Yesterday was supposed to be the day we concentrated on my scene with Anna, and I was completely prepared." He looked directly at Lisa, daring her to challenge him. "Now I don't know if my concentration has been broken—"

"Gee, you mean you may need to go back to using your book?" someone said sarcastically from the back of the crowd.

"Who said that?" Victor screeched. "How dare you!" His eye caught little Sally Carter, giggling at him behind her hand.

"How dare you!" she mocked him, in that childish way that children have.

"You little monster!" Victor sputtered. "Where's your mother?"

"Where's your mother?" the girl mimicked.

"Darling," Simon whispered to me. "I think the natives are getting restless."

"All right, cut it out!" I yelled.

Silence.

"Victor, grow up. Sally, behave yourself."

Inspector Yahata stepped out of the wings. "Mrs. Fairfax, if I may say a few words?"

The crowd turned to him, possibly the only man in a room full of performers who could actually command their attention.

The detective spoke in his standard clipped, precise tones. "Yesterday, a body was found in the theater." There were little yelps as hands flew to cover mouths. The detective went on briskly. "It was the body of

Brian Dexter, who had been hired to direct this play."
Yahata waited for the shocked murmurs to subside.
"My officers and I will be here all day, asking you to
think back to anything that may provide some insight
into this affair. Thank you." He turned and walked
back into the shadows of the wings, where I could see
his investigative team had gathered.

The silence lasted exactly three heartbeats. It was
followed by pandemonium.

"Oh, that poor, dear, boy!" Olivia moaned in her
most sell-it-to-the-back-row voice. "Killed in the
prime of life!" As far as I knew, she'd never met the
poor dear boy.

"And just like the playwright, what's-her-name."
This was contributed by the sound engineer.

"Someone's got it in for us! Someone's going to kill
us all!" I don't know who said that, but it seemed to
set the mood for the whole group.

"Well, I'm not going to stick around to be picked
off by some serial killer," called Paris' master carpenter. "And anyone who does is crazy!"

Everyone began shouting at once. I looked around
in desperation and caught sight of Flank, in the orchestra seats, with his gun drawn. I knew the cast and
crew were quickly becoming an angry mob, but they
didn't pose a threat to me, and pulling out a gun was a
good way for my bodyguard to get shot by the police.

"Stop!" I yelled. I meant it for Flank, who looked
at me with surprise and reluctantly holstered his gun.
But my shout had also had the effect of silencing all
the yelling onstage. I took advantage of that.

"Everybody, just stop panicking. We don't know if
there is any connection at all between the death of
Nancy Tyler"—I stressed the playwright's name for the
benefit of the sound engineer—"and Brian Dexter."

"How can they not be connected?" a voice called.
It was the wigmaster. "They were both working on
this play. Just like the rest of us." He looked around
for confirmation.

"The point is"—I spoke over the muttered agreements—

"that both Nancy and Brian died several weeks ago. And nothing suspicious has happened since." At least nothing I was going to tell them about. Cast and crew began exchanging uneasy glances.

"This is a horrible thing to have happened, but we can't let it stop us from doing the very best we can to help the police, and doing the very best we can to put on this production." I saw Olivia about to protest, and stormed over her words. "I know you're probably thinking we can't go on. But we have to." I tried not to sound desperate. "This is the only play Nancy Tyler ever wrote. Her whole family is going to be here on opening night to see her dream come alive." Her whole family was one sister and an orphaned cat, but I was on a roll. "We can't let her down."

Help came from an unexpected source. "Charley's right!" Regan said. "What is this play about but overcoming obstacles and following your dreams? We have to follow this through. We have to put this play on. For Nancy and for all of us!"

The cynical part of my brain, which is the larger part, knew that this play also provided a fabulous role for Regan, and that the publicity surrounding the murders would guarantee her maximum exposure. There was also the possibility that she had either committed the crimes or was working for the person who had. But she was agreeing with me, so I let it go.

"You heard what the lady said," Paris called out. "If any one of my crew wants to leave you just go on out that door. Who's going? Come on, speak up!" The group of builders, carpenters, stagehands, electricians, scenic artists, and engineers looked at each other uncomfortably. Since most of them were union employees, they weren't exactly free to walk without legal ramifications. Still, Paris' challenge set the right emotional tone.

"Well, we're staying," the lead stitcher called, the tailor and wigmaster nodding enthusiastically. "We won't abandon Martha!"

"I'm absolutely staying," Lisa spoke up with determination. "Nothing can keep me from finishing this job." She turned to the cast. "How about the rest of you? Olivia? Victor? Paul? Sally?" She looked at each of the actors in turn.

Victor spoke up loudly. "I want police protection!" he declaimed. "I won't stay in this theater without it!"

"I think we can count on Inspector Yahata to maintain a police presence for the time being." The detective met my eyes. Yep, we could count on a police presence all right.

"I'll have to ask my mom," Sally said.

"I'll talk to her about it," I reassured her.

"I'm in," Paul said simply.

"Then we're all staying!" Olivia trumpeted regally. As if she had been the force for keeping the group together. And then she uttered the inevitable line. "The show must go on!"

I returned everyone's hugs and handshakes gratefully in the general surge of enthusiasm that followed. But I couldn't help wondering if, by convincing these people to stay at the Rep, I had just put them all in horrible danger.

"Mrs. Fairfax."

I'd felt Yahata's presence before he'd spoken my name. I looked up from the desk in the theater office to find him standing in the doorway.

"Inspector. Thank you for your help down there."

He inclined his head a fraction. "Of course." He took a quick survey of the room. "Is your husband here?"

"No. Can I give him a message?" I was dying to know what those two talked about when I wasn't around. "Come in."

The detective moved into the room. "We have learned something about Brian Dexter which might be important."

"Oh?"

"Your colleagues were correct in their assessment that he had lied about much of his experience."

"Oh." Was that all?

"It seems Mr. Dexter had worked mainly in television. In fact, his most recent job was as a producer of a television reality show."

"You're kidding."

The detective looked at me with mild surprise. Of course he didn't kid. "The name of the show was *Cheaters Paradise*. The premise was that couples were invited to a luxury resort. At the resort a group of actors, posing as gigolos, seduced the women away from their husbands."

My jaw dropped.

"Mr. Dexter's responsibility was to provide the actors."

The real impact of Yahata's statement took a few seconds to hit me. When Macbeth had needed an actor to seduce Cece . . . I gulped. Brian had been working for Macbeth.

I stared at the detective. "I'll tell Jack."

"Thank you." And he was gone.

Chapter 25

After the meeting, the cast and crew pulled together in a way they never had before. There was less bickering, less backstabbing. And when a week passed with no further corpses turning up, people gradually stopped jumping at the slightest noise and abandoned the use of the buddy system when going from dressing room to stage. We were making steady progress, and the production was coming together. Which was good, because we opened in two weeks.

Jack had learned from Yahata that Tom Nelson had indeed been one of the actors on Brian's list of rejected applicants to *Cheaters Paradise*. So had a man named Blake Blaine, who had admitted to having been hired to romance Nancy Tyler.

"His story is almost identical to Nelson's," Jack told me. "He was hired over the phone, given instructions over the web, and told to take Nancy to the hotel that night, then leave her in the room while the TV crew explained that it had all been a show."

"Does he have any idea who actually came to the room? Who actually killed Nancy and brought her to our room?"

Jack shook his head. "He has no clue."

Just like the rest of us.

At least I was finally getting into the directorial thing, possibly because it provided a convenient distraction from my complete lack of progress in the murder investigation. In any case, it gave me something else to obsess about.

Currently I was obsessing over a line from a poem by Shelley that Regan's character, Anna, quoted in Act Two. I couldn't figure out how much significance to give it. Had our playwright not been murdered, I could have discussed it with her.

"Jack?" I reached over and nudged him a little. It was a Sunday, and I wasn't going to the theater until the afternoon, so we'd both slept in.

"Mphrrmmph?"

I chose to interpret that as "Yes, my beloved?"

"Do you know much about Shelley?"

Jack rolled onto his back, blinking. He cleared his throat. "Shelly who?"

"Percy Bysshe Shelley." I have a degree in English literature, but I've never been sure how to pronounce the man's middle name. "The poet."

Jack sat up on one elbow, rubbing his eyes. "Shelley the poet. Do I know what about him?" Sometimes Jack wakes up slowly.

"Can you place the quote 'Gives grace and truth to life's unquiet dream'?"

"Can I place it?"

"Do you know what poem it came from? I need to know what gives grace and truth to life's unquiet dream."

He looked at the clock. "At eight in the morning?" He slumped back into the pillows. "Pumpkin, I hate to say it, but it's possible you married the wrong guy."

"Like hell I did," I reassured him. "You have other uses."

His mouth twitched. "Oh, sure. You just want to have your way with me, then you'll cast me aside to go buy a book of poetry or something."

"The bookstores probably don't open until noon on Sunday."

He eyed me speculatively. "Think that's long enough?"

*   *   *

Later, after Jack had left for Mike's, I yawned and stretched and wondered what to do with the remains of the morning.

I'd been toying with the idea of bringing all the suspects together, the way they do in the movies, and waiting for someone to incriminate themselves. So far the suspects included only Regan and Paul, but still . . . I felt it was time for a dinner party.

Harry had liked the plan when I'd mentioned it to him, and had offered the use of his house. Dialing his number, I was hoping the offer would include the use of Gordon's culinary skills. It was Gordon who answered.

"How are you, Gordon? How's Cece doing?" It had been a little over a month since Cece's rescue, and our paths hadn't crossed since.

"Your cousin is . . . out for the morning," Gordon said.

I didn't like the little pause in his sentence. I sat up in bed. "She's out? At eleven-thirty on a Sunday morning? Don't tell me she's at church," I joked.

There was a distinct silence on the phone.

"She's at church?"

"In a manner of speaking. Miss Gee has taken her to a women's retreat. 'A day of mindfulness and meditation' is, I believe, how she described the event. At a spiritual center somewhere near Big Basin."

That sounded like Brenda. She'd dragged me along on more than one occasion to sit in the woods with a collection of natural-fiber-clothing types who clearly got more out of the proceedings than I did. I was surprised Cece had been talked into going. And I thought I detected a smidgen of disapproval in Gordon's voice.

"Don't you believe in meditation, Gordon?" I fished.

"As a matter of fact, I have a daily practice which facilitates a great tranquility of the mind."

Oh. "Really? Then why do I get the feeling you're not altogether thrilled that Cece's gone with Brenda?"

Could he be jealous? It wasn't the first time I'd wondered if Gordon was developing a thing for Cece.

He paused before answering. "It isn't the fact that your cousin has gone with Miss Gee which troubles me, it's that your uncle has seen fit to accompany them."

Harry? At a women's meditation retreat? The mind boggled.

"He felt they needed his protection away from the house," Gordon added. "So he went . . . ah . . . undercover."

"Please don't tell me he's in drag."

"Please don't think I would have allowed that," Gordon answered smoothly. "He is masquerading as their driver. He is acting as their bodyguard."

Somehow, once I'd pictured Harry in a floppy hat and peasant blouse, seeing him as a Flank wanna-be wasn't nearly as amusing.

"Well, I'm sure they'll be fine." I wasn't, really.

"I'll tell them you called," Gordon said.

"Wait, Gordon. I actually wanted to talk to you."

A pause. "Yes?"

All of a sudden I was nervous. "Um, I'm planning a little dinner party for a week from today."

"Yes?"

"And Harry has offered to let me use the house." Before he could say "yes" again, I went on. "So I was wondering if you might be available."

"Why, thank you," he said. "I'd be delighted to attend."

Oops. This was proof that I wasn't meant to organize my own parties. I stammered. "Oh. Oh, well, that's . . . that's just . . ."

Did I hear laughter from the phone? Not laughter exactly, but definitely a soft chuckle. "Please," Gordon stopped my babbling. "I apologize. Of course I understand that you'd like me to cook for your party, and I'd be happy to do so. I was just having a little fun with you."

I stared at the phone. Gordon had a sense of

humor? Gordon could tease? Who knew? "Oh, um . . ." I recovered beautifully.

"Shall we discuss the menu?"

After Gordon and I had weighed the various attributes and drawbacks of sea bass, reduction sauces, and seasonal greens to his satisfaction—and a bit beyond my comprehension—I hung up and made my next call.

"Simon?"

There were muffled sounds of activity on the line, but no voice had spoken.

"Simon, it's Charley." I waited.

Finally, "Charley," breathless, "darling. What time is it? I thought we weren't meeting until two-ish." More muffled activity and a distinct thump. "Ow. Stop that."

"Is this a bad time?"

"No!" I wasn't sure if that was meant for me or his companion. "Charley, hang on a minute." Another thump and what might have been a slap. "What is it, darling? What's happened?"

Assuming that was addressed to me, I said, "A dinner party."

"How lovely. Did you have a nice time?"

"I didn't go to one, I'm having one."

"Oh, even lovelier. And I'm invited?" Then he placed his hand over the mouthpiece, which didn't stop me from hearing, "No, run the bath. I'll be right there."

"You are invited," I told him. "A week from today. At Harry's house in Hillsborough."

"Excellent. And who have you invited for me?"

"The primary purpose of the evening isn't to find you a date," I told him.

"You're very cruel sometimes, darling. What is?"

"What is what?" I asked.

"What is the primary purpose of the evening?"

"To have a nice time?"

"Just that?"

"What else would there be?" I said innocently.

"Not, for example, to ferret out a killer?" Simon enquired. "Not to trap an unwary villain? Are we all to be characters in some Agatha Christie-inspired dinner drama?"

"It'll just be a friendly little get-together with the gang and a few assorted extras," I lied.

"I'll try to believe that."

I'd just put down the receiver when the phone rang.

"Charley?"

"Eileen! I was just going to call you."

"I haven't dared ask how things are going," she said. "But how are things going?"

I brought her up to speed on the production.

"And no more bodies?" she asked.

"I'd have told you."

"I'm not so sure of that. What were you going to call me about?"

I invited her to the party.

"Next Sunday? That's perfect. Anthony gets back from his dad's a week from tomorrow, so your party will be my last free evening for a while." I hadn't seen Anthony since before I'd left for London, but I'd heard all about how much he'd grown and how well he'd been doing in school. Apparently he was studying Japanese. An underachiever, like his mother.

"I can't wait to see him again. He must be getting so big." What else can you say about someone's son?

"You'd better bone up on your PlayStation trivia," she warned. "That's all he wants to talk about these days." She paused. "I miss him."

"One more week," I said.

Eventually I dragged myself away from the phone and out of bed. I showered and dressed in the jeans and long-sleeved tee that was becoming my standard uniform, then tucked the Walther into my waistband. I'd gotten used to carrying the gun in the small of my back. I suppose I should have gotten a real holster, but I hadn't made the time.

I was rummaging through the mess at the bottom of the closet, looking for the mate to my most comfortable Cole Haans, when I came across the box containing the gun Harry had loaned me, the Smith & Wesson. I was already carrying one unlicensed concealed weapon, so I didn't really need another. But then, I didn't need five pair of black high-heeled strappy sandals either. I took the .38 out of its box, checked to make sure it was loaded, and tossed it into the messenger bag.

Flank and I walked to the theater, as usual. But in a stunning turn of events, San Francisco was experiencing a genuinely sunny summer day. It was a shame I'd be spending the rest of it in a dusty old theater basement. But just because I was, everyone didn't have to.

"Flank," I said, "it's just going to be Simon and Paris and Martha and Chip today. We're just going to look over the props and costumes for a few hours. It seems silly for you to hang around for that. Why don't you go enjoy the sunshine? Go to the park or something."

Flank nodded several times and said something that was probably "No way." He held the door open for me.

"Your loss," I told him.

I found Chip and Paris onstage with a measuring tape and clipboard, respectively.

"Hey, Charley," Chip greeted me. "We thought we'd get started without you."

"Go for it." I watched them work for a while, and eventually was joined by Martha and Simon.

Martha had only stayed away for a few days after the discovery of Brian's body. She'd come back subdued, and had enveloped herself in black ever since, but I don't suppose anyone really noticed. The biggest change, according to the head stitcher, had been in the redesign of most of the costumes. "They're still fifties," she had reassured me as we'd munched lunchtime salads a few days before, "but darker somehow. As if it's the fifties of the Communist witch hunts and the Cold War, rather than of Elvis and *I Love Lucy*."

That made me just a little bit nervous. I couldn't imagine a professional like Martha making any drastic changes without my approval. But when I'd asked her about it, she'd said "Trust me." Never a good sign.

The costume and properties workshops were in the basement of the theater. I didn't like it down there. Probably because I'd grown up in earthquake country, I get uncomfortable below ground. It was unusual to have a basement in a San Francisco building as old as the theater. It had been an addition, scooped out during a seismic retrofitting sometime in the eighties. That should have made me feel better, but it didn't.

Martha had done her best to cheer up the costume shop by hanging sari silks on the walls and using lots of floor lamps instead of the cold overhead fluorescent lights, but fabric could only do so much to soften concrete.

Martha and her staff had dressed five dressmaker's dummies in outfits to be worn by Regan, Paul, Olivia, Victor, and little Sally. As soon as I saw the clothes I knew what the stitcher had meant. The costumes were darker somehow. Emotionally darker. It was as if everything, from the fitted bodice on the party dress for Regan to the stiff fabric of Victor's suit, was just a little harsher, a little more confining, than it had been before.

"What I'm going for," Martha explained, "is the sense of being held captive by the clothing. It looks beautiful, but it restricts movement, even restricts breathing a little." She looked at us expectantly.

"This one's pretty," Chip said, gesturing to the party dress.

Martha gave him a look of grave disappointment.

"I see it," Simon said. "It's a commentary on the society of the time. The repression, the conformity that Regan is rebelling against." Martha and I stared at him in amazement. "What?" He looked a little ruffled.

"Nothing, Simon," I said. "You expressed it beautifully. And Martha, they're wonderful. They'll add a whole new emotional dimension. It's subtle, but on a subconscious level—"

"Thank you," Martha cut me off. Clearly, she was uncomfortable with compliments.

"Girl, they're perfect," Paris declared. "Now, who wants to see the props?"

"Hang on," I said. "Aren't there more?"

She nodded. "In the walk-in. I took these out just to show you. Everything else stays in the closet until it's time to use it. This basement is so damp," she said to Simon, somewhat accusingly. "We need to keep dehumidifiers running all the time to make sure the clothes aren't damaged."

She opened a door on the back wall, behind an enormous padded table. I followed her into a large closet.

"Wow," I said when Martha flicked on the light. "This is a lot of costumes."

"It's everything we've done for the past three seasons, sorted by period and gender." She sounded proud and I could see why.

"It's so clean," I said. "And organized."

Martha smiled. "Remember before you went to London when I asked you for budget to have it fitted out?" I didn't, but that didn't seem to matter. "We covered the walls with moisture-repellant materials and had the dehumidifiers installed. It's temperature-controlled, which is more than I can say for the workroom. We were also able to get some shelving and a cedar floor. The only weaknesses are the doors."

"Doors?" I looked around but could see only one.

"This one down here leads to an electrical room." She pushed some Elizabethan dresses aside to reveal a painted metal door. "I think you'll like the takeoffs on the bowling shirt that we did for Paul." She rolled a rack of costumes toward me. "Here's everything for this production, sorted by actor."

We looked through the clothes, and, although I had a few suggestions, the overall impression was that Martha was a genius.

Across the hall in Paris' realm, it was harder to figure out what was going on. Everything was stacked on top of everything else, with furniture, kitchen fixtures, and trees thrown into the mix seemingly at random.

The actual sets had been constructed off-site, then loaded into the theater. In the onsite workshop, Paris' crew built the furniture and other props to be used in the sets.

The bits and pieces scattered across the properties shop looked like something from news footage of a tornado's aftermath. Paris picked out a kitchen chair and began to describe how it integrated into the overall artistic vision. I looked around at the rest of the collection.

It was going to be a long afternoon.

I didn't stop talking all through dinner. Jack took me to Moose's in North Beach, which was sort of a shame because I love Moose's and I was so caught up in telling Jack about the sets and costumes that I didn't even notice my fig and goat cheese salad or my steak with horseradish mashed potatoes. But by the time the blueberry tart with homemade marshmallows arrived, perhaps because that coincided with finishing the bottle of wine, I had slowed down enough to ask Jack if he'd made any progress on the hunt for the killer.

His lips tightened slightly. "It's possible."

I dropped my fork. "Are you serious? And you let me just go on like that about the stupid show?"

"It isn't stupid and I couldn't have stopped you if I'd tried."

"Well, that's true." I dipped my finger into the creamy marshmallow. Jack sighed and gave me his fork. "Thank you. Now tell me everything."

"It may not be anything," he frowned. "But Mike may have traced something to a bank in the Cayman Islands."

"He followed the money," I said sagely.

"He did."

"What money?"

"The money Macbeth used to pay the actors."

I almost dropped Jack's fork. "So it's true? Macbeth set everything in motion before he was killed?"

Jack ran a hand across his face. "Working with someone on the outside, yes."

I let it sink in. "Brian? Refrigerated Brian? Do you think he was Macbeth's contact?"

"We know he used Brian to find the actors." Jack paused. "But I don't believe Brian and Macbeth were full-fledged partners. Brian was probably useful at first because Macbeth was looking around for your weak spots, and the Rep was an obvious place to start. The fact that Brian had lied about his background might have made him easy for Macbeth to manipulate, and his list of actors who'd do just about anything without asking questions was an added bonus. But from what Yahata's been able to find, Brian wasn't a killer."

I pushed the remains of the tart away. Something about Macbeth having looked for my weak spots took my appetite away.

Jack went on. "It worked for a while. Brian was able to report on what was happening at the Rep. That's how Macbeth would have found out about Nancy. She was single and local, and perfect for what he had in mind."

Okay, it was possible I'd never have an appetite again.

"But eventually Brian got cold feet. You told me Chip and Paris were skeptical about him. He probably knew he'd be found out eventually."

"And when he tried to back out of his deal with Macbeth . . ."

"He'd outlived his usefulness."

I tried not to think of the body tumbling slowly

out of the refrigerator. "So, with Brian gone, Macbeth needed someone else to infiltrate the Rep."

"Right." Jack waited for me to make the next logical leap.

Which only took a moment. "That bloody blond bitch!"

Jack signaled for the check. "If that's your way of referring to the lovely Regan—"

"Has Mike been able to find out anything about her? Why she's dating Rix, for example?"

"As a matter of fact, he has found something." Jack grinned.

"Are you going to tell me?"

The grin got wider. "Pumpkin, how do you feel about porn?"

"That's not a very smooth way of changing the subject."

"I'm not changing the subject." He gave me raised eyebrows.

"Regan?" I got it. "The princess is a porn star?"

"Which I'm sure she doesn't want you or anyone else to know."

"And which would explain why she used a sugar daddy instead of an agent to get cast in the play." I wondered if Rix knew.

"And which also would have made her a fairly ripe candidate for blackmail by Macbeth."

Our eyes locked, and I said it again. "That bloody blond bitch."

When we got back to the hotel there was a wrapped gift on the bed.

"What's this?" I'm ashamed to say my first thought was to send for the bomb squad.

"Open it," Jack said. "It's not ticking."

It's possible he was getting to know me too well.

I pulled off the ribbon and paper. It was a book. *The Collected Poems of Percy Bysshe Shelley.*

"Jack! When did you get this?"

"Today," he said as he vanished into the closet. "There are a lot of bookstores in Palo Alto."

"I didn't think you were even paying attention. . . ." I opened the cover and saw that Jack had written something on the first page.

Charley, you idiot, you give grace and truth to life's unquiet dream.

I looked over at the closet. "Like hell I married the wrong guy."

Chapter 26

We were thirteen for dinner. I should have known better.

The week had passed in a blur of activity. Rehearsals had gone on for at least eight hours a day, followed by production meetings and endless discussions that lasted into the night. We had done some tricky scheduling around Sally because of child labor laws, but everyone else had worked until they were ready to drop.

The schedule was taking a toll on Paul. I'd had a hard time trying to get into the dressing room he shared with Victor, because the two of them were rarely onstage at the same time. But eventually I managed it, and looked behind mirrors and under drawers and everywhere else that Gordon had suggested I search for evidence of drug use. In spite of the fact that Paul's erratic behavior had gotten worse, I had found no proof of a drug problem.

I did find half a dozen empty vodka bottles in Victor's closet, which explained a lot.

But despite the miscellaneous substance abuse among the actors, things were going well. I was convinced I'd heard Olivia say the words "pot roast" for the last time, which in itself was enough to keep me going.

Regan just got better and better, damn her.

And then she brought Rix to dinner.

*   *   *

I had invited her, Paul, Victor, and Olivia. I had explicitly not said "and guest." Along with Harry, Cece, Brenda, Eileen, Simon, Mike, Jack, and myself, we were supposed to be twelve. A nice even number. Some suspects, some spies, and a few friends just to make things go smoothly. No bastard ex-boyfriends on the list.

They were the last to arrive. The rest of us were assembled in Harry's great room. Because of the party, the household ban on alcohol had been lifted for the night, although I noticed Harry continued to stick to club soda.

I was shocked when I saw my cousin Cece. She was a different woman. She'd put on enough weight to fill out the hollows under her eyes, and for the first time since she was about fifteen, she looked healthy. She'd gotten a sleek blond bob of a haircut, and kept her use of black eyeliner to a minimum. She was wearing a powder blue strapless dress made out of a filmy, wispy fabric that made her look like a latter-day ex-junkie Grace Kelly.

"Hey, Charley," she greeted me. "Who the fuck are all the losers?"

Some things didn't change.

"You look fabulous, Cece. Really good." I was determined not to let her pull me into a childish argument.

She plucked at her skirt. "It's a Jasper Conran. Brenda picked it out."

"Well, it's just great to see you doing so well."

"A lot of good it'll do me with this crowd. You could have at least invited one good-looking man besides your husband."

That's when the doorbell rang and Regan arrived. With Rix. Harry brought them into the room, his face wearing a look somewhere between get-me-a-knife-and-I'll-cut-this-bastard's-heart-out and I'm-playing-it-cool-because-this-may-be-part-of-a-plan. He was about to go into spasms.

"Shit, Charley, this may turn out to be a fun party

after all," Cece said. Then, "Hi, Rix. Long time no see." She gave me the kind of look she used to save for the moment just before she'd set fire to my bed or pour honey in my underwear drawer. Then she slid her arm into Rix' and pulled him away from Regan, saying, "I don't think you've met Charley's husband, Jack."

"Regan, sweetie." My smile probably looked something like my uncle's. "I didn't know you'd be bringing your boyfriend. How—"

"Nice." Brenda stepped quickly beside me. "How nice he was able to come. I'm Brenda Gee, I'm a friend of Charley's. And this is Eileen Scotto."

Eileen magically appeared on my other side. "Pleased to meet you. Charley's told us so much about you."

It's good to have friends. Regan probably never knew how close she had come to being decked by her director on Harry's hardwood floor.

"Excuse me, Mrs. Fairfax." Gordon came out of nowhere to tap me on the shoulder. "If I may have a word with you about the glazed oysters?"

Bless him. We weren't having glazed oysters. I followed him to the dining room while Brenda and Eileen maneuvered Regan into a corner.

"Take this." Gordon placed a drink in my hand. I had no idea what it was. "Iced vanilla-infused vodka," he informed me when I hesitated. "It's possible you may need more fortification than champagne cocktails can provide."

I downed the drink just as Mike opened the dining room door and slipped in. "That guy is Rix?"

I nodded. "It was bad enough to invite Regan here. Don't forget that if she is connected to Macbeth, while we're watching her she's watching us. And now she's in our—"

"Inner sanctum?" Gordon offered.

"Whatever." I looked at them both. "Which is dangerous enough, but Rix—"

"Is nothing to worry about." Jack joined us through

the kitchen door. "We've taken plenty of precautions for Regan, and they'll work just as well for Rix."

Mike spoke up. "We'll sweep the whole house for bugs after everyone's gone. And they don't know it, but they've already passed through a metal detector to get here."

"On that subject." Gordon brought a list out of his pocket. "Flank thought we should know that Victor was carrying a metal hip flask. Olivia had a tin of candies and a metal-handled hairbrush in her purse. Simon had—"

"Hey! We're not worried about Simon," I interrupted.

Gordon looked up mildly. "Of course not. I'll omit the rest of the friends." He consulted the list. "Regan had nothing. Rix had his own hip flask as well as what looked like a good-sized pocket knife." He looked at Jack significantly. "But no gun. And Paul—" Gordon folded the list as he finished—"had a zippered case with a hypodermic needle in it."

"Okay," Mike said. "Um, Charley, do you think you're ready to get back out there?"

"That's some metal detector," I said. "Are you sure about Paul?"

Gordon's face was expressionless. "There's no mistake."

"Mike, you go first and stick to Regan," Jack said. "We'll follow." Gordon had vanished into the kitchen.

When Mike left, Jack gave me a searching look. "How are you?"

"Peachy. Now that we know Paul is on drugs, we go back to the fact that someone could be exploiting his weakness, right?"

"Right."

"So Paul the addict, Regan the porn star, and Rix the slimy bastard."

"We don't know Rix is anything other than Regan's—"

"But he is a slimy bastard and I wouldn't put anything past him."

"Granted. So we have three possible leads to Macbeth, and to the person who's picked up where he left off."

I cleared my throat and squared my shoulders. "Right. Let's go see which of them will crack first."

We fell into groups. Brenda and Eileen kept Regan occupied until Mike wandered over to them. Harry endured a barrage of what Olivia must have considered to be flirtation while Victor looked on and signaled for continual refills of his glass. Rix and Simon were circling each other with hostility when Jack joined them and somehow smoothed things over. Cece was talking to Paul. That couldn't be good. I mingled.

Gordon had hired wait staff for the party, so I wasn't surprised to see a flock of white-coated servers. But when we were summoned to the dining room and I caught sight of the figure to the right of the kitchen doorway, my step faltered a bit. He bulged at every seam and his top collar button was in danger of popping across the room into the centerpiece. Roughly three inches of furry wrist were visible below each cuff. When he saw me looking at him he gave me an enormous wink.

"Flank is undercover?" I muttered to Jack.

"He's become very attached to you. Should I be jealous?" He didn't wait for an answer before turning to pull Eileen's chair out for her.

Harry insisted that Jack sit at one end of the long table, and I at the other. He took a center position, manfully staying with Olivia.

Gordon had outdone himself. He'd prepared five courses, beginning with a seared foie gras served with caramelized red onions and black mission figs, then moving on to the fish, herb-crusted salmon medallions. For the entrée, duck breast with plum compote and a potato-cauliflower puree. Then assorted cheeses accompanied by walnuts and honey, and crème brûlée for dessert. It was not a light meal.

There was wine with every course, and Gordon brought out a bottle of Harry's 1955 port with the cheese. Cece was right next to me, so I could see that she stuck to water, but Harry broke his resolve when the port went around.

Unfortunately, the food and liquor had the effect of loosening the wrong tongues. Victor dominated the conversation, at least at my end of the table, with tales of his illustrious career. He kept me so occupied I couldn't overhear what Cece and Paul were talking about. Olivia ignored him to focus on Harry, so I was left as the sole audience for the sloshed old actor.

I kept stealing glances to the far end of the table, where Jack, Simon, and Rix were still in conversation. I wished I knew what they were talking about. Mike and Regan seemed to be getting along, I observed with satisfaction. I know it was petty of me, but if Mike's goal of monitoring Regan's activities might result in pissing off Rix as well as ferreting out information, I could live with that.

By the time the wait staff came around with coffee and little cookies, I had made a decision. "Excuse me, Victor," I said, interrupting something about Olivier telling him, "Please, I'm not Sir Laurence to you—call me Larry."

"Why don't we take our coffee back in the great room?" I suggested. "We'll be much more comfortable." And I'd be able to shake off the sodden actor who was now, alarmingly, tearing up.

As the rest of us stood, a large white form appeared behind Victor. Flank grabbed him by the shoulders and lifted him to a standing position, then looked at me enquiringly. "Just put him anywhere," I said. Flank half carried, half propelled the actor to a solitary chair under a potted palm tree. Good old Flank.

I looked around the room and saw Simon meandering towards me.

"What were you three talking about?" I said with a bright, fake smile.

"Golf, mainly." Simon sipped his cappuccino. "Excellent dinner, darling. Lord, that man can cook. Why doesn't he open a restaurant?"

"What do you mean, golf?"

Simon looked surprised. "You know, the tiny little ball you bash about with a stick. Golf."

"That's all?"

"What am I missing, darling? Were they supposed to be fighting over your honor or something?"

"Of course not, but—where are they?" I looked quickly around and saw everyone but Rix and my husband. When had they disappeared?

"Toddled off to the game room, I think. Harry does know how to live, doesn't he?"

"The game room?"

"I think that's what they said. Something about a set of clubs Jack wanted to show the swine." Simon grinned. "You don't think he's going to take a whack at old Rix, do you?"

"Well that's the fun of a party, isn't it?" I said bitterly. "Anything can happen."

I mingled, making small talk until I bumped into Simon again at the bar. Brenda and Eileen joined us. "What's going on?"

"I wish I knew."

"Mike seems quite taken with the ice queen," Eileen observed. "Is she—"

"Good Lord," Simon interrupted. "He's leaving."

We followed his stare. Rix was leaving. Jack closed the door behind him and sauntered over with his hands in his pockets and a satisfied look on his face.

"What's all this, then?" Simon was finding himself very amusing.

"Oh, Rix? He had to go." Jack smiled innocently. "Pumpkin, can I see you for a minute?"

I followed Jack down the stairs to Harry's office. I waited until he'd closed the door before I pounced. "What the hell is going on? What did you say to him? What did he say to you? Did he admit anything? What happened?"

Jack silenced me effectively but temporarily with a rather dashing kiss. "Something you'd like to know?"

I stamped my foot. I literally stamped my foot. "Cut it out! Tell me what happened!"

Jack, looking more pleased with himself than I'd ever seen him outside of the bedroom, lounged on the arm of the red leather sofa. "Your friend Rix and I had a little chat about golf over dinner."

"He's not my friend," I said through clenched teeth. "And Simon has already told me about your fascinating dinner conversation."

Jack smiled coolly. "And you know, when you talk about golf, eventually you get to talking about how expensive the good courses are, and how pricey memberships to places like country clubs are."

That sounded a little more promising. "And?"

"And I happened to mention that it was the sign of a true theater lover that Rix would donate his money to a risky proposition like the Rep when he could enjoy it so much more in so many different ways."

"Ah ha!"

"Not quite, but we're getting there. I hope you noticed that the waiter kept Rix's glass full at all times?"

I hadn't, particularly, but I nodded.

"With that much wine and talk of money, eventually, one of us was bound to be indiscreet." Jack raised his hands helplessly.

"I'll assume it wasn't you." I sat cross-legged on the sofa and looked up at him.

"It wasn't. After dinner I invited him down to the game room to look at Harry's new clubs—they're Ping, by the way, and completely wasted on him—and then I asked Rix for money."

"You what?" I was horrified.

"An investment. Since he's a patron of the arts. I told him I was opening a gallery and needed a couple hundred thousand just to tide me over."

"What did he say?"

Jack slid down the arm of the sofa until he was facing me. "That's when he got all man-to-man with me. Told me that I should understand, being a guy with no money and being married to yours."

"To mine?" I said incredulously. "Not to me, but to mine?"

Jack shook his head. "Seriously, Pumpkin, I don't know how you ever let a prince like that get away."

"Shut up and tell me what happened."

Jack grinned. "He confessed. But only to making an ass of himself over Regan. He told me he'd won a huge amount of money playing poker a couple of months ago, and that Regan had been there with some other guy. When her date lost all his money, she left with Rix."

"How romantic," I said. "Where does Macbeth fit in?"

"Nowhere, yet. Up until this point it really does seem like just a bizarre coincidence. Rix says Regan wanted to get out of porn, and she figured if she could be 'discovered' in a small play put on by a small company, nobody would look any further into her past. The Rep seemed like the perfect place to start, but it apparently never occurred to her to just try out for a part. Instead, she talked Rix into investing in the theater so he'd have enough influence to get her cast."

"And Rix did it?" I shook my head "Nobody's that stupid."

"Apparently the lady is quite persuasive," Jack said. "And it was also a way for Rix to make you think he had money. He wanted you to owe him."

"I wish he hadn't gone. I'd like to give him a swift kick," I muttered.

"And I'd like to see you do it." Jack flashed another grin. "Now do you want to hear where Macbeth comes in?"

"How? When? What—"

Jack didn't bother to let me frame a coherent question. "After getting Regan situated nicely at the Rep, Rix did the one stupid thing he could be counted on doing."

"There are lots of stupid—"

Jack cut me off again. "He kept gambling."

"Oh," I said. "And . . ." I didn't get it.

"And he lost," Jack continued. "He lost a lot. To a lot of people. And he was just thinking his best option was to leave town when he got a phone call."

"From Macbeth—wait, was Macbeth dead by then?"

"Yes, this was only a couple of weeks ago. The guy who called said he was working for an 'interested party.' He said this party had bought all Rix' debts, and Rix now only owes one person, but he owes a little over four hundred thousand dollars."

"And the interested party is Macbeth's accomplice."

Jack nodded. "He told Rix how he could pay off the debt."

"How?" I didn't like the look on Jack's face.

"By ruining the Rep."

"What! How—"

Before I could do anything other than sputter out incoherent questions, Jack went on. "Don't worry, I took care of it."

I stared at him. "Tell me what happened. Tell me exactly what happened."

Jack nodded. "Rix was told that if he made all sorts of allegations about financial improprieties at the Rep, and ruined your reputation, his debt would be paid."

I swallowed. "He can't do that. We're not a publicly held company. We don't have to answer to anyone—" I stopped. "At least we didn't until we took his money."

"Don't worry," Jack said again.

"What did you tell him?" My voice shook. The Rep may occasionally drive me crazy, but to have it vulnerable to attack from outside made me completely insane.

"I was very sympathetic."

"Great."

"And then I bought him off."

"You what?" I yelled. "You gave him money?"

"Here's the thing," Jack said calmly. "If he doesn't owe anyone money, he doesn't have any reason to ruin the Rep."

I swallowed. Or I may have choked. "You didn't give him four hundred thousand dollars?"

"No, I rounded up." Jack got that pleased-with-himself look again.

"Jack! You didn't!"

"Pumpkin, you know I wouldn't lie to you." I was speechless, which Jack took a moment to enjoy. Then I got it.

"It's a trap."

"Ten points to the gorgeous woman in black. Have I told you how good you look in that dress?"

I refused to be distracted. "You'll follow the money."

"Mike will. And we'll see if we can find out where Macbeth's partner in crime is currently stashing the cash."

"And that will tell us who it is?"

"It will help." Suddenly Jack became serious. "And that's when things will get dangerous."

And here I'd been thinking that murders and kidnappings were already pretty dangerous.

"When will all this happen?" I asked.

"As soon as Rix can make contact with whoever owns his debts."

"Jack! If he's going to find this guy we should follow him! When did he leave? Where was he going?" I jumped up and headed toward the door. Jack didn't follow me. I turned around to find him crossing his legs comfortably.

"Gosh, I wish I'd thought to have him followed."

"Oh." I deflated. "All right, you're better at this than I am." I put my hands on my hips. "Maybe you married the wrong girl."

He grinned. "Like hell I did."

I never claimed to be a great hostess. We'd probably been gone half an hour by the time we rejoined the others.

Harry had put Victor in a cab soon after he'd started snoring from his seat under the potted palm.

Then, ever the gentleman, Harry offered his car and driver to Olivia, who seemed to think that was as good as an engagement ring. "Charley, dearest, I've had such a lovely evening," she said, looking at Harry. "Such delightful company." She floated off in a haze of Obsession.

"Guess I'd better be going too," Paul said. "I'll be there bright and early tomorrow, Charley." He turned to Cece. "Can I count on you to come see me on opening night?"

"You're awfully cute," she told him, running a manicured finger down his tie. "But I can't think of anything more boring." She didn't wait for him to leave before turning away and going upstairs.

It was right about that time that Regan seemed to notice Rix's absence. "Would you allow me to take you home?" Mike asked her. He seemed all masculine and protective but at the same time a little star struck. It worked for him. I wondered how many of her films he'd had to research.

"Thank you," she said. "I can't imagine what happened. Charley, thank you so much for such a lovely time." Her manners were impeccable. I wanted to squash her like a bug.

"Well, old thing, I guess that's our cue." Simon slung his arm around Eileen. "Shall we run away together?"

"My son's coming home tomorrow," she told him. "I'm not running anywhere."

"Didn't think so. How about a lift home, then?" He kissed me on the cheek and shook Jack's hand.

"Are you two staying over?" Harry asked when they'd gone. "And you'd better say yes, because I haven't got a goddamn clue what went on here tonight."

Gordon, whose timing was even better than his crème brûlée, appeared with a tray of after-dinner liquors.

"Stay," Brenda said. "I'm dying to know what you said to Rix."

We stayed.

* * *

Later that night, when I woke up at my usual three o'clock thinking time, it occurred to me that I should ask Jack where he'd gotten the half million dollars he'd given Rix.

Chapter 27

Opening night. At least it would be in twelve hours. We'd had our one and only preview the night before. Not a disaster. I'd held my breath for the entire performance. Then Chip and I had kept the cast until almost one, giving notes and encouragements.

Jack dropped me off in front of the theater in the morning with Flank and a subdued little black Donna Karan that I planned to change into before the performance. Flank carried a purple shoebox which I hoped contained my Stuart Weitzman stilettos and not munitions of some sort.

"Break a leg," Jack said.

"Save that for later. Right now just tell me everything's going to be fine."

"Everything's going to be fine," he said dutifully.

I took a deep breath. "See you at six?"

"I'll be the incredibly handsome guy in the new tux."

The plan was for the company to break at six, two hours before curtain. Jack would come by then and stop me from running away from it all. Which is what I felt like doing. I'm pretty sure everyone involved in the production did, at that point.

"You won't do anything stupid between now and then, will you?" I asked.

"Probably not." He said it lightly, but his face betrayed a flash of frustration. We'd learned nothing since the dinner party. We'd had Rix followed and monitored his bank account, hoping to trace the half million. Nothing. We'd had Regan followed, and when she wasn't at rehearsals or obsessing about her part to the pathetically infatuated Rix, she was at home, either working out or sleeping. We'd had Paul followed, and although we now knew the best places in the city to score heroin, we were no closer to an answer.

Jack squeezed my hand. "Everything will be fine," he said again. He's a very good liar.

If the saying "bad rehearsal, good show" was true, we were in luck. Victor knew his lines by now but was having trouble with his shoes. They seemed to snag on the stage and he tripped constantly. Sally was having a major case of opening-night jitters. She spent most of the morning sniffling in her mother's arms. "Don't worry," the mom assured me, "she's a trouper. She's got it in her blood." Right. That stopped me from worrying.

Paul was fine early in the morning, but got increasingly high-strung and irritable as the day wore on. We all did, I suppose, but I assumed he'd take something at the six o'clock break and be fine for the opening. If it turned out he wasn't plotting to kill someone, I planned on getting him to a rehab center as soon as I could manage it.

Thank God for Lisa. She seemed to be everywhere, doing everything, keeping a different crisis at arm's length every five minutes. Chip had always been a good stage manager, but Lisa was amazing. I couldn't imagine how we'd have gotten along without her.

When I'd seen Simon first thing in the morning he'd had his usual opening-night case of nerves. "Charley, we're completely sold out. Completely! Is it too early in the day to start drinking?"

"It's nine in the morning. Have some coffee. Decaf."

He'd taken a deep breath. "Everything will be fine?"

"Everything will be fine," I'd told him. And I'd kept repeating it to everyone I came in contact with all day. Until the electricity went out.

Four o'clock in the afternoon. Four hours until curtain, and the theater was plunged into darkness.

I only had the time to think, "What the hell?" before I was tackled and thrown to the ground. I would have yelled, but for the first time I realized what it meant to have the wind knocked out of you.

The bright white safety lights flickered on a few seconds later, and I got a look at my attacker.

"Flank, get off of me," I wheezed.

"Stay down," he ordered. His gun was drawn and he crouched protectively by my side. It seemed he was only intelligible when his gun was out. I didn't have time to speculate on the Freudian implications of that, because Olivia, who had screamed when the lights went out, screamed again when she saw him.

Flank's entire security team had swarmed to the stage. It looked like the last scene in a John Woo movie. Everyone who had a gun was pointing it at someone else with a gun. Gradually, they all realized they were on the same team and began calling "Clear!"

"Can I get up now?" I asked Flank. I'd recovered my breath enough to notice how much my butt hurt. He holstered his weapon and held out his hand to help me up.

"Thanks," I muttered. Then, addressing the group at large, "What the hell happened?"

"Um . . ." I heard a voice from backstage. "I think I did it."

Paris let out a volley of obscenities that shocked even me. The electrician who stepped out from behind the scenery was a brave man. "It was the fan," he explained. "For the breeze in Act Three. It must have overloaded the circuit."

"Then fix it!" This was bellowed by the lighting director, who then gave Paris a challenging stare. Who was allowed to yell at whom was a matter of strict union rules, and the electrician belonged to him, not Paris.

The electrician dashed back behind the scenery. "Where's he going?" I asked Paris, trying to distract him from what promised to be an all-out testosterone war. "Isn't the electrical room downstairs?"

He glared at me. "And just what in the hell do you think you know about anything electrical?"

Great. "Paris, sweetie," I said evenly. "Don't worry about it. He'll fix it. Everything will be fine."

I received a snort in return as Paris stormed away.

Lisa stepped out from behind a tree. "Don't worry, Charley, this should just take a minute." I followed her gaze upward. I could see the electrician climbing a metal ladder bolted to the wall behind the stage. The ladder led to a platform in front of a bank of metal boxes on the wall.

"Where's he going?" I asked Lisa. "What's up there?"

"Electrical stuff," she said. "All the circuit breakers."

The electrician got to the platform and began opening various boxes and flipping switches. "Here it is!" Suddenly the normal lights were back.

"Okay, everybody," Lisa called. "One more run-through of Act Three for lighting cues and then we'll break. Is everybody ready?"

At five-thirty we'd had enough. I sent the cast to their dressing rooms to rest, if they could, and prepare themselves for the curtain. Lisa had ordered a buffet of sandwiches and snacks, and had set everything up on a long table backstage. It was a nice thought, but against our policy of bringing large amounts of unattended food into the theater. We had a minor rodent problem, as most theaters do, and we didn't want it to get out of hand. But when the cast and crew started swarming around the table, I figured there wouldn't be enough leftovers to cause a problem.

Sally's mother brought her a hamburger meal from

the fast food place down the street. I didn't tell her what a bad idea I thought that was. The kid had pre-performance butterflies in a big way. But I ruffled the girl's hair and told her everything was going to be fine. Then I told Martha to make sure not to dress the child until she'd inevitably thrown up.

Flank followed me up to the office. I expected to find Simon, surrounded by public relations and publicity people, in a frenzy of activity, but the room was empty. "Where is everybody?" I asked.

Flank tapped his earpiece and mumbled into his sleeve. Then I think he said "Box office." I considered asking him to take out his gun and repeat himself, but it wasn't worth the effort.

"Look," I told him, "I'm going to lie down with a cold compress on my eyes for about twenty minutes, okay? So don't worry about me. Go get something to eat or something."

Flank looked doubtful, but he nodded and left.

Quiet. Solitude. Bliss.

I soaked some paper towels at the water cooler, squeezed them out, and lay down on the couch with the wet compress over my eyes. It was hardly a day at Elizabeth Arden, but it would have to do.

I wished I'd paid more attention at those meditation things Brenda had taken me to over the years. It would be nice to be able to summon a quiet mind whenever I wanted to. Of course, it would also be nice to summon a cast that wasn't full of drug addicts, porn stars, and possible killers. The only one with any real talent was Regan, and she was only using us to cover up her past.

Nevertheless, she was a damn good actor. And I was having a harder and harder time casting her in the role of Macbeth's accomplice. Whoever was running things now, aside from being a sociopath, would have to be intelligent, organized, efficient, and capable of managing multiple operations simultaneously, all while keeping his or her identity a secret. As talented as Regan was, she just didn't seem that smart.

I took a deep breath and tried to put it all out of my thoughts until after the performance.

My mind drifted to Paris' little outburst. I knew tension was running high, but did he really resent the fact that I didn't get into the technical details of putting on a production? Did everyone? Even Lisa knew where the electrical stuff was, and she was the newest staff member at the Rep. Martha probably hated me too. I hadn't even cared enough about her costumes to go see that fabulous closet I'd bought for her.

I felt queasy. It wasn't nerves. Nerves make me hungry. This was the kind of queasy I get when I wake up in the middle of the night and realize I've forgotten something, or said something tactless, or done something stupid. What? What had I forgotten? If it was anything important it would be on Chip's three-page checklist, but still. Queasy.

Was it something about Chip? He'd speak up if there was anything wrong. Simon? He'd lost all sense of perspective, but he always did on opening night. Paris? The sets were fine, even if he was furious with the lighting director, and maybe me. Martha? Something about Martha. There was something nagging me about Martha, but I couldn't pin it down.

Then another name popped into my head. Lisa. No problems with Lisa, of course. She was amazing. No matter how many things Chip and I passed off to her, she could handle them. Hiring her had been Chip's smartest move ever.

I took the compress off and sat up. When exactly had Chip hired Lisa? I had no real idea. Sometime while I'd been gone, but when? My gaze wandered past the battered desk to the file cabinet. It would be easy enough to find out.

I sighed and threw the compress away as I crossed the room. I opened the drawer marked *Staff*, pulled Lisa's file, and took a look.

The date seemed to rise off the page, burning itself into my vision. I still saw it after I shut the file, dropped it back into place, and closed the drawer.

Chip had hired Lisa just before I'd come home from London. Just before Cece had been kidnapped and Nancy had been killed. Just after Macbeth's death.

I shivered. Where was Chip? I needed to ask him about Lisa. Had he known her before she showed up at the theater? If so, I was out of my mind and Lisa was just an extremely competent professional. But if he hadn't . . .

Seriously, where was Chip? This close to curtain he could be anywhere. I braced myself and called his cell phone. He didn't pick up and I didn't leave a message. I couldn't think of one that wouldn't make him doubt my sanity.

This was crazy. I should file it away and tell Jack about it after the performance. What else was I going to do? Ask Chip if he thought maybe he'd unintentionally hired a psychotic killer? Or pull Lisa aside and drill her with questions during the most hectic two hours of her career?

Yes. That's what I was going to do.

I dialed her number. She picked up immediately. "Lisa," she said briskly.

"Lisa, it's Charley."

"No!" she shouted. "Not there! Stage right!" She turned her attention back to me. "Charley, what's up?"

Damn. She was in the middle of chaos. I shouldn't do this. "Lisa, I need to speak to you in private. Where are you?"

There was a slight pause. "Right now I'm on my way down to the costume shop with Victor's shoes."

Victor's shoes! I slapped my forehead. That's what had been nagging me about Martha. She needed to get Victor's shoes fixed before the curtain went up.

"Charley? You still there?"

"Still here," I said. "Look, I'll meet you in the costume shop, okay?"

" 'kay." She hung up.

The short conversation made me feel better. Criminal masterminds do not say " 'kay" when confronted by their accusers. Not that I was accusing her of anything yet.

"Oh, hell," I said to the empty room. "Hell."

I headed downstairs and saw most of the crew and some of the actors milling around the buffet table, scarfing down little croissant sandwiches and cheese cubes on sticks. I headed for the basement.

I could hear Paris in the workshop yelling at someone. I was a little worried about that. We had three more plays to get through this season. He couldn't have a breakdown for months.

When I got there, the costume workshop was empty and I felt ridiculous. I didn't even know how to approach Lisa. I didn't think "Hey, did you ever know a spy who really hated my husband?" would set the right tone.

I looked around the shop, wondering if Lisa had been waylaid by yet another crisis. The costumes were all up in the cast's dressing rooms, so there were just odds and ends lying around. And a pair of men's shoes—Victor's. Damn. Lisa must have already come and gone. She was probably so busy she couldn't wait around for me.

All right. Enough. This was some cosmic way of telling me to forget about it until after the performance. I looked around the room one last time and noticed the closet door was open. Great. With as many pains as Martha had taken to create a sealed environment, I didn't imagine she'd like the door left open.

I went over to close it and hesitated, suddenly queasy again. The other door, the one inside the closet, was visible beyond the Elizabethan dresses, and it too was open slightly. Martha had said it led to an electrical room, but I'd seen that afternoon that the electrical stuff was mounted on the backstage wall. Of course, Paris was right, and I didn't know anything about anything, so it was likely that there was more electrical equipment in the room behind the closet. Generators or boilers or something.

I went into the closet. Was I crazy or was there a faint hum coming from the door? Electrical, no doubt. I put my hand on the handle and paused. The last time I'd gone into a deserted room in the theater I'd found Brian's body in a refrigerator.

I shook my head. Ridiculous. I simply had a monumental case of pre-performance jitters. Lisa wasn't a maniacal killer and there was nothing behind the door but a generator or furnace or something. To prove it, I pushed the door open.

The room was large and brightly lit. One wall seemed to be covered with stacks of video monitors and computer consoles. But that wasn't what I noticed first. What I noticed first was Lisa. She was looking at me speculatively, and said, "Well, I guess this means it's Plan B."

That's when I saw the gun.

Chapter 28

"It's good to finally get things out in the open, Charley," Lisa said, advancing towards me. "I've been wanting to talk to you, but the time just never seemed right. And there's a lot to talk about. You. Me. Jack. Dave." With each name she came a step closer.

My mind didn't seem to be working at full capacity. "Dave?" I said stupidly.

"I'll take your bag now." She reached towards me.

Run. Scream. Too late, I tried to do both. I felt something pull me back through the doorway and for the second time that day I was lifted off my feet and thrown flat on my ass.

She didn't let go of the messenger bag strap. She used it to drag me inside the room. I screamed. I yelled for Paris, hoping he'd hear me from his workshop across the hall. I kicked at the doorway and tried to hang on to it with my feet. I tried to reach behind to pull her arms away.

Then I heard a sharp crack and felt my head open. Or at least my scalp. It didn't knock me out, but it disoriented me enough for her to get me in the room, kick the door closed, pull the messenger bag off me, and bind my hands and feet with silver tape.

"Yell as much as you want, Charley. Everybody's upstairs pigging out on free food. Why do you think I brought in a buffet?"

She shoved me onto a leopard-print sofa that I recognized as one we'd used in *The Way of the World* three years ago, and used an electrical cord to tie me to its arm. I sat up, still woozy. I felt blood trickling down my face. Lisa stood at a table, another piece she'd apparently scavenged from the prop room. Behind her was the wall of monitors.

My brain felt fuzzy. Nothing made sense. "Who's Dave?"

She dumped the contents of my bag onto the table. "Come on, Charley. Even you must be able to figure that one out. Didn't Jack ever tell you his name? Dave Miller?"

Macbeth. Dave Miller was Macbeth. Which made Lisa . . . what? The criminal he'd had an affair with? The one who—according to Jack—had killed him? I shook my head and the pain brought a little focus. Whatever Lisa had been to Macbeth before his death, she was obviously the one who'd been carrying on with his plans since then.

She picked the cell phone and the Smith & Wesson out of the pile of my things on the table. "Everything I need to deal with Jack." She turned to me. "It was obvious, you know, from the way you kept this bag with you, that you carried your gun in it."

My head cleared a little more, probably from the surge of panic that hit me. "You're not going to kill him."

"I'm not?" She looked at me with raised eyebrows.

"He's going to kill you," I said.

"Really?" She paused. "I don't see how."

I suddenly felt completely insane. This could not be the same woman I'd been working alongside for the past six weeks.

"And trust me," she went on. "I see everything." She glanced at the monitors behind her and I realized what they were.

Video feeds. Of the inside of the theater, mostly. The hallway leading to the office. The stairs and halls of the basement. The costume shop. The closet. The stage and backstage areas from various angles. Then there was the hotel hallway with the door to our room. And Harry's front door.

"You see," she said, "I've been watching you."

"All along," I said, dazed. "Everything."

"Call me the Phantom of the Rep." She looked at the screens with her head tilted. "Whoops, we've got a visitor."

I looked at the monitors. It took me a minute to figure out what she'd seen. It was Flank. In the costume shop. Looking worried.

"Poor guy. He's about to become unemployed," Lisa said.

"Don't hurt him," I said sharply.

She kept her eyes on the monitor. "I have no intention of causing a scene if he doesn't." Then, absently, "Not yet."

"You won't get away with this, you know. Jack's going to be here any minute, if he isn't here already. And the box office opens at six, and the doors open at seven. This building will be filled with people, and Jack and Flank will call the police, and Jack—"

"Yep," she interrupted me. "Here's our star now." She tapped a screen with the barrel of the .38. The video showed the stage door, where Jack had just walked in. He spoke briefly with the security guy, who then said something into his sleeve. In the costume shop, I saw Flank respond. He headed for the stairs.

"Fun, isn't it?" Lisa observed me watching.

"What are you going to do?"

Something flickered over her expression too quickly for me to read. "Anything I want."

My hands were taped at the wrist, and tied to the sofa. Which was a shame, because I still had the Walther tucked into the back of my jeans. Apparently Lisa was so smug about figuring out I carried a gun in my bag she hadn't felt a need to look for another. I just had to get my hands loose to get at it. I saw Flank talking with Jack. They moved from monitor to monitor, making their way to the office. They stopped outside the door when they saw I wasn't there. Jack brought out his phone and punched a number.

I jumped when my phone rang. Lisa had left it on the table.

"What do you think?" she asked. "Do we let it ring and make him worry, or do you two kids want to talk?"

Second ring. Third ring. I knew after eight it would go to voice mail.

"I think we'll just let him worry," Lisa said.

"No!" I had an idea. "Let me answer it."

Her eyebrows raised a fraction. "I thought you had more guts." But she picked up the phone. "Fine. Tell him where you are. Let's get this over with."

She flipped the phone open and held it to my ear. "Jack!"

"Charley!" I heard his voice an instant before I saw his lips move on the monitor. "Where are you? Are you all right?"

"I'm fine, Jack, I went to the bar on the corner. Meet me—"

Lisa swore and snatched the phone away, snapping it shut. On the monitor, Jack said something to Flank, who shook his head violently. They retraced their path through the monitors to the stage door. The security guy also shook his head.

"They know you didn't leave," Lisa said, recovering her cool efficiency. "They would have seen you."

We watched the screens. The security team was everywhere. Jack disappeared for a moment, then showed up on the lobby monitor. He banged on the box office door until Simon opened it. Then he went in.

"How long shall we give him?" Lisa asked. "How long shall we let him run around the theater, crazed with worry, until we tell him where you are?"

I hated that she could see every move Jack made. That she could follow him like a rat in a maze. I had to distract her. I had to let Jack do something, go somewhere unobserved.

"Were you Dave Miller's lover?"

It worked. She turned away from the screens. "What do you know about it? What do you know about anything?"

Not enough, clearly. "I know he was selling secrets to someone." I spoke quickly. "I know he was sleeping with someone who talked him into betraying Jack and the others, who used him to—"

"I never used him!" Her chin snapped up defiantly. "We were in love. Whatever he did, he did to help me."

Something told me to back off from that touchy subject. I tried another approach. "Why did you kidnap Cece?"

Her expression mellowed a little. "That was Dave's idea. It was brilliant. He knew Jack wouldn't have told you anything about his past, so he set up a situation where Jack wouldn't be able to resist playing the hero—where he'd have to show himself for what he really is."

Oh. Well, I had to admit it had been effective. Jack's actions on the night of Cece's rescue had not been those of a meteorologist. "But why did you go to all that trouble? Hiring an actor and making Cece fall in love with him? Couldn't you just have snatched her?"

Lisa looked impatiently at me. "We were making our plans as we went along. At first we just wanted to watch a few key people. Dave set things up so we'd be prepared to deal with anything—anyone—at a moment's notice."

"Like you dealt with Nancy Tyler?"

"Nancy Tyler?"

Good Lord, did no one ever remember her name? "The playwright," I explained. "In the bathtub."

"Oh, her." Lisa left the monitors to come closer to me. "That was my idea. I wanted to have a little welcome home message for you and Jack."

"You killed her just to warn us?" I squeaked.

"Warn you? What makes you think I'd want to

warn you?" She squatted down to my eye level. "I just wanted to say—'Look. Look how easy it's going to be when I kill your wife the way you killed Dave's.' "

"What?" I stared at her.

"Oh, didn't he tell you?" Lisa spoke softly. "I'll bet there's a lot he didn't tell you." She met my eyes for a moment, letting her accusation sink in. Then she must have seen the sick horror on my face, because she smiled, mission accomplished. She stood.

"Killing the playwright was easy. Once I had a maid's uniform I was pretty much invisible. And it was so simple to just wear Nancy's clothes out of the hotel and drop the uniform down the laundry chute when I was done."

She seemed to expect me to congratulate her. I was too busy trying to blank out what she'd said about Jack. "Did you hire someone else to date my friend Eileen?" I tried to stay focused, tried not to let her see how badly I was shaken.

She gave me an appraising look. "I wasn't sure you knew Eileen's guy was one of mine. He messed everything up so early in the project."

"I wasn't sure. Why did you set her up?"

"Because she's a bitch." Lisa's eyes flashed. "She came into the theater one day—it was the day she took the money from your old lover Rix—and she treated me like shit."

My head was spinning, and not just from the whack Lisa had given it. "What? You set her up just because you didn't like her? Were you going to kill her too?"

Lisa shrugged. "Probably not. I figured I'd have the guy frame her for some embezzlement or something, and ruin her financially. I hadn't really worked it all out yet when he messed it up anyway." She made a face. "You know, you can never believe what agents tell you about actors."

"No shit," I agreed. "But you must have known that. Because you must have had experience working in theaters before this."

For the first time she showed a flicker of regret. "Some," she said. "A long time ago."

"You're good," I told her. I didn't add "for a crazed psychopath."

"Thanks," she said. "It was fun. And not just the part where I planned how I'd watch you squirm." She gave me a hard look, and I probably squirmed. "The job was fun too."

"How did you get the job?" I asked. "Did Brian tell you Chip was looking for an assistant?"

"He told me Chip had already hired someone, a woman from LA."

"You?"

"Of course not. But I called Chip pretending to be the woman he hired and told him I'd found out I was pregnant and didn't want to move anymore. Then I recommended someone else for the job."

"Yourself."

"Myself." She inclined her head in a mock bow.

"What did you do with the woman he'd actually hired? Did you pay her off?"

"Don't be an idiot," Lisa said dismissively. "I pushed her under a bus before I made the call to Chip."

"You—" All the air left my lungs and the room took a half turn. I swallowed hard. "What about Brian? How did you and Dave control him? Just because he lied about his experience?"

"You make everything so complicated." She shook her head in irritation. "We just paid him to tell us what was going on."

Oh. That was much simpler. "Then you killed him when he lost his nerve for what you were doing."

Lisa looked at me like I was an imbecile. "You really don't understand anything, do you? He didn't lose his nerve. He wanted more money. The little prick thought he could blackmail me about the playwright, what's-her-name."

"Nancy," I said through gritted teeth. "Her name was Nancy."

"Whatever. None of that matters now, does it?"

She looked at the monitors. Jack was back in the lobby with Simon and Flank.

"Wait a minute," I said wildly. "What about Rix? Where does he fit in all of this?"

"Rix is an idiot," Lisa said flatly. "What did you ever see in—"

"Never mind." I was hardly going to take criticism about my love life from a psycho who'd been sleeping with a traitor. "Are you the one who bought all his gambling debts?"

She froze. "How did you know that?"

"He told Jack." I probably shouldn't have sounded quite so smug, but I couldn't help it. It felt good to know something she didn't know.

"When?" She looked at me sharply.

"Sunday. I suppose Regan is the one who told you all about Rix's gambling in the first place?"

But suddenly Lisa wasn't allowing me to stall her any more. "Let's get moving." She picked up my phone and punched a number. On a monitor, I saw Jack answer.

"Hi, Jack? This is Lisa? Charley's stage manager?" she said, sounding for all the world like my hyper-efficient employee. "Charley says hi."

Jack said something but she cut him off. "Oh, and Dave says hi too."

Jack's face froze. Lisa continued. "I know you have some friends with you, so I want you to pretend this is a normal call. Maybe it's Harry inviting you to a game of golf, or Mike, asking you to a ball game, okay?"

I could see Jack utter one word.

"Good. Now I want you to get rid of your entourage and meet me on your own. If you let them know where you're going, I'll see it and I'll kill her. If you do anything except what I tell you to, I'll see it and I'll kill her. But if you come down here like a good boy, I'll only kill you. Is that clear?" This was all spoken in the same bright, capable voice that had reasoned Olivia into peace over her pot roast speech.

Once again I saw Jack's mouth form one word.

"Good. Now make up some plausible story for your friends. Then lose them and come down to the costume shop. Alone. And open the closet door. Be here in three minutes or I'll kill her." She hung up. "Let's watch."

I watched. Jack hung up the phone and looked relieved. He said something to Simon, who ran his hands through his hair and dashed back into the box office. Then he said something to Flank. Flank's back was towards me, but I didn't see a release of tension in it. Whatever story Jack was telling him, I don't think he bought it. But he tapped his earpiece and said something into his sleeve.

On all the theater monitors, I saw security agents relax. Then I saw something that made my throat close. The door to Harry's house in Hillsborough opened, and Harry and Brenda came out. The camera that filmed them must have been hidden in the trees somewhere across the street. It gave a perfect view of them walking to the waiting limo in the driveway.

"Great," Lisa said. "Your family will be here to share your big moment."

We saw Jack making his way down the stairs to the costume shop. He came in the room and looked around. He stopped at the worktable before going into the closet. He took a gun out of his jacket, held it up, and then put it on the table.

"Good boy," Lisa murmured. "Now come in."

Jack walked into the closet and saw the door to the back room where we waited. He approached the door and looked around it. He looked directly into the camera, then reached up. The monitor went blank.

Chapter 29

"Jack!" I screamed, "Don't come in! She's got a gun!"

Jack opened the door. His eyes widened when he saw the blood on my face. "Are you all right?" His voice was low and steady.

I took a breath. "I'm just looking for a handsome guy in a new tux."

His mouth twitched. His eyes swept over the room. He seemed to notice Lisa for the first time. "Nice setup."

"Get in." Lisa kept the gun on Jack but stepped back, motioning him into the room. "That's far enough." She closed the door and frisked him thoroughly, which probably meant he wouldn't be carrying anything I could use to free my hands.

"Now," Lisa said. "Hold out your hands." Jack complied, and his hands were taped together at the wrists like mine. Then he sat down next to me and extended his legs, his eyes never leaving her face. She bound his ankles and grabbed another electrical cord to tie him to the opposite end of the sofa.

"There. That's better." She remained crouched in front of us, seeming to take stock of the situation. Lisa's attitude had changed completely when Jack had entered the room. She'd dropped the last shred of the mask she'd worn as my stage manager. She now looked equal parts wired and exhausted. There was a manic energy about her. When she spoke again her voice was husky. "The legendary Jack Fairfax."

Jack spoke. "Charley, I take it your stage manager is related in some way to the man we've been calling Macbeth?"

I answered automatically. "It's bad luck to say that name in a theater."

Lisa's eyes flicked to me. "I think we're a little beyond that, don't you?"

I looked at her and performed the only part of the ritual I could. I spat. She sprang to her feet and wiped her face. If we hadn't been tied up, it would have been the perfect time to take the gun away from her. She glared at me but addressed her next words to Jack.

"I think you know who I am."

Jack's gaze flicked over her. "Miller's whore?"

She was motionless. When she spoke it was in a fierce whisper. "He loved me. I loved him. You can't cheapen what we had."

"Maybe not, but I think you cheapened it when you and your associates killed him."

"Them, not me!" She leapt towards Jack, bringing the gun level with his face. "They didn't trust him. They didn't believe me when I said he was one of us. He would never have talked. He cared about us, and he cared about—"

"Money?" I interrupted. I've never been a fan of monologues. Or of guns pointed at my husband.

Lisa gave me a look of pure venom. "You think everything is about money."

"If it wasn't about the money, why didn't you two just disappear?" Jack asked. "You knew Miller's wife had found out about you."

Lisa's face twisted. "We were going to go. As soon as we'd made that last deal. And then *she* had to ruin everything. And *you* had to ruin everything."

"You could hardly have expected either of us to turn a blind eye," Jack said mildly.

Lisa put the gun to his face again. "You made her talk. You used her and then you let her pay the price. You may as well have drowned her yourself."

But he hadn't, apparently. And hearing that, something in my chest untied itself. "Dave killed her," I said.

"You don't know anything about him," she accused me. "He didn't kill her, they did, just like they killed him."

Jack gave Lisa a curious look. "You expect me to believe you weren't involved in Miller's death?"

Her eyes clouded over as she moved away from us. "I thought I'd convinced them," she said hollowly. "I thought they believed me when I told them Dave would never sell us out. But they killed him anyway. And when they told me about it afterwards, I left."

"You left?" Jack said skeptically. "I don't think so. I don't think you can just resign from your line of work."

"Nor you from yours."

They stared at each other. She had a point.

"How did you get away from them?" I asked. Not that I knew who "they" were, specifically.

Lisa leaned forward over the table. "I'd been in contact with Dave all along. He'd been able to set everything up from prison. He'd targeted your family and your business, and he'd hired Brian to tell us what was going on inside the theater."

"And Brian gave you the names of the actors to use for Cece and Nancy," I prodded.

"And Miller arranged for the house in Mill Valley where Cece was taken, and the hired thugs who took her," Jack went on. "But you? What were you doing all this time?"

"I was in LA," she said. "They'd sent me there on some—" She stopped for a moment before continuing. "I was there when I found out what they'd done to Dave." She turned away, her face twisted in pain.

I didn't press her. I didn't know if Jack had a plan for our escape, but he seemed just as interested in getting Lisa's story out of her as I was. Eventually, he spoke. "So you left them and you came here."

Lisa answered with her back to us. "Brian had told

us about the woman from LA who was being hired
into the Rep. I took her place."

With the help of a bus. I knew that much already.

"I needed a new identity," she told us. "So I took
one. And they didn't know anything about what Dave
and I had been planning, so I was safe here." She
looked around the room. "Safe."

Maybe I should have left well enough alone, but I
couldn't. "Why?" I asked. "Why did you target me
anyway? When Dave started asking Brian questions
and hiring God-knows-who, I'd barely even met Jack.
Why on earth would you two think I was the best way
to get to him?"

Lisa got a warm gleam in her eye. "Because Jack is
completely predictable," she said. "And Dave knew
him." She looked at Jack. "You showed your hand early
in the game, Jack. You showed your hand the minute
you sent Gordon to check up on Charley's background."
She turned to me. "You should be flattered."

Stunned was more like it. I turned to Jack. "I've
always known nothing good would come of having me
spied on."

He flashed me a quick look. "Sorry, Pumpkin."

I wasn't sure whether I wanted to kiss him or kill
him, but circumstances prevented me from doing
either.

Jack looked over at Lisa. "So what now?"

"Why? Are you in a hurry?"

Jack shrugged. "My wife's play begins in a little
over an hour. I don't want to miss it."

She checked her watch. "I think you will." She put
the gun down, reached under the table, and brought
out a metal briefcase I hadn't noticed before. It looked
like the sort of thing that would carry a bomb in one
of those Bruce Willis movies. "Do you recognize
this?"

Jack cleared his throat. For the first time in this
whole episode he began to look uneasy—which didn't
fill me with confidence.

"Jack, what is it?" I asked.

He kept his eyes on Lisa. "An explosive device. Mike and Miller developed it."

Not good news.

"This is what it was all about, isn't it, Jack?" Lisa said. "If you'd just let us trade a few dozen of these for the gold shipment, everything would have worked out fine."

Gold shipment? A few dozen bombs? Jack was going to have quite a story to tell me some day. If we lived through this.

I licked my lips. "All right, Lisa, why don't you just tell us what you want?"

"I want Dave back!" She brought her fist down onto the table with enough force to make the briefcase jump. Probably not a good thing.

She drew a ragged breath, then turned to face Jack. "Tell her what I want, Jack. Tell her why I'm here."

"Because you're a sick and bitter woman?"

Lisa moved suddenly, striking Jack's face with the barrel of the gun so quickly it was over before I even realized what was happening. Jack barely acknowledged the blow that sent blood spilling from his lip.

"What, Lisa? What do you want?" I spoke quickly, wanting to get her talking again. As long as she was talking she wasn't hitting and she wasn't doing anything with the bomb on the table.

"Never mind, Charley," Jack said steadily. "Whatever she wants, she's not going to get it this way."

Lisa brought the gun up to hit him again, but I yelled, "Wait!"

Her arm still raised, she looked over at me—which would have been great if I could think of something to say. The three of us stayed frozen for a moment.

Jack broke the spell. "What are you planning to do now?"

Lisa slowly lowered her arm. She turned and picked up the suitcase. "What do you think?"

"You can't!" I yelped. "Lisa, you can't blow up the building. The doors will open any minute! We're sold out! You—"

She set the bomb down with a thud. I jumped and shut up. "You're right," she said. "I can't blow up the building. This was designed for maximum effect in a small area, like a coffee shop or classroom." She stopped to take a breath and suddenly I saw a shred of the calm-in-any-crisis stage manager again, competently summarizing the facts. "But it will destroy this room, and probably the costume shop. Fire will spread across the hall—lots of flammable material in the design workshop, as you know—and of course . . ." She looked up. "The stage is just above us."

"The stage?" I whispered.

She nodded. "And maybe the first two or three rows of the audience. Who will be in those seats, I wonder? Your family? Your friends? The poor grieving sister of the murdered playwright?"

"Stop it," Jack ordered. He leaned forward. "What are you really after?"

Lisa looked surprised. "This," she said. "Just this." She gestured to the bomb. "And in a way, I have to thank you. You've helped me make an important decision. I've been struggling over whether it would be worse for you to die or to live on without your wife, knowing that you'd caused her death and the deaths of so many. I did think letting you live would be a fair exchange—your wife for my Dave—but in the end—" she looked at me—"Charley made the decision for me."

I swallowed. "What were you planning to do—go for a break in the second act and watch from outside as the bomb went off?"

"Actually, I thought I'd wait for the curtain calls," she said. "That way I'd be sure you'd be on stage. But now you've messed up all the cues . . . And despite what you think, I'm not going to be outside when . . ." Her voice cracked and she stopped. And suddenly I understood. Dave Miller might not have committed suicide, but Lisa was going to.

She turned to the briefcase and opened it. I half expected to see a big digital clock, counting the minutes we had left to live. "Well, it's been great working with you, Charley, but I've really got to be going now. They need me upstairs, and—"

In one quick motion Jack twisted his body and somehow freed himself. Before I realized what had happened, he was holding a thin blade at Lisa's throat with one hand and keeping the gun she had grabbed pointed away with the other.

"No!" Lisa shouted. A line of blood appeared on her neck. "No!" she cried again as Jack succeeded in taking the gun from her.

He took one step back, keeping the gun and his eyes on her, and sliced through the cord that bound me to the sofa. Then he held the knife out to me. I hesitated, not wanting to touch Lisa's blood, then took it with both hands. I cut my feet loose first, because it was easier, then awkwardly turned it to saw through the tape at my wrists.

Lisa was leaning against the wall of monitors, staring at the gun Jack held on her and moaning a low, rhythmic incantation. "No, no, no, Dave, no . . ."

"Lisa," Jack said sharply.

She looked up without seeming to focus. "How did you do that?"

"I'm a professional. And didn't you just tell me I was completely predictable?"

I stood behind Jack. "What are you going to do?"

At this Lisa seemed to pull herself together. "Yeah, Jack," she repeated. "It's your move now. What are you going to do?"

Both of them were breathing heavily after their short struggle. Jack didn't answer.

Suddenly, horribly, a knowing smile appeared on Lisa's face. She looked from the gun to Jack, wiping the blood from her neck. "You can't. You are predictable. You'd never shoot a woman." She took a step back.

"Don't be stupid," Jack said. "The theater is full of police. What do you think Flank has been doing all this time?"

Lisa's back had been to the monitors, but now she spun to look at them. Uniformed police were swarming all over backstage, in the seats, in the lobby. The only place I didn't see them was downstairs in the workshops. "You won't get away," Jack said.

"Of course I will." Lisa took another step back. "Look at me. I'm one of the guys. I work here. Everybody knows me. Hell, they're probably going crazy without me." She moved slowly toward the door, walking backwards. "And you and I both know," she said, turning, "that you wouldn't shoot a woman, especially in the back."

She reached for the handle.

"Oh, really," I said, my hand moving to the small of my back. "I would." I pulled out the Walther, popped the safety, and shot her in the ass.

Chapter 30

As it turned out, shooting Lisa wasn't really necessary. Because as it turned out, Flank and Inspector Yahata were waiting in the closet.

"Pumpkin," Jack asked, taking the gun out of my shaking hands, "do you really think I'd have let her get away?"

I looked at him. My ears were ringing. "What?"

"Why do you think I took out the camera at the closet door?"

"Oh."

Lisa was screaming and swearing and bleeding all over Flank. Jack looked at her dispassionately. "Although, if you had to shoot someone . . ." Flank snarled something and dragged her out to the costume shop.

Inspector Yahata asked for the gun.

"Am I going to jail?" I asked him.

I felt the heat of his eyes on me, but his voice remained cool and clipped. "Not tonight, I think. But I will want your statement."

That was going to be tricky, but I was saved by a policeman shouting "Jesus Christ—It's a bomb!" Then Inspector Yahata's cell phone rang and gave us all a collective heart attack. Mike popped his head into the room. "A bomb? I learned a little about bombs in the Navy. Do you want me to check it out?" The detective waved him in and answered his phone.

We watched Mike tinker with the wires for a few

minutes. It occurred to me that there was no reason to stay in the room, but before I could suggest anything to Jack, Mike looked up with a smug expression on his face. "All done."

Inspector Yahata ended his call. "Mrs. Fairfax, Mr. Fairfax," he said, "I . . ." He looked like he was about to say something, but he just gave us a fleeting frown. He tried again. "I don't suppose you know why this woman was so hostile to you and your family."

No way in hell was I touching that question. Jack answered smoothly, "I have no idea."

The detective studied my husband for a minute, and a quick flash of . . . something . . . crossed his face. Then he snapped his notebook shut. "Come down to the station tomorrow to make a full statement. And"—he paused—"come up with a story by then."

As he left the room, Mike spoke softly. "I think we can guess who was on the phone." He and Jack exchanged a look. Something told me they knew someone with even more clout than Harry. I allowed myself three seconds to feel bad for Inspector Yahata. Then I realized Jack had probably told him a lot more than he'd ever told me—off the official police record.

I might have collapsed right about then if Simon hadn't yelled from somewhere outside the door. Under normal circumstances a person might have called something like "Are you all right?" But this was, remarkably, still opening night. Simon shouted, "Charley! Half hour to curtain!"

I grabbed Jack's hand and made for the door. The costume shop was a madhouse of police, Flank's security people, and crew members straining to see what was going on. Simon was getting ready to yell again. "Char— Good Lord!" He recoiled when he saw me. "What happened? Are you all right?"

I'd forgotten my scalp wound and the blood all over my face. "Get me a damp cloth and tell me what's going on upstairs," I ordered him.

"And maybe a hat or something," Jack suggested, pulling the silk handkerchief from his breast pocket.

Jack cleaned the worst of the blood off my face and hands while Simon wound a piece of fabric around my head like a scarf, babbling all the time. "There, very Isadora Duncan, darling. Now all you have to do is get upstairs and give the cast their final instructions before you collapse. Everyone's convinced you've found another body down here, and some of them saw Lisa being carried out to the ambulance. Victor said he heard a gunshot, but nobody believes him. Of course I'm dying to know what the hell you've been up to, but that can wait until you've stopped the actors from rioting. Are you ready?"

I was still bleeding a little and shaking a lot. I'd been conked on the head and nearly blown up. I'd just shot someone and lied to the police.

"Of course I'm ready."

Chip had gathered everyone together for a last-minute pep talk. Which he'd pretty thoroughly lost control of, given the fact that there was a steady stream of police and assorted official-looking technicians rushing from the stage door to the basement stairs and back again.

Olivia saw me first. "Charley! I demand to know—"

I stopped her before she got up a head of steam. "All right, everybody. Half hour! Now I know you're all going to do your best tonight, and you're going to give the performances of your lives—"

"Charley, what the hell is going on?" Victor bellowed.

"Um . . ." I suppose I couldn't ask them just to ignore the police, but maybe I could distract them. "Um, I don't think everyone here knows my husband, Jack."

Jack looked startled as twenty people turned their curious eyes on him, but he recovered quickly and gave a little yes-I'm-her-husband wave.

"Jack," I continued, "isn't like us. He isn't from the

theater, and doesn't know all our traditions. So earlier this evening he accidentally said the name of the Scottish play."

Murmurs, some of disgust and some of alarm, ran through the crowd.

"Did he know what to do?" Sally asked. "I know what to do because my mother told me. You have to turn around three times—"

"Yes," I interrupted, "but he didn't know that." I addressed the group. "He was with Lisa downstairs in the costume shop at the time, and she was so surprised when she heard . . . the M word . . . that she stabbed herself in the leg with a dagger." I tried to assess how well it was going over. "She'd taken it from one of the costumes in the wardrobe closet and . . . well, these things happen."

I saw the wigmaster about to point out any number of things fishy about the story, but Martha, bless her, gave him a fierce glare accompanied by an elbow to the ribs. He didn't speak.

"What are we going to do for a stage manager?" Chip asked, unhelpfully.

"Well . . ." I looked to Jack for inspiration but received none.

"Can you do it?" Simon demanded from behind me.

Chip looked dazed. Then he took a deep breath. "I guess I have to."

Amazingly, the cast and crew burst into applause. There's nothing like backstage drama to get theatrical blood really pumping. I tuned it all out as I sagged against Jack. He spoke to Simon. "Think we can get her out of here now?"

While we were busy telling outrageous lies, Mike had gone out to the lobby to intercept Harry, Brenda, and Eileen when they arrived. Everyone was waiting for us in the office.

"Goddammit!" Harry shouted when he saw me. "Where is he? What did he do to you? What in the holy hell went on here tonight?" He pulled a gun from a shoulder holster and started waving it around. "I'll kill the sonofabitch! I'll—"

"We got her," Jack said simply.

"You got her? *Her?*" Harry repeated, cut off in mid-rant.

"We got her," Jack said, taking the gun lightly from Harry's hand. "Charley shot her." I couldn't tell if it was pride or amusement in his voice.

"Oh my God!" Brenda rushed towards me. "Charley, are you all right? Sit down. Are you hurt?"

I sat on the couch and winced a little as I took off the scarf. "It's just a little—"

"If I may?" Gordon said from the doorway.

"What in the hell are you doing here?" Harry demanded.

"I thought this might prove useful." He held up a first aid kit and made his way over to me. His fingers were surprisingly gentle as he explored the wound. "I don't suppose there's a very high likelihood of you agreeing to go to the hospital for stitches?"

"After the show?" I negotiated.

He muttered a few phrases that ended with "as bad as Jack," and started taking things out of the first aid kit.

He had just dabbed on something that stung like hell when I heard a strangled cry from the doorway. Flank staggered in and threw himself to the floor at my feet. The only phrase I could isolate in his half-sobbed monologue was "forgive me."

"Don't be silly. There's nothing to forgive," I told him, looking to Jack for a little assistance. "It was all my own fault for wandering off without you."

"Right," Jack said, pulling the man to his feet. "And I don't know what we would have done if you hadn't managed to get Yahata here and put everyone in position the way you did."

There was a huge sniff, and Flank wiped his face with his sleeve. Or the hair on his wrist. Then, with as much dignity as a damp grizzly wearing Armani can muster, he said, quite clearly, "I'll never let you down again," and left.

"That's a damn fine man," Harry commented.

"Everybody out," I said. "Go watch the play."

Ethel Merman would have been proud of us. From what I was told, it was one hell of a performance. Still in the office, Jack and Gordon and I started hearing the audience's laughter soon after the curtain went up. Gordon made tsk-ing sounds and applied butterfly bandages to my scalp. Then he ordered me to go wash up in the ladies' room down the hall.

When I got back Mike had joined them, holding a fist full of wires and electronic-looking things. "Are those the cameras?" I asked.

"Yeah."

"Isn't that tampering with evidence or something?" Mike looked uncomfortable.

"They're not exactly over-the-counter equipment," Jack said. "It's best if they're not traced."

Right. I sat on the desk and took the Tylenol that Gordon handed me. Then I took a deep breath and looked Jack in the eye. "You knew."

Gordon and Mike exchanged looks and backed away.

Jack faced me. "I knew."

"For how long?"

"Since yesterday, when we were able to trace the owner of the bank account where Rix sent the money we gave him."

"Rix—that's why she was so shocked when I told her we knew she'd bought his debts."

"Right. She must have figured there was a chance we'd found out about her, so she had to speed things up a little."

I swallowed. "Why didn't you just tell Yahata and have her arrested?"

"There wasn't enough evidence. There wasn't anything to tie her directly to any of the crimes. Once we found her little hideout in the costume shop we could have—"

"You knew about that too?" I stared at him. Then I flashed back to how Jack had rescued us. "You had a knife hidden in the sofa, didn't you?"

Mike spoke up. "We had weapons hidden all over the place. And microphones and cameras. See, we figured whatever she was planning would happen on opening night. We just had to wait and watch her and, um, catch her in the act." He'd started his speech all proud of himself, but by the end he'd melted slightly from the look I gave him.

I turned back to my husband. "And you didn't think it might be a good idea to tell me any of this? That my stage manager was the psycho killer who'd been stalking us?"

"I thought you'd be safer if you didn't know." I noted this was not phrased as an apology.

"Right. We can see how well that worked out."

Jack grinned. "I have to tell you, Pumpkin, when Flank told me where you were tonight I could have killed you myself." He shook his head. "How did you figure out it was Lisa?"

"I'm brilliant, remember?"

He put his hands around my waist and slid me off the desk. "I'll never forget that again."

Things got a little fuzzy after that, but at some point, I suppose, Mike and Gordon left us alone.

At intermission Brenda and Eileen came upstairs and sent Jack away to meet Harry at the lobby bar.

"Where's your dress?" Eileen took charge. "You've got to be ready for curtain calls. You're going to say something, aren't you?"

I'd prepared a few words to say in memory of Nancy Tyler after the performance. I suppose that was when Lisa had planned to blow me up. "I have to do it, don't I?"

"If you're not up to it . . . ." Brenda began.

"Of course she's up to it," Eileen snapped. "What

kind of makeup do you have with you? What can we do with her hair?"

It took their best efforts, but my friends got me dressed and presentable in time for the curtain calls. The cast was flushed with victory. Chip was practically dancing with glee. He grabbed me in a ferocious hug. "Charley, it was great! Everybody was great! You should have seen Victor! And Regan . . . she was . . . I just can't . . ." and then it was our turn to join the cast onstage.

I paid my tribute to Nancy. Part of me wanted to announce from the stage that she hadn't killed herself, and that her killer was now on her way to justice, but I decided Inspector Yahata should have the privilege of telling the family the news. So I stuck to my script, and got embarrassingly choked up as I ended my words with the hope that everyone would remember Nancy's name. Regan gave the playwright's sister, seated in the front row, a bouquet of roses. It was very moving. I couldn't wait for it all to be over.

I don't recommend walking across a stage in three-inch heels after you've had the kind of day I had.

There was one last surprise waiting in the wings.

"Inspector Yahata." I doubted he'd come back to the theater to congratulate me on a great show.

"Mrs. Fairfax."

Jack joined us. "Inspector. What can we do for you?"

Yahata, always so careful with his words, seemed to be at a loss for them. "I have to tell you—I'm sorry to say—"

"What's happened?" Jack asked. I began scanning the crowd for everyone I loved, a hundred horrible fears about what might have happened to one of them all popping into my mind at once.

"It's the woman." Yahata seemed to pull himself into focus. "Lisa."

I snapped my head around. "What did she do?"

"She escaped," he said. "The bullet wound was

minor, and when she'd been bandaged up in the emergency room, she knocked the doctor unconscious and—"

"Where is she? Did you catch her? What—" But something in the inspector's face stopped my questions cold.

"She made it out of the hospital to the street, managed to run a few steps, and was hit by an oncoming truck. She was killed instantly."

Killed. Instantly. The noise of the crowd rose around us, people laughing and congratulating each other. "When did it happen?"

"Only a few moments ago."

During curtain calls. Despite everything, she'd managed to kill herself right on schedule.

Chapter 31

When I got to the theater the next morning I found Chip and Martha in conversation onstage. I was just about to join them when we heard a shriek and a loud crash from somewhere upstairs.

Chip looked at me in alarm. "Simon's in the office."

We ran up the stairs and came clamoring down the hall to find Simon red-faced and gasping over a broken lamp. He stared at us wildly.

I looked around for a snake or tarantula that Lisa might have left as a parting gift, or at the very least another bomb, but couldn't see any immediate danger.

"Simon? Sweetie? What's wrong?"

He grabbed a piece of paper from the wreckage. "That bloody blond bitch!"

Regan. A completely different kind of snake.

"What did she do?"

"She's *gone*." Simon gave the paper a vicious twist, then began tearing it into pieces. "She left us a *note!*" He thrust the crumpled mess at me.

I picked out a piece at random.

but I know you won't be angry with me when I tell you my fantastic news. A casting director saw my performance last night and made me an offer to be in a movie with

"Oh, hell."

"What is it?" Chip asked. "Has she been kid-napped?"

"I wish," Simon said. "She's dumped us." He kicked the desk, yelped in pain, and slumped into the battered sofa.

"I'm not surprised," Martha announced. "She's a user. She used that guy—Rix—to get here, and then she dumped him when he lost all his money. And she used us to get into the movies. Of course she dumped us."

I knew this wasn't Regan's first time in the movies—just her first time with her clothes on. But I didn't think I'd accomplish anything by sharing her sordid past. Besides, something else had caught my interest. "Regan dumped Rix?"

Martha looked surprised. "I thought you knew. I thought everyone knew. She went on and on about how he lost all his money gambling and what a loser he was."

"When was this?"

"A couple of weeks into rehearsals. But then something happened and she took him back."

Something had happened, all right. Lisa had bought all Rix's debts. She must have learned about his gambling losses the same way Martha had.

"She broke up with him again the night of the preview," Chip said.

"How do you know?"

He blushed slightly. "Because I saw her making out with Paul at intermission, and so did Rix. He rushed Paul, but Paul decked him. Then Regan told him she never wanted to see him again, and he left."

All the best drama happens offstage.

"I didn't know Regan and Paul were an item." Martha sounded disappointed.

"I did," Simon said hollowly. "I read it in her note."

"Simon, you're not saying . . ."

"Yes, darling. Our leading man is gone too."

A few days later Brenda moved back into her house. I went with her to help clean it up after being abandoned for almost two months. Well, I went with her to keep her company while she cleaned. But Harry had gotten there before us. He'd sent a maid service over the day before to make sure the place sparkled and to put fresh flowers in every room.

"He's even had someone take care of the garden," she said, looking out at her tiny backyard.

"Brenda," I began, but didn't quite know how to go on. "Are you sure you want to move back here?"

She turned from the window. "Are you asking what I think you're asking?"

I was profoundly uncomfortable. But she was my best friend. "It's just that you seemed like you were pretty happy at Harry's." I took the plunge. "Pretty happy with Harry."

She crossed the room and hugged me. "Oh, Charley. Thank you for that. He's a good man, you know. Deep down."

I resisted the impulse to say "way deep," but I'm pretty sure she knew me well enough to feel it.

"So . . . ?" I asked.

She rearranged one of the bouquets he'd sent. "He knows where I am."

"And you're okay with that?"

"I am." She put her hands on her hips and looked around. "Now where do you suppose my Birkenstocks are?"

The play was up and running, featuring hastily rehearsed stand-ins for our two leads, and I had a few weeks before casting for the next show would begin. I made a huge to-do list, including everything from joining a gym to finding a house. But I've never really been a to-do list sort of person. And I was starting to think the whole house-hunting thing should probably be postponed until after the season. It was just such a gigantic effort.

Jack was keeping busy with Mike, helping him work on the business plan for his new company—for real this time. They named it MJE, for Mike and Jack Encryption. I could only hope what they lacked in creativity they'd make up for in computer and business skills.

He'd been gone a lot, so I was surprised to come back from a particularly enjoyable girl-type lunch with Brenda and Eileen and hear the sound of the shower. I went into the bedroom and found a large, beautifully wrapped gift on the bed. I arranged myself next to it and waited for Jack.

He emerged from the bathroom dripping, with a towel riding loosely on his hips. It was a sight I'd never get tired of.

"Why don't we go away?" I greeted him. "On a sort of honeymoon? The traditional kind without people trying to kill us? Someplace where you can be naked and wet all the time?"

He grinned. "I can be naked and wet here, see?" The towel dropped.

"Very nice. And is this for me too?" I nudged the box with my toe.

"Open it."

I pulled the paper off and was baffled to find a state-of-the-art six-cup French press coffee maker. "I don't get it."

"It's for when we get a house."

"Oh." Warning lights flashed the words Dangerous Topic in my mind. "Great. Now why don't I go get naked and wet, and then we can—where are you going?"

Into the closet, obviously. Leaving me quite alone with my wet and naked thoughts. "To get dressed," he called. "We have to be ready in an hour."

"Ready? For what?"

He popped his head out. "You'll see."

"I've had quite enough mystery from you lately," I called after him. "I expect you to be completely forthcoming with me from now on."

He came out wearing black slacks and a bare chest.

He looked directly at the spot where I'd dripped Bolognaise sauce on my white linen blouse at lunch. "You might want to change."

I looked down. "Brenda said I'd gotten it all out at the restaurant."

Jack sat on the bed next to me. "Brenda's sweet," he said, circling the remains of the stain with his finger. "But you can't believe a word she says."

"Unlike you," I answered.

He gave me a look of unadulterated innocence. "Have I ever lied to you?"

"Would I ever know?"

"Excellent point."

"You know," I said, "I've been thinking."

"Why does that make me nervous?"

I ignored him. "I've been thinking about Nancy and Cece and Eileen, and how they all met these fabulous men and had these whirlwind romances, and how these men all turned out to be complete fakes, and—"

"Are you going somewhere with this?"

"I am."

"Okay." He left his exploration of the stain and began concentrating on a spot behind my left ear. It's possible there was spaghetti sauce back there too, but I doubted it.

"I'm just trying to say that I'm glad you're not a fake. Even if you are more full of shit than any man I've ever known."

He pulled away to give me a pleased smile. "You're not so bad yourself."

"Jack," I said softly, hoping he was too preoccupied with the buttons of my blouse to pay attention to what I was saying. "How much about everything did you tell Inspector Yahata?"

Jack's ministrations ceased. He eased himself away to lie on his back. "How much do you think?"

I'd thought about it a lot. About why the inspector, who had been suspicious of Jack at first, had suddenly seemed to trust him for some reason. And why he'd let us off the hook so easily on more than one occasion. And who might have been on the other end of the phone call that he'd taken in the costume shop that night. "In my experience," I told Jack, "when the police suddenly start looking the other way it generally has something to do with my uncle."

Jack appeared to be thinking it over. "Harry is very influential in this town."

"Mmmm." I scooted closer to him and joined him in his perusal of the ceiling fixtures. "But."

"But?"

"But . . ." I waited.

Jack cleared his throat. "I suppose it's possible Harry wasn't the only one watching our backs."

"I thought not."

"It's possible I still have a few friends who have a few friends . . ."

"In high places?" I asked.

"In a variety of places," he said dryly.

"Jack, there's something else."

"I'm shocked."

I looked over at him. "I've been wondering where you got the half a million you gave Rix."

"Have you?" He frowned. "It was pretty much my life savings, plus Mike's and Gordon's."

"Jack." I was horrified. "You have to let me pay it back—"

"That's very sweet of you, Pumpkin, but not necessary. Mike was able to get it."

"Mike?"

"Remember how he traced it to Lisa's offshore account?"

I sat up. "He took it out? How?"

Jack grinned. "Sometimes it's best not to ask Mike how he does things with computers. The point is we all got our investments back, and there was some left over."

"How much?"

"Enough for Gordon to open a restaurant." Jack rolled over on his side to look at me. "I don't know what Harry's going to do without him."

"Anything else?"

"Enough for Mike not to worry about finding investors for MJE for a couple of years."

"And?"

Jack brushed a stray strand of hair off my face. "If you're asking what I think you're asking, I decided to pass."

"Pass," I said.

"I didn't really think we needed any more money, and I kind of figured you might think it was ill-gotten gains, or something, so—"

I cut him off by planting my mouth firmly on his. Eventually I told him, "You kind of figured right."

At that extremely inconvenient moment, the phone rang. Jack struggled rather ungallantly to get away from me. "It's for you." He reached for the phone.

"How do you know?"

"Because I told her you'd meet her in the lobby." He handed me the receiver. "It's the realtor."

Damn.